ANYONE *for* SECRETS?

*For Ella.
Happy Christmas
with warmest
wishes from a
xo*

FIONA CASSIDY

POOLBEG

This novel is entirely a work of fiction. The names, characters and incidents portrayed in it are the work of the author's imagination. Any resemblance to actual persons, living or dead, events or localities is entirely coincidental.

Published 2012
by Poolbeg Press Ltd.
123 Grange Hill, Baldoyle,
Dublin 13, Ireland
Email: poolbeg@poolbeg.com

A catalogue record for this book is available from the British Library.

ISBN 978-1-84223-464-8

Typeset by Patricia Hope in Sabon 11/15

Printed and bound by CPI Group (UK) Ltd, Croydon, CR0 4YY

www.poolbeg.com

About the Author

Fiona Cassidy (better known locally as Fionnuala McGoldrick) lives in Galbally, Co Tyrone with her partner Philip and their collective children – Colm, Úna, Ciarán, Áine and Orán (in a very noisy house that she wishes had an inbuilt self-cleaning mechanism!).

Fiona is a full-time mother and creative-writing workshop-facilitator and tutor, teaching writing to adults, young people and children as a recreational activity, and to people who have suffered trauma as therapy. She has also worked as a mentor for aspiring writers.

She is the author of two other novels: *Anyone for Seconds?* and *Anyone for Me?* To find out more about Fiona you can follow her blog and visit her at www.fionacassidy.net, become a fan on Facebook or follow her on Twitter: https://twitter.com/_FionaCassidy_

Also by Poolbeg

Anyone for Me?

Anyone for Seconds?

Acknowledgements

Of the three books I have written I have to admit that I found this the most difficult – not because I don't love my craft but quite simply because life was difficult and you have no idea how hard it is to write comedy when you feel overwhelmed and burdened. Well, actually, you do end up writing but your characters are all murderous individuals who are very angry, swear a lot and enjoy slapping people . . . *hmmm*, perhaps the least said about that particular draft the better . . . *ahem!*

There are certain people who I have to thank for helping me stay sane and giving me the encouragement I needed not only to complete this book but literally to stay standing in the face of adversity. Carrie-Ann McKay, I don't know what I would do without you. Thank you for always being there with your straight and honest approach to life that never fails to comfort and inspire me – and, as for your little godson, Orán, he thinks you're pretty amazing too! Thanks also to your hubby Gary (known locally as Mr Bubbles as he has the best carwash in the country!). A special mention must go to Adrian Kelly as well who I would trust with my life and whose help has been invaluable, and to Ciara for all her support.

Rachel McRory is also a girl in a million who has the gift of knowing what to say at the right time!

To my longstanding best friends Noeleen, Katrina and Joanna. I'm so lucky to have you, love you all to bits and always look forward to the nights out and the midweek chats!

Melissa Mellon, Geraldine Quinn and Jim Hamill, you all know what you mean to me and how much I value your friendship! People are always brought into your life for a reason and I rejoice in the fact that you're all in mine!

My mammy and daddy, Peter and Eileen, are the best in the world and I don't know where I would be without them! Thank you for always being there and loving us all and giving your time and energy so willingly to your grandchildren when my laptop is calling and the house won't clean itself!

To Jane McGlinchy, Geraldine Donnelly and the McNulty clan . . . good neighbours and baby-sitters are hard to find, therefore we count ourselves fortunate to have you all so close!

I dedicated this book in loving memory of my mother-in-law Maureen McGoldrick who died last year. Colm, Úna and I will always treasure the memories we have and never forget the kindness shown to us by this wonderful woman and her husband Seán, which was extended towards the rest of our family also.

Thanks to my sisters-in-law Edel and Brigid Ann, and Paul and Michele for being great friends and to Edel and Brendan for giving me the privilege of being Daniel's godmother for the precious time he was with us.

During the last year I also lost another special lady, my

aunt Mary Clarkson, who I have no doubt is looking down and smiling on us all with my lovely Aunt Ann. Mary and Ann, I will always remember your visits home from St Louis, Missouri, with great affection as you created some of my best-loved childhood memories. All my love to the Grahams and Clarksons – and as always thanks for taking care of the American book marketing for me!

Thanks also to John Pat and Margaret and my McAllister family both in Glengormley and Sydney, Australia. Stephen, we miss you so much and can't wait to see you again but know that you're in good hands in Oz with Veryan and the extended gang! Thank you for leaving us with great friends Joe, Gary and Claire as a reminder of our get-togethers.

When writing this book I had to be sure that I was getting my facts straight about certain elements of the storyline and thank Kathy McCausland for sharing her knowledge and insight with me.

Where would I be without my fellow writers who are a source of great comfort and craic? Claire Allan, you have become a true friend and I love our wee chats! A shout out also to Emma Heatherington and Sharon Owens, my other Northern compatriots!

Huge gratitude to all the booksellers throughout Ireland who house my books but special thanks to TP and Madeleine from Sheehy's bookshop, Cookstown, who have provided books for my launches and work tirelessly to promote me as a local author. Appreciation also to Eason's in Craigavon and Belfast and to Elizabeth McAleer of Libraries NI for inviting me to speak and read at events throughout the north.

A grateful mention also to all the local, regional and national media for the TV and radio interviews, reviews and articles and features that have been written and helped to raise awareness not only of my writing but other subjects that are close to my heart like adoption. A special thanks to Davina Sands for all her hard work and talent in dealing with a sensitive issue and writing about it beautifully.

As well as writing myself, I also love teaching others to explore the art of creative writing and I'd like to thank all the organisations that have employed me as a tutor or workshop facilitator. I have enjoyed myself immensely, met some fantastic characters, been inspired by people's stories and the reasons why they write and learnt a lot myself! Hello, Greg (see, I did mention you – good luck with your writing!). And Sharon Dempsey, I just know I'll be reading your first book of fiction some day, you amazing woman!

I wouldn't be here if it weren't for the lovely people from Poolbeg who publish my work. Thanks to the encouraging and understanding Paula Campbell, Sarah Ormston and David Prendergast for all they do to make it come together, and to my editor Gaye Shortland for being fantastically supportive, having a razor-sharp eye for detail and the ability to take a piece of writing and make it the very best it can be.

To my agent Emma Walsh I extend huge appreciation for the wonderful job she does. Her friendship, support, encouragement and unflinching faith in my ability continue to motivate me daily! Thank you for everything as always . . . you truly are one in a million!

Last but not least, I give my thanks to my family.

Philip, I am so proud of you and love you with all my heart . . . that which does not kill us will only make us stronger and here we are still standing tall together! To our amazing children who I would be lost without – thank you all for making our family unique and special – and for making me laugh and reminding me why being a mother is such a worthwhile job!

To you, my readers, who were so enthusiastic about *Anyone for Seconds?* and *Anyone for Me?*, I hope you enjoy this one – the last book in this series. Thank you for all your kind emails and messages which have made me grin broadly . . . I love making others laugh and being able to connect with people through my writing. Enjoy!!

∾

In loving memory
of
my mother-in-law
Maureen McGoldrick,
died 9 July 2011,
a cherished friend and a wonderful grandmother.

And

her grandson
Daniel Woods,
19 May 1996 – 24 June 1999,
my godson and a treasured little boy who will live
on in the hearts of those
who loved him forever.

Heaven is only a whisper away.

∾

Please visit www.phraselibrary.com to find out more
about a service that has been created in their
memory which hopes to eradicate language barriers
within palliative care on a global scale.

1

Jodi

I carefully counted out the change and picked out a piece of pocket fluff and a rogue mint before I begrudgingly handed it over to the waitress. I was officially now the saddest person on the planet – sitting in the bistro of the Swiftstown Arms Hotel with the jobs section of one of the weekly newspapers open, ready to circle with a red pen anything that looked feasible. In the old days I would have been very selective. Only putting a mark against anything that I deemed appealing or worthy of my knowledge and qualifications – now it didn't matter if I ended up washing dishes or scrubbing toilets (executive toilets, that is, I wasn't homeless just yet) as I was heading at mounting speed towards utter hopelessness. I didn't even feel like working. All I wanted to do was to crawl into a black hole and stay there with all my horrible thoughts, but unfortunately holes of the black variety were scarce on the ground and, if I was going to continue living, I needed to eat and pay rent. I had fantasised about buying a litre bottle of vodka (with no mixer) and drinking it straight from the neck. It wouldn't cure anything but it might numb the pain for long enough to allow me to forget who I was and why I had, unbeknownst to myself, apparently included the words 'treat me like a piece of scum and walk all over me' in my wedding vows.

I took a deep breath and tried to stem the flow of tears that were about to cascade down my face in the manner of Niagara Falls. I had never felt so lonely or out of control in all my life and what was worse I hadn't the first clue about how I could make it better. But then I supposed that I could comfort myself with the notion that it couldn't possibly get any worse. I had hit rock bottom and the only way was up (the only problem was I didn't think I had the right equipment with me and mountain climbing had never been my strong point).

I scanned the paper and ignored the ever-curious glances from the other diners. Most of them were regulars who knew each other well and I had ascertained over the last number of weeks that the three men who sat at the breakfast bar in front of the till were stalwarts who must be immune to caffeine and its effects. The small one was called Ringo. He was a recovering alcoholic who had seemingly replaced his addiction to the demon drink with one for chocolate ganache, as he ate cupcakes like they were going out of fashion. Jockey had messy hair, wore a paisley waistcoat (circa 1973) and had a cigarette permanently tucked behind one ear. He was a serial gambler but not a very good one as he always lost, much to the amusement of the other diners who made comments about it being more likely for Shergar to be found than for Jockey to actually win anything. The third man (term used loosely), Jamesie Mac, was worse than a woman when it came to spreading idle gossip and talking about everyone; all he was missing was a headscarf and a handbag. He travelled the length and breadth of the town every day calling into all the shops and pubs and spent his time finding out what everyone else's business was. Of course, when he was imparting the gossip back in the bistro I was sure that there had been ten yards added on to every story so I took everything I overheard with a mountain of salt.

I was probably driving them all mad as no matter what they asked me or how they tried to strike up conversation I remained polite but resolutely quiet about my circumstances and how I came to be there.

This morning they had nodded their usual greeting and, since I had walked in twenty minutes previously, I had heard the intimate details of a man called George whose reputation could have rivalled that of any choirboy – until he came home from England wearing a dress, that is (more power to him, I say). A woman called Janet had just started HRT treatment and was threatening to kill her husband, so confused were her hormones (that's not hormones, love, that's just nature's way of telling you you've been too much of a pushover all your life). They were discussing another story as well. Something about a local adopted girl who had got married last year and had her birth mother at the wedding.

At the mere mention of a wedding I felt my eyes start to sting again. When was I going to stop letting innocent remarks that weren't even anything to do with me affect me so badly? When was my chest going to stop tightening and my heart stop threatening to beat its way out of me when I thought about having to start all over again? Alone.

I had no doubt that, as the locals had no details about my life (or how ludicrously messed up it was), they would probably make it up. I would most likely find myself cast in the role of 'your woman who comes in here for coffee, the jittery-looking one, the stranger'. This would, if present observations were anything to go by, be greeted with intense speculation and I would probably end up being a bi-sexual ex-convict who was opening a burlesque parlour on a quest to corrupt half the town.

Little did they know that I forced myself to go out for fear that if I spent long enough alone I'd end up in the madhouse gnawing my arm off and talking repeatedly with a malevolent grin on my face about how much I'd enjoy killing my husband. Pardon me, ex-husband.

I took another sip from my oversized cup and paused to look out the window. I could see my reflection and felt disgusted. Gone were the shining blue eyes which ordinarily would be full of sparkle, waiting in anticipation for the next challenge. Gone was my coiffed and glossy raven-coloured hair, my crowning glory that had always earned me such compliments. Instead it was now carelessly tied up with stray wisps escaping around my face. Gone was the flawless complexion, and the make-up that had always made me feel fully dressed. Gone were the sharp tailored suits, the briefcase and the aura of authority. Gone was my life as I knew it.

It was a cold and miserable Thursday afternoon at the end of February and people were rushing from shop to shop, hoods and umbrellas up and heads down to avoid the rain that was splashing on them in large droplets. There was a flower shop opposite and I noticed a man coming out brandishing a large bouquet of lilies and was nearly sick. He was probably going home to schmooze his unsuspecting (very stupid, gullible and simpering) wife who would probably be delighted at the unexpected surprise, not realising that far from being a gift it would simply be a conscience-easing gesture that would make him feel better about the secret life he had been leading.

I had been so stupid and so unbelievably naïve and trusting. I should have suspected that something was amiss from the moment that he had suggested we get married on a remote Caribbean island – just the two of us. I mean, who does that? Who gets married without a single friend or family member in sight and then doesn't even have a reception to mark the occasion when they get home "because it would spoil the intimacy of our experience abroad, darling". I do, apparently.

"Are you alright, love?" a voice asked, making me jump out of my skin while simultaneously spilling hot liquid over the only pair of jeans I had that weren't sitting in a bin-liner waiting to go to the 'pay by the load' laundry down the street. "It's just that you don't look very well."

I started to over-breathe and a brown-paper bag was looking like an attractive prospect. The woman who was talking to me had now started to back away while obviously regretting ever having opened her mouth.

"I'll be fine," I squeaked. "I mean, I am fine. Great. Couldn't be better. Top of the world."

I stood up quickly, banging my knee off the corner of the table, swore in a stage whisper, grabbed the newspaper and my bag whose strap was wrapped around the chair, subsequently knocking it noisily to the floor, and eventually made an unceremonious exit while everyone looked on in apparent amazement.

"You mark my words, boys, there's something mighty strange going on there," I heard Jamesie Mac mutter just before the door swung closed.

I left the building, red-faced, and made for the fleapit I couldn't afford the rent for. My new abode was a cramped two-bedroom semi situated in Westvale Estate on the outskirts of town. It took me about ten minutes to walk back and I didn't remember until I entered the freezing cold hall that the reason I had gone out for a cup of coffee in the first place was because I was famished with the cold and the central heating didn't work. The landlord had promised all week he was going to fix it but still nothing had been done. Mr Peebles was a horrible, sleazy little man who looked like the type who, on doing you a favour, would ask for it to be returned in kind.

"*Yeeeeuccccchhhh!*" I said, hearing my voice echo around the sparsely decorated living room (the feng shui was definitely up the left here).

I sat down heavily on the lumpy uncomfortable sofa that had questionable stains that I didn't want to dwell on all over the cushions.

I looked at the newspaper again and to my dismay discovered that it had got a bit wet in transit. The only job I had encircled with a red pen as an option had now been smudged and I couldn't make out the phone number to ring them and get an application form.

I sighed heavily, squinted at the soggy page and could just about make out an address. It was situated on the other side of town so I had better get a move on.

Putting on two pairs of socks and a pair of walking boots, I prepared to make the journey there on foot as I wasn't about to spend the meagre savings I had on taxis when God had given me a good pair of legs as transportation.

I was soaked to the skin and probably looked like a bedraggled rat by the time I arrived at my destination. My hair had frizzed to twice its normal proportions and was impersonating a whin bush that had got entangled around my face. My coat was sodden so that my T-shirt had started to stick to me (and not in an attractive Daisy *Dukes of Hazzard* way either), and what was worse I had started to sneeze and had a thumping headache to boot.

"Can I help you?" a sickeningly polished receptionist asked.

"I'd like an application for the position of PR Assistant, please," I said, sneezing into my hand as she wrinkled her nose in disgust.

"The closing date has already passed for that, I'm afraid," she answered primly. "All application forms had to be with our personnel department by four o'clock yesterday afternoon."

"You cannot be serious," I complained in a groan worthy of John McEnroe.

She shrugged her shoulders and went back to tapping keys on her computer.

I took the page I had torn out, which was now more damp than ever from being in my pocket, and studied it, which was when I discovered that the part that must have stated the closing date was completely illegible.

It was just my luck that the only appropriate job advertisement had now closed.

"Fine. Thanks anyway," I said, feeling disappointed in the extreme but not surprised. Everything else in my life was going wrong so why shouldn't this too?

I turned to leave but was stopped at the door by a petite, pretty, blonde lady who motioned for me to follow her into another room.

"I heard you asking about the PR Assistant's job. May I see your CV?"

"Em, I don't have it with me – I need to update it," I improvised. What would she think if she knew I was looking for a job without one to hand?

"Well, what experience do you have?"

I looked at her open face and into her blue eyes which were sparkling with interest and knew that it was a genuine question. I was terrified of anyone who knew me finding out I was here and wanted to keep as low a profile as possible. I wouldn't have put it past him to have me followed. All I wanted was to be allowed to forget. I wanted somebody to erase the last five years from my memory and give me a blank slate so that I could start afresh (this time with my brain in gear).

I pushed my wet hair behind my ears and in a stilted voice listed my qualifications and previous employment experience.

"Wow. That's very impressive," she said once I had finished speaking.

We were now in a private room and she was sitting opposite me.

"If you don't mind me asking a personal question, why did you leave your last job and what are you doing here?"

I opened my mouth, closed it again feeling flummoxed, and tried to think of a way of answering the question without making it sound like I was acting out a scene in a particularly far-fetched soap opera or one of Jeremy Kyle's shows probably entitled 'I trusted you, I made sacrifices for you, I was the perfect wife, but you stabbed me in the back and if I wasn't such a mess I might have the energy to kill you'.

"It's a bit complicated. Erm . . . my . . . erm . . . I just felt that I needed a new start. I used to work in the same company as my husband and things got a bit complicated after Ashley – after he – he – he –"

What the hell was wrong with me? Minutes before I had been listing out my relevant expertise, speaking in a reasonably even tone and making a good fist of it considering that the question had been asked unexpectedly, I wasn't prepared and looked like a partially wrung-out dishrag. Was this going to happen every time he was alluded to or merely hinted at in a conversation?

"I tell you what," the lady whispered, "to be honest we didn't receive the response I had been hoping for, so, just this once I'll make an exception given the fact that you have so much experience."

She handed me an application form.

"Fill this in and have it back to me tomorrow with your CV. I'll take a look at it and have a letter sent out to you to come for interview at some stage next month – assuming that you meet the criteria of course."

I opened my mouth to protest and say that I could do the job with my eyes closed and one hand tied behind my back, only to find that she was smiling broadly at me.

"Try and keep it dry though. Presentation is very important in Redmond House College. I'm Frances by the way. Frances McCormick but people usually call me Frankie."

"I'll have it back to you tomorrow and I'll do my best to keep it dry. And my name's Joanna." I took a deep breath. "Joanna McDermott but you can call me Jodi."

2

Frankie

Before I left the office I did what I always did these days and rang home first to see if anyone needed anything brought in or was going out, as I seemed to spend my time alternating between being 'Mammy' (AKA Wonder Woman) and moonlighting as an unofficial (unpaid) taxi service.

As I waited for an answer I looked at my engagement ring and decided that it needed a good clean. Owen and I hadn't got round to discussing actually getting married but if we ever did (we were in no rush as we'd both been there before) it would be nice if my diamonds were sparkling as opposed to being dull and tarnished.

"Hello?"

"Hi, love," I answered, hearing the voice of my stepdaughter Angelica on the other end of the line.

"Hi, Frankie," she said cheerily. "Will you be home soon?"

First of all I was shocked that she was in such a good mood and secondly she wasn't usually that enthusiastic about me coming home as I normally had a string of things for her to do. It wasn't easy being the seventeen-year-old eldest child of a family that had two younger step-siblings and a toddler in it. I sniffed the air and was overcome by the essence of rat.

"I will but first I want to know who needs to be picked up, dropped off, where, when and how and what you'd all like for tea."

Angelica who knew the drill well enough by now was already prepared for my barrage of questions and gave me the necessary information.

"Ben needs his football gear washed because he has a match tomorrow and he has to be at the basketball club for six o'clock tonight to practise before the game. He's playing at six thirty and he wants to know if you're going to come and watch him."

"Yes, yes and no," I answered swiftly. "His football gear will be sparkling for tomorrow and I will drop him to the club but, unless he wants me to bring the washing machine to the game with Jack strapped to my back, then I'm afraid that my being there to watch just won't be possible."

"You wouldn't have been able to go anyway as Carly has ballet this evening and is, as we speak, trying to put a tutu on inside out over her head, and is now stuck."

I listened in amusement as Angelica dropped the phone and started to chastise her younger stepsister as she helped her out of her predicament.

"*Aooooowwwww!* Angelica, you tugged my curls!"

"Well, your curls would have been fine if you'd stepped

into it like a normal person and why are you wearing your mammy's eye shadow?"

At this my ears suddenly pricked up as the only eye shadow I didn't carry with me was the really expensive one that I kept in the drawer of my bedside locker. It had cost a fortune and even Angelica had problems asking permission to use it but I had eventually given in as we shared most things and I enjoyed being able to trust her with it.

"The tutu's ripped at one corner and she's covered herself in purple eye shadow and given herself the most beautiful green blush on both cheeks but apart from that we're good to go."

"Can you do the needful, please?"

"I have a wipe in my hand and she will be pale and interesting again by the time you get back."

"Good. What would you like for tea?"

"Well, the kids have already eaten at your mother's house so they don't need anything and, as Dad's working late and will be getting fed at the college, I reckon that you and I should get something nice later like a big fat burger or a nice curry."

"Do you now?" I answered, thinking that it was a nice idea.

"I do," she responded. "Besides, I've got something to tell you."

My mind, at that point, decided to do a double-pike, high-flip somersault and came to the conclusion that it had to be bad news. Why else was she being so agreeable and reasonable? I was starting to imagine all sorts. She wanted me to talk to her father because she had decided to go and visit her free-spirited mother in whatever corner of the world she was currently calling home (which he wouldn't be happy about). She was in trouble at school and she needed me to soften the blow for her before she broke the news that she'd failed all her exams (he would be fuming and she would be grounded for the rest of her life). She was pregnant (he would quite likely be in need of resuscitation . . . oh *feck*!).

"Frankie, are you still there?"

"Yes, I'm here," I answered in a tight voice. "You are alright, aren't you? This thing that you need to talk about isn't going to give your father a heart attack, is it?"

"No, it's quite good news actually. I think you'll be pleased."

There was another silence.

My idea of good news and a hormonal teenager's idea of the same were probably on very different planes.

"I'll put the kettle on and have the tea ready for you coming home," she said pleasantly.

Oh my God, she *was* fecking pregnant.

"You're home quick," Angelica said as I fell through the back door (lucky to be still in one piece after having driven through one red light and possibly broken the speed limit on several occasions).

I had a quick look around and felt my stomach lurch even further. Normally the clean-freak within me had a mini-meltdown upon my arrival home from work as the house usually looked like a tornado had ripped through it, but today it was actually clean and tidy. My kitchen which had the look and feel of a country cottage with its cream coloured units, large oak table and ornamental beams on the ceiling had been neatly organised. The

14

throws on the armchairs that sat around the stove had been fixed the way I liked them and the mats had been hoovered. I should have been delighted but instead felt even more scared. Angelica detested cleaning and only ever did it under severe duress so for her to have done such a thorough job only made me think that the problem was much worse than I had first suspected.

I had yet to collect Jack but had rung my childminder and asked her if she could keep him for an extra half hour as I had something important to do.

"Are you alright?" I asked, scrutinising her appearance. I had already wracked my brains for possible signs that had been staring me in the face that I had chosen to ignore but had come to the conclusion that, if she had been having morning sickness or putting on any weight, she'd been hiding it very well. However, as teenagers had the capacity to dupe you at every turn-around, so cunning were their mindsets, I still wasn't convinced.

"I'm fine, Frankie. Why are you looking at me like a deranged person?"

We didn't get to discuss just how deranged I was capable of becoming were my suspicions confirmed, as Ben and Carly arrived into the kitchen arguing loudly about who was going to get dropped off at their place of leisure first.

"Shut up, Carly, it's only your first night of ballet practice in the Community Centre – it's hardly a performance of *Swan Lake* in the Waterfront Hall!"

I smiled in spite of myself. At fourteen my son was starting to have a very strong mind of his own and was more than capable of shouting down his seven-year-old sister.

"But Mammy will be taking me first and she'll stay with me cos she doesn't like stupid basketball!"

15

I held up my hands like a traffic controller and silenced them with one of my 'looks' that Owen maintained could have debilitating consequences if I stared at you for long enough.

"If you don't stop fighting I'll not be taking anybody anywhere. I'll be staying here and putting my feet up and watching the soaps like a normal person who doesn't have demanding children. Besides, I was just in the middle of a rather important conversation with Angelica and now you're interrupting me and annoying my head with your arguing."

They stood there looking at me until I opened the door and motioned for them to get out. If Angelica was about to tell me that I might or might not have to get used to the title of step-granny at the ripe old age of thirty-seven, I'd rather have a hissy fit followed by a breakdown in private thank you very much.

"Frankie, you're acting really weird. The only reason I wanted to talk to you is because I've met someone. His name is Jerome Devereaux and he's totally gorgeous and all my friends are really jealous."

"And what have you been doing with him?" I asked, narrowing my eyes not, mind you, that I wanted the intimate details, but still it would be best to be honest about it and if it had been a one-night mistake then I could try and make Owen recollect what he was like as a reckless (horny) teenager.

"We've only been out a few times so far but I definitely know that he's 'the one'."

She was now pirouetting on the spot and hugging herself gleefully.

I laughed which was probably not the best reaction but

I couldn't help myself. She was seventeen! What the hell did she know about finding 'the one'? As far as I was concerned 'the one' lived in the same angelic realm as unicorns and dragons and other mythical creatures, primarily because he simply didn't exist as quite frankly all men were flawed in one way or another.

"Angelica, you're seventeen years old, love, and you have many years of living to do yet before you find the right man. I'm very glad that you've met someone nice but please don't kid yourself that this is it because it isn't. Now, getting back to what's really important, have you and this boy, this Jerome person, been doing things?"

"Like what?" Angelica demanded huffily.

I knew that I had probably hurt her feelings by being brutally honest but it was for her own good. I didn't want to see her marching down the aisle barely out of a gymslip only to realise several years later that she had made the most humongous mistake of her life and married the biggest prick available who she mistakenly thought was 'the one' (and, yes, I am talking about myself here funnily enough – how'd you guess?).

Tony (the scumbag ex who decided to run off with an American stick-insect) had taught me a few valuable lessons in life – the first one being that you don't accept the first man who is nice to you as they're only doing that because they're looking for something, or several things maybe. My other learning experiences had come from the fact that I had to stand on my own two feet after relying on someone else for a long time or at least until I'd met Angelica's father Owen, who, when it came down to it was the nearest there could be in life to 'the one' even though he did bite his nails, snore quite loudly and truly believed that Angelica was still a little girl, perfect in every way with no diva-like qualities at all.

"Like have you been doing things you shouldn't be doing? Has your relationship progressed beyond second base?"

She looked mystified and I concluded that the terminology had changed significantly since I had been doing what I shouldn't have been doing behind the proverbial bike shed many moons ago.

"Have you had sex with him yet?" I demanded loudly which was quite unfortunate as that was the moment that Owen decided to burst in through the door in a fluster, looking for student papers he had been marking the night before.

I looked at him, he looked at me and then we both turned to face Angelica who announced in a strangled voice that in future when she had news she would be sure to tell me over the phone if I was going to make such a deal out of everything.

"And, no, I haven't been getting beyond third step or fourth base or whatever they used to call it in the primitive years. We're taking things very slowly because Jerome says I'm special."

And with that she flounced out, leaving me to explain to Owen why I appeared to be harassing his daughter and demanding details about things he'd rather not imagine.

Welcome to the Addams family.

3

Angelica

I had decided to go for a walk as I wanted to put as much distance between Frankie and myself as possible. Who did she think she was, speaking to me like I was some sort of child who didn't know her own mind? And why did she think that she was qualified to lecture me on what love was? She hadn't exactly been successful in that department herself. Her husband left her and ran off with one of his work colleagues, therefore I think she had a cheek laughing at me. I *did* know how I felt. I was in love. Jerome was the one for me.

I was still puffing and panting by the time I arrived at my friend Katie's house. I would have gone straight to see Jerome only I knew that he was working and had told me that his mum and dad weren't keen on having unannounced guests as they liked to be properly prepared for company. I thought that this was quite strange as my own house was like a railway station most of the time and my dad and

Frankie didn't seem to mind, but I supposed that everyone had their own way of doing things.

"What's the matter with you?" Katie asked as I stood on her doorstep scowling.

"I'm so annoyed with Frankie."

"I thought you and she had been getting on okay lately?"

"We do get on alright when she's not making fun of me and completely dismissing my feelings. I couldn't wait to tell her about Jerome. She's usually so cool about stuff like that and I could always talk to her about anything. I can't believe that she's made me feel so bad."

Katie held the door open and I walked into her hallway.

"She laughed at me and told me that I didn't know what love was. She has some feckin' nerve. If it wasn't for my dad she would be on her own bringing up two children while her ex-husband paraded his new fancy piece in front of her face."

Katie motioned for me to follow her into the kitchen where she poured both of us a drink and we sat down.

"Okay, so aside from the fact that you're pissed with Frankie, how are things going? With the lovely Jerome?"

I grinned and arched an eyebrow. I loved the fact that all the other girls thought he was gorgeous.

"We're getting on really well. I've gone out with boys before but nobody has ever treated me the way he does. He makes the most amazing plans for us when we go out. I told you how last weekend he took me out for a meal and then we went to see Taylor Swift live in concert and I even got to sit in one of the corporate boxes and the view was amazing."

Katie's expression was tinged with envy as she sat with her glass in mid-air.

"His father's marketing company is really successful," I continued, "and he has lots of great contacts through that. We're going to a film premiere next month. I don't know what it is yet but it'll be an exclusive with all the trimmings laid on."

"Oh wow! Maybe you could ask him if he could get tickets for us as well. We'd pay for them of course."

I nodded but had a sneaking suspicion that Jerome wouldn't like that idea. He hated anyone else being there when we went out. He said that he loved spending quality time with just me.

Katie had a faraway dreamy look on her face and I knew that she was nearly sick with jealousy. Who wouldn't be? I had found the perfect boyfriend. He was handsome and showered me with gifts and attention, and as an added bonus I was the envy of all my friends at school who couldn't believe that I had landed myself such an unbelievable catch.

We had met outside the cinema one night purely by chance. I had been waiting for Dad to pick me up after meeting my friends and watching a film but he had got the time wrong and was fifteen minutes late which ordinarily I would have been cross about but on this occasion had been very thankful for. Jerome had been the ultimate gentleman and offered to stand with me until Dad arrived to pick me up and I hadn't argued. He was very easy on the eye with his floppy blonde hair, strong physique and sexy smile. We had chatted easily about bands and music and the films that we had respectively gone to see and then he had asked me if I had a Facebook page and the rest was history. We chatted solidly online for a week before he asked me if I would like to meet him for

21

something to eat. I readily agreed and by the time I had got home from our first date I was both full and deliriously happy.

My phone rang and I looked at my screen in disgust as I saw that it was Frankie ringing me.

I made a face at Katie.

"What?" I answered abruptly.

"Don't be like that, Angelica," she said in a tone that was obviously meant to humour me (but which I was determined wasn't going to work). "Look, I didn't mean to upset you."

"Well, you did!" I snapped, staring mutinously at the wall clock in Katie's kitchen. "I'm not five years old. I don't need you telling me what way I should feel or how I need to behave. Do you know how many people in my class have been going steady now for years?"

"I'm sorry, Angelica," Frankie said softly. "I tell you what, why don't you ask Jerome if he'd like to come over for dinner some evening this week? If he's so special then your father and I would like to meet him."

I silently contemplated this for a moment while Katie looked at me with raised eyebrows.

"Fine," I answered sharply. "I'll ask him but tell Dad that he's not allowed to embarrass me."

I hung up and grinned at my friend.

"You have the two of them wrapped around your little finger," she said, shaking her head.

I nodded in agreement and started to think about what I would wear for my very own episode of *Meet the Fockers*.

4

Ruby

I looked at the clock and sighed. It was time to set off for my appointment, the last one of the day at the clinic. I wasn't enamoured of the notion of attending in the first place. To me it was totally unnecessary. I was not into the process of baring my soul to complete strangers and wasn't looking forward to this. My doctor, however, had different ideas and she strongly recommended that I seek out some emotional guidance with regards to what I had in mind. Apparently even *I* wasn't infallible, even though I could be quite strong-willed. Sonia Bernstein had better be damn good at her job or my doctor was getting shot.

I checked my appearance in the mirror and decided that I looked normal enough. My hair (which was at the bad stage of growing into a longer length and looked mad) was tucked behind my ears. I had put on a little kohl eyeliner and rubbed some Vaseline on my lips and was dressed in a pair of brown linen trousers, a cream Rugby shirt and brown flat-soled boots. I put on my jacket, lifted my brown satchel bag and took a deep breath. My phone buzzed with a message and I looked and grinned as I saw it was a smiley face and a row of kisses from Luke. I sent him a kiss and hug back and instantly felt marginally brighter. I had the most amazing husband who was so supportive of everything I did.

After a short drive I arrived at the clinic five minutes before the appointed time.

I went in, gave my name to the receptionist and took a seat in the waiting room. I sat there fidgeting and screwing and unscrewing my hands.

I suppose you're wondering why I needed an appointment with a counsellor. After all, I was happily married, loved my husband to pieces, owned my own house, had a job I really enjoyed and had the most brilliant friends. Note I haven't mentioned my parents or rather my mothers to be exact. When I say 'mothers' I'm referring to Isobel and Georgie. Isobel is the one I call Mammy. She's the one who has always been there for me. She's bandaged my knees, sang me to sleep and kicked my arse when it's been required (which was and is quite often). Then there's my 'birth mother' Georgina (we call her Georgie for short as she hates sounding like she just wandered out of a Jane Austen novel). To make matters even more confusing she also operates under the name Sarah Larkin as she is an award-winning artist. All my life I've been nuts about all things arty which everyone thought was completely hilarious for some reason (probably because I've always been an irrepressible tomboy) so it made sense when I found her and we discovered where the artistic appreciation genes came from.

My mothers don't always see eye to eye, however, and

quite often I feel like an 'abandoned/adopted/reunited with birth-mother and in fear of offending adoptive-mother' child in the middle. They liked each other really but there was always tension, especially when I needed an opinion or advice on something. If jumping out of your skin to offer an answer in the quickest time was an Olympic sport, I had no doubt that they would both have been gold medallists at this stage. To give Georgie her due, she was very respectful of Isobel's position as my longstanding, longsuffering 'mother' but at the same time she was dying to make up for lost time and, as she belonged to a younger generation and was a creative woman of the world, I always liked to have her point of view. Isobel was also very respectful of the fact that Georgie had given birth to me and therefore had played an integral part in my 'being here' but could be quite defensive as she wasn't keen on being replaced and still thought she knew best. In fairness she'd known me since I was a baby therefore had an advantage and usually did know best (but I would never ever admit that for fear of constant reminders and permanent earache).

One of the proudest and most heart-wrenchingly emotional moments of my life had been when they both walked me up the aisle on my wedding day to meet Luke who was waiting at the altar for me. The day was totally perfect and couldn't have been made any more special, aside from the fact that I would have traded in all my teeth to have had my daddy with me. He died when I was eighteen and I'd never got over it. I'd learned to cope but I thought about him every day. If I had been able to choose my own dad, I would have picked him. In the words of Tina Turner he was 'simply the best'. He could never be replaced. It didn't stop me thinking about the 'real one' however, from a purely 'curiosity might kill me instead of the cat' perspective. I hadn't given it much thought before I found out about Georgina. I suppose I was too preoccupied thinking about tracing *her* but, now that I had, I was hungry for more information and didn't see the harm in finding out the whole truth about my parentage. After all, it was my right to know who I was, who I had inherited my features, my temperament and my funny little idiosyncrasies from. As for my hair, Georgie was entirely to blame. We both had wild untameable locks which were red in colour. I had a temper to match but, as Georgie was on the whole very mild-mannered, I could only assume that my father was responsible for that. I hadn't broached the subject in a long time as I was trying to work up the courage to do so. It was not the type of thing you could drop into a conversation between the starters and main course. 'By the way, Georgie, in order to create me who exactly did you shag and just out of interest where did the conception happen?'

I had an intrusive image in my head of a Ford Cortina with a creaky suspension but kept shoving it away as it didn't fit in with what I knew of Georgie. She didn't seem like the type of woman who would have casual sex in the backs of cars or anywhere else for that matter. She seemed like someone who was quite sensible and loving and caring and not at all like the sort of person who would give up her own baby. It didn't surprise me, therefore, to find out that it hadn't been her decision. Her family weren't exactly supportive. 'Not exactly supportive' being the operative phrase for people who cared so little about their own flesh and blood and so much about their reputations, money and standing in the community that they willingly cast me out into the cold without a second thought.

I had only ever mentioned my father once to Georgie and that had been in the early days after we had first met. I had simply asked her if she could tell me who he was but she had looked terrified and I had told her not to worry.

She told me hesitantly that she would tell me more about 'him' when she was ready but that we needed to concentrate on getting to know one another for now. I knew that this made sense but the impulsive, 'eager to find out' side of me was dying to know more and I couldn't help the way I felt. I would, however, have to learn to curb my enthusiasm and respect Georgie's wishes which would be easier said than done. I suppose in a way this was why I was here waiting to see a counsellor now. Finding Georgie had been a wonderful experience but had left me feeling emotionally drained and I felt, having begrudgingly accepted the advice I was given, that before I embarked on anything else I needed to brace myself. I hadn't actually told anyone about my intentions with the exception of Luke and Frankie but they were accustomed to simply agreeing with me at this stage as they knew that to argue would be futile.

"Ruby Reilly, please," the receptionist called.

I felt as if everyone was looking at me and wondering what I was doing there. They weren't of course. They were all probably too preoccupied with their own reasons for needing to be there. (I was nothing if not totally paranoid.)

I was shown into a bright and airy office where a

pretty dark-haired girl was sitting writing in a notebook. I quickly glanced around and noticed that there wasn't a couch or a straitjacket in sight (my mind had been going slightly into overdrive of late).

"Ruby. Lovely to meet you. I'm Sonia." She smiled warmly at me with an open and engaging expression and I was instantly left-footed. For some reason I had anticipated that the counsellor would have a foreign accent, be wearing her hair in a taut and severe bun and have a large pair of spectacles hanging from a chain around her neck which she would put on while swinging a pendulum in front of me and telling me to count backwards from ten. (Perhaps the crazy view I had on life was why I needed feckin' counselling in the first place.)

She invited me to sit in the armchair opposite her, and then said softly, "I have some information in front of me which tells me a little about the reasons you've been referred to me, Ruby. But before we explore those issues I'd like you to tell me in your own words what you would like to achieve. Why are you here?"

I looked at her, stared at my hands, and my eyes fixated upon a photograph on her desk which pictured a man holding a small girl who was looking into his face and laughing.

"I'm here to mentally prepare myself for finding my father," I said matter of factly.

5

Jodi

I followed the library assistant as she directed me towards a free computer. I switched it on, called up a blank document on the screen and began to create a CV. My fingers flew over the keys as I listed my qualifications and experience and I knew that it was an impressive combination that would create a good impression with prospective employers. I thought back to all the times when I had been in the position of hiring and firing and what I had looked for. Qualifications were indeed important but a good attitude and the will to succeed and be the best were also attributes that I valued and admired.

It seemed that those were things that *he* had looked for all those years ago when I had arrived at Digital Concepts for a job interview. Little did I know that I was going to end up with a lot more than I had bargained for and I wasn't just talking about the public relations post, the petrol allowance and the discount at one of Belfast's most prestigious Lisburn Road boutiques. I had always thought that it had been a stroke of luck that he had been on the interviewing panel that day. Global sales managers aren't usually present when a prospective marketing manager is being recruited, but apparently he was called in at the last minute as the company had been let down by another senior member of staff. However, now, instead of viewing it as some type of good fortune I tended to think that my life had been sabotaged by the devil himself. I hit the keys on the computer harder than I had intended as a sudden moment of anger engulfed me but it left as quickly as it had arrived and was replaced with the usual sadness and misery that had been my constant companions of late. The noise, however, incurred the wrath of a cross-looking librarian who cleared her throat with a superior and disapproving air and looked sternly in my direction.

I studiously looked at the screen, trying to ignore the fact that her eyes were boring into my downturned forehead. If only she knew what I'd been through, she would be offering to go and sort him out for me. If it had been as simple as an affair, a momentary slip in judgement or a stupid meaningless fling, I would still have been crushed but might have been able to work through it (although the likelihood of him having retained all his manhood if my father had got hold of him would have been slim). That, however, was most certainly not the case. His deceit had been so great and so calculated that it had taken the very breath from me and forced me to leave my home with not much more than the clothes I stood up in.

It was too late when I remembered that I had very little money as I had invested most of my hard-earned cash in a fixed-term savings account that I couldn't touch for a year. To my dismay, however, my rainy day had come a lot sooner than expected and brought thunder and lightning and destruction in its wake. All I had left was £2,000 in my personal account and I had taken it all out the day I had left. It was slowly dwindling away but one thing was for sure – I'd rather die as a pauper in a cardboard box before I withdrew anything from our joint account. Other women might have been happy to clear it out and leave him with nothing but my hurt and disbelief had been so raw that I wanted nothing connected with him. The one thing I had desired he hadn't given me and I didn't want anything else.

Everything I had worked for and treasured was still in the house along with my clothes, shoes, gorgeous costume jewellery and designer accessories. But what did it all mean? It meant nothing in light of what he had done and how little he must have thought of me. How could he do it? How could he treat me in such a terrible way?

I didn't know if he had looked for me or tried to locate me but he would have had a job. Not only had I arrived in a tiny backwater town in deepest Tyrone but I had gone back to using my maiden name and cut up all my credit cards so that I wouldn't be tempted to use them and be traced that way. I didn't know if my sudden disappearance was causing him much suffering or not, but I sincerely hoped that it was making him feel moderately anxious and above all that he was looking foolish and stupid. He would hate that more than anything else.

I used to have a close network of friends when I was younger but with time everyone had moved on and gone their separate ways and I hadn't been in contact with any of them in many months as my work had started to take over my life. I had also got the distinct impression that they all thought I'd crawled up my own arse, so high was my own opinion of myself, which wasn't strictly true but looking back I think I took my lifestyle and the people involved in it a lot more seriously than I should have. Therefore it was no surprise that nobody apparently had noticed I was gone. My friendships were just another casualty of my extremely questionable decision to become involved with a deceitful underhand manipulator. I had had one or two missed calls from the office but, as the last thing I wanted to be reminded of was him, I had ignored them completely while shuddering at my own stupidity.

I completed the application form in my neat handwriting, printed off my CV and on a wing and a prayer popped it in an envelope and started to walk back to the college where I planned to kiss it, drown it in holy water and hand it into reception in anticipation of some good news soon.

I curled up on the sofa that evening with a polystyrene cup of tea (because I didn't trust the chipped mugs in the fusty cupboard – I really must splash out on a new mug) but all the delicately flavoured Darjeeling in China would not have persuaded me to go back to the plush three-storey townhouse I used to reside in on the Malone Road in the south of Belfast. There were some things that were just too highly priced and I was not willing to sell my soul to the devil for a fancy house and a few bits of designer gear. My stomach lurched just a tiny bit when I thought of my beautiful clothes and walk-in shoe cupboard that housed all my babies. At the mere thought of babies of any description a frisson of annoyance shot through me and I tried to chase the unwanted thoughts and images out of my head. He had always told me that children were never to be part of the deal and I had reluctantly accepted that. I comforted myself with the notion that I was young and ambitious, and losing my figure and having to take precious time off work didn't really appeal to me, although I think I could have been persuaded had we discussed having a family at some point. I remembered the dolls I used to have as a child and how I used to dress them and do their hair and rock them to sleep. I was a wonderful mother to my dolls and had I been given the chance I could have been a good role model and provider for my own children. But like everything else he had taken that away from me too. He hadn't lost out, of course. He'd had his cake and stuffed it down his throat all in one go, and as usual I was the one who had made the sacrifices, probably while he laughed up his sleeve at me and congratulated himself on how cunning he was.

My mobile rang and I looked at the screen, sighed and pressed the button that would ensure that the call was ignored. It was my mother who, no doubt, would be ringing to remonstrate with me yet again about my actions and to demand to know where I was hiding, which I had no intention of telling her. She had told me the last time I spoke to her that I was going through a phase and it would pass.

"Every woman is unhappy with their lot at one time or another, Joanna darling, but you just have to stick with it instead of running away. If your father had stayed with me for a bit longer and tried to work things out, instead of having a mid-life crisis and going to live in the bloody Lake District to collect antiques, our marriage might have survived. But he never gave it a chance."

I had shuddered both at her words and the sound of her voice which was condescending in the extreme. She hadn't the first notion why I had taken the action I had nor had she taken the time to find out. She just presumed that I was overreacting about something.

Unlike her, however, I wasn't prone to wanton acts of drama for no good reason and I could've been a hell of a lot more dramatic, believe me. My ex-husband loved nothing more than being the centre of attention, especially at work, where he seemed to think he was running the show. He loved regaling the staff with stories of the exotic and foreign places he visited and how he was able to clinch deals that a lesser man would have lost. He was cocky and confident but with a likeable cheeky streak that had drawn me to him in the first place. I didn't want to think about him in that way, though. He had destroyed that and as a result I could have provided our colleagues with a hell of a lot of office gossip. The secretaries could have got mileage out of his activities for weeks. The only reason I didn't do it at the time was because, after a lot of thought, I reasoned that revenge is a dish best served cold. I was going to think long and hard about my actions. There were people I needed to see and facts that required further investigation before I made any more decisions.

I fiddled with the silver Celtic cross around my neck which was something I always did when I felt lost and needed help. It was a wonder that the design was still there and that it hadn't been rubbed off as I had been handling it a lot lately. It was very precious to me as it had belonged to my brother Paul. He had been dead now for a long time but I could still feel his presence around me and I liked to think that when I was in trouble he was there, putting a comforting arm around me and having a word with those in control of our destiny to tell them that I needed a break.

"Hurry up, big bro," I whispered as I kissed the pendant and let it fall back to its usual position on my neckline.

The most important thing for me to do at the moment was to get back on track and become independent again. I had become spoilt and pampered in the last number of years and had started to take my way of life for granted. I had been brought up in a middle-class household and had never wanted for anything but had never experienced anything like the luxury that my married life had brought to me. My now 'ex' husband had inherited considerable wealth as he was the only son of a prosperous farmer and, as he had sold the land before the property prices fell, we wanted for nothing. My family had benefited as well which was precisely why my mother was so keen for me to 'sort things out and remember my vows'. Perhaps her weekly game of bridge wasn't as much fun when she wasn't able to keep her friends regaled with stories of new cars, fancy holidays and what shoulders her daughter was rubbing against at the various functions she attended as part of her job.

My heart was beating like a brass drum, I could feel beads of perspiration forming on my brow and the polystyrene cup which had been in its entirety before was now lying shredded to bits beside me in a heap while I continued to fidget in agitation.

"Stop it," I commanded myself firmly before taking the disintegrated cup and leaving the room. In the kitchen I threw it in the bin before spraying all surfaces with bleach and vigorously wiping them down.

I finished what I was doing and ascended the stairs to my cold and lonely bed. It was as hard as a board and had the squeakiest mattress in the country, but it would have to do for now. The bed in my marital abode had been a sleigh-bed made from the finest leather and boasting linen made from the highest quality and softest material. It had been comfortable and my husband and I had enjoyed many satisfying nights in it but those days were well and truly over now. I had been a gullible idiot. A trophy wife. A fool.

I turned over on my back, looked at the ceiling, closed my eyes, pictured my brother's face and willed him to give me the courage I needed.

You are master of your own destiny now, Jodi, so be strong. Stand tall and look the world right in the eye. You've done nothing wrong but you still have everything to prove.

6

Frankie

I was strangely preoccupied as I flicked through the application form that had just arrived on my desk. I smiled as I looked at the neat handwriting that I had already predicted Jodi would deliver and nodded my head and pursed my lips in approval as I read down an impressive list of her qualifications and relevant experience. Then I frowned as I noticed that her references were well out of date, none of them relating to her work experience in recent years.

I was very curious about Jodi. There was most definitely a story there that needed ironing out. She'd had a very good job and several promotions within the company she'd worked for and her education and skills were exemplary which therefore begged the question of what on earth she was doing here in Swiftstown looking for a junior position in a college. I was aware that she was looking for a new start but was seriously questioning her motives in thinking Swiftstown would be the right place to begin whatever journey she was on.

"What are you doing?" Ruby asked as she sauntered into my office and plopped her bum on the corner of my desk, which meant she wasn't simply calling in for a quick hello but that she wanted a full-scale catch-up on all the gossip with a bit of ridiculing of our workmates thrown in for good measure.

"Don't tell anyone but I'm looking at a late application that has just come in."

"Oh, you rebel," Ruby said, sucking air through her teeth and tutting. "People always told you that you'd end up being corrupted, hanging around with me too much. So what's so unique about this one then that he or she is getting such specialist treatment?"

"Oh, I don't know. She's got lots of experience and I feel like I should give her a chance. She looks like she's had a tough time and needs a break."

"And we all know what that's like," Ruby sighed, looking at her hands and swinging her legs.

"Shit. I almost forgot. How did you get on with your counselling yesterday? Was it good?"

"As good as anything can be when you're made to feel like a fecking loony-bin and forced to expose your feelings to complete strangers who take notes about what you're saying and make sporadic comments about your body language and how uptight you appear. I bet if I had scratched my arse and picked my nose it would have meant something sinister that she could have told a story from. 'You need to learn to relax, Ruby. Give yourself a shake and loosen up all your muscles and breathe.'" Ruby finished her speech in a bizarre foreign accent that sounded partly German.

"Is your counsellor not from here, then?" I asked,

thinking that having to decipher what someone was saying in broken English would have almost certainly tipped her over the edge altogether and required her to go straight from therapy into anger-management sessions.

"No, she's from Belfast, I think."

I raised one eyebrow and fixed her with a penetrating stare.

"I had this picture in my head of someone who would be talking in a funny accent and telling me to lie down on a couch and whatnot and now I can't get rid of it," Ruby said in an exasperated tone while flapping her hands around her.

I could tell that she'd had to explain the same thing to Luke who no doubt was just as confused as me.

"Even though she's from here and you sat looking at her for the entire session," I surmised.

"I'll say it before you do. I know it's no wonder that I need counselling." Her tone of voice was resigned. (She had obviously heard that before too.) "Blame my lack of knowledge about my father for screwing so badly with my head."

"What did she say about all that?" I asked, leaning forward in my seat. "Does she think you're doing the right thing?"

"That's the thing. They're not there to tell you what to do. They're only there to advise you on the best way to handle certain situations, but she reckons that if finding my father is going to give me closure and make me a happier, more well-rounded person, then that's what I should do. Of course she advised caution because not every situation works out the way you'd like it to but I, above all people, know that so I'm already prepared. You should have seen her face when I told her what had happened with Georgie. I'll bet she's heard some weird and wonderful revelations in her time but I think even she was shocked."

"Who wouldn't be?" I murmured, thinking of all the trauma that Ruby had been put through at the hands of other people who had created a web of lies that both she and her birth mother had been badly affected by. It seemed that some people would stoop low enough to do anything if it meant saving their own skins and reputations, but thankfully it had all worked out in the end and they had both triumphed through adversity.

I suddenly thought of Ruby's longsuffering mother.

"And how does she think that you should handle breaking the news to Isobel who may well have a heart attack at the thought of any more manhunts or wild-goose chases?"

Ruby groaned and I knew that even she didn't want to think about that particular scenario.

"One thing at a time, my dear. I'm having a hard enough time getting my own head around this situation without involving anyone else at this point."

"Surely you'll have to involve Georgie though? After all, she's the one who's in possession of the necessary information about your birth father."

"I know, but she acted like a scalded cat when I brought it up before so I'm a bit wary, but as you say I'll have to broach it with her at some stage. I'm just trying to time it right. It's a bit delicate. I can hardly just casually drop it into the conversation after discussing the weather. 'By the way, Georgie, I assume that I'm not a test-tube baby or that you didn't use a turkey-baster, therefore if you wouldn't mind could you tell me who fathered me?'"

I raised my eyes to heaven and came to the conclusion

that Ruby must have been born under a particularly unlucky moon as nobody else in the world led a life that was so completely and totally complicated. Of course it was always very useful to have a friend who led such a colourful existence as there was never a dull moment and it also served to remind you that you weren't the only one who had problems. Angelica's boyfriend was coming for dinner this evening and I still hadn't interrogated her as to his tastes.

In fact, on reflection, it had been a very stupid idea (but at the time it was necessary to stop World War Three from breaking out). One wrong move could have very unpleasant consequences and I could find myself even more unpopular with Angelica than I already was. I could cook the wrong thing and a) make him violently ill, b) insult his possible vegetarianism, or c) make him dump her with whatever I concocted.

Shit.

I went home and placed Jack in front of the Disney Channel, in what we commonly referred to as 'the den', as we had transformed the room that had once served as a spare bedroom into a snug playroom for the children. With its brightly painted walls, comfy sofas, bean bags and boxes of toys I could have cheerfully joined my son and vegetated in front of the television for the rest of the evening but unfortunately I needed to be busy.

I ran upstairs to the bedroom, swiftly changed out of my work clothes into tracksuit bottoms and T-shirt and viewed myself in front of the large mirrored wardrobe that was positioned between the vanity unit and the door that led to our en suite bathroom. I looked tired and drawn and decided that before I met Angelica's boyfriend I would have to apply some make-up and make myself altogether more alive-looking. And wear something flattering, of course.

Once downstairs again I started to raid the food cupboard, wondering what on earth I was going to make for a complete stranger who could have any amount of weird tastes.

"Have you got dinner on yet?" Angelica demanded as she came in and threw her bag on the kitchen table, looking flustered.

"Hello to you too," I greeted her.

"*Helllooooo*," she said with a sway of her shoulders as she came and stood beside me. "You're supposed to be impressing Jerome this evening."

"I'm not snogging him," I answered indignantly. "Therefore it's not up to me to impress him."

"Well, is there any chance of you getting something prepared for him at least," she responded, totally ignoring me (she suffered from an advanced case of selective hearing which I believe is prevalent in those aged between thirteen and twenty-one). "I don't want him thinking we're a bunch of saddos that can't cook, y'know."

"Well, you could help me in that regard by actually telling me what he likes to eat. I'm not psychic."

"He doesn't like red meat, not fussed on vegetables, hates soup and won't eat salad," she informed me in an annoying sing-song voice.

"Note that I said tell me what he *likes*," I emphasised pointedly.

"Well, I was helping you by telling you what he *doesn't* eat so you can figure it out. Oh my God, I've so much to do. I have to put on my tan and straighten my hair and can you iron my white skinny jeans for me?"

I held up my hands to emphasise the point that I did indeed only possess two of them and wasn't a multi-tasking octopus but sadly was showing them to the back of her retreating blonde highlighted head as she disappeared out the door.

So I did what I always did in a crisis: I lifted the phone.

"What the hell do you cook for somebody who doesn't eat red meat, hates vegetables and won't entertain soup or salad?" I demanded, cradling the phone under my chin as I rifled through the fridge which was filled with all the ingredients I apparently didn't need.

"Your telephone skills definitely need to be more finely tuned, Frankie, as that is certainly not the recommended way to greet someone."

"Hello, Ruby. Now what the hell am I going to make for dinner? Fecking Angelica and her bloody boyfriends. A glass of wine and a foot-rub is what I want this evening," I muttered, fantasising about lying my length across the sofa instead of donning an apron and having to play host to a boy I'd never met before but who was in the very centre of Angelica's world and was therefore important.

"*Ahem!* Frankie, are you listening to me?" Ruby demanded.

"Sorry, honey, what were you saying?"

"I said you should make chicken noodles. Get some chicken and mushrooms and stir in noodles and lots of soy sauce. You can't go wrong with that. I didn't hear any mention of him not liking those ingredients. Talk about fussy. Why are you cooking anyway? You're not the one that wants to fumble with him."

"She says she's not doing anything with him and I believe her. Apparently they're taking things slowly because he wants to get to know her properly and she's special."

"Oh please!" Ruby scoffed. "If ever there was a line designed to make a girl drop her knickers, that's it!" She continued in a simpering voice. "'I'll wait, darling. I'll not put any pressure on you. We'll move at your pace and when you're ready then we'll get down and dirty and you'll do anything I want because I've behaved like such a gentleman even though I'm a horny little git with only one thing on my mind!'"

I opened my mouth to protest but realised that she had a point. I would have to have another talk with Angelica about how naïve and gullible her behaviour could potentially be and how boys of a certain age always have ulterior motives for being nice because they're so full of hormones that they'd jump on a cracked plate if it would respond accordingly.

Two hours had passed and miraculously I had managed to cook dinner, become Angelica's tanning consultant, iron her clothes, take Ben to a football match and change into something more appropriate myself. Owen was laughing at me as I had told him that I didn't know how Jerome was feeling but that if he was as nervous as I was then we already had something in common.

"Why are you nervous?" he asked as I patted the oversized cushions that lay on the corner sofa in the mocha-and-cream living room and straightened the family photographs that took pride of place above the limestone mantel-shelf.

"Because I want everything to go okay. Angelica really

likes him. She's talked about nothing else since she first mentioned him and I don't want to be responsible for messing things up. You *are* aware that if the night turns out to be an unmitigated disaster it will somehow end up being my fault?"

Owen put his arms around me and kissed me on the nose. "Dinner will be wonderful as always. Angelica will be happy just to have her boyfriend here and see you making the effort to impress him. Stop giving yourself a hernia. It's not good for the digestion."

"*He's here!*" Angelica screeched from the hall while simultaneously fluffing her hair, applying lipstick and straightening her top as she scrutinised her appearance in the large ornate mirror that hung on the main wall opposite a cushioned church bench.

"Jesus, there wouldn't be as much fuss if the feckin' pope called in," Owen complained.

"*Sssssshhhhhhhh!*" Angelica hissed before going to answer the door.

He wasn't at all what I had expected but then I always did get it wrong. I never was good at listening to voices or hearing about people and then being able to guess what they looked like. If they were tall with black hair I would without fail picture them as being stumpy and ginger. As for Jerome, he was of average height with floppy blonde hair and blue eyes. He had a broad chest and shoulders and carried himself confidently and, as soon as he saw Angelica, his face lit up and he treated her to a one-hundred-watt smile that would have made any teenage girl swoon. I could see the attraction right away and why her friends were all obviously a variety of shades of green.

"This is Jerome," Angelica beamed as if she was a farmer showing off a prize bull that had just won every rosette at the fair. "This is my dad Owen."

"Pleased to meet you." He shook Owen's hand and smiled.

"And this is my step-mum Frankie," Angelica said as she presented me like it was the queen who had just entered our humble abode.

"Hello, Frankie," he said, shaking my hand brusquely. "I've heard a lot about you."

I hoped that what he had heard was good but, as he didn't meet my gaze when I smiled at him, I had a sinking feeling that I had been painted as the interfering stepmother who was out to obstruct the path of love's young dream.

I had a notion that life was about to become very stressful and my hunches weren't usually wrong.

7

Angelica

I was delighted to see that Jerome and my dad were getting on so well. They were currently talking about the state of the economy and I noticed that Jerome seemed to be very knowledgeable in this area.

"And what is it that you do exactly?" Dad asked him between mouthfuls of noodles.

I noticed that Jerome had barely touched his dinner but was instead pushing it around his plate which I knew would drive Frankie absolutely insane. I could see that she had gone to a lot of trouble in laying the dining-room table with the best glassware and dinner set that normally only came out on special occasions. The scent of fresh lilies wafted from the sideboard beside a lit ornate candle.

"Don't you like your food, Jerome?" she asked as she came through to the dining room carrying a bottle of sparkling water and some glasses.

"It's fine," Jerome said dismissively and I could almost feel her bristling as tension descended.

"Well, if you don't like it I'm sure I can fix you something else," she replied much to my surprise.

I say 'surprise' because Frankie has been known to throw things (usually at me) when people (usually me) turn their noses up at dishes that she has lovingly prepared.

Jerome was still talking to my dad and didn't answer.

Frankie continued to tidy around the table and then to my relief I heard Ben calling her and she disappeared upstairs.

"Jerome's just telling me about some new clients that he's made for his father's business," Dad said in an impressed voice. "It all sounds very exciting and he's also told me that his dad has a corporate box at Anfield and that the next time Liverpool is playing he might be able to get me a few tickets!"

Dad's eyebrows were bobbing up and down at a rate of knots and he was grinning like an eejit.

Some people reckon that the way to a man's heart is through his stomach but in my dad's case give him a red scarf, the promise of attending the next live match and a rousing chorus of 'You'll Never Walk Alone' and you've automatically made a friend.

Frankie came back into the room and apologised for having to leave.

"Sorry about that. Ben was just getting his football gear together and he needed some help packing his bag."

Jerome nodded in response and then went back to playing with his food.

Frankie gave me a forced smile and sat down again although she looked extremely uncomfortable (think poker up the arse) which irked me. Why couldn't she just relax and try and enjoy herself? Why was she being so uptight? If anyone should feel under pressure it was me. I had just introduced my boyfriend (the love of my life, the cheese to my pickle, the jelly to my ice cream) to my parents and so far I thought that things had gone reasonably well.

"So, Jerome, what do you work at?" Frankie asked.

"God, Frankie, play catch up," I said. "We've been talking about his father's business for the past half hour."

"Oh, I'm sorry," Frankie responded, looking embarrassed. "All part of being a mother, I'm afraid. When football gear has to be sorted the world stands still. But I'm sure your mother does the same for you, Jerome. Mothers and their sons and all that."

Jerome made a funny face and didn't answer and I knew that Frankie had also noticed this and was looking at him quizzically. She looked like she was about to say something else but changed her mind.

Dad and Jerome started back into Anfield talk and Frankie sat silent – but that didn't last long. She soon started to ask Jerome questions about his past schooling and what he liked to do for fun and I willed her to stop acting as if he was supposed to be trying to impress at a job interview. I could see that he looked strained and noticed his tone of voice become sharper.

Then Frankie insisted on making Jerome a ham sandwich (without butter as he doesn't like it) and after dessert (which he didn't eat) he and I excused ourselves and went for a drive.

I felt as if forty tonnes of concrete had been lifted from my shoulders.

"That went well," I said as more of a statement than a question.

"I suppose it did," he answered. "Your step-mum's a bit of a handful, isn't she? Does she usually ask so many questions? It's a good job I like you so much or that could seriously put me off, y'know."

I must have looked stricken as he touched me on the arm and smiled. "I'm only messing with you. Don't look so worried. Your dad is a nice man and we had a lot in common, especially when it comes to football."

I grinned and nodded excitedly. "Yeah, you did really well there. Your efforts to impress worked really well!"

Jerome made a noise that sounded like a snort. "I've only said that I'll try and get him a few VIP tickets. It's no big deal. I'd do that for anyone if I wanted something from them in return."

"Oh really?" I said questioningly. "And what exactly would you like from my father then?"

Jerome indicated and turned down a dirt side-road that I knew led to an old quarry. "I'd like to be with his lovely daughter. I'd like to get to know her a lot better."

Jerome took a series of twists and turns once we had entered the grounds of the quarry until we came to a particularly isolated spot around the back.

"I've never been here before," I said before realising how stupid that sounded. Why would I ever have had reason to have been there? It was a quarry after all.

He smiled as he stopped the car and turned to me.

"You, on the other hand, seem to know your way around here very well," I added.

He smiled again. "Oh, I know lots of dark corners where people can have a lot of fun."

As he began to kiss me and fumble with the buttons on my top it occurred to me that he must have been here before and, as his hands began to wander lower, I wondered for a split second who he had been with and whether or not he had promised their fathers tickets to any premiere football matches.

8

Ruby

Luke and I arrived home at exactly the same time and as usual had a race to see who could get the better parking spot (we're mature adults really – we're just very good at hiding it). It was three o'clock and we had both finished early and I was looking forward to a nice relaxing afternoon and evening.

We had been married for a little over a year and everything was going smoothly. We had a lovely home, enjoyed our respective jobs, got plenty of breaks away thanks to the fact that our parents were considerate enough to live in particularly scenic (my mother lived in Donegal) and hot (his parents had retired to Turkey) tourist spots and I had become something of a whiz in the kitchen much to everyone else's amusement. This was as far as my expertise extended, however, as I was still a mucky pup when it came to anything else that required domesticity so Luke's position as resident cleaning lady was safe. Even though I was loath to admit it, being with

Luke had also created a more mellow me. Frankie loved to remind me of times where my infamously quick temper had got the better of me but I just wasn't that person any more. I was generally more settled and happy these days. Luke was good to me and for me and I loved him so much it hurt. I still had my feisty moments, mind you, but they were a lot less frequent these days.

I closed the car door, took the bags from the boot and made my way into the house which smelt of sandalwood thanks to a radiator sachet in the hall permeating my home with its scent. I reached the small but compact kitchen in time to see that Luke had obviously beaten me to it and was unloading steaks, potatoes, mange tout and baby sweetcorn from a bag.

"Not today, darlin'," he said. "I have the immersion heater on for a bath which you are going to go and lie in now, then you are going to change into something more comfortable after which you are going to be served your dinner in style and maybe we can have a chat."

I liked the sound of his suggestions. All apart from the last bit as chats which were preceded by dinner and wine and Luke being all lovey-feckin-dovey could only be about one thing. The one thing in the world that I'd rather not talk about.

I sank gratefully into the lavender-scented bubbles and breathed deeply to let the stresses of the day wash over me. I loved relaxing and in order to indulge the water baby in me Luke had installed a large corner-bath in the house after we had got married. With its white units and walls that were a delicate shade of lavender with towels and mats to match, our bathroom was a very restful place to be – which was good as I needed somewhere I could try to ease the disquiet in my mind. Work was hectic and the management were constantly adding to my duties but I relished a challenge and didn't mind dealing with the students who were always coming to me for advice and guidance. If only I was as good at steering my own life, I'd be alright. I shut my eyes tightly and thought about what the counsellor had said. No one could force me into doing anything I didn't want to. I was to take one day at a time and think carefully about my actions and the far-reaching consequences they might have.

The bathroom door opened and Luke came in carrying a glass of white wine which looked like it had been chilled to the right temperature of perfection as the condensation was literally glistening tantalisingly on its sides.

"That looks divine," I said as I took the glass from him and drank deeply. "Yum."

"Dinner won't be long, love." He sat on the side of the bath.

I hated it when he hovered and I hated the hovering even more when I knew that it was liable to end up in a row because the whole reason why he was hovering was because he was trying to pluck up the courage to say what was on his mind.

"I saw Mandy earlier on today."

"Did you?" I said, resisting the urge to sigh loudly because I knew what he was going to say before he uttered the words. Mandy was his only sister and she had just got married.

"She's looking amazing. She has the most fabulous glow about her. Does that happen to all women when they get pregnant or just a select few?"

"I couldn't possibly say, Luke. I don't know the first thing about pregnancy." And I didn't plan on finding out either. If it was a glow he wanted he could go and get himself a halogen fire.

"She's so excited. They've already started to plan ahead. She's talking about doing up the spare bedroom as a nursery and I think they must have found out what sex the baby is at the last scan because she was very coy about it all."

"That's lovely," I said stiffly, wishing to feck that he'd close the door and get out. My bath was starting to get cold, I was starting to resemble a prune and I was becoming increasingly uneasy.

"She was asking about you. She was actually wondering if there was any chance of her baby having a little cousin some day."

I stood up abruptly and both myself and three gallons of water jumped out of the bath, soaking Luke in the process.

"*Oi!* What the hell did you do that for? What is your problem, Ruby? Why do you always have to act like this?" He followed me as I dripped down the hall and into our room.

Luke was starting to strip out of his wet clothes and ordinarily the two of us being semi-naked in the bedroom would have been an attractive prospect. Lately, however, any bedroom activity had started to lose its appeal as for Luke it had become a one-way street to making a baby which was something that was guaranteed to wilt my desires in seconds.

"You know how I feel, Luke, but still you keep pressurising me. What is so wrong with the way we are?

Is it so terrible for you to think that it might only be you and me in this family? We're alright on our own, aren't we? Why do we need anyone else?"

"You make it sound like I want to move in an illicit lover instead of talking about you getting pregnant," Luke responded in a hurt tone. "Why is the idea of having a baby so repulsive to you? Is it my genes? Are you afraid that our child might turn out to be a drunk like my father or are you scared that if we have a girl that she might be a lush like my mother?"

(That was indeed a frightening prospect but it wasn't the biggest problem.)

"Genes? Genes?" I shouted at him. "Don't talk to me about being scared of what the gene pool might hold when I don't even know where half my genetic make-up has come from!"

"I'm sorry," Luke said. "That was insensitive of me. I didn't mean to say that but it really upsets me that you're so unwilling to even think about it. I've watched you time and again with other people's children and you're a complete natural. You only have to look at the way that Ben and Carly treat you and, as for little Jack, he trips over himself to get on your knee whenever you're around – and you treat them like they're your own."

"But they're not my own, Luke. That's the beauty of other people's children."

He sat down heavily on the bed and I heard him sighing in a resigned and defeatist fashion and immediately was engulfed by guilt.

"Don't do this, Luke," I said, feeling close to tears. "It's not that I don't love children. You know that I do. The problem in this case lies with me. It's very complicated and hard for me to put into words but I have my own reasons for not wanting to get pregnant and have children of my own."

"You keep saying that but you never tell me why and I can't help you if I don't understand what the problem is."

"Please believe me when I say that I love you more than life itself and that I'd do anything for you but please don't ask me to do this because there could be so many far-reaching repercussions for so many people."

"What has this got to do with anybody else?" Luke said in exasperation. "This is about you and me. It doesn't involve anyone else."

"But, you see, that's where you're wrong, Luke. It does involve other people because it might affect the way that I view them in the future. I've only just found my birth mother and we're getting on alright and believe me when I say that I don't want that to change."

"I don't know what you're so scared of," Luke said as he approached me and put his hands on my shoulders. "But I promise that I will do everything in my power to make you feel better. I do beseech you, however, to rethink this decision. Nothing would make me happier than to see you carry and give birth to our child. A new life that would be wanted and needed and worshipped."

I didn't answer but instead thought about what it must be like to feel that you're wanted and needed. It must be nice to think that your birth was planned as opposed to viewing yourself as a huge nuisance that everybody wanted rid of as soon as you appeared.

9

Frankie

"I'm not sure about him," I said, taking a drink of my cappuccino. I didn't know why I was so bothered because, at the end of the day, if Angelica got suitably paired off it would mean that she'd be out of my hair. For my sins, however, I did care and even though my hair would be very grateful to be set free there was something irking me about the boy on whom the sun seemed to rise and set in Angelica's world.

"What's wrong with him?" Ruby asked, taking another bite of her sandwich.

"He never made eye contact with me once, he hardly spoke to me, seemed annoyed that I was interested in him and kept giving me snappy one word answers when I asked him anything. Correct me if I'm wrong but if you want to be a girl's boyfriend surely it's in your best interests to try and get along with her mother?"

"Maybe he was just nervous and completely in awe of you," Ruby suggested. "You are pretty amazing."

"It wasn't that he was nervous as such," I said

thoughtfully. "It was more like he was dismissive of me, as if I didn't matter or that I had no right to be interested in him. He talked away to Owen and even suggested getting him tickets and seats in the corporate box for the next Liverpool match so it wasn't as if he wasn't making the effort for him."

"How does he treat Angelica?"

"If Angelica were any more besotted she'd be on her knees and hanging off his ankle. It's pitiful to watch. But as far as I can see I have to admit that he's quite good to her. Gives her lots of presents and takes her out a lot but I don't care about any of that. There's more to a relationship than just the material end of it and, although I can't put my finger on it, there's something I don't like about him. He's definitely attractive but has very hard eyes."

"Hard eyes?" Ruby repeated with a smirk. "And how did Angelica think it all went?"

"She was quite animated last night while he was in the house and then they went for a drive and she was quiet when she came home. I tried to ask her how the night had gone but she said that she had a headache and just wanted to go to bed. I can't help worrying about her. I do hope she's alright."

"Are you sure you're not turning into your mother?"

I opened my mouth and then shut it again. Very tightly. I was digesting what she had just said and hoping fervently that it wasn't true. They do say that as you get older you start to get like those who brought you up . . . *nooooooooooooooooooooooooo!*

"Not that there's anything wrong with your mother," Ruby said quickly, obviously mistaking my silence for annoyance (instead of pure and unadulterated fear).

"I know there's nothing wrong with her technically," I mused. "She's just a bit of a loose cannon with her opinions and rather over-protective of her children."

The last bit was said in a slow mechanical voice as I thought about it.

Shit.

Ruby looked at me, looked away and then started to laugh.

"Don't worry, you're not that bad, Frankie, and anyway I think it's very admirable of you to care so much. After all, if Angelica's got herself a boyfriend, think of all the free time you'll have. She'll spend all her time with him and leave you alone."

"It's not as simple as all that though, Ruby. She's Owen's child and I do love her and if she is going to get into a relationship then I'd rather it was with a normal person who doesn't display signs of being potential trouble. Besides, if current circumstances are to be taken into account, I'm actually doing more for her now between slathering on false tan, cooking meals and providing entertainment for her and her boyfriend who by the way didn't eat my noodles yesterday because apparently soy sauce makes his lips swell. That was your suggestion, by the way."

"So what did he eat?" Ruby asked, her sandwich poised in front of her mouth in mid-air.

"I ended up making him a ham sandwich with no butter on white bread. I thought only Angelica was a fussy eater. She's the best food connoisseur in the world in comparison to this boy. And as if that wasn't bad enough, I offered him a piece of my home-made Malteser cheesecake that everybody loves, which has always earned me nothing but compliments, and he turned his nose up at it as if it was a pile of dog-shit heaped on a plate."

"So is that why you've taken a spite against him then?"

Ruby, who knew that people who were pernickety about their food were a pet hate of mine, obviously thought that she had it all figured out except she hadn't. Annoying and frustrating as the food situation had been (I had battered the ham to within an inch of its life before it had been slapped between two pieces of bread and sawed in half in a frenzied manner), that wasn't my main concern.

I looked around the hotel bistro that was bustling with Saturday shoppers and sighed. Angelica wouldn't thank me for prying into her business and would no doubt accuse me of trying to ruin her fun as she seemed to think that I was on a permanent mission to be a killjoy.

A mobile phone rang in the vicinity and we heard a girl sigh loudly. I glanced at her in time to see her pressing a button in an abrupt manner and throwing the apparently offensive item in a bag.

It was only when I took a second glance that I recognised the girl who had presented such a bedraggled image in my work several days earlier and, apart from filling in an impressive application form, she didn't appear to be any further forward.

I was in two minds whether or not to approach her as I didn't want to appear intrusive but curiosity got the better of me and I moved my chair back and stood up.

"Where are you going?" Ruby asked in surprise. "You haven't finished your baguette yet."

"It's okay, Rubes, I'm not leaving. There's just someone I want to say hello to."

I moved over to the girl's table.

"Hi, Jodi," I said gently but obviously not gently enough as she jumped half a mile in the air with fright and managed to practically douse herself in what looked like hot coffee.

"Shit! I'm so sorry. I didn't mean to frighten you. Hold on and I'll get you a cloth."

"It'll be fine," she protested but there was already a waitress on her way over.

"Are you alright, love?" she asked in a concerned tone of voice. "That was bound to be scalding. Are you burnt?"

"I'm fine, honestly," Joanna said, looking furtively around her, obviously hating the fact that she had been made the centre of attention (by me).

She looked most uncomfortable and I chided myself for not leaving well enough alone. I shouldn't have gone near her. I should have maintained a professional distance and left it up to her to come over to me.

"I'm fine, honestly!"

"Why don't you let me buy you another cup of coffee?" I said, faltering and feeling more and more like a bright-red stewed eejit by the second as I watched her lift her stuff and prepare to go.

"No. I'm fine honestly," she said firmly before walking away without looking back.

"Cheeky fecking cow!" Ruby announced as I walked back to the table. "You wouldn't have to ask me twice and I think I'd have the manners to say thank you as well."

"Ruby, if somebody scared the shite out of you and made you spill hot coffee over yourself, you wouldn't say thank you. You'd have them up against the nearest wall by the throat and well you know it."

"That's very much beside the point, Frankie. It's nice to be nice. Besides, I'm not as violent as I used to be. They'd maybe only get a small slap and a stern ticking off."

"Are you sure it was counselling you went for and not anger management or hypnotherapy or something?" I asked, looking quizzically at her. Ruby was very lovely and the most loyal friend in the world but a force to be reckoned with who didn't suffer fools gladly and was quite liable to thump you if you annoyed her as people in the past had found out to their peril. I did agree, however, that she was a lot less scary these days but, given the right provocation, I still reckoned she could frighten any opponent into submission.

"Yes, it *was* counselling, smartarse. So what's the story with Miss Attitude who has no manners?"

"She's the girl I told you about. She was going to apply for the job of PR Assistant but was too late for the closing date."

"Frankie, have you lost your marbles entirely?" Ruby demanded while spraying me with crumbs.

"No, I haven't. You should see the experience she has," I said, ducking to avoid another attack.

"In what exactly? People who work in public relations are supposed to have a personality that doesn't frighten or offend people, or had that little fact escaped you?"

"I know, dear, which is precisely why you work behind the scenes with the students and not with the public."

"Oh, ha feckin' ha."

"Look, I know a good asset when I see one! Her curriculum vitae reads like the perfect example of what a PR professional should be. She had a really good position in one of the biggest computer logistic companies in Belfast, for God sake!"

"So she's sitting here looking like one of our poverty-stricken students why? Is her company not missing her?"

"That's the funny part," I said thoughtfully. "She's left a really good job and doesn't seem to be in the position to explain why, although apparently it had something to do with her husband. They worked together, y'see, and must have split up. I can see how that would be awkward. If Owen and I fall out over breakfast I find it hard to meet him in the corridor in the college later in the day. I still feel like smacking him one but have to be nice to him no matter what because you have to be professional at all times."

"I do think that your common sense has gone on extended leave, Frankie. She left a major company to come here and apply for a junior job role in a college for a salary that probably just about covered her petrol allowance in the past and you don't think she could be on the run from the police? She's probably an embezzler or wanted for fraud or maybe she's involved in drug trafficking and is running for her life from the heroin lords." With every word Ruby's voice rose an octave and at the mention of drugs the entire bistro were now giving us their undivided attention.

"You've been watching too many late-night thrillers, Ruby. I'm going to have to speak to Luke about this again," I hissed, trying to avoid the looks being thrown at us by our fellow-diners.

Ruby snorted and looked at me in disgust while the waitress lifted the crockery from our table and gave us the bill which Ruby took before fishing her purse out of her bag.

There was a low whistle, a grunt and much tutting and

sucking of teeth coming from the breakfast bar where Jamesie Mac and his two cronies Jockey and Ringo were perched, drinking coffee.

"What are you tutting about, Jockey?" Ruby said. "Is there not a lame horse somewhere that you should be putting a bet on?"

Everybody laughed while Jockey fixed Ruby with a particularly mutinous stare.

Jamesie Mac looked as if he might explode if he didn't come over and talk to us. He was a renowned gossip and would have given the *Swiftstown Chronicle* a run for their money when it came to delivering the latest exclusives.

"I see your daughter's stepping out with Lewis Devereaux's boy," he said, after he had lumbered across to lean over our table.

Immediately I felt irritated. If *he* saw it, then why did he need confirmation from *me* about it?

"That's right," I snapped.

"He's a very shrewd businessman is Lewis Devereaux. He's made a great name for himself but from what I hear he's a cutthroat merchant when it comes to negotiations."

"And you'd know all about negotiations, Jamesie," Ruby drawled sarcastically. "The only difference between you and Lewis Devereaux is that he doesn't conduct his business on street corners or interrogate people for information so that he can impart their business to every Tom, Dick or Harry walking down the street."

As well as having a pronounced gift of the gab, it seemed that Jamesie Mac also suffered from an advanced case of selective hearing and continued talking to me as if Ruby hadn't spoken.

"Your girl'll be wanting to hold on to him, Frankie.

He's the only son and they're rolling in it." This statement was accompanied by much rubbing of fingers and thumbs and served to annoy me even more.

"Well, I'm sure when we're looking for a suitable beau for our daughter we'll take other things into consideration apart from the size of his bank balance."

"Yeah, you'd want to know what size his other packages were too!"

Much lascivious laughter and slapping of knees later and he finally stopped talking, which was a good job really because a wired jaw isn't nice on anybody.

"Jamesie, seeing as you are the resident Swiftstown oracle, what's the *craic* with your woman who just sloshed coffee around herself?" Ruby asked.

He sat down, looked all around him furtively and then motioned for us to come closer. We leaned towards him in the manner of people who were about to be told of the findings of a US top-secret mission.

"That one's in here all the time, y'know," he said, continuing to peer round him. "She's always jumpy and nervous of herself and never talks to anybody and every time her phone rings she throws it away. We reckon she's an ex-convict who's come here to make a new life for herself. Some of the locals are convinced she's here to cause trouble in town and there's been a few questions asked about which team she bats for, if you know what I mean. She doesn't seem to like men. You should see the way she looks at me and some of the other regulars. We might as well be a pile of earwigs."

(In fairness the men in question could indeed have passed for a pile of earwigs, but that was just my opinion.)

Ruby gave me a superior knowing look before folding

her arms and settling back in her seat with an air of smugness.

"Thank you for that, Jamesie," I said before he got too comfortable, making it sound as much like a dismissal as I could.

"Any time, ladies," he said as he went back to his friends who were looking at us curiously.

"Ha!" Ruby said.

I smacked my forehead with my hand and groaned. "Okay. I tell you what, we'll do a wee bit of homework on our friend and see what we can find out and, if there seems to be anything at all suspicious, then I'll call her for interview but not entertain the idea of giving her a job. Nobody is safe any more, Ruby. If she's been involved in anything then Google is sure to know about it."

10

Jodi

I towel-dried my hair as I looked towards the TV and watched as Jeremy Kyle tried to control a panel of rowdies on his show who all looked like they were about to kick the hell out of each other. I flicked my head back and began to comb my long hair. I could give him an excellent story that would have his viewers positively sitting on the edge of their seats with curiosity and suspense but, as even I didn't know how it would all end, there would be little point – although I would love to see the bastard squirm. I could just hear Jeremy (we were on first name terms these days) giving him a lecture about the sanctity of marriage and see the old biddies in the audience shaking their heads in disbelief as they sucked mint humbugs and tried to take it all in.

I took a deep gulp of strong coffee and thought about how much my life had changed. I'd heard people talking about daytime television before and had always scoffed in their general direction as I could imagine nothing sadder or more mind-numbing than sitting looking at a box in the corner when I could have been at work, glossy and preened and ready to take on the next challenge. In my opinion in my former life, people who had time to watch television between the hours of nine to five were lazy scroungers who needed a well-positioned boot in the general direction of the job centre. Like everything else in my life, I had taken my qualifications, my will to succeed and the strong work ethic that I inherited from my father for granted. Looking back now, I realised that I had never taken the time to consider that people might not have simply been lazy, that there could have been extenuating circumstances which prevented them from being able to work. Obstinate about my own point of view, I never explored these possibilities, preferring instead to look down on others from on high in my glass tower. My glass tower that had now come crashing down around me in a spectacular fashion. It probably served me right for being self-absorbed and stupid enough to let that prat get under my skin and carry me away.

The more I thought about it, the more resentful I became. *He* had reduced me to this. Here I was in a grotty house in a less than attractive estate, that a student would probably turn up their nose at, all because I had been stupid and gullible and naïve.

I suppose I could have stayed on in my job and continued to live in the house and pretended not to notice or care. In fact, if you had presented me with the hypothetical scenario I would have probably told you in a determined voice that no man would ever drive me away from what I had worked so hard to achieve. I was a fighter not a quitter. But you just don't know how you're going to react until you're presented with the situation and in my case I couldn't have predicted the depth of the pain and hurt I felt and how strong the urge to run away and pretend it hadn't happened had been. The day I received the phone call and everything had been revealed, I had been devastated and my first reaction had been to leave. For the sake of my sanity I had to put as much distance between him and me as possible and, as long as it stayed that way, I reckoned that I could cope. Just about.

I stood up and began to pace up and down. Why did this keep happening? I could go for hours and be reasonably content (or as content as one could be when one's life had just collapsed) and then something would happen that would bring me back to square one again and I'd start feeling miserable and alone and literally want to lock myself away.

I willed myself not to give in to my distressed emotions. A walk would do me the power of good. It would hopefully distract my mind for long enough to allow me to function normally for a while.

I loved being out in the fresh air and exploring the quaint little shops that Swiftstown had to offer. The town boasted various outlets that sold period furniture and antiques to which I was particularly partial. My interest probably stemmed from the fact that I used to help my father when I was younger. I loved going to work with him on a Saturday and hearing him talk in what I called his 'racing-car voice' as he invited bids and shouted out the prices being offered before banging down his gavel and declaring a sale. He was an auctioneer for a local firm that dealt in antiques, paintings, houses and the like, and I used to be fascinated by the things that would be going up for sale. My daddy always used to tell me that every piece of furniture and every painting had a history. There were all sorts of reasons for things being auctioned. People died and sometimes unwitting relations dumped off boxes of what they thought was old tat only to discover later that their family heirlooms had made them a tidy sum. Other things were there as a result of repossessions or debt management and some simply seemed to fall into the auctioneers' hands with discarded boxes being left outside their doors with notes telling them to give the proceeds to charity.

My father was lovely. It was he who had taught me the value of work by taking me with him and paying me if something I had scrubbed or polished managed to make him a sale or if there had been a big lot to be auctioned and I played his assistant and shyly held up items while the punters appraised the items before raising their fingers to register their interest.

Daddy had never been a big fan of my husband's. My father was the sort of man who tried to get on with everyone but I knew instinctively that he hadn't been very fond of my choice of partner. He had never said that he had a problem with him as it wasn't in his nature to act like a dictator and tell me how to live my life (Mother did a good enough job of that for both of them). My parents had been divorced for a number of years and my father retired to live in the Lake District in England. I spoke to him a lot but hadn't told him about the mess I was in as I didn't want to worry him or let him down. He had always been so proud of my achievements and I wanted to continue to prove that I could look after myself against all odds.

Dad had no contact with my mother nor would she dream of contacting him, so I knew that he wouldn't find out about my predicament that way, which was a good job as she'd have probably only ended up blaming him for it anyway. If I ever did anything wrong I was always 'his daughter' while any achievements naturally were always down to her and the perfect upbringing that she had insisted I had. Neither did my father ever ring my house or my work because of his antipathy to Ashley, so he wouldn't find out that way either.

Ashley and I had clicked so easily into a relationship and I had foolishly been so swept away by his charm and attentiveness (save for the routine trips away to foreign offices that now made a lot of sense) that I had foolishly let my guard down and allowed him 'in' which was very stupid indeed. If only I had paid more attention to my father's apparent reluctance and less attention to my mother's delight that her daughter had become a Belfast socialite overnight. My mother had found it difficult to cope after she and my father had separated but had gradually settled back into her routine and was hardly ever in the house as her diary was constantly full of an endless stream of engagements pertaining to her bridge nights and her involvement with the local amateur dramatics society. I had often joked that she was well suited to the theatre as she was quite highly strung and it gave her an outlet for all her nervous energy and excitement.

As I stopped walking and entered one of my favourite browsing spots, Quinn Antiques, I managed to quieten my disturbed brain which had started going into meltdown.

The shop was quite dark at first but, as my eyes grew accustomed to the light, I began to look around me with interest. Anything new that had been brought in was always placed to the front in an antique shop so that it would be readily seen by the customer (a fact gleaned from working under my father's tutelage). There was an ornamental lamp, a tea set, an old jewellery box and a material-covered stool that was balancing on two legs as the third one had broken.

"Can I help you?" a male voice asked.

Usually the shop was manned by a lady in her sixties who looked exactly like she had been born into the right job with her hair tied back in a tight bun and a pair of ornate spectacles hanging from a chain around her neck.

I turned around and saw a man, in what I estimated to be in his mid to late forties, approach me. He had a pleasant face, a welcoming smile, was tall and had dark hair that was peppered with grey (which on a woman would have looked like she was a lazy cow who couldn't be bothered doing her roots but on a man looked distinguished).

"I'm just having a wee look," I answered, knowing full well that even if anything did interest me it would just have to be left behind as I had very little money left and what I did have wasn't being squandered on an antique no matter how striking or unusual it looked.

"That's fine. Take your time. You must be new in town. I haven't seen you around here before. Fabian Quinn at your service." He finished with a proffered hand.

I immediately stiffened and looked at his outstretched arm like it was an offensive weapon before limply shaking his hand while wishing to God that people weren't so pass-remarkable. So what if he hadn't seen me before? You didn't have to live in Swiftstown and have had four generations of your bloody family there to be allowed entrance to the shops, did you?

"I'm Joanna," I said.

He must have sensed my unease as he pursed his lips and retreated behind the counter, picking up a mug from it and sipping from it while he fiddled with a small TV that was positioned there.

"I like to keep up with what's happening in the world," he said by way of explanation as the jingle of the local news was played.

I raised my hands in surrender to let him know that I didn't have a problem with this and hoped fervently that this would keep him occupied and stop him from asking any more difficult questions.

I had just spied something which I thought would be very interesting when my blood ran cold and I felt like an invisible force was tying me to the spot.

"And in other news today. Fears are growing for the safety of a young woman who has been reported missing. Joanna Crozier was last seen on the fourteenth of January when neighbours near her Malone Road residence saw her leaving her home around 2.30 p.m. . . . ."

Fabian Quinn had turned the TV around closer to him and was peering at it, then looking at me and scratching his head in a rather confused manner.

My mind went blank and I didn't even hear the rest of the news report – except for the final sentence: *"Police have asked anyone who knows the whereabouts of Joanna to get in touch with them immediately."*

11

Frankie

"Oh my God," I murmured as I saw the face of the girl who had called for a job application form flash before me accompanied by a story that seemed to indicate that she was a missing person.

"What's wrong?" one of my colleagues asked as I continued to sit rooted to the spot at the canteen table with my lunchtime sandwich going limp in my hand.

Everyone started to look towards the TV and I found myself wanting to distract them as for some reason I felt strangely compelled to protect the girl who hadn't been able to tell me why she had abandoned her job.

"Sorry, guys, I'm just a bit distracted but I'm fine now honestly." And with that I got up, threw my partially eaten sandwich in the bin, went straight to my office and turned on the computer.

I hadn't got round to Googling her yet as I'd been too busy but had told Ruby that I had and found nothing. I didn't know what it was but the girl had a vulnerable quality about her and I really believed that she needed a chance to prove herself.

"Ha! I told you that there was no big mystery," I'd said. "She's just a newcomer and because this damn town is so small and parochial there has be the equivalent of the Spanish Inquisition to find out who she is, where she comes from, why she's here, who her parents are, what colour of feckin knickers she's wearing and when the last time she felt the urge to pee was."

"Alright, alright, get off your high horse," Ruby had countered. "Her story might not have made it to the worldwide web yet but trust me when I say that there's something going on."

I typed in the name Joanna Crozier and had to hunt through several other people with the same name until I found the one I was looking for and when I saw her profile on a logistics company website I had to view it several times to make sure that I wasn't hallucinating. The woman beaming out at me from the internet looked happy. She had a dazzling smile. She was impeccably dressed with perfect long glossy hair and subtle make-up and had a healthy glow about her. The Joanna I knew couldn't have been further removed from her former self. For one thing she had lost a lot of weight and couldn't possibly pose for a photograph now and give off the same aura of authority and self-confidence. She looked anxious and strained all the time and the effects of whatever she had suffered had definitely taken their toll on her. And she was so desperate to keep her whereabouts a secret and had done such a good job in effectively disappearing that she was now being reported as a missing person. What did somebody have to do to you to make you want to run away from your job and your marriage and your life?

I looked away and looked back at the photo and suddenly felt angry on her behalf. It was obvious that she had been broken by whatever had happened and the fixer in me wanted to help put her back together again but not before I found out more about the toe-rag that had left her in this state. She had blurted out the name Ashley when I had first met her and I surmised that that must be the delightful character she had married. I typed in the name and another profile appeared. Ashley Crozier was a global sales account manager and it appeared that his job was to fly all over the world and ensure that systems were working correctly. I studied the photo and wished that I could print out a poster-sized copy to make a dartboard from. He was good-looking. Very good-looking. Probably too good-looking and therein lay the problem. It seemed to me he had an underlying air of smugness about him and I wondered what on earth his wife had ever seen in him. But then we all make mistakes. My ludicrous marriage to Tony bore testimony to that.

Decisive action needed to be taken but before I did anything else I buzzed into the main office and spoke to the secretary.

"I left an envelope in there to be posted earlier. I wonder has it been sent yet? It was an interview request letter made out for the attention of a Joanna McDermott. Could you check for me?"

Five minutes later I had the letter in my hands and was perplexed as I pondered what I should do with it. Technically the girl hadn't done anything wrong and I had been delighted to be able to offer her an interview but I was now feeling understandably uneasy as something was very much amiss.

I lifted the phone and rang Owen's office but was greeted with the message that told me that he was teaching all afternoon and wouldn't be available to return messages until the following morning so instead I rang his mobile which promptly told me that unlike him his answer phone was available.

I let out a low growl and threw the letter into my bag for safe keeping because I didn't want it to go into the post yet. I needed time to think. I didn't want to mention anything about it to the senior management just yet as they were liable to all have heart attacks, so great was their desire to do everything by the book and I didn't think employing someone whose face was likely to show up on the side of a milk carton would go down at all well.

Why could nothing be straightforward or easy at the minute? I thought that I had struck gold when Jodi walked in that day looking like a bedraggled duck desperate for a job that she was overqualified for, but it like everything else seemed to be going wrong.

My home life had descended further into discontentment, and things had gone from bad to worse with Angelica who had reacted in a not entirely reasonable way when I suggested that Jerome perhaps wasn't the boy for her (to be accurate her mood at the time could have been described as psychopathic) and because I had upset her she now wasn't talking to me and Owen kept asking me in an accusing fashion what I had "done to her". "I haven't *done* anything to her as you so nicely and sensitively put it," I had snapped. "I was just trying to help but as usual it's all gone pear-shaped and as usual I'm the worst in the world and she's now doing her Cinderella routine and behaving like I've nicked her tickets to go to the ball to meet Prince Charming."

"But what's wrong with him?" Owen pressed. "I thought he was alright. He seemed perfectly friendly and normal to me and anyway it's not like they've just announced their engagement. There'll be plenty more opportunities for you to worry before she meets 'the one'."

"You," I said pointedly, "just don't want to be robbed of the chance of acting like a football hooligan at a Liverpool match. He might be able to charm you with promises of seeing Anfield but I'll not be so easily bought over."

"You're just jealous that he didn't promise you anything," he said.

"You know what, Owen," I answered, "I would have been happy if he had taken any notice of me at all instead of pretending I wasn't there. Angelica must have told him that I was the Wicked Stepmother. I wonder how her real mother would have fared. Would she have got any more respect?"

"Oh, come on, Frankie. That's taking it just a bit far now. You know that Angelica loves you and appreciates everything you do. I don't think she primed her boyfriend to act in a particular way just to upset you."

When he put it like that he made me sound like I was being an overprotective and unreasonable fusspot who was just out to ruin Angelica's fun, which definitely hadn't been my intention but unfortunately seemed to be the case according to everyone else.

"I don't know what it is, Owen. I just have a feeling that there's something not quite right about him."

"And on the basis of your amazing intuition you decided to tell her that he wasn't right for her thereby turning her into the hormonal young female from hell who has now been given a reason to act like the hormonal young female from hell? Well done, you."

I had snarled something inaudible at him in response but Owen hadn't stopped to listen. He had simply walked out of the room shaking his head and leaving me wondering if he had a point.

Living in the house had been miserable over the last few days as there was an atmosphere that a chainsaw would have had a hard time penetrating. I had no choice. I would have to do my least favourite thing in the world and admit that perhaps I had been a bit hasty in my judgement and agree to give Jerome another chance. Angelica would no doubt get great mileage out of the fact that I was having to apologise and Owen would also be reminding me about this for the rest of my life anytime I offered an opinion on anything else.

I didn't care though. I was sure that something wasn't quite right but I knew it was true that me giving Angelica my opinion about not liking him would only encourage her to go to him more because that's what teenagers will do just to spite you and assert their chronic need to be independent.

Ben and Carly had also sensed that something was wrong and seemed to be tip-toeing around in an effort to render themselves invisible so that they wouldn't get caught up in the crossfire. They were getting a break this weekend, however, as they were going to stay with their father who apparently had lots of nice plans for them (and although there was no love lost between Tony and me, I was tempted to ask if I could come too simply because the prospect of peace and two days without griping or arguing sounded like heaven).

I made a plan in my head which involved me making something nice for dinner, taking Angelica aside and apologising for the fact that I had obviously hurt her feelings and that if she was happy then that was all I cared about but I would always be there if she needed me. God, but I was too reasonable for my own good. Ruby would kick my arse if she knew that I was being such a walkover.

There was, however, something I needed to do first that didn't involve any of my family but did need my urgent attention. Someone was in trouble and I wanted to see if I could help and I fervently hoped that this time the person would be more receptive to my suggestion of having a cup of coffee.

12

Angelica

I sat in my maths class and tried to concentrate on what was being explained but my mind kept wandering back to the fact that I had let myself down.

I had always said that I wouldn't have sex until I was totally ready and Jerome had always told me that it wasn't an issue and that he would wait for me. So how the hell, I wondered, had I ended up doing what I promised myself I wouldn't in his car in a horrible setting?

I had really wanted to tell Katie and the girls but I was afraid of what they would say. I had always been very insistent that I wouldn't be doing anything until I was ready and they had all been very impressed by Jerome's willingness to wait.

"He really does like you just for you," Katie had said, looking extremely envious.

"It would appear so," I had responded happily.

That had been a week ago and now all my smugness had disappeared.

To make matters worse he hadn't been in contact as much as he had been before the event and I was beginning to wonder if this was the beginning of the end. He used to always send me a text in the morning, one in the middle of the day when he knew I'd be on the bus on my way home and then we'd usually meet up at some stage in the evening. I had only seen him once since although he had reassured me that it was simply because he was busy helping his father and didn't have the time to spare.

Frankie was being a pain in the arse as well. She had told me the day after the meal that she didn't think that Jerome was right for me and I had accused her of just being pissed off because he hadn't eaten her food and then we had an almighty row that my dad had to eventually step in and sort out.

We hadn't really spoken much since and that, for me, was probably the best outcome, as any time Frankie and I did speak lately it always ended up in us having words. (When I say 'words' what I really mean is that we exchanged insults and screamed at each other until my dad reminded us that there were children in the house who had not chosen to live in a war zone.)

I was suddenly jolted out of my thoughts by my neighbouring classmate giving me a dig in the ribs. I looked up and to my chagrin saw that Miss Roach was looking at me in a seriously peeved fashion.

"I'm so sorry, Miss Byrne. Are we keeping you awake?"

I looked up and felt my cheeks colour.

"If you'd care to come up to the whiteboard I'd like

you to show the class how you worked out the equation. You have done it, I presume?"

"Angelica, where is your head today?" Katie demanded as we sat eating our lunch in the school canteen.

I looked at her, sighed and threw my practically untouched salad roll onto my tray.

"I'm just having a few problems at home. It's no big deal. I didn't sleep well last night and you know what I'm like when I'm tired."

"Yeah, and I also know what you're like when you're not telling me the truth. I've seen you falling out with Frankie a hundred times before but I've never seen you this distracted."

"I'm just annoyed that she doesn't like Jerome. He behaved brilliantly and even went out of his way to get on well with my dad and still she finds fault with him. According to her he was rude and unmannerly and didn't try hard enough to be pleasant. She reckons that he's not good enough for me."

"Oh my God," Katie said in disbelief. "Is she blind? I bet if she was twenty years younger she'd have a go at him herself! He really is beautiful to look at. I never saw a man blessed with such amazing eyelashes and cheekbones."

I felt the familiar buzz as I saw the other girls at the table exchange glances.

"And the fact that he agreed to wait for you is just so sweet. Most boys are only after one thing and then when they get it they dump you and tell everyone how easy it was to get you to put out."

My heart skipped a beat and I stole a glance at my phone which had remained silent so far that day.

I smiled in response and then got up, excusing myself, as I was getting tired of this conversation.

"What's the matter with her?" I heard a voice whisper as I left. "Maybe he *has* dumped her."

"God, wouldn't you be devastated if you managed to land him and then he got rid of you because something better came along?"

I heard a ripple of laughter and felt worse than ever.

This was all Frankie's feckin' fault. If she hadn't made things so awkward at dinner then maybe I wouldn't have felt the need to make things up to him afterwards and he wouldn't be viewing me as a cheap thrill now because I was no longer a challenge.

I just wanted to be liked. Especially by him.

13

Ruby

I heard the phone ringing and knew that the call must be for me when I heard Luke padding up the stairs as he spoke to the caller.

I was sitting at my desk trying to prepare a report for one of the students in my care who needed a work placement.

"It's Georgie," he mouthed at me as he handed me the phone.

"Hello," I said cheerfully.

I hadn't been speaking to Georgie in a few days as she had been hosting an artist's retreat at a local tourist spot in Donegal – I was dying to hear all about it.

"Ruby . . . I . . ."

I heard the catch in her throat and laboured breathing.

"Georgie," I said in alarm, sitting forward abruptly. "What's the matter?"

There was silence.

"Talk to me," I commanded in an urgent tone. "Please. You're scaring me."

"It's my father," she said softly. "Your grandfather Charlie. He's very ill. The doctor thinks he may have developed pneumonia from a chest infection that he had. It's not good. He's an old man. He could never survive that."

"Who's with you?"

"I'm on my own right now. I rang around the others and I'm sure they'll be along when they can."

I closed my eyes and tried to think of what to say but there was nothing that could make this situation any better. Words were futile. What was needed was action. I knew what it was like to lose my father and I never had the luxury of saying a proper goodbye to him because he had died so suddenly. I wasn't going to let the same thing happen with the only living grandparent I still had.

"Right, I'm going to get dressed and drive down to you now. I'm owed a few hours' time in lieu from the college so I'll take them over the next few days."

"I couldn't ask you to do that," Georgie said quickly. "Luke just told me that you had locked yourself away to do some work. I don't want to be disturbing you. I'll be fine."

"Georgie, quite frankly, if you think that I'll be able to concentrate on my work now that I know what you're dealing with, then you overestimate how thick-skinned I must be."

"Your mother will have a fit," Georgie said quietly.

I was used to this reaction now from both of them. They always tried to pre-empt each other's actions and whether or not their own actions had the capacity to cause offence (which they usually did even if there was none intended) and as a result I always ended up like piggy in the middle trying to console, reassure – stay sane.

Georgie continued in an urgent voice. "She'll think that I'm expecting too much of you and taking advantage. No, you stay where you are and I'll keep you posted from here. I just wanted you to know what was happening. Say a wee prayer, though, won't you?"

"You leave my mother to me," I said, thinking of the elderly but sprightly man that I'd met on a number of occasions and grown fond of. He had always greeted me with warm eyes and an open heart and held my hands tightly. "This is too important and I've missed so much already and I'm not prepared to forego this. If my grandfather is as bad as you say he is then I should be with him and with you too. Not another word. I'm on my way."

I hung up before she had the chance to protest any more and turned off my computer before going into the bedroom and throwing a spare set of clothes into an overnight bag.

"What are you doing?" Luke asked, standing at the door looking bewildered.

"I need to go to Mulroy Cove to be with Georgie."

"Now?" he spluttered.

"I'm sorry that it's at such short notice but I have to be there. My grandfather is seriously ill and Georgie doesn't know how long he's likely to have left. It's all very difficult for her especially as the rest of her stupid family seem to think it's entirely her job to look out for him."

"How are you going to cope if you run into them, Ruby? It won't be the easiest situation to deal with and under pressure you can be dangerous and you don't want to make things worse for Georgie. She'll have her hands full enough without you kicking off as well."

"Well that's just charming, Luke. I'm offering to go and help Georgie because I think she could do with my support and all you're worried about is how I'm likely to react to everyone else. I'm not a bull in a china shop, y'know."

Luke rolled his eyes and continued to look unconvinced.

"I promise I will not cause any scenes. My main priority is to be there to help."

My husband kissed me on the nose and then enveloped me in a hug. "I'm sorry. I don't mean for it to sound like I don't trust you to behave. It's just that you've been so justifiably annoyed about everything and hospitals can be quite tense and emotional places and I don't want you getting hurt."

"I won't. I've found Georgie and as long as I have her the rest of them don't matter to me. I'll tolerate them but honestly I couldn't care less any more."

Less than an hour later I was packed and ready to go and Luke was waving me off at the door. He had offered to come with me but I had told him to stay where he was as it would give Georgie and me an opportunity to spend some time together. There was something that I had to do before that though.

It was dark when I arrived in Donegal. I had made the journey in two hours and twenty minutes which was a new record.

The hotel that my mother owned, the Manor House Hotel, was situated in the picturesque seaside village of Smuggler's Bay, not far from Mulroy Cove where Georgie lived. (Having the two of them in such close proximity to each other while I wasn't there terrified me.)

Smuggler's Bay was not a big place but I loved being there as it exuded peace and serenity and obviously a lot of the tourists that frequented the old Manor House, which my mother had lovingly restored to its former glory, thought the same. The old house had been threatened with demolition at the hands of the last greedy owner who wanted to turn it into a modern monstrosity that required exclusive membership fees but, alas for them, fate had stepped in and it hadn't happened. The hotel boasted sea views, its own piano bar and a tour guide was on hand to take patrons on guided tours and explain how the house's former inhabitants had put in their time . . . and some of the stories were rather . . . shall we say . . . colourful.

I know it sounds very grand to say that your mother owns a hotel but believe me if you knew the story behind it and all the grief she had to put up with from the previous owners then you'd know that she had earned it. She had been left the small cottage in the hotel grounds as an inheritance from her great-aunt and had never really taken any great interest in the old Manor House, but she had ended up having to react when she had become the victim of a campaign to have her removed from the property that was rightfully hers. She had never actually wanted anything to do with the hotel per se. It had just sort of fellen into her lap and, as it turned out that she had a natural flair for hospitality management after all her years in the catering industry, it seemed that the right things had happened.

"Hi, Mum!" I shouted as I entered her office in the hotel.

"Hello, darling," she answered in surprise, giving me a tight hug and a kiss on the cheek before closing the door and taking her seat again. "I wasn't expecting to see you here until the weekend at least."

"And I wasn't expecting to see you still at work at this hour of the night. Do you have no home to go to?"

"I wish," she sighed, "but we're being audited and the auditor could be here any day so I need to make sure that all the paperwork's in order. And speaking of the hour," she finished, looking at her watch, "what are you doing here? What's wrong? Please tell me that you haven't fallen out with Luke again? That poor man must spend half his life living on his nerves."

"Eh . . . charming," I said, feeling rather hurt that my mother had such a low opinion of me. "I'd actually rather not be here to be honest. Georgie is extremely upset as her father is very ill and she rang me earlier in a terrible state and I said that I'd come down here and give her some moral support."

I immediately gauged by the stiff way that my mother was holding herself and her lack of communication that she wasn't best pleased with this nugget of information.

"I'm sad to hear that Charlie isn't well," she said.

What had been left unsaid was the fact that she was raging that I had come all this way to support Georgie when in her opinion it wouldn't be necessary.

"Poor Georgie has had to deal with so much on her own that I didn't want her to have to try and sort this out by herself as well," I said in the vain hope that she would try to be understanding and not go off on one of her tirades about how we had only known each other five minutes and I shouldn't be getting so involved.

Mammy looked up at me sharply and I knew immediately that I'd said the wrong thing.

"And here's me with a million people waltzing around me every time I have a bit of bad news or something troublesome to deal with. The only difference between us is that I wouldn't go ringing you at the drop of a hat to drag you the whole distance from Tyrone to Donegal just because I'm incapable of coping!"

Mammy sniffed in a dismissive fashion and I wondered why the hell I had thought it was a good idea to come here in the first place. But that reason was obvious, wasn't it? I couldn't have allowed myself to be in the vicinity and either risk Mammy finding out from Luke, which would have created merry hell because I would have been accused of doing things behind her back, or worse still had her bumping into Georgie herself to be told that I had been there.

I sighed. "Mammy you are a completely different person and you've had a different life – which hasn't always been easy either. But you're strong and you have lots of friends and staff around you, not to mention Gabriel," (my former flamboyant wedding planner and now her events manager) "if there's a problem or you need anything. Georgie literally has nobody. She isn't really in touch with her family that much and unlike you she doesn't have a boyfriend."

Yes, that's right. My mother is at an age where she should be retiring and taking it easy but instead of that she's too busy entertaining and making plans with her boyfriend (who in my opinion should be referred to as her gentleman friend as she wasn't sixteen and snogging behind the bike sheds, or at least I hoped she wasn't). I found this concept very hard to get my head around when it first came to light last year and had actually been quite resentful of the gentleman in question, Donal O'Donnell, as I had got it into my head that he was trying to replace my father. Nothing, however, could have been further from the truth and, once I had learnt to accept that, we had become good friends. I had come to respect him greatly for what he did in looking after my mother and keeping her happy. Pity he wasn't here now to lavish some attention on her which might take the focus off me and what an apparently inattentive and traitorous daughter I was being in trying to be supportive of the woman who had given birth to me.

Mammy looked at me and fiddled with her hands and I knew that she was pondering on what I had said.

"I can appreciate that perhaps I'm in a better position than Georgie, Ruby, but at the end of the day you still need to be careful. I don't want anyone taking advantage of your good nature just so as they can benefit. You've really only known her five minutes . . ."

I'd known it was only a matter of time before I heard those words . . .

". . . and already she has you like a puppet on a string at her beck and call."

I looked at Mammy and willed her to understand and not to berate me any more. "Whatever I do, I do because I care and I want to help, and please believe me when I say that I don't do anything to hurt you. I know that this hasn't been easy for you but don't think that anyone will ever take your place. You are my mother. You've always been there for me through good times and bad times and my memory is big enough and strong enough not to ever let me forget that. You will never be replaced. Just please understand that sometimes Georgie will need me too and, as we've both missed out on so much, I think it's important that we're there for each other when it matters."

"You make me sound like a petulant child," Mammy complained. "It's not that I'm jealous or that I don't want you spending time with her – I'm just worried about you getting carried away and I don't want the rest of her family ever to look down their noses at you or think that you're in any way inferior."

"Jesus, what is it with you and Luke tonight? I wish you'd all stop worrying about the rest of that family and let me concentrate on Georgie who's the important one. I couldn't give a stuff about the others and I'd tell them that too but just don't tell Luke I said that. I'm trying to persuade him that his calm approach to life is brushing off on me."

"It has indeed brushed off on you but he's not a miracle worker in possession of a tranquiliser gun, Ruby, so I'm not shocked that the old you is still in there somewhere."

We exchanged grins and I inwardly breathed a large sigh of relief. I thought that I had finally managed to convince her that she was still 'Top Dog Number 1 Mum' (yet again) but I had to admit that it did get rather wearing having to constantly reassure her.

I was glad that I had been honest with her though and I wanted to maintain my current honest approach as I had come to a very important resolution that was likely to affect us all.

14

Jodi

I don't know who had been more flustered or embarrassed. I had been rooted to the spot for what seemed like hours but was probably only seconds or a minute at the most. The newsreader had announced a break and I could hear the jingle of a familiar advert and decided to move (as inconspicuously as possible).

In my haste, however, I managed to trip over a vintage footstool making a quiet and swift exit somewhat impossible.

"Excuse me, I'm sorry to ask but was that you they were talking about?" Fabian Quinn looked stricken.

"Of course not, don't be silly. Do I look like a missing person to you?"

"Anyone can be missing if the people who care about them don't know where they are and that photograph was definitely you and you just told me your name is Joanna. Are you in trouble? Do you need help? Is there someone I can call?"

"I'm perfectly fine, thank you," I said before leaving with as much self-respect as I could muster under the circumstances.

The walk home from the antiques shop had been akin to a military operation as I took to the side streets, hid behind bushes when I saw anyone coming and basically acted like the fugitive I was. Now I knew how criminals felt when they were described on the news as being 'unlawfully at large'. Speaking of the news, I was astonished that I had actually been mentioned on it. My photo had been shown and footage of the street outside my house had been aired. I had always said that I wanted to make my mark on the world but I certainly hadn't intended on doing it this way! I didn't want to be notorious for running away or synonymous with being missing or lost. I shook my head and wondered what I should do in order to draw the least attention to myself and then balked as I suddenly realised that the frequent patrons of the Swiftstown Arms Bistro were bound to all be sitting there right now at this moment, waiting for the news to come back on. Jamesie Mac would be holding his tea in mid-air as he listened open-mouthed to every word, as he'd be on a mission to make sure everyone knew before morning that the missing girl was right here under their very noses and that all their suspicions had been correct. Yes, indeed, she was hiding something but she bet that not one of them could even hazard a guess as to how wrong they all were in thinking *she* was the criminal.

I groaned and flopped on the sofa after entering the house (by the back door which involved climbing over a padlocked gate in a most unladylike fashion) and pulled a blanket over my head. I'd probably have to get used to covering my face now. Perhaps I should pretend to be a refugee and go around with a Muslim-inspired veil covering me. Maybe that wouldn't be so bad. I wouldn't have to worry about make-up or the annoying spots that appeared at certain times of the month or chapped unsightly lips in the winter and, as for my hair, it could go unwashed for a week and I'd save a fortune on colours and styling. Then there would be the benefit of being able to conceal my facial expressions. If anyone pissed me off they'd never know that I was curling my lip or sticking my tongue out at them.

I removed the blanket from my face and promptly burst into noisy tears that induced a spasm of heavy breathing and snorting and eventually a coughing fit that made me choke and wheeze.

What the hell was I supposed to do now? Was I facing a lifetime of hiding in the shadows and dodging around corners and would I never be able to have contact with humans again for fear of them pointing at me in horror and saying 'there's that missing girl, the one that has been presumed dead as she's never been found and I must be seeing a ghost . . . *aaaaaaaagh!*'

I started to wail and held my head in my hands which meant that I didn't hear the door opening. That, in turn, meant that when I stopped sobbing and looked up to see Frankie McCormick staring at me in horrified fascination I nearly had a coronary which would have been very handy and could have solved a whole lot of problems. A swift, painless, well-timed heart attack would have been very welcome right then!

"I'm sorry, Joanna. I didn't mean to startle you. It's just that you obviously didn't hear me knocking but I could hear you . . . erm . . . and when I tried the door it wasn't locked and you're very . . . erm . . . you're very . . ."

"Disturbed. Insane. In the middle of a very big pile of shite that I'm not quite sure how to climb out off. Yep, I'm all those things as well as apparently being fecking missing despite being very much here."

"I don't think you're missing, Joanna," Frankie said gently. "I just think you've lost your way and need someone to rescue you."

I wasn't expecting Frankie to be so nice to me. In fact, I was only realising that she was actually here in my horrible grotty sitting room and the first person to show me that they actually cared since I left stupid Belfast. Cue another bout of noisy tears. Although at least this time I knew I wasn't alone as Frankie took me in her arms and held me until my sobs had subsided and my breathing had returned to normal.

"I'm really sorry," I said, rubbing my eyes, flicking my hair back and feeling decidedly idiotic.

"Nothing to be sorry about, pet. We all go through bad times although I must say that when you do it you certainly do it in style. There's not too many of us actually get a portion of the lunch-time news devoted to us."

I looked at Frankie and saw that she had a quizzical expression on her face – she was obviously begging for an explanation. I felt the usual irritation creep up around my back and neck as I fought off the urge to tell her to mind her own business, but logic prevailed as I reasoned that she had every right to know what was going on as she mightn't now be in the position of being able to employ me. Besides, she had been genuinely nice to me. My trust had been severely knocked but I knew that Frankie wasn't here to gossip or gloat.

"If I put the kettle on and make you a nice cup of coffee, will you promise not to throw it over yourself or me?" Frankie asked as she removed her coat and rolled up her sleeves.

I smiled weakly and nodded my head which had now started to pound with a mixture of stress and the result of the heavy bout of crying.

I followed Frankie into my horrible kitchen, suddenly conscious that she could see that my living conditions were extremely poor.

She didn't react, just filled the kettle and switched it on.

"It's rotten, isn't it?" I said as I hunted in a cupboard, hoping to find a packet of headache tablets but finding nothing but anti-decongestant tablets which I needed a lot as the house was freezing and I seemed to be permanently coughing and sniffling.

Frankie walked out of the kitchen and bustled in two seconds later, hunting in her bag for something before eventually heeling its contents out on my grungy worktop.

"*Aha!*" she said suddenly as she produced a strip of paracetamol and handed them to me. "I knew I had some somewhere." She ran the tap and filled me a glass of water, then made me sit down on a kitchen chair.

I was amazed. I never realised that a complete stranger could be so kind and my eyes started to well up again before I checked myself sternly for being a wimp and ordered my emotions to behave.

"You've obviously been through a lot, Joanna –" Frankie started as she busied herself preparing the coffee.

"Frankie, could you do me a favour and call me Jodi, please. My ex-husband and my mother were the only ones

99

who ever gave me my full title and for obvious reasons I'd rather not be reminded of that."

Frankie nodded. "Jodi it is then. If you don't mind me asking . . . will your mother not be worried about you? Does she not know where you are?"

"She knew I had left but I stopped answering her calls about a week ago because she was annoying me so much. She just doesn't seem to understand how I feel. Everything is black and white with her and she leaves no room for grey areas. She sees my ex-husband as my meal ticket for life and can't understand why I would want to sacrifice that for a few principles. She thinks I'm overreacting over nothing and hasn't even taken the time or the trouble to ask exactly why I left in the first place."

There was a pause where Frankie handed me my coffee before sitting down and looking at me expectantly again.

"Frankie, I'm really sorry. You've been nicer to me than I've deserved after the way I've behaved and I appreciate you turning up here like my guardian angel and making me coffee and supplying me with pain relief, but I'm afraid that I just can't talk about it. I'll maybe tell you someday but for now I have to work things out in my own head. Besides, it's just too painful and saying it out loud will probably only make it worse."

"I'm not pressing you for details, Jodi, and I certainly don't want to intrude into your business but I think that you need to let people know that you're alive and well and not lying dead in a ditch somewhere. I don't know what your husband has done to you but, for the sake of your family, I think you should phone the police and ask them to let them know that you're okay. As a mother myself, I can assure you that it would be bad enough to think that something has happened to one of your children but not to know and to be left imagining all sorts of things would be ten times worse."

I turned away and closed my eyes and felt instantly guilty. Perhaps I had taken things too far. I hadn't meant for everything to get so dramatic and messy, it had just happened. One thing had led to another and, hey presto, I had gone from unhappy and betrayed runaway wife to missing person whose face was all over the news.

"You're absolutely right," I said in resignation. "Things have got out of hand and I'll sort it now."

I was just about to lift my mobile when I noticed the time and realised the tea-time news was about to start.

"Maybe we should watch the news first and see what they're saying now," I suggested.

We lifted our mugs and went back into the living room. I flicked on the TV and we sat down.

"Northern Ireland plunged into water crisis . . . Stormont in uproar over ministerial expenses . . . and fears continue to grow for the safety of an up-and-coming young PR executive from Belfast – we hear from her family."

Shit.

I was cringing already at the thought of the performance my mother would no doubt put on. Too many years in the amateur dramatic society would have her wailing and putting her hand on her brow and having to have people hold her up.

I listened impatiently as the rest of the news was read out and jiggled the remote control in my hand in the hope that my actions would somehow speed up events.

"And after the break we will hear a heart-rending appeal from the family of Joanna Crozier who are desperately wanting news of her whereabouts."

The family? Well, obviously nobody had been in contact with my father. The ads came on and I studied my feet, feeling that I couldn't look Frankie in the face at the moment. She was probably regretting coming here at all and I was more embarrassed than I think I've ever been in my life. What must she think of me? She probably thought I was an attention-seeking little drama queen that had no regard for anyone but myself. I peeked at her from the corner of my eye and saw that her brow was furrowed and she had a very concerned expression on her face.

The ads ended and my heart started to thump. The newscaster told the sad story of a young woman who had mysteriously disappeared and then the face of Ashley came on the screen, dabbing his eyes with a tissue. I couldn't believe it. How could he take such a risk in the circumstances? Was there no end to his arrogance? Did he think he was untouchable – or was he simply insane?

"Joanna is a wonderful woman. She is my life and I dread to think that someone is holding her."

"Holding her?" I exclaimed angrily, sitting bolt upright. "Yeah, you would think that. It wouldn't occur to you that you pushed me so far that I literally just left with nowhere to go and no plans for the future! Someone would need to hold me back to stop me from giving you exactly what you deserve, you low-life arsehole!"

I was outraged and filled with a fire that I hadn't possessed in weeks. I had spent so much time feeling sad and bereft that the anger which had been slowing bubbling and simmering under the surface hadn't had the proper opportunity to come out. Until now. There he was, sitting on TV, delivering an Oscar-worthy performance of being concerned when I knew that he was doing it solely for the benefit of his colleagues and business associates who no doubt had been asking questions. The rat-bag had probably practised it in front of the mirror while examining his face to see if his eyebrows needed plucking or his nose-hairs trimming. He was a vain self-absorbed idiot – a fact that had been evident in his every action up until now. I wanted to punch him in the mouth. I got to my feet and started to pace.

"*And have you a message for anyone who has any information or who might know of her whereabouts?*" the newscaster prompted compassionately, obviously spectacularly taken in by the sob story and the crocodile tears.

"*Please let the police know where she is and above all don't hurt her. I just want her home safely where she belongs.*"

Where I belonged? Where he bloody wanted me in order to protect his reputation more like! I wondered what the other woman in his life was making of all this fuss. He had obviously had to come clean with her after I went to see her on receiving her phone call the day I left. He'd thought he was so smart but he was obviously not smart enough. Most men thought one woman was hard work but this dickhead thought that he could dupe two of them at the same time. Hell hath no fury like a woman scorned (or in our case hell was crowded out by two women who had not only been scorned by the same man but royally led up the garden path and shat upon from a great height to add insult to injury).

The screen then left Ashley's tear-stained face while a number where police could be contacted appeared and was read out along with an appeal for information.

I was about to jot the number down when Frankie handed me a piece of paper with the number on.

"Ring them now and let them know you're safe."

I punched the number into my mobile and in a stilted voice told the policeman on the other end of the phone that I was fine, that I had a legitimate reason for leaving and that he should ask Ashley to join my mother at her drama club as he would be brilliant at acting out any tragic scenes they had going.

"You can also ask him to closely examine his own conscience and, while you're at it, ask him if there's anything he'd like to tell you? I have been wronged in the worst way possible and I want nothing more to do with him – *ever*."

I put the phone down and glanced at Frankie who was looking a cross between relieved and bemused.

"I'm glad that you've cleared that up although I'm not sure that the policeman will be able to repeat all of your message in the interests of good taste."

I had gone on a bit of a rant, to be fair, so the policeman probably wouldn't repeat all my words but I did hope that he'd say enough to make my darling (ex) husband realise that I was not playing a game of hide and seek but trying in earnest to stay as far away from him as possible.

"Frankie, if and when I get round to telling you what that sorry excuse for a man has put me through, believe me, you will understand."

"I'll probably understand more than you think and I'm not sitting in judgement over you either. It's obvious that you didn't deliberately set out to hurt anyone."

Frankie got up and put her coat on and I followed her to the door.

"I'm here if you ever need me. Here's my business card and I've also written my personal mobile number on the back for you. Oh, and by the way I have something for you."

I watched as she produced a white envelope from her bag and smiled as I read its contents and realised that I was being asked for interview.

"Thanks for giving me a chance," I said gratefully.

"No problem," she answered quietly. "Just do me a favour and give yourself a chance as well and ring your mother and put her out of her misery."

I smiled as I saw her out, then lifted my mobile again and took a very deep breath.

15

Angelica

What was it people (usually Frankie) said about watched kettles never boiling? Obviously the same idea applied to mobile phones that stayed resolutely silent no matter how much you looked pleadingly at them, tutted, sighed and willed them with silent prayers to ring.

I'd had one stilted and awkward conversation with Jerome the night before and gone to bed feeling thoroughly miserable and resigning myself to the fact that I had been all but dumped without the words actually being spoken. He probably wouldn't even do it to my face. He'd lost so much respect for me that he'd send me a text to let me know he'd moved on or write the words on a post-it note and paste it onto the windscreen of our car or onto our front door just to add to my complete humiliation. The girls in school would have a field day with this one. He was the most eligible man in Swiftstown and I had managed to win the ultimate prize by actually going out with him – only to ruin it all with one stupid act.

I didn't usually (ever) listen to Frankie but one thing she had said had turned out to be true.

"You need to have some self-respect, Angelica. No matter how much a boy wants you, and believe me they'll let you know in no uncertain terms, you have to be the stronger one. Don't let any boy take advantage of you or use you because, you mark my words, once he's had his wicked way with you you'll no longer be a challenge and he'll think you're nothing more than a cheap thrill and have moved on to his next conquest before you have time to straighten yourself. And that's before we even talk about the dangers involved. What if you got pregnant or ended up with a horrible disease down below?"

At the exact moment where Frankie had screwed up her face and started to point ominously to her nether regions to illustrate what could lurk there in the aftermath of a dangerous liaison, I had scoffed and made a swift exit. There was nothing more cringe-worthy in this world than having your parents lecture you about having sex. Like, seriously, what the hell did they know about it? Or on second thoughts don't go there. They did it too bloody much if the sounds emanating from their bedroom sometimes were anything to go by. The two of them giggling and telling each other to shush, followed by other veiled moans and wails. Actually I've changed my mind. When it comes to cringing, there's nothing worse than thinking about your father having sex with your stepmother. 'The talk' comes a close second though.

I threw my phone behind the sofa only to perform a cartwheel to swiftly retrieve it again. Sighing, I switched the computer on and it hummed into life. A quick browse on Facebook told me all I needed to know and sorrowfully I stared at my relationship status that would probably soon say 'single'. Pity there wasn't a 'dumped for being stupid' option on the drop-down menu as that would have fitted the bill nicely. Or maybe there should be an option for citing your stepmother as the cause of all evil in the world.

I banged down the lid of the laptop and sat back with my arms folded and thought of how Frankie had inadvertently sabotaged my night. She probably only invited him around in the first place so that she could have a good gawp at him before labelling me an imbecile that didn't know her own mind and determining that I should get rid of him.

Dark thoughts started to enter my mind. When it came to messing things up for me Frankie was a dab hand at either dropping me in it or just being totally un-cooperative. She was always telling me what to do and thinking she knew best and I'd had to swallow my tongue several times to stop myself from screaming at her that she wasn't my mother and she should shut the hell up before I shut her mouth for her. Auntie Brenda reckoned I had been very restrained when I told her about the few altercations we'd had.

"I'd have told her to mind her own business and look after her own children," she had sniffed with unveiled contempt. "She's not a drop's blood to you and hasn't earned the right to tell you what to do. She's a poor excuse for a mother, that one. I could do better myself."

It had been on the tip of my tongue to actually enquire why my aunt hadn't thought of looking after me more when I was younger if she felt so strongly about it, but I didn't like to bring it up, especially not when she looked like she might possibly murder someone. Anyway, I knew why. Brenda was an incorrigible workaholic. She worked every hour God sent and hoarded every penny she got. It wouldn't surprise me to learn that she had an off-shore bank account somewhere as with all the hours she'd clocked up over the years she must be worth millions.

My phone vibrating suddenly into life instantly dragged me away from my musings and it was with nothing short of sheer delight that I saw that Jerome was phoning me. The happiness was short-lived, however, when I realised he was probably only ringing to tell me we were no longer a couple.

"Hello," I said nervously.

"What's the matter with you?" Jerome demanded. "You sound funny."

Yes. I probably did. Anyone would sound strange if they were talking and holding their breath at the same time. I straightened myself and tried to speak in a more cheerful tone.

"I'm fine," I announced brightly. "What have you been up to? I thought you'd forgotten about me."

"I've been busy, Angelica. My dad needed me to sort out a few things for him. I can't be at your beck and call all the time, y'know."

There was a silence as I digested this and I felt annoyed and nervous all at once. I didn't like his tone of voice and felt like a berated needy child that had been put in its box for being too clingy.

"I'm sorry," I spluttered. "I didn't know."

"So how have you been?" he asked in a more companionable tone.

"Fine," I answered morosely. I hated being chastised

and could feel a monumental huff descend upon me as a result.

"Why don't we meet up later?" he said. "We could go for a drive or out for pizza if you like?"

Pizza I liked the sound of. Drive I didn't. I was too afraid that the bumper would lead us down a deserted road again and there was no way I was giving a repeat performance of that particular occurrence. I didn't know what all the fuss was about. Everybody raved about their first time being this huge all-singing all-dancing experience where the earth moved and nothing was ever the same again. I beg to differ. It had been sore and uncomfortable and I felt weird and almost unclean after it. The fact that it had happened in the car in the grounds of a disused quarry and I hadn't been prepared hadn't helped matters. I didn't mind a bit of spontaneity in the grand scale of things but when it comes to life-changing events such as losing your virginity a girl needs some warning.

"Pizza," I answered quietly. "We'll go out for pizza."

"I'll pick you up at seven."

"No. I'll meet you there." The last thing I needed was another row with Frankie who no doubt would have some comment to make about me going out with Jerome.

"Fair enough. See you later then."

The phone clicked off, signalling the end of the conversation and, although I should have been the happiest girl in the country, for some reason that I couldn't quite fathom I wasn't.

I was waiting for Jerome to meet me when Paddy McCourt, a boy I knew from school, leaned against the window sill of the packed pizzeria to talk to me. We were discussing how much we hated our principal and how the school's football team hadn't had a good season when Jerome arrived. I obviously didn't see him instantly as it was with a shock that I registered him sitting watching me intently with the engine off and his lights dimmed.

I waved to greet him but he didn't wave back.

He got out of the car and came over to meet me whereby Paddy bade me farewell and sloped off to meet his friends in the snooker hall.

I then noticed that his jaw-line was tight and he was wearing a most disgruntled expression.

"What are you doing standing on a street corner talking to him?" Jerome asked without smiling.

"He only stopped to chat for five minutes while I was waiting for you." I answered. "He's in the year above me at school."

Jerome turned me to face him and took my face in his hands. "In future I'd like you to wait inside for me. I'd rather you were warm and not being chatted up by every Tom, Dick and Harry on the street."

His touch and the intense way he was looking at me made me feel warm and fuzzy inside and all my earlier worries disappeared in a flash. He was so sweet and kind and considerate and I was chuffed to bits to now discover that he could also be jealous of other boys taking my attention away from him.

Perhaps my Facebook status would remain the same after all.

16

Ruby

I had been signalling wildly at Georgie as Gabriel had been talking animatedly about his latest project and I hadn't had the heart to interrupt him and hang up the phone. He had got into the habit of ringing about once a week where we would have a chat about what was going on in our lives and about once a month arrange when we were next going to meet up. He and Frankie and I usually went for drinks at least once a month or so for a "good old bitching session" or "girlie night out", as Gabriel referred to it. We always tried to go somewhere different and usually ended up being the centre of attention. Gabriel didn't exactly blend into the background or behave like a wallflower. If truth be told, he should come with a government health warning and 3D glasses as his appearance and behaviour were both so loud.

Gabriel was my wedding planner and to say that we hadn't hit it off in the beginning would be a huge understatement, as I had despised him and his camp attitude and his attempts to get me to wear high heels. Eventually, however, we gained a mutual understanding and respect for one another and now were good friends. Despite all my reservations and the blistering arguments we used to have, my wedding day had gone like a dream and I knew that it probably wouldn't have been half as good without him. Don't get me wrong, Luke and I still would have got married even if Gabriel hadn't been involved but there would have been a real chance that the event would have taken place in the form of a dawn ceremony with me in jeans and a reception organised in the local pub where we would have drunk beer and eaten pork scratchings and peanuts as opposed to the lavish meal we had been served at the fabulous venue in Donegal. Having said that, and although I was grateful for what had turned out to be an amazing day, Gabriel knew not to try and advise me on how to dress as a general rule, as that was a recipe for getting a punch in the mouth. He now worked at my mother's hotel in Donegal where he got to parade around in coat tails and organise all the events and functions there, and as she loved him like the son she never had, and allowed him to give her fashion advice, she was now the trendiest and most colourfully dressed (think traffic lights) hotelier in the country.

After I eventually persuaded him to take a breath (and shut up) he agreed that we would meet up within the next few weeks and wished me all the best and told me to give my regards to Georgie who was busy gathering things together to take to the hospital with us. She had already been to the hospital earlier but had come back to collect things that her father would need.

I watched her as she moved swiftly around, packing things into a bag while ticking the items off a list she had made. She looked exhausted but was still very pretty. I had inherited my red hair from Georgie and had the same sprinkling of freckles over my nose and chest and arms as she had. She had a wide gentle smile and I always thought that her dress sense exuded her creativity as she was partial to long flowing skirts and colourful scarves.

She looked at me and I could see concern etched on her face.

"Are you sure you want to come back with me, Ruby? You do know that the others will be there?"

I moved towards her and put my arms around her in a tight embrace then kissed her on the cheek.

"All the more reason why I want to go, Georgie," I answered quietly, taking a step back to look at her earnestly. "It's about time I got to meet the rest of the genetic connections and they got to meet the missing link. I will be perfectly pleasant and nice and won't let the past and what happened bother me."

I hoped that she couldn't sense the ball of nervousness in the pit of my stomach that seemed to be expanding by the second.

With regards to my adoption I hadn't fared badly at all as I had ended up with wonderful adoptive parents and had led a charmed existence. That is, if you didn't take into account the constant hankering and need to know where exactly I had come from, which resulted in me having a crap identity-crisis-filled teenagedom and my long-suffering parents probably wanting a refund for their bad choice of a child. As for poor Georgie, she had suffered dreadfully. She had carried a child for nine months, given birth to her baby and taken her home with the best intentions of looking after her only to be accosted by Social Services who accused her of being some sort of a scarlet woman with a penchant for men and drink and drugs before carting me off and leaving Georgie scarred for life. Not only did she not know what had become of her baby but she was also left in the horrible position of knowing that she would probably never find out as information would probably be passed on that would deter her child's adoptive parents from ever wanting anything to do with her. The evil plan had nearly succeeded too, apart from the fact that nobody had banked on me being as stubborn and nosy as I was. It was a good job that I was headstrong (I do try telling Luke and my mother this all the time but they tend to disagree) or else a lot of people could have gone to their graves badly hurt and haunted by the fact that they needed answers to questions that would never leave them.

"You're doing that thing with your hands again," Georgie said, looking pointedly at my lap where I was screwing my hands into balls and attempting to pull my fingers off.

It was a habit I'd had since I was a child. I hated my stupid hands as they always gave my mood away. I only did this when I was anxious and, even though I might be smiling, people who knew me were never fooled. Georgie, in the short time that we had been in touch, was getting to know me pretty well and was quite intuitive when it came to reading me. Of course, if my mother heard me saying that she wouldn't be long pointing out that, even though *she* hadn't given birth to me, *she* knew me better than anyone else in the world (these words would be accompanied by a ferocious nodding of the head and possibly a stern wagging of the finger – therefore I kept my thoughts to myself as I was a big fan of having a peaceful life).

"I'm fine," I said.

"Sure you are," Georgie said with a wry smile that at an ordinary time would have lit up her face. But her face was now masked with sadness at the thought of losing her father who was the one person in the whole equation who had not approved of how she and I had been treated. Unfortunately, however, as Charlie Delaney had been only one voice in a rather large crowd, some of whom had the ability to shout louder and better, his views had been dismissed. He was told his older daughter had other ideas which would benefit Georgie and me better in the long run.

Charlie hadn't had any visitors since Georgie had left. We learned that the rest of the family would be along when they had the chance. Translated, of course, this meant that they knew Georgie would go and do all the hard work, while they arrived later trying to be the epitome of concern.

I gasped as I saw Charlie for the first time, after being led into the room by a kindly nurse who had patted Georgie's arm and looked at her sympathetically. His skin was ashen and he looked clammy and uncomfortable. He was sleeping but moaning in a low and weak tone at the same time. I looked at Georgie and saw that she had tears welling in her eyes.

I touched her on the elbow and motioned for her to sit down on the chair beside Charlie's bed.

"Maybe you should talk to him," I said. "I'm sure he'll

be able to hear you. Let him know that you're here. Give him something to fight for."

Georgie sat down and looked thoroughly miserable. She blew into a hankie and then roughly wiped her eyes with the sleeve of her cardigan, a determined look on her face.

"Daddy, I know you can hear me. Please get better. I couldn't bear to lose you. You're the only normal person in our family, the only one who's ever loved me for me, who hasn't tried to control me or judge me. I need you."

I could feel my own eyes start to fill as I watched the desperation become more and more evident on her face. What she said was all true (apart from the fact that she thought that Charlie was her only normal relation – she had me – and I was perfectly sane and normal).

She began to stroke his hand and whisper to him and I felt strangely like it was a private moment that I shouldn't be witnessing so I decided to leave in search of a coffee machine. It could be a long night.

I sipped my coffee and punched in Luke's number as he would no doubt be wondering what was happening.

"Hi, pet."

"Are you alright?" he asked anxiously. "How's Georgie?"

"I'm fine but Georgie's very upset which is to be expected."

"How's Charlie holding up?"

"It's not looking good to be honest. Although you'd think he was grand and fighting fit if the actions of the rest of his useless family were to be taken into account. As usual Georgie is the only one here. It makes me so cross."

At that moment I was nearly run over by a deluge of people running into the hospital and had to quickly side-step them to avoid being squished.

117

"I'll give you a ring later, love. I just wanted to let you know what was happening. I'd say we'll probably be here all night. I'm sorry for running out on you at such short notice. I'm sorry about dinner and after you went to all that trouble too."

"It's fine, pet. We'll have a nice quality night together soon."

I grimaced and got the familiar fluttery panicky feeling in my stomach.

"We will," I answered without conviction.

After we had exchanged goodnight wishes and I had gone to the drinks machine to buy another cup of coffee for Georgie, I made my way back to Charlie's room where to my dismay there seemed to be a lot of commotion going on.

I approached the door which had been left partially ajar and saw that the room was full of people. I spotted *her* straight away. She looked like a bulldog chewing a nettle and when she spoke it appeared that she expected to be obeyed.

"Georgina, this is a time for family only. We don't need strangers here on a night like this. Our father is very ill."

"I second that," another woman answered, raising herself to her full height and going over to peer into Georgie's face in a most intimidating manner. "You've got to agree that you're putting the rest of us in a rather awkward position. There is a time and a place for such things but now is certainly not one of them."

"I don't think there will ever be a time or a place actually," the other woman said harshly.

"The past is the past and should stay that way. Done. Dusted. Forgotten." The last three words were said while the speaker rubbed the palms of her hands together which seemed to indicate that whatever she was talking about could easily be got rid of or dusted off – and it was at that precise point that I decided I couldn't keep quiet any longer.

I threw open the door in a manner that made everyone jump.

"Here, Georgie, I brought you a coffee. You've got to keep your strength up. Would you like a sandwich or anything?"

Everyone stood rooted to the spot and nobody seemed capable of speaking.

"I'm Ruby, by the way," I announced to the room. "I'm Georgina's daughter. You know, the one that you thought it would be a good idea to get rid of? And lying in that bed is my maternal grandfather who was very nice to me when he met me. He didn't view me as a stranger. He was very welcoming as it happens and he asked something of me that day. He asked me to look out for Georgie, which is exactly what I'm doing now, so if you don't mind I think we'll stop being nasty and playing games and just deal with the situation in hand."

Luke would have been exceedingly proud of me as, given half the opportunity, I'd have rather introduced myself by shoving some heads in bedpans and sending some others spinning while giving them a roller-coaster ride on the electronically controlled beds.

Nobody spoke. They all looked like they had been smacked across the face with a rubber chicken, but as I glared around the room my eyes connected with my nemesis who I had long been waiting to meet and neither of us moved as we stared at each other through narrowed eyes.

17

Jodi

I appraised my reflection in the mirror and tried to look at myself through the critical eyes that would no doubt be viewing me in less than an hour. I was thinner than I had been which showed in my face, but with the help of some make-up I hoped that I had adequately disguised how pale I was. I had always enjoyed going to the hairdresser's but my hair hadn't been groomed now in weeks because I simply couldn't afford it and instead of swinging thickly around my shoulders I had tied it up in a knot and put an ornate clip in to secure it.

We had arranged to meet up at a coffee shop in Lurgan. My mother had objected to being forced to travel so far but, as I was unwilling to set foot anywhere near Belfast and didn't want to meet anywhere in Swiftstown for fear of being seen and interrupted, she had had little choice in the matter. She still didn't know where I was staying and I knew that the curiosity was about to kill her.

The search had now officially been called off and an announcement made to the public to indicate that I had been found safe and well. I didn't know how much of my message Ashley had received but I had ended up having to get a new SIM card in order to change my number as he had morphed into a scary stalker type who was ringing every five minutes, begging to be given a chance to explain everything.

Ashley was a smart man who was an undoubtedly talented and charming orator, but if he thought that all he needed was five measly minutes to explain away the mess that he had created then he had an overinflated view of his own abilities. It would take a hell of a lot longer than five minutes but, in any case, as I wasn't prepared to give him the chance there was little point in dwelling on it any longer.

Since I'd had my phone switched off I had been having nightmares about being tracked down by a private detective who would drive at a snail's pace beside me as I walked down the street or be up a tree with a camera where he would get photos of me in my underwear (which would be most unfortunate as all my nice stuff was still in my Malone Road townhouse so if he was looking for a lace-induced thrill he'd be sadly disappointed).

I glanced at myself one last time and then threw my hands in the air as I came to the conclusion that she would find fault with my appearance no matter what lengths I went to so there was little point in worrying unduly about it.

I had rung my father after I had spoken to my mother the night of the news appeal. I should have just told him that Ashley and I had been having problems instead of letting things grow and fester to the extent they had in my mind, which rendered me incapable of speaking about them. He was angry with me when I said that I didn't want to let him down and had told me that he was more upset about the fact that I had felt that I couldn't confide in him.

"Your career is important, Jo, and you've worked hard to succeed, but your health and wellbeing are worth a hell of a lot more. I always knew that you were far too good for that fellow but you had to see that for yourself. Stop hiding away like a hermit and hold your head high. You've done absolutely nothing wrong so stop acting like you have."

"Why did you never tell me that you thought Ashley wasn't right for me? I might have listened."

"I did try in my own way to let you know that I didn't think he was suitable but I didn't want to interfere too much. You seemed so happy in your job and I thought that in time he'd prove himself."

"Well, he did that all right. He proved himself to be completely and totally untrustworthy and he also proved that I was easy to dupe."

"Don't be too hard on yourself, Jo. The best lessons you learn in life are those that you create yourself, my darling."

"Will I see you any time soon?" I had asked, overcome by a desire to spend some quality time with him.

"You'll see me next week. I had already planned to come over anyway but this gives me even more of a reason."

I couldn't wait to see my dad and was even planning on taking him to Swiftstown as he was the one person who would allow me to be myself and not judge my decisions or actions. I had become tired of always trying to please everyone else and live life to their standards as opposed to my own and, since my face had become plastered across the TV, I had resolved to just be me and stop feeling that I had to hide away. I had never been a secretive person and had always been outgoing and sociable and was finding it hard to maintain the aloof character that I had become of late. From now on I was going to take my father's advice and smile more and feel less intimidated by people. Besides, who minded if everybody found out what a scumbag Ashley was? Certainly not me. He had brought it all on himself. Why the hell was I protecting him? I had nothing to lose by holding my head up and telling people the truth when they asked me why I had moved away from Belfast to start a new life. On the contrary I had everything to gain and Ashley had everything to lose.

I had checked the bus timetable and knew that I had about twenty minutes to kill before I was due to board the one that would take me to my destination (and unfortunately my mother).

I had only just stepped outside when I spotted my landlord coming waddling down the street. He had a beer belly and a greasy comb-over and yellowing fingers from smoking copious amounts of cigarettes. All that was missing was the string vest and he could have been Rab C Nesbitt's best friend.

I contemplated ducking into the house again and running out the back door but reasoned that I couldn't avoid him forever and that it was better to get whatever it was that he wanted out of the way.

"Ah, Mssssss Crozier," he leered, leaning up close to me just so that I could have the pleasure of being engulfed in the delightful aroma of body odour mixed with the whiff of stale cigarette smoke.

I smiled tightly and tried not to gag. He was the most odious little man who now insisted on referring to me as Mssssss Crozier because he had seen my husband's heartfelt TV performance and come round that evening calling me Mrs Crozier and demanding to know if there was a reward for finding me, like I was a missing Labrador pup. Naturally, I had not been in a receptive mood and told him abruptly that I was not Mrs anything at which point he had started to call me Mssssss which was just around the time where I had lost the will to live.

"Is there any particular reason why you're here?" I gasped, recoiling away from him and trying to breathe into the material of my top so that I could avoid vomiting.

"I just wanted to let you know that from next month on I'll be putting your rent up, Mssssss Crozier."

I stopped and stared at him, my jaw dropping with shock and disbelief.

"And why do you think you can do that?" I asked.

"Well, it seems to me that I've been charging you too little. I was looking up pictures of you on the internet today and you were looking very well at one of your work functions and wearing some mighty fine bling. I liked your dress. It showed off your figure to perfection."

As he said this he looked long and hard at my chest and licked his lips while I looked at him in horror. I wasn't actually sure what I found more abhorrent – the idea he thought he could increase my rent without good reason or the fact he'd been looking at photographs of me which probably depicted me in an array of revealing evening dresses, as part of my job entailed entertaining clients and attending various functions on behalf of the company where networking opportunities could lead to future business.

My mind temporarily wandered as I recalled the preening I used to do before each event. I used to spend hours getting waxed, manicured and coiffed until the big day would arrive and I would stand in my dressing room slathering myself with expensive body lotion and applying tit-tape with excruciating precision before I stepped into whatever elaborate gown the Lisburn Road boutique couriered over. I had enjoyed all the fuss at the time and had looked upon it as one of the perks of the job but now it all seemed meaningless. I thought of Frankie McCormick and her upturned handbag that had spilled over my counter-top the night that she had called to my house. She'd had no gold credit cards or fancy pens or membership slips indicating that she was affiliated to any exclusive gyms or clubs. Instead I had seen family photographs, a dummy and a cheap lip gloss, but suddenly it seemed to outshine and outclass anything that I had lived for or achieved in all the time that I was married.

My mind slipped back to the present where Mr Peebles was still staring at me with his lascivious gaze resting on the skin that was visible above the first button on the shirt I was wearing.

I grabbed my jacket tighter around me and looked directly at him with growing frustration.

"You can't do that," I said wearily, feeling a headache start to pound behind my eyes. As if meeting my mother wasn't pressure enough for me to cope with in one afternoon, now I had to deal with a leering landlord with financial control issues. "You can't just come around here telling me that you're raising my rent for no good reason other than the fact that you've made a pile of assumptions about my financial state and saw some photographs on the internet. This is ludicrous. If I took this to a solicitor you'd be laughed out of court for going against every law relating to landlord tenancy agreements."

He grinned at me again and I swallowed, feeling sick to my stomach, knowing precisely what he was going to say before he uttered the words.

"And do you remember signing one of those, Mssssss Crozier, because I must admit that my memory of that particular event is failing me?" He took a step closer and breathed on me.

I took a stumbling step backwards and felt the wall behind me. I tried to give him my most deadly look but decided I was too tired and felt a lump form in my throat which was partly borne of frustration and partly borne of fear. I shoved him away and tried to side-step around him but his large bulk prevented me from moving.

"What the hell do you think you're doing accosting me on my doorstep in broad daylight and making threatening demands?" I snapped, feeling anger build in me. I'd had just about enough of bloody men thinking that they could behave in whatever way they liked without having to face any consequences.

I thought that shouting at him might make him move on as there were people walking up and down the street but instead of deterring him he seemed to be getting a thrill out of it and it was with mounting horror that I realised that his breathing was becoming increasingly laboured as his hand moved suspiciously inside his trouser pocket.

"Oh my God. Do whatever you want, you horrible

little prick! I'm late and will miss my bus if I don't leave now."

I slammed the door shut and unfortunately missed catching his chubby fingers in the hinge before marching past him feeling aggravated and violated in the extreme.

"It's the first of the month two weeks from Friday, Mssssss Crozier, and I look forward to coming to collect my rent from you although if you don't have it all I'm sure we could come to an alternative arrangement that would satisfy me."

I walked down the street, feeling like I might cry in the manner of a toddler who is so confused and annoyed that they deem it necessary to scream and kick until everyone is aware of how upset they are.

Why? Why me? So much for holding my head high and not feeling intimidated.

I could feel tears prick my eyes and angrily wiped my face with the back of my hand, realising too late that I had smeared my make-up. Not that it mattered anyway. If Elizabeth Arden herself had prepped me for meeting my mother, the woman would still find something to criticise and complain about.

"Hello again."

I heard a voice behind me and tentatively turned around to find Fabian Quinn looking at me. "How are you? Have you been okay since I saw you last?"

"I'm safe and well if that's what you mean," I answered in a sharper tone than I intended.

"I'm glad to hear it." He looked uncomfortable and sounded a bit weary and started to turn away with a cursory nod.

"I'm sorry," I sighed. "Thank you for your concern."

"Don't mention it. I got a nice delivery of things in yesterday that you might like to look at. If nothing else it would take your mind off things?"

"I'll bear that in mind."

I watched as he walked away and wished I could have accompanied him back to his shop there and then. I would have cleaned an eighteenth-century woodworm-infested storage-box with my own toothbrush if it meant I wouldn't have to deal with my mother.

I boarded the bus and spent my journey to Lurgan puffing and panting and fantasising about how nice it would be to knee Mr Peebles in his peebles and leave him feeling as hurt and victimised as I felt. Fecking men – they were all the same – they all wanted to screw you one way or the other.

I arrived in the town, asked directions to the coffee shop, and with a heavy heart saw that my mother was already there looking strained and disgusted in equal measure. She was wearing a long coat and an expensive scarf and looked totally uncomfortable and out of place sitting in a snug by the window. I had hoped that she might have changed her mind or that she would have at least been late and allowed me to get settled before she came and gave me the once over and started to berate me for behaving the way I had.

I breathed heavily and walked inside and saw the shock register on her face as I approached her table.

"Oh my god! You've lost so much weight, Joanna, and look at your hair! Why have you let yourself go like this? Why are you doing this to me?"

(Oh yeah, that's right. I forgot that I had done all this just to annoy her.)

"Hello, Mother," I greeted her stiffly. "It's nice to see you too. Thank you so much for your concern."

She visibly blanched at the harshness of my tone as I slid into the seat opposite her without hugging her or kissing her on the cheek as I was accustomed to doing.

I caught the attention of a waitress and asked for a coffee. Strong and black and preferably served with a dose of sedatives in it to help me get through this meeting.

"What aperitifs do you have?" my mother asked the young girl in a snooty voice, only to have the poor waitress blush and look sheepishly at her as she shrugged her shoulders.

I snorted. "It's a daytime café, Mother. You're not on the Malone Road now. She'll have a cup of coffee and a scone, thanks."

The waitress looked worryingly like she might collapse with the relief of not having to figure out what my stupid mother was talking about.

"There's no need to be so rude, Joanna," my mother said sharply, looking wounded and annoyed at the same time. "All these establishments should have aperitifs. A little drink before your lunch aids digestion and goodness knows with all the worry I've had lately I've probably developed an ulcer and would need something to help me."

I was thinking that a *big* drink would do *me* the world of good. There was nothing little about the pile of bullshit I was having to listen to – and from someone who was apparently supposed to care but hadn't even asked how I was, why I'd felt the need to run away or indeed what had caused the weight-loss she was apparently so shocked about.

"You've changed, Joanna, and not for the better if first appearances are anything to go by. You need to sort yourself out and decide what you're going to do to make this up to Ashley. He's dreadfully upset and has been distracted beyond belief lately."

I swallowed slowly and cracked my knuckles one by one (which I knew would irritate her).

She winced and I smiled.

"I will not be apologising to Ashley for anything, Mother. He's the one that would need to be working on his grovelling technique, not that it would work anyway. He could stay on his knees from now until the end of time and I still wouldn't touch him with a bargepole. He has behaved like a complete bastard and I have no intention of ever having anything to do with him again. Why don't you go back and ask him about his secret life? The one that didn't involve me. Ask him about the day I left and what I discovered when I answered the mobile phone that was hidden in a drawer so that I wouldn't find it. Ask him about Pamela and see what he says."

That evening I phoned Pamela. For some reason I really wanted to know how she was.

18

Frankie

"What's wrong with you?" my mother asked as I pursed my lips and swallowed the urge to hurl my phone at her kitchen wall.

"Nothing at all, Mammy. Everything's grand thanks," I said, sounding a little too bright even to my own ears.

"There's nothing worse than your own daughter ignoring you and feeling that she can't talk to you. That would cut any mother to the bone."

Mammy adopted her most wounded expression and I again questioned my logic in thinking that it would be a good idea to call in. The warning signs were all there that she was in one of her moods. I had met Daddy out walking the dog as soon as I turned into their road and he had been marching along, undeterred by the mizzling rain, as if the devil and all the ghouls from hell were after him. Our dog Banjo used to be a bit on the chubby side but could now give any greyhound a run for its money he was so athletically fit from all the exercise Daddy gave him. When Daddy needed a reason to get out of the house (and out of Mammy's way) he grabbed Banjo and off they went. He had actually turned it into a bit of a career now and did dog-walking for other people who weren't able to get out and about due to ill-health or work commitments which Daddy thought was desperate altogether. Although, mind you, Daddy would think it terrible not to be able to escape as he knew without a shadow of a doubt that if he didn't he might very well find himself bearing the brunt of the Wrath of Mammy which was not something anybody in their right mind wanted to incur.

Mammy had started to cut hunks of soda bread as if she was sawing a tree trunk in half.

"Things are just a bit stressful with Angelica," I relented at last, splaying my hands in front of me and stretching as I spoke.

"Well, now, there's a change!" Mammy snapped. "Frankie, why couldn't you have made life easy for yourself and got a man who didn't have as much baggage? Owen is lovely but the issues that daughter of his has would take up the entire luggage compartment in a jumbo jet."

"Mother," I said in a controlled voice, "perhaps you've forgotten but I myself come with a humongous suitcase in the form of your grandchildren. I'm sure Owen's mother says the same thing to him about me and I'm sure any other potential suitor's mother would have been issuing a warning as well so, to be honest, I'm quite glad that not everyone looks on a partner having children before they embark on a relationship as necessarily a bad thing."

"It depends on the child," Mammy answered, refusing to back down. "That Angelica one is a spoilt little minx. She's got so many chips on her shoulder I'm surprised

McCain's haven't branded her. She knows exactly how to work the pair of you, and you, like the pair of fools you are, let her away with it."

"I do not let her away with anything," I said abruptly.

"Well, apparently, as always, you know best, dear, so I'm glad you think so."

I was bristling with irritation and decided that the best course of action would be to head for home before I said something I would regret that Mammy could claim mileage from for the next four years. Mammy could store up wrongdoings and hurt forever and remind you about them at any given time when she thought you deserved it.

"Look, Mammy, I'm going to head on here."

"Going so soon?" she asked as if she was genuinely shocked.

"Oh yes." Fecking sure I wasn't staying about here to be picked on and abused. I had children who could perform that particular ritual for me while I was in the comfort of my own home.

I looked at my mobile again and wondered if I needed to grow a thicker skin and stop letting the slightest little thing annoy me regarding my stepdaughter. I had texted Angelica to see if she would like anything in particular from the shop for tea but all I got was what I had interpreted as a grumpy one-word retort. I had apologised for being so hasty concerning Jerome but that had hardly registered which had left me positively livid as I knew I was right and was actually only trying to smooth things over for Owen's sake. And so the saga continued. I tried to act normal even though the strain might kill me and in response she behaved worse than ever and her father continued to blame me. Great.

Angelica was getting more and more difficult to deal with and I was tired of everyone (with the exception of Mammy and Ruby) telling me that it was her hormones. Hormones, my feckin' arse. It was a combination of being spoilt and having an unfortunate set of genes that meant she was prone to fits and bouts of bad-tempered and irrational behaviour just like her bloody Auntie Brenda, who had 'helped' care for Angelica when Angelica's mother Jane had done her Houdini act all those years ago. When I say 'help' what I actually mean is manipulate, try to apportion blame and earn herself an honours degree in the art of causing as much trouble as possible to the most people with maximum impact. I had always thought that it must be very sad being her and waking up in the morning with the sole aim of wondering who to hurt that day. What a sorry life to have and what an unhappy person she must be within herself to act in such a way.

In fact her behaviour was so unfathomably nasty and her personality so completely skewed that she had earned herself a nickname. Ruby and I referred to her (affectionately) as 'Brutal Brenda' and we thought that the name represented her in all her poisonous glory. She was tall and thin and had a permanently fixed sneer on her face. She exuded toxic contempt from every pore and thought nothing of eating small children (well, okay, I made that bit up, but I wouldn't have put it past her). She was the most vindictive woman I had ever met and when it came to holding a grudge and making you suffer she was a master at what she did. Obviously deeply unhappy and more than a tad unhinged but very talented in that respect nevertheless.

Over the years I had tried to get Angelica to see that

there was another life out there where people could be nice to each other and everyone could get along well and to some degree it had worked, but lately I felt as if she was slipping away from me again and reverting to form by acting like the stroppy unappreciative brat she had been when I had met her for the very first time. I always tried to make allowances for her, though, as losing her mother at such a young age and suffering all the disruption it caused couldn't have been easy. And when I say 'lost' I don't mean that she died. I mean that she got up one morning and went on an adventure. She decided that she wasn't mothering material and spent many years hot-footing it around the world with a backpack until she eventually returned home several years ago and saw Angelica again for the first time. Since then they kept up minimal contact but for the most part Angelica seemed to be happy with the arrangement. I think she probably would have simply accepted the situation and moved on had it not been for Brenda's insistence that Owen was somehow to blame for everything and, as for me, I had been branded as some sort of interfering nobody who had no say over anything Angelica said or did as I wasn't her mother. Brenda never even took the time to get to know me, she just wanted to believe the worst and at this stage I was inclined to let her, in the hope that in her bad temper and bad grace Angelica would finally see her for the scheming troublemaker that she was.

I gave myself high credit for not running for the hills and gave Owen even more for somehow being such a catch that I thought he was worth fighting for. I still believed that of course. I only wished that he would be more agreeable sometimes and give in to my infinite female wisdom and intuition when I said that I was unhappy with something, or in this case somebody.

It wasn't that I disliked Jerome exactly. It was more that I didn't trust him. Not that I was making this about me. It was all very simple really. I just didn't think that he was good enough for Angelica and I didn't care how much he was worth. Because when all was said and done, even though she was difficult, Angelica was still Owen's daughter and a girl I considered to be one of my children.

Just as I was getting into the car to leave, my phone vibrated and I saw that the incoming text was from Jodi who was very grateful for my earlier visit but seemed highly embarrassed at the same time, as she used the words 'sorry' and 'idiot' at least four times in her message.

I snapped my phone shut and decided that I would text her later when my mind wasn't preoccupied with other things. I was glad, however, that I had been able to help or be of some comfort to her as I sensed that she didn't trust too many people and hadn't had too many visitors to her rather dilapidated house since she had moved in.

I did my shopping and arrived home to find the living room in disarray and Angelica sprawled on the sofa and had to stamp hard on the clean-freak within me so as not to overreact completely. I knew that on this occasion Ben and Carly were not to blame as their father had picked them up from school and wouldn't be dropping them home until later on that evening. I would never, in a million years, understand why Angelica felt the need to be so messy. She had built-in wardrobes in her room, plenty of shelving and had her own sacred space decorated to her specific requirements (everything was black and pink, making her room look like a bat cave that had been sprayed with Pepto Bismol), but still the house seemed to take on the appearance of war-torn Beirut when I left her in it alone for any length of time. Actually war-torn Beirut was probably tidier and the militants there were probably easier to feckin' reason with than a grumpy teenager (I wondered if they needed any negotiators as I was bound to be an expert at this stage).

"Angelica, could we possibly tidy up a bit?" I said, trying not to let the peevishness I felt creep into my voice.

"Yeah, *you* possibly could," she answered snappily before standing up abruptly and leaving the room.

I followed her out into the hall, listened as she stomped into the den and threw herself on a beanbag in there, and subdued the urge to empty my shopping out and start firing tins of soup and packets of pasta at her insolent head. Instead I took my groceries into the kitchen where I began to unpack them in a frenzied fashion while inwardly counting to five thousand lest my head explode in bad temper.

Things had been good between us for a long time and perhaps I had become complacent about it and taken it for granted instead of continually working at it.

I sighed wearily and continued to unpack my bags and fill my cupboards.

"Angelica, would you like a cup of coffee?" I shouted out, flicking on the kettle and resolving to try harder to appease her (because I was the adult and as such had to keep a cool sensible head at all times . . . bah!).

No answer. Oh good, now she was ignoring me! Though perhaps that would have its advantages as at least, if she wasn't answering me back in the smart-arsed, all-knowing fashion she had adopted of late, I couldn't get so riled that I would fantasise about wrestling her to the ground and smacking her head off the floor in an attempt to knock some sense into her.

I went out into the hall and found Angelica sitting on the bottom stair staring at her phone with a distressed look on her face.

"What's the matter, honey?" I asked, all thoughts of rugby tackles banished to the back of my head, as I could see how upset she was.

"What do you care?" she retorted, jumping up and brushing past me, heading for the living room again.

I followed her. "Of course I care, Angelica," I said with my hands spread out (I read in a magazine once that that was supposed to let the other person know that you were open to a discussion and hoped that she had read the same one, as I was tired of talking).

"Jerome can't see me tonight," she said. "He says he's busy but didn't say what he's doing. He's been acting really strangely and I don't know what to do. I bet he's going to dump me now. Sophie Johnson fancies him and she better not be involved or I'll be deflating her boobs for her."

I opened my mouth and then closed it again as I needed to think before I made any response. I didn't want to make things any worse than they already were.

"You're probably reading too much into it, love. And, anyway, it's not good to be living in each other's pockets all the time. A night off will do the pair of you the world of good. It will make him look forward to seeing you the next time even more."

Okay, so when I said I might make things worse I wasn't banking on the fact that she'd end up being a snottery mess which resulted in me having to sit outside the door of the downstairs toilet for an age. I was trying to coax her to open it, as naturally she had locked herself in there because I had upset her by daring to suggest that a night off would be a good thing since there was nothing in this world that she wanted more than to live in his pocket.

Dear sweet Jesus, I thought, please give me strength and preserve me from all teenagers and their innate ability to annoy the shite out of you and test your patience to its limits.

I had to get out of the house and away from her.

"Angelica, I need to go and collect Jack. Are you going to be alright? I hate leaving you while you're in this state."

"No, please go," she said in a less distressed, more stroppy voice. "I'd rather be on my own."

Excellent. Now Owen would come home to find her sobbing into her pillow and lying across her bed like a tortured soul (still clutching her phone obviously) but now instead of it being Jerome's fault it would all be mine and she'd hate me even more and her boyfriend would be completely vindicated even though he *was* probably out with Sophie Johnson and her big knockers while I was being painted as Public Enemy Number 1.

Perfect. Just shaggin' perfect.

19

Angelica

I heard the door close and was glad Frankie had gone. I crept out of the bathroom, ran upstairs and threw myself on top of my bed.

Tears were streaming down my cheeks and I had never felt so confused in all my life.

I heard the front door opening again and footsteps on the stairs and as my bedroom door was opened I hurled a pillow at it and shrieked in annoyance.

"Why can't you just leave me alone? I never wanted a mother! Dad and I were fine on our own. If it wasn't for you maybe things wouldn't be going tits-up with Jerome. You just don't want me to be happy!"

I let out an agonised wail and pushed my head further into my pillow and continued sniffing. I was suddenly aware that there was someone in the room with me and realised with a jolt that it might not be Frankie after all.

Shit.

I looked up from my mascara-stained bedding to see

Katie looking at me with a concerned frown. She held out her arms and I half-wriggled half-stumbled off the bed and into them where I felt able to unleash all my hurt and anger.

"Okay, chick, start from the beginning," she said once my sobs had ceased. "What's happened now? I met Frankie on the path and she told me to come in and try to talk some sense into you because she had given up."

"Oh yeah. Sure. That's right. Let everyone think I'm the one in the wrong as usual. Stupid silly Angelica who can't do anything right and is so worthless that she can't keep a boyfriend. But then again why would that surprise anyone? Her own mother didn't think enough of her to stick around so why would anyone else?"

I felt my voice break and a torrent of emotion spilled out that shocked me. I'd had moments throughout the years where I'd felt the absence of my mother particularly keenly but now that I had met someone who I felt I could love and was in danger of losing, all the old memories of abandonment and betrayal had come back to haunt me.

Katie was quiet and contemplative. I don't think she knew what to say so she did what every good friend should do and simply stayed with me and stroked my hair.

I finally sat forward, rubbed my eyes and hung my head in despair. Why did everything in my life have to be so complicated? Why could I not just be normal? At school I looked around me and saw other girls my age. They had the same mother and father that brought them into the world and they didn't have to cope with all the shit that a marriage break-up created, although of course this wasn't a simple separation where the parents still strove to do their best for the children and both parties saw them on a regular basis. That would be too ordinary and too easy for my world. In my world my mother had to walk out on me when I was seven years old. A little girl in pigtails who, according to my father, had been cute beyond belief with a lisp and a penchant for washing her doll's hair in the bath and painting pictures of fairies. Presumably, however, my mother hadn't looked on my cuteness with quite as much fondness. Instead, she had decided that concentrating on herself was more important. She said she had felt stifled. As if she was drowning in responsibilities and duties that she had never wanted. She had loved my father and he alone had been her world. She had never bargained for anyone else to come along to upset the balance of things. She had never really wanted children though she claimed that once I had come along she had loved me very much. She said that that was why she had to leave. She had to leave before she came to resent me and what my being there had done to her life.

The doctors had said that she had been suffering from post-natal depression after my birth but in those days you didn't talk about it. In those days you had a baby and you cared for it regardless of how lost or inadequate you felt. Then, as the years went by, the depression deepened.

Auntie Brenda blamed my father for it all. She said that he failed to notice my mother becoming more and more depressed and then when she left he accepted all the sympathy that was given to him without so much as a thought for his wife who was so tired of living and drowning in a bubble that she saw no other option but to leave. Daddy said that Auntie Brenda hadn't had the first clue about what she was saying because she hadn't been there then. As always she had been away working and only jumped on the bandwagon when she came home to find her sister gone because she had never liked her brother-in-law and enjoyed a good row anyway. Things hadn't changed much. They still hated each other with a passion although Daddy never stopped me from seeing Brenda as he reckoned that I had needed some link to my mother and it would have been cruel to cut me off from her only sister.

"Are you ready to tell me what's wrong yet?" Katie said softly. "What's brought all of this on? This is so unlike you. You're usually the one picking everyone else up and putting things right for them. We've always looked up to you because you're so strong and smart and you've coped so well with everything you've been through."

I snorted and thought that if only she knew how stupid and weak I felt she'd be taking her admiration and respect elsewhere to someone more deserving of it.

"What's happened with Jerome? I thought everything was going really well with him? Have you had a row?"

"No. I've just been incredibly stupid and mucked everything up. I had sex with him in his car after the disastrous dinner here."

"*Oooooh*." She digested this piece of information and seemed to want to say something but then thought better of it.

"And it's not all it's cracked up to be. It's crap if you must know and I'll not be in a rush to do it again. Earth-shattering, my arse."

Katie shook her head in apparent disbelief at what she was hearing and then allowed herself to get back to the point in hand.

"You said he was willing to wait for you and that you

143

were never going to do anything like that until it was special and the time was right. And you told me that the dinner had gone really well and your dad was over the moon because Jerome was arranging to get him into the next Liverpool match."

Katie was a great one for stating the obvious, I thought in irritation. I had wanted my first time to be special. What girl didn't? Who in their right mind would want to lose their virginity in the passenger seat of a sports car when they could have had roses and candles and nice things?

I brought myself back to the current discussion.

"It was fine up until Frankie started trying too hard and when he didn't respond the way she wanted him to she automatically wrote him off as being the wrong one. I heard her talking to Ruby on the phone the night after and she made him out to be some sort of shifty no-good waste of space that was only after one thing."

I smiled bitterly as I realised that she could possibly have been right about the last bit but then that had been her fault. She had driven me to it. I had to try and make it up to him some way so that he'd still like me.

"Is that the reason why you're so upset then?" Katie said, trying to understand. "Frankie says she doesn't like him and you've taken it badly." Katie gave me a searching look. "I'm surprised you're getting so worked up about it. Sure you don't usually pass a blind bit of notice of what she thinks or says. In fact you usually go out of your way to do things just to spite her."

I smiled ruefully. It was true. Perhaps this was karma coming to call and I was finally being made to pay for all those times that I'd had her hopping in temper at my insolence and deliberate disobedience.

"It's hard to explain," I said, twisting the corner of my quilt cover between my thumbs. "This is probably going to sound like the daftest thing ever."

"Go on," Katie prompted, moving closer and staring at me expectantly.

"It's just that Jerome is the first person – well, apart from my friends obviously, but that's different – to like me for me. He isn't constantly trying to make up for the past, the way I feel my daddy and granny are. I look at them at Christmas or on my birthday and remember every school play and every piano recital when I could almost feel them jumping out of their skin to try and make me forget that there was someone missing. Then there's Frankie. She tries to be what she thinks I need. She's good in her own way but most of the time she just annoys me. I know she thinks that I'm a nuisance who does nothing but cause her trouble. If she could have had my dad without me her life would have been perfect. Everyone else treats me in a certain way because they think they have to, but to Jerome I'm just Angelica. I'm not the unruly stepdaughter with a bad attitude. I'm not the little girl with pigtails whose mammy left her. I'm just me and I like that. I like him, I really like him and not just because he's eligible or because I'm the envy of everyone at school although those are added perks. I like him because he treats me normally and with him I feel like I'm normal and I don't want to lose that feeling."

I don't know if Katie did understand. I wasn't quite sure that I understood it all myself but one thing was for sure – what I had found was something special that made me feel good and I wasn't about to lose that for anyone.

20

Ruby

I woke up in the most awkward position known to man and with a crick in my neck that would have made a contortionist cry. You would swear that the masochistic fecker that had designed the hospital chairs had had a wee chuckle to himself and thought: 'Right, the people who are sitting in these will be annoyed, anxious and sleep-deprived – so, just to add to their discomfort I'm going to create chairs that will stretch and strain muscles they never knew they had and have them walking like Quasimodo for a week!'

I looked around me (with great difficulty as my neck was broken) and saw that Georgie was nowhere to be seen but that Charlie didn't seem to be any worse than he had been the previous night.

I placed my hand on his, said a prayer and willed him to pull through. The doctor had said that he had contracted pneumonia which was difficult for the hardiest of people to recover from but I prayed that Charlie would find the strength to overcome it, if for no other reason than to be there for Georgie who so desperately still needed him.

I remembered meeting Charlie for the first time like it was yesterday. I had been a bag of nerves and was like a jumping bean by the time we arrived at Georgie's childhood home where Charlie still lived at that time.

"It'll be fine," she had said in her soft Donegal accent. "He still can't believe that you found me again and he's dying to meet you. He's probably just as nervous as you are, if perhaps not more so."

Just as Georgie had predicted, it had been a pleasant visit. I had found Charlie to be a very open, honest and nice man who seemed very regretful about the way that events had unfolded.

"I promise you, my dear. My daughter loved you very much and never would have wanted to be parted from you. I heard whispers of something being discussed before it happened but never thought that they would actually go through with it. You were a lovely little thing. No trouble at all. Neither of you deserved what happened to you, and I, for one, am very sorry for what you've both been through."

With the mere mention of the lovely Marcella I had stiffened and looked at my hands. I had never met the woman but I had already made my mind up about her. Anyone who could be so hard-nosed as to behave in the way that she had, deserved nothing but contempt. Charlie had tears in his eyes and Georgie had left the room although I could still see her through the glass doors that led from the kitchen to the conservatory. She was staring out the window and dabbing her eyes with a tissue, looking wistful and sad at the same time.

It was at that moment that Charlie had leaned across to me and made me promise that I would always be there for her.

"I know it's a lot to ask," he'd said, looking uncomfortable, "but I won't always be here and Georgie was always the one who needed help the most but never asked for it because she never wanted to be a bother to anyone. I know you must find all this very hard to believe and difficult to understand, Ruby, but believe me when I say that it wasn't her fault."

All the talk of faults and blame had made me uneasy which was when I had decided to tell him about my parents who had been so good to me. I wasn't a victim. I hadn't had an unfortunate childhood that was spent in care or in an unhappy home. I had been lucky and I had wanted him to know it.

"I'm glad that you found such wonderful parents," he had said. "I just wish that Georgie could have known that too. I know that she thought about you each and every day. She would disappear around the time of your birthday each year for a few days almost like it was a sacred anniversary and I knew that she had gone to remember you and probably mourn you. She never said a lot because I doubt that she could have put her feelings into words but I knew that her heart was broken and it hasn't healed yet. Her art probably saved her life as it allowed her to express her emotions in a way that could give her some sort of release."

I'd had a lump in my throat the size of a golf ball and was overcome with feelings of guilt. There I had been, for years, safe and secure in my adoptive family home, feeling sorry for myself and berating my birth mother for her selfish actions in giving me away, when in actual fact nothing could have been further from the truth.

Charlie, at the time, had mistaken my silence for some type of ill feeling on my part and had immediately started to apologise.

"I'm sorry, Ruby. I know that this whole experience must have been dreadfully difficult for you too and I didn't mean to focus solely on my daughter's feelings. You were the innocent party in all of this."

At that moment I had leaned forward and taken his two hands in mine and looked deep into his eyes as he had continued to stare sadly at me.

"I think that instead of focussing on the past we should concentrate on the future and all that it holds," I had said. "I can swear that I don't blame Georgie for any of this. I will always stay in touch with her and I'm also looking forward to getting to know the rest of the family."

It was at that point in the conversation that Charlie's face had become guarded and taken on a worried expression and, having now met his other daughters (who must have been adopted themselves as I couldn't understand how such a nice man could have played any part in producing such evil children), I understood entirely where his fears came from.

That was the one and only time that we had ever discussed my adoption but I was glad that we had and that he hadn't swept the actions of his family under the carpet like they were of no importance. I had seen Charlie a few other times after that and loved my visits to his house with its extensive gardens where we would have high teas out on the patio with scones and jam and buttered ginger cake and talk about Georgie's paintings, my work at the college and Charlie's obsession with classical music. Of course those days were now a thing of the past as Marcella had taken it upon herself to place Charlie in a nursing home after he'd had a fall and broken his hip. "It's for his own good," she'd been quoted as saying.

Now where had we all heard that before?

As I looked over at Charlie now and at his chest which was rising and falling in a rhythmic but wheezy manner, I resolved to change things. Charlie might have been too old or too soft to stand up to his daughter and Georgie might have been too afraid but I was here now and there was no way that I would allow things to continue in that way. I didn't want to cause waves (well, actually I would have liked to have created a tsunami but that was beside the point) so I couldn't delve in and try and take over, but I was determined that this reign of terror wouldn't continue.

"You're awake," Georgie said as she appeared in the room armed with coffee and muffins from the little tea shop which was located at the front of the hospital.

"Awake and as stiff as a poker." I manoeuvred my neck around as I spoke and longed for Luke and his magic fingers to come and relax all my aching muscles with his touch.

A nurse poked her head around the door and announced that there was someone here to see me and that she would show them to the corridor outside the room as she didn't want Charlie being overexcited or unnecessarily exerted by too many visitors.

Georgie followed me out into the corridor as I think she may have been fearing that her sisters were planning on having a gentle word in my ear about my presence there.

But, instead of having to deal with my demon aunts, I had to deal with my mother. She had just rounded the corner carrying a picnic basket that would have fed the entire ward and saved a sizeable chunk of the budget allocated to patient meals.

"Hello, darling," she said in a business-like manner and I felt my heart sink into my shoes. She was in uber-efficient mode which was very dangerous as that was when she was most likely to go finding fault with things. "You look dreadful. Did you not get any sleep last night? *Tut-tut*! That's terrible. I would have made sure that I got you a bed. After all, you've been good enough to come all this way to offer your support."

I could see Georgie looking longingly at the ground and guessed that she was probably wishing she was wearing a pair of ruby slippers that would beam her away from my mother's fussing.

"Have you eaten yet?" Mammy enquired.

Georgie made an attempt to prove herself worthy: "Yes, I've already been down to the coffee shop and bought tea and muffins."

I looked at Georgie's animated, eager-to-please face and felt a rush of affection for her. I then looked at Mammy and willed her to keep her mouth closed but of course that was too much to expect.

"Muffins?" she scoffed in the same tone of voice that war veterans probably use to speak of rations and powdered eggs. "What good are muffins for giving you the strength you need to look after someone and spend all day in hospital? What you need is proper food." And with that she lifted the top of the picnic basket to reveal pork pies, slices of quiche, a selection of sandwiches and rolls, homemade buns and a flask of what smelt like freshly percolated coffee.

My stomach made a loud gnawing noise and Mammy looked at me in triumph.

"I knew you'd be hungry, pet," she said. "There's enough there for both of you," she said, facing Georgie again.

"Thank you, Isobel."

"How's your father now?"

"He's still critical but we're praying that he'll pull through."

"I'll light a candle for him when I get home. I presume that you'll be going back to Swiftstown this evening, Ruby. Poor Luke will be pining without you and there's only so much time you can have off from your work." With that Mammy shoved the basket into my hand, kissed me on the cheek and left.

I looked at Georgie, shrugged my shoulders and gave her a wry smile. "She means well, you know. Her heart's in the right place even if she does allow her mouth to run away with itself and is just a tad overbearing sometimes."

"Oh, I know she means well," Georgie said. "She loves you very much and still wants to look after you and why shouldn't she? It's been her job for long enough."

And as if in complete defeat she turned around with her shoulders slouched and walked back towards the room where Charlie lay barely conscious.

I followed with the food.

As Georgie started to pour coffee from the flask she spoke in a low, even but firm tone. "You'll get a good night's sleep tonight, Ruby. You need to go home. You've done your bit by just being here for me last night but your job and family are in Swiftstown, pet, and God knows how long Dad's going to be here or indeed if he'll ever get out."

She looked sadly in the direction of her father which only strengthened my resolve. There was no way I was going to leave her at the mercy of her sisters who were behaving like a pack of slobbering baying wolves and ganging up on her.

"My family and job will be fine, Georgie. They aren't going anywhere and neither am I. Unlike the rest of your family, I know what my priorities are and won't be shirking them either. You need me right now and I'm here for as long as it takes. Please don't pay any attention to my mother. She's just worried that things will be falling apart without me at home but I can assure you they're not. Luke is probably having parties every night to celebrate the fact that I'm not there creating a mess for him to clean up, and I had time owing to me from work so they can't say a word. Besides, I should be asking for my time with you to be counted as Special Family Leave as that's exactly how I view it."

My words and resolve were strong but inwardly I was dreading telling both Luke and Mammy of my decision to stay with Georgie longer as I knew that they would both yap as a result but for different reasons.

Mammy would no doubt be disapproving as she would tell me that Luke was my priority and that I should be with him (but what she really meant was that I'd had a life before Georgie entered it and I should focus on it). In fairness, I knew that she was concerned about me getting hurt, but I also knew that she had an inbuilt but totally unfounded fear of being replaced.

Luke would also complain but in his case he would think that I was going to extraordinary lengths to avoid any more well-planned dinners that would initiate intimate chats that would lead to other things. Just to be clear, so as you know, I have nothing against sex. I love sex, in fact. I just have a bit of a hang-up about its side effects, which was precisely why I was on the pill and never intended to come off it. Ever.

21

Jodi

"Are you sure you don't mind?" I asked Frankie who was shaking her head at me in an easy-going fashion.

I had been on my way to the bus station when Frankie pulled up beside me for a chat and it seemed that yet again she was prepared to be my saviour.

"I'm going to Belfast to a marketing meeting anyway and I can drop you off at the airport on the way. I think there's a bus that will take you into Belfast city centre and then you can get another connection straight back to Swiftstown from there."

"That's brilliant. I really want to meet my father at the airport. He rang me last night to say that he had decided to come earlier than planned. I can't wait to see him." I climbed in beside her and put my seatbelt on.

"I hope I'm not speaking out of turn but am I to take it that you're closer to your father than you are to your mother then?"

"Are you joking me?" I said, laughing. "He kept me

sane when I was living at home. My mother is very hard work and that's putting it mildly. It's no wonder Daddy eventually walked out and left – given the circumstances it didn't come as much of a surprise. She's always been rather highly strung but she got a lot worse after my brother died and the pressure got too much for both of them to bear and it took its toll on their relationship."

"Oh God, I'm sorry to hear that," Frankie said with a shocked expression. "I assumed you were an only child as you never mentioned having siblings before. Did this happen long ago?"

"Paul died eighteen years ago when I was fifteen and he was seventeen. I can still remember the last words I said to him. I asked him if he wanted a cup of tea before I went to bed the night before we found him and he told me that he was fine but that I could wake him up with one in the morning so that's what I did. I went in to wake him and found him dead. He'd had a brain haemorrhage during the night."

"That's awful. You poor thing! How on earth do you cope with something like that? I have one sister and to be honest I simply don't know what I'd do without her. She lives in Scotland and I miss her dreadfully."

"You get used to it and learn to come to terms with it although you never actually get over it as such. I miss him but I like to think that he's in a better position to help me now . . . although I'd like to know what's keeping him at this moment in time."

"I lost a baby several years ago," Frankie confided. "I had been pregnant with twins and lost one and the surviving one is my little Jack but I like to think that my other baby is helping me out. I talk to him all the time and

156

ask for his help and when things don't turn out the way I want them to immediately I always assume that it's because I have a lesson to learn or because there's a reason why I have to wait for things to happen, and that is usually the case."

I thought about what she had said and it made more sense than anything had in a long time. Obviously there must be another plan but I prayed and hoped that things would become clear soon.

After Frankie dropped me off I walked through the airport and as I did I remembered all the times that I'd been there in the past dropping Ashley off or picking him up. I often used to wonder why he had quite so many trips when he had a sales team employed for that purpose and had voiced my feelings about this on several occasions, only to be told that the personal touch was essential in business. He had given the personal touch alright. It was just a pity that the recipient hadn't been one of his tycoon friends but someone else entirely.

I was still daydreaming as I reached the arrivals lounge, only for an announcement to be made that told us that due to a fuel problem the British Airways flight from the Midlands had been delayed.

I sighed and flopped down on a seat in irritation and prepared to sit it out, although I really needed to get home and do some preparation as I had my interview for the job in the college tomorrow. Frankie had told me just to be myself and I'd be fine. She wasn't actually going to be on the interview panel though as they were bringing in someone from the Public Relations department in Belfast.

I found a magazine discarded on a seat and settled down to wait for my father's flight to land.

I had been flicking through the pages for about fifteen minutes when I suddenly felt the urge to look up. The sight that greeted me floored me completely and made me want to be sick with panic.

Ashley was standing looking directly at me with a suitcase in one hand and a piece of hand-luggage in the other.

He stopped and looked at me and his face must have mirrored my own expression of blind fear. I hoped nastily that the sudden rush of adrenalin would make him have a heart attack and that it would be excruciatingly painful, unbearable and have the side effect that his bits would all fall off.

My discomfort mounted further as I watched him approach me and my grip on the latest edition of *Heat* magazine tightened (although what use being beaten with a rolled-up celebrity glossy that depicted Katie Price on the cover would do, I didn't know).

"Joanna, what are you doing here? Are you going somewhere? You look . . ." (there was a long pause) ". . . well."

I gave him the filthiest look I could muster and got up abruptly with the intention of shifting to another seat (preferably beside a security guard who would be built like a brick shithouse and who would thump him).

"Please, can you give me five minutes?" he said. "Just five minutes is all I ask. I know that, in your eyes, I probably don't deserve that and maybe you're right but I need to try and explain. I never meant to hurt you. Things just got out of hand."

"*Out of hand?*" I squealed, my resolve not to answer him weakening as a result of my anger at his pathetic excuses. "You're not sorry that things got out of hand at all. You seemed to be quite enjoying the challenge and the secrecy. Lies dripped off your tongue like they were of no consequence, but that's the thing with liars, you see, their actions come back to bite them on the arse eventually and, boy, did you royally screw yourself over! Did it never occur to you that I'd find out or that she would ever need you like she did? Did you seriously credit us with so little brainpower that you thought neither of us would catch on to your games eventually?"

He seemed to have momentarily forgotten that he was in an airport but, as my voice rose an octave with every accusation, he was brought back to reality and was now furtively looking around him as if he wanted the ground to swallow him up.

"Oh, I'm sorry. Does the truth hurt? Or, more to the point, are you worried about the fact that some of your fancy upmarket high-class friends might see you and discover what a shit you really are?"

"Please, Joanna, give me a chance to explain everything, but not here. Why don't you let me take you home? I love you so much and the house hasn't been the same without you in it. I don't feel complete without you. You were my world and if it's any consolation when I was faced with a choice I chose you. The fact that I was prepared to go on national TV and beg for you to come back should have been testament enough to that."

"What do you want me to say, Ashley? Do you want a medal or a pat on the head for being a good boy? It doesn't please me that other people are suffering as a result of your actions and that unwittingly I've been an accessory to your behaviour for a long time. The fact that now you think I'm worth devoting all your time and energies to is of no interest to me at all. It's too little too late. It means nothing just like you mean nothing."

He was obviously more deluded and up his own arse than I thought as he looked shocked that I wasn't jumping on him in a loved-up fashion and thanking him for making me 'the one'.

"You've got to believe me, Joanna. You are my life and my world and I love you. Please, please believe me. I never meant for anyone to get hurt." He was sounding increasingly desperate.

"You never intended for anyone to find out would be closer to the truth," I spat. "What was it you always said – oh, that's right – the eleventh commandment: Don't Get Caught."

"I used to say that with regards to business. I was never talking about my personal life," he said quietly.

"Well, I think it applied quite aptly," I retorted. "You definitely give a whole new meaning to the concept of having your cake and eating it."

"Don't think that I enjoyed any of it, Joanna. I never meant for things to get so complicated. I used to lie awake at night and wonder how everything had got so messed up. It hasn't been easy for me either."

I waited for approximately thirty seconds before I lunged at him.

By the time the security guards (who were indeed built like brick shithouses) pulled me off him he had scratches all over his face, I had torn his shirt and was wielding clumps of his hair in my hands and feeling most satisfied.

My satisfaction was short-lived, however, as it was at that particular moment that my father appeared through

160

the door of the arrivals gate. He was looking around, obviously to see if he could spot me, and when he finally did he looked more than a bit perplexed to see me being manhandled by airport security, red in the face through sheer exertion with my hair in a mess and my clothes dishevelled while my (ex) husband looked roughed-up and angry.

"Do you wish to press charges, Mr Crozier?" one of the guards asked. "We're obliged to ring the police and I have to say that you have a cut-and-dried case for assault. We can run back the tapes and get the CCTV footage and there are a lot of witnesses."

"Sure, go ahead and charge me with assault," I snarled. "I've been dying to have a word with the police anyway but haven't had the chance so this will give me the perfect opportunity to put some very interesting facts to them."

"I don't want to press any charges," Ashley said. "She's my wife."

"I'm his *ex*-wife," I growled through gritted teeth. "And just so as we're clear, I don't normally go around battering people in public places – but if you had any idea of what he's done you'd understand why hitting him felt so damn good."

"Joanna, what the hell is going on and what is he doing here?" my father demanded, giving Ashley a dirty look.

"I have no idea what he's doing here," I said airily, "and much less do I care. What he does is no longer any concern of mine. Come on. Let's go and get something to eat and get the hell out of here."

Three hours later and we were on our way home. We'd had three cups of coffee each, cleared the coffee shop of tray bakes, and I had told my father absolutely everything and to say that he had been shocked to the core would have been an understatement.

My heart had descended into my toes when I had first seen Ashley at the airport and I still felt a bit nervous and anxious, but I also felt strangely vindicated and calm and was glad that it had happened. It was almost as if I had been cleansed. I had told Ashley what I thought of him, I had seen his reaction and I felt nothing. I had loved this man with every fibre of my being but he and his actions had caused me such heartache that any love I'd had for him had turned to contempt.

The day I walked out on Ashley I had arrived in Swiftstown because that's where the bus I had boarded was going. For the first time in my life I hadn't had a plan to follow and I had been scared out of my wits, but what my time in Swiftstown had given me was the opportunity to think. But the time for thinking was now over and the time for acting was upon me and I planned to give this scene everything I had.

I had reached a new crossroads in my life. I was now free to move on and I hoped that this chapter would be less turbulent and more peaceful than the last.

Frankie had been right. Everything was happening as it should and, even though I hadn't understood or wanted to understand, it was all for the best.

I kissed the cross around my neck and thanked my brother for his divine assistance.

22

Frankie

I had stopped smoking a long time ago but was seriously tempted to go into the shop, order a packet of Marlboro lights and puff the head off myself. Or perhaps I might just send a few smoke signals in the general direction of Owen which would translate as 'Go and feck yourself, you absolute arsehole!' He had annoyed and upset me beyond belief with his failure to even pretend that I had a point of view, an opinion or indeed the right to provide my side of the story.

Angelica had been giving me filthy looks now for days and when my last nerve snapped and I told her what a spoilt, selfish, immature little brat she was, Owen rounded on me in front of her and told me never to speak to *his* daughter like that again.

The look on Angelica's face spoke volumes. She was triumphant in the wake of her father's complete demeaning of me in front of her. She would never take me seriously again and, if she had been of the opinion that I knew nothing before then, he had just well and truly cemented the fact in her head. One parent belittling another in front of a smug teenager was never going to be a good idea and this definitely hadn't been one of his better plans and the abject look of terror on Owen's face betrayed the fact that he knew this.

"Angelica, you wouldn't give us a moment, please?" he had asked in a terse voice.

His daughter had been most obliging and skipped past me wearing the most delighted expression of one-upmanship.

"It's customary to ask a child to step out of the room before you berate one of their parents but perhaps that courtesy only extends to birth parents and not pathetic excuses for stand-in ones who have been doing their best but obviously don't make the grade."

Owen squeezed his eyes shut and held his hands out. "Look, I'm sorry. I shouldn't have said that. I didn't mean it the way it sounded. I just think you're being very hard on her at the moment and, whether you've noticed it or not, she seems preoccupied and distracted and I'm worried about her. I know you don't like the company she's keeping right now but maybe if you laid off her a bit she'd see that maybe he's not right for her and it would fizzle out. Teenage girls are notorious for doing the exact opposite of what you want them to do just to spite you so perhaps if you pretended to like Jerome she'd instantly lose her infatuation with him."

"And what makes you such an expert on teenage girls?" I demanded. "At least when I speak I know what I'm talking about because I actually have had the experience of being one."

"Where are you going?" he asked as I put my coat on and lifted my bag.

"Me? I am going as far away as possible from you and *your* daughter. *My* children are staying with my parents tonight as I have an early meeting in the morning and you are teaching so you don't have to worry about them and I trust that putting *our* son to bed for a change won't be too challenging for you?"

He started to speak again but I didn't stop to listen. I had never been so hurt in all my life. I had worked so hard to try and earn Angelica's respect. More fool me to think that my efforts had been appreciated or noted by her or anyone else. For once my mother appeared to be right. A man minus baggage was now looking like a very attractive prospect.

I got into the car, started the engine and for once didn't have anywhere pressing to be. I was just going to drive and put as much distance between myself and Owen as possible.

Owen and I had triumphed against all the odds. Our relationship was built on strong foundations that had been formed due to the fact that we had to fight to be together against everyone else who was hell-bent on keeping us apart. His mother hadn't thought that I was good enough for her precious son until I had produced her grandson who had been named after her late husband – which was when she suddenly seemed to think I wasn't that bad. Then there was Brutal Brenda who hated me with a passion and made it her life's mission to demean Owen where possible to try and discredit him, without truly giving Angelica's feelings a second thought. Not to mention Angelica herself who had gone to terrible lengths to try and break us up with her constant troublemaking and outrageous behaviour. Owen's words made all the sacrifices and heartache all the more pointless. It was the latest in a string of arguments which all had one common denominator . . . Princess Angelica.

I arrived in town, stopped the car and slumped across the steering wheel, letting out a huge sigh of exasperation. Why did life have to be so hard? I was a good person. I tried to be nice to everyone. I was glad to see others happy. I wasn't claiming to be the best mother in the world but compared to some of the excuses for mothers out there I thought that I would pass as half-decent.

I gathered myself with a start when someone abruptly tapped my driver's window and nearly died of shock when I saw none other than my friend Gabriel standing there. Gabriel O'Sullivan was flamboyant in the extreme, as mad as a hatter, as camp as *Hi-de-Hi* and gayer than a Christmas tree, but he was also a tonic who instantly made you feel better and at the very sight of him I could feel my spirits rising.

"Gabriel! Oh my God! What are you doing here?" I asked, getting out of the car and enveloping him in a bear hug.

"Steady on, Frankie," he admonished. "People will talk, y'know, and the last thing I want is for some ridiculous rumour to get out that I'm straight or something."

"That's hardly feckin' likely," I answered with a laugh as I took a step back and surveyed him. He was wearing a tweed cap, riding breeches, a tartan waistcoat and knee-length boots that boasted a heel that was taller than any jockey would ever have use for.

I had first met Gabriel when he had been assigned the

unenviable task of being Ruby's wedding planner the year before. I had been chief bridesmaid and as such had witnessed some of their most terrifying and eye-watering arguments which started mostly because Ruby was an incorrigible tomboy who Gabriel had wanted to transform into a Barbie doll (Chucky the devil doll was about as much as he had accomplished). Eventually, however, due to circumstances and a few common bonds in relation to identity and 'fitting in' they had come to a mutual understanding and we were all now good friends.

"I was going to call and see you but I didn't expect find you sitting in your car in a state of collapse. Have you no home to go to?"

"It's a long story," I said wearily, running my eye down Gabriel's ensemble again.

"I know," Gabriel said as he watched me eyeing his clothing and performed a perfectly executed spin on one magnificent heel. "It's fabulous, isn't it? I planned a wedding recently for an English earl who has decided that he would like to live in Ireland now and he sported the most delicious outfits. In fact, I'm just coming from meeting with him now. He lives in an old manor house in Fermanagh so I thought I'd call in on you on the way back."

"Was it a normal wedding?" I asked.

"What do you mean – normal?"

"I mean was he marrying a girl or was he one of your funny friends?"

"I'm glad I know you too well now to be offended by that remark," Gabriel answered. "If you must know it was a same-sex wedding so, no, it wasn't one of your boring 'normal' weddings." He made inverted quote-marks with his fingers while rolling his eyes to heaven and pretending to stifle a massive yawn.

"I never would have guessed," I said, laughing, as I gave him another hug, feeling suddenly emotional and teary-eyed. I was missing Ruby dreadfully as she was still in Donegal and I didn't want to disturb her with my problems at such a sensitive time – and I badly needed the comfort of a friend.

"Are you alright?" Gabriel asked, holding my shoulders and giving me a penetrating look.

"I'm fine," I lied.

"Sure you are and I fancy girls and have suddenly developed a liking for big boobs."

I looked at him and my eyes filled again with tears.

"Hey, what's the matter?" he asked, hugging me close and rubbing my back in a comforting circular motion.

He smelt of musk and I nuzzled into his shoulder, breathing it in and wishing that I could always feel so secure and loved.

"Frankie, you're leaving a damp patch on my shoulder, sweetie, and it doesn't really blend in with my country-gent look. If I had known you were going to be so upset and needed a girl-to-girl chat I would have brought my nail-art set and curling tongs and we could have made a proper night of it."

I smiled despite myself. Gabriel didn't have to do much to make you laugh. In fact, looking at him was normally enough!

"So, tell me what or who has been upsetting you but don't expect me to react like Ruby and threaten to beat anyone up because you know that is *sooooo* not my style. I could maybe bitch-slap them into touch but I find that being an actual bitch is normally much more effective."

I rolled my eyes and blew hard into a tissue.

"Owen just completely annihilated me in front of Angelica. She's being a little nightmare of late and I finally snapped and told her a few home truths and Owen barged into the middle of it and told me never to speak to *his* daughter like that again."

I pronounced the word *his* with particular emphasis and as I said it I decided that the two of them were welcome to each other because I'd had enough of being used and abused.

"Bitch," Gabriel muttered in an outraged tone (and for a moment I was unsure which one of them this was aimed at). "You say she's been a little nightmare recently, darling, but correct me if I'm wrong – has there ever been a time when she hasn't been one?"

I sighed and, as I thought of some of the closeness we'd shared, I felt an overwhelming sadness envelop me. I mightn't have had the stretch marks or the scar as proof of parentage but it had never stopped me from trying to do my best for her or looking on her as one of my own.

As my emotions threatened to get the better of me again Gabriel sighed and placed a comforting arm around me.

"Frankie, darling, you're just going to have to learn to ignore her. She's manipulating Owen and, God love his cotton socks, he doesn't realise that he's being played. But, what you don't realise is that by reacting in this way you're giving in to her and letting her win. You need to toughen up, girl, and learn to play her at her own game."

"*Aarrrrrrgggghhhhh*!" I squealed in complete

frustration, making Gabriel nearly overbalance in his precarious footwear. "That's the feckin' problem! I don't want to play games. I'm an adult and this isn't some stupid trivial situation that revolves around one person getting the better of the other one. It's about a little girl who's been badly hurt and who unfortunately enjoys taking her frustrations out on me and it's also about my relationship with her father. Why can't Owen see my point of view? Why is he always so quick to jump to her defence and so quick to believe the worst of me? It didn't use to be like this. I don't understand what's changed."

As I said the words I could feel something inside me snap and my shoulders began to heave with huge wracking sobs. For the first time in a long time I felt insecure and afraid. What if Owen suddenly decided that I was the problem and that he wanted me out of his life and away from his daughter?

"I can read your mind, Frankie," Gabriel said, still rubbing my back. "Owen loves you, babe. He loves you very much. He's not going anywhere and neither are you and don't worry about Angelica – she's always been a problem. If she didn't cause you bother, your life would be very boring and we'd have nothing to talk about on our nights out."

Gabriel pulled me close again, affectionately stroking my hair while peppering my cheek with light feathery kisses.

"Come on, you," he said. "I know what you need."

He took my keys from me, locked the car, gave me my bag and held my hand as he led me across the road.

"Gabriel, where are we going?"

"I saw something on the way in that looked quite

interesting and wanted to check it out and now I have my perfect excuse. You need to be cheered up and I am your agony aunt."

"Uncle," I corrected.

"No, Frankie. I am most definitely your agony 'aunt', my dear."

We rounded the corner which led on to a street where I saw a sign advertising Cocktails and Tapas.

"Good grief," I said. "This used to be an old man's pub, Gabriel. I'd say I've only been in it twice in my life. I'd forgotten it was here actually. I wonder who owns it and why they've decided that a cocktail bar would be a good idea for Swiftstown. It's not exactly the most exciting place in the world. I mean, you'd hardly call it the cosmopolitan capital of the world, would you? Or even in the running?"

"Whoever had the idea has been pretty smart about it actually," Gabriel said, surveying price lists, menus for food and the special opening offers that the new bar was boasting. "Swiftstown might not be an urban metropolis full of night clubs and expensive bars but, hey, that's the beauty of it. It's something different in a small town where you can get peace and serenity as well as a slice of city life. I like it a lot. Besides they serve normal drinks as well so it's sure to appeal to everyone."

At that point a man in his late forties came out the front door and started to wipe the chalk board down with a damp cloth.

"I must say, old boy, this is a jolly nice place you have here," Gabriel said, adopting the worst English accent I had ever heard while swaggering in his tweed attire with his nose in the air. He looked most peculiar. Eccentric gone wrong.

I was going to have to have a word with him about this. Or rather, I was going to have to tell him to lose the clothes, the accent and the ridiculous poses before Ruby got her hands on him as she had a very low threshold for people behaving like eejits and would end up trying to kill him.

"Ehhhh . . . yeah. It's something new I've decided to try," the man said, trying very hard not to look too shell-shocked and astonished.

"Hi, I'm Gabriel. Gabriel O'Sullivan but you can call me Gay for short."

The man's eyebrows were practically touching his hairline as he shook Gabriel's outstretched hand.

"Nice to meet you, Gabriel, I mean Gay. My name is Fabian Quinn and Pitchers, my new cocktail bar, will be officially opening at the end of the month and you and your friend here are more than welcome to come along."

"Don't you run the antiques shop on the main street?" I said suddenly as I remembered where I'd heard the name before.

"I do indeed but my uncle used to run this place and wanted it kept in the family so I decided to try and liven things up a little!"

"You'll definitely do that alright," Gabriel said. "You'll be encouraging all types of new clientele with this menu. I must spread the word."

Fabian Quinn looked scared and I grinned in spite of the anguish I was feeling, thinking that Gabriel and his particular brand of zany energy should be bottled and sold for when you needed a swift pick-me-up.

"By all means bring your wives, husbands, partners whatever and enjoy the fun."

172

"Sod that," Gabriel said. "We'll tell Ruby and make it a girlie night with just the three of us."

Fabian Quinn smiled before thrusting a sample menu in Gabriel's hand.

"*Ooooooh!* Sex on the Beach at the end of February," Gabriel announced in his campest voice to the whole street. "I can hardly wait!"

23

Angelica

At last the battle was over and I had come out on top. I was victorious. A winner. I had finally got what I wanted and when I told Auntie Brenda all about it she had cackled so hard that I thought she was in danger of cracking a rib.

"Oh, what I wouldn't have given to have been a fly on the wall!" she said for the fortieth time.

I hoped in earnest that she wasn't going to ask me to repeat what had happened again as I was getting tired of talking about it.

"I don't have that much time for your father, Angelica, but this is one occasion where I'd like to shake his hand for a job well done. It's about time somebody taught that bitch a lesson and brought her down a peg or two. She's had that coming for years."

Brenda's face contorted in anger, making her seem harsh and ugly and suddenly I felt tired and wanted to leave.

"I have to go. I need to head home and pamper myself for tonight. We're going to a flash new restaurant and I want to look extra special. Jerome told me the kind of thing he'd like me to wear and everything so I want to make sure I get everything right for him."

"He's very decisive, isn't he?" Brenda said approvingly. "I like that in a man. He sounds like someone who knows what he wants. Hold on to him and you'll do well. He's set to inherit a fortune too. His father's business is booming. You'll be set up for life."

My worries about Jerome going off me had apparently been unfounded as we had met the night before which was when he had said that he wanted me to accompany him to dinner tonight. He too had been delighted to hear that my father had put Frankie in her place.

"Sounds like everything's working out the way it should. You don't need her breathing down your neck and telling you what to do. You've got me and that's all you need."

My heart had started to sing at his words. Katie had been right. I had been reading far too much into it all and had allowed past events to distress me. Jerome wasn't going anywhere. He said he liked me and was showing me how much by finally introducing me to his parents.

I always planned my outfits very carefully when I was going to be in Jerome's company. He had distinctive taste and wasn't a big fan of the tank tops and skinny jeans that I had worn before I met him. In this case he had mentioned the black dress he had seen me wear the other night. I pulled hangers apart looking for it but concluded that it must be in the wash and, as Frankie and I weren't exactly on speaking terms, now wasn't the time for grovelling and asking the Laundry Fairy to do me any favours. I would wear my red dress with the sweetheart neckline and the wide black belt along with my highest heels and loosely curl my hair the way that he liked.

"Dinner's ready," I heard Frankie calling from downstairs.

I didn't bother responding as I wouldn't be eating anything anyway. Jerome's parents were entertaining a major new client at dinner tonight and I was lucky enough to have been included. Jerome had told me that if they managed to impress this man he could send a lot of work their way. I was going to order a Chicken Caesar salad and drink water and not have any dessert. Jerome had said that he loved my figure and wouldn't like to see me putting on any excess weight so the chocolate treats that I used to love were now a definite no-no.

My door opened abruptly.

"Your dinner is ready, Angelica. Everyone else is sitting at the table. Do you need a special invitation and a loud gong rung in your ear?"

"I'm not having dinner, Frankie. I'm going out with Jerome and his parents this evening."

I gave her a dirty look and then continued to apply my make-up. Not too much eye liner (as Jerome hated the Gothic look), a hint of mascara to accentuate my long lashes and some lip balm.

"You could at least have had the manners to tell me that you weren't going to be around this evening, Angelica."

With that she closed the door and I could hear her padding down the stairs in her socks, back to the kitchen to where the rest of the mob were sitting waiting to be served. I could hear her relaying to my father that I was going out and sighed as I heard more footsteps on the stairs.

"Going out for dinner, I hear. *Meet the Fockers* night, is it?" Dad said jokily.

"Something like that."

"You look very well," he said. "It's nice to be able to actually see your eyes for once and that's a lovely dress. You look great!"

"Thanks, Dad. Apparently we're going to a posh new restaurant in Armagh. Somewhere near the theatre."

"Well, you'd best have some money on you though I presume they'll be paying if they invited you? Here you are, sweetheart." With that he took fifty pounds out of his wallet and handed it to me.

"Thanks, Dad," I said, feeling a rush of affection for him. "I'm sorry about all the trouble I've caused." I felt regretful for the first time.

"Don't you worry about it. It'll all sort itself out soon, I promise. Frankie mightn't be your mother, Angelica, but she's the closest thing you've had and she's been very good to you. I was tired and cross when I shouted at her the way I did and I shouldn't have. She has all of our best interests at heart and without her I don't know where we'd all be."

I successfully managed to control the urge to snort loudly and laugh. Where would I be without Frankie? I'd be living life to my own tune and I'd have my father to myself just like old times and I'd be a hell of a lot happier without her constant interference.

"Oh yes," Dad said as if he had just remembered something, "I forgot to tell you that your granny is coming up from Dublin on Friday evening for the weekend so why don't you tell Jerome to come for dinner on Saturday?"

"Are you serious, Dad? It was the last dinner here that nearly caused World War Four and I'm not up for a rematch, thanks."

"You leave that to me, sweetheart. I'll talk to Frankie and make sure that she makes something nice and is on her best behaviour."

"Well, I suppose I could ask him and see if he's free."

"You do that and I'll keep my end of the bargain."

As it turned out Jerome wasn't very keen on the idea of going to my house for dinner again so soon and who could blame him?

He had picked me up at exactly seven o'clock as he was nothing if not very punctual (another attribute that my daddy appreciated greatly). He had looked at me with a critical eye when I had got into the car but instead of complimenting me as he usually did he simply told me that I'd "do".

I tried not to take it too seriously but felt a bit put out as I'd gone to a lot of trouble to try and please him.

"Are you okay?" I asked eventually.

"I'm fine. I just hope that this meeting goes well tonight. If it goes according to plan and we agree all the necessary figures for the contract then it will boost our business significantly."

"So who are the people that we're meeting then?"

"Angelica, darling, my father and I are meeting with them. My mother and you are simply going to be eating and looking pretty."

I smiled back at him and tried to be happy that he thought that I was pretty enough to be invited along to an important meeting but something got in the way of my joy.

We arrived at the restaurant at the same time as Jerome's parents. I could see immediately where he got his good looks from. He was very like his father who looked important and distinguished with his trimmed moustache and fair hair. Jerome's mother on the other hand was nothing like I had expected. I had anticipated her to be a highly glamorous lady who would be stunningly good-looking and polished with perfect hair and nails. She wasn't. Although she was well-dressed and tidy, to me she looked tired and had a timidity about her that surprised me.

"Dad, I'd like you to meet Angelica. Angelica, this is my father Lewis."

I almost felt like I should curtsey or perform a dance or something.

He scrutinised me for a moment before shaking my hand and nodding curtly.

"Hello, son," he said. "We'd better get inside and prepare ourselves. We'll see you two in there. Don't be late."

I stopped in surprise at his tone which was hard and brusque and directed mostly at his wife who nodded at him.

"I'm sorry, I don't know your name," I said after they had left, realising that neither Jerome nor his father had introduced me to her.

"I'm Marian," she said. "And I'm very happy to meet you. It's nice to have company for a change. I hate these stuffy old dinners."

I warmed to her immediately and was glad that she wasn't the uber-trendy yummy-mummy type that I had been expecting. Warm and friendly was much nicer.

"Come along, Angelica. Let's go inside and prepare to be bored rigid all night."

24

Ruby

"We've been praying for a miracle," Georgie breathed as the doctor examined Charlie.

"Well, it would appear that you may well have a direct line to God then," the doctor answered. "Your father seems to be responding well to the intravenous antibiotics we've been treating him with. He's very lucky though. Do you realise how many people his age can die from pneumonia? I'm sorry to be blunt but it's one of the biggest killers amongst the elderly in this country. It was a good job that the nursing home used their own discretion and brought him here. If they had waited for your sister to sign the relevant documentation we could be telling a rather different story, I'm afraid."

"Excuse me?" Georgie said, looking shocked and confused. "What do you mean?"

The doctor looked wary and seemed to realise that he might have inadvertently stuck his stethoscope in it.

"Look, perhaps you better take it up with the nursing

181

home. I'm in the middle of my ward round and need to go," he said hastily. "Just be assured that your father is coping well at the minute but that he needs a lot of attention. He'll be very weak and the slightest infection or complication could literally be fatal for him. He'll need careful nursing and regular check-ups."

"He'll get the best nursing there is," Georgie said with uncharacteristic brusqueness. "He'll be moving in with me and if anyone has a problem with that then they'll just have to get over themselves."

The doctor left, looking alarmed, and I started to clap.

"About time you started sticking up for yourself. I'm impressed. Perhaps my, kick-ass genes are not wholly down to my father after all."

I nearly swallowed my tongue as it dawned on me that sometimes I needed to put my brain into gear before I went opening my mouth.

"Sorry," I said, squinting with one eye opened and the other closed. "Did I actually say that out loud?"

"You did," Georgie answered, her usual quiet manner restored.

"I did, didn't I?"

For a short time neither of us spoke, both of us lost in our own thoughts.

Georgie looked pensive and withdrawn and I was wondering how I managed to say the wrong thing on a regular basis either intentionally or by accident.

"Look, I'm sorry if I spoke out of turn. I didn't mean to be so flippant about it. I know that you'll tell me in your own good time and I'm prepared to wait. Just, please, have a heart and don't make me wait too long. I'm the most impatient, impulsive person in the world."

Sitting in the hospital and watching someone sleep didn't present many opportunities apart from plenty of time to think and, as the subject of my father was ever present in my mind, it was hardly surprising that it had cropped up, even if it was an accident.

Georgie looked at me and nodded.

"When everything is sorted out Ruby I promise that I'll put you out of your misery but for now I'm sure you understand that I need to devote all my energies to looking after Dad and getting him away from that nursing home. I don't care what Marcella says, he's not going back there."

"I wasn't actually intending on bringing it up right now, Georgie. It just happened, as things tend to do with me."

There was a short awkward silence before I spoke again. "What was all that stuff about the nursing home using their own discretion as opposed to waiting for your sister? I thought you told me that you were down as Charlie's next of kin and that they were to contact you if there was a problem?"

"That *was* my understanding. It was agreed when he went in there that, because I was nearby, I would be contacted if they needed a signature on anything or there was a problem but obviously all that has now changed. Pity nobody thought to tell me."

Georgie looked most put out and for a moment I was trying to visualise what she would look like if she were to behave like a raving lunatic and tell her family exactly where they could go and what they could do with their domineering attitudes and relentless need to control everything and everybody around them. I tried to imagine her unleashing the years of anger that she had managed to bury but couldn't. Unlike me, she was far too placid and mild-mannered for such a display of temper. She would, instead, no doubt, try to resolve things her own way which might seem ludicrously reasonable to me but then again we were two different people who reacted in very different ways to things.

"A penny for them," Georgie said.

"I was just thinking about how different we all are," I responded. "Everyone has their own way of looking at things and dealing with other people. I don't know what you're planning on doing about this situation with your father but I'd like to see you being assertive and not bowing down to Marcella. She seems to be manipulative in the extreme and doesn't seem to care what consequences her actions provoke. What happened to your life and mine is a prime example of that."

Georgie looked uncomfortable and sat down heavily in the high-backed chair beside her father's bed.

"I don't intend to take any abuse from anyone, Ruby, but you have to understand that a lot has happened over the years. Things that don't involve you or that you don't have to concern yourself with. I have to be careful about what I do."

I could feel myself getting prickly and annoyed.

"Why do you always feel the need to be the peacemaker, Georgie? After all that those people have done to you throughout the years, I think that your loyalty is remarkable. It's okay to feel wronged. You owe them nothing. They destroyed your life. They might well have destroyed my life too had things been different. They're trying to do it again with Charlie. Suiting themselves for whatever reason and to hell with everyone else. Please don't let them walk all over you because I won't have it."

There was a deafening silence.

Perhaps I had said too much (very unlike me).

I knew that Georgie wasn't prone to reacting badly to things but, if the way that she was moving her mouth around and sucking in her cheeks and jigging her leg was anything to go by, then I'd say she wasn't best pleased with me.

"I'm sorry," I began.

"No need to be sorry," she answered in a tight voice. "Everyone is entitled to their opinion."

(I must stress at this point that when I was encouraging Georgie to stand up for herself I wasn't actually asking for her to practise on me.)

"Oh Georgie, the last thing I want to do is to annoy you. I'm sorry if I sound insensitive but I'm the outsider looking in at this family. My birth family. And, believe me, it makes for disturbing viewing. I don't want to see you being hurt any more but I won't say another thing. I'll be out here if you need me."

I went outside and did what I always did when I was annoyed: I reached for my phone and punched in Luke's number.

"Hello," he answered cheerily. "Are you planning on coming home anytime soon? This house is far too big for a bachelor on his own, y'know."

"Oh, I don't think you'll ever be a bachelor, Luke. I wouldn't allow it. I wasn't planning on coming home for another few days but on reflection I think that it mightn't be a bad idea if I leave here and put some distance between Georgie and myself."

"Oh dear."

I could just imagine Luke sitting wondering exactly what I had done to create this situation. At the very least he would be surmising that I had been a large contributor to whatever unrest there was. And, as usual, he would be right.

"I think I may have upset Georgie. I didn't mean to. It just sort of happened." I paused and considered. "Look, no, I can't just leave. I think I'll phone my mother and ask her if I can come and stay with her for a few days. She was here earlier and was complaining about me having no bed and not getting enough food so she'll have no argument if I say that I'm going to compromise and spend some time with her as well as with Georgie."

"You could always come home, y'know," Luke responded in a huffy tone. "I do miss you."

"And what's to stop you from joining me in Donegal?" I asked in an equally huffy voice. "I don't want to be too far away just in case anything happens. Besides, whether Georgie realises it or not, she actually needs me. That feckin' family of hers are up to something again and you can bet that she won't go snooping to find out what it is. Just like before, that will be down to me. Like I keep telling you, it's a good job that I'm a stubborn mule who doesn't give up easily."

Luke muttered something under his breath about knowing exactly how stubborn I was and didn't he know it because he was on the receiving end of it most of the time.

"Look, I'll leave it with you," I said. "Do try and free yourself up and come down. I'm sure that Mammy would be delighted to see you."

"And what about you?" he asked accusingly.

"And I'll be glad to see you too. I do love you, y'know."

I put my phone back in my bag and prepared to enter my grandfather's room again but decided that maybe I should leave it a bit longer and give Georgie some space with her father before I said anything else I would regret.

I was wandering around the large foyer of the hospital with its clinically white walls, flower shop and fruit stall, when I spotted the doctor that had been attending my grandfather getting what looked like the third degree from none other than Marcella and a man who I presumed must be her husband.

I decided to walk closer as they looked like they were having a very heated debate about something and you didn't have to be Einstein to work out what. I managed to position myself behind a large pillar where I strained to hear the conversation without looking conspicuous.

"In future, doctor, I suggest that you keep your big mouth shut," said Marcella. "You've probably gone and upset my sister now. The only reason why I changed the details with the nursing home was because Georgina might not be around a lot of the time as she has her painting to do and exhibitions to organise. She didn't need to know anything about this. I was just looking after her interests."

The doctor gave his sincerest apologies and went on his way, leaving Marcella and her companion standing there.

"That girl needs to be stopped," Marcella said suddenly in a hard, brittle voice.

"Which one?" her partner asked.

"Both of them if necessary. Georgina is far too gullible to be allowed contact with her."

"Her daughter, you mean?"

"Daughter?" she sneered and laughed nastily. "She's nothing to this family and no matter how she tries to worm her way in I won't allow her to get close. I've met her type before. She's not interested in Georgie really. Meeting Georgie was just to satisfy her curiosity. Now she's more interested in getting her hands on Father's money. Georgie must have told her about it which is why she's hanging around a dying man's bed."

I nearly jumped out at that point and was shaking with annoyance as nothing could have been further from the truth. I didn't have the first clue what they were talking about but could categorically state that I didn't care about money, or land, or property or anything else that they might have owned. The only thing that I was interested in gaining from them was an acknowledgement of my existence and some type of human decency that might actually indicate that they knew that both Georgie and I had been badly treated in the past. That, apparently, was asking too much and I felt tears prick my eyes as I was overcome with a mixture of anger and sadness.

"That girl is nothing more than a chromosomal genetic link that I thought we had taken care of years ago but not well enough. Pity we couldn't have got Georgie on a boat to England in time, then we wouldn't be having any problems now."

I breathed in sharply and tried to stem the flow of tears that were already spilling down my cheeks. This woman, my own flesh and blood, really did truly believe that I was nothing. She hated me so much that she was wishing that I had been destroyed before I was born. Why? Just so that she wouldn't have to worry about anyone else getting their hands on some money, which was all she seemed concerned about. I brushed the tears off my face in agitation. I wasn't going to allow her or her words to stop me from pursuing this further and if she thought that she'd seen the last of me or that I'd give in without a fight then she was sorely mistaken and, somehow, without annoying Georgie any more I had to warn her to be on her guard as it seemed that I wasn't the only one being targeted.

The woman spoke again and her voice and the callousness in it caused my blood to run cold.

"Father is a sentimental old fool and Georgie always was his favourite but things are about to change. My darling little sister has ignored me for the last time. I'll teach her to overrule me! And, as for that mistake of a daughter of hers, she's going to learn a tough lesson too. I'm going to tell our father exactly why we had to take the decision we did all those years ago and, once he hears the truth, I wonder will he still think that his precious Georgie is so pure and innocent?"

25

Jodi

I looked at Frankie and she didn't have to say a word. I knew exactly what was coming.

"I didn't get it, did I?"

"Jodi, please believe me when I say that you did nothing wrong. Your interview was faultless and I, for one, from the feedback I've received from the panel, would have given you the job in a heartbeat, but unfortunately it wasn't my decision to make. You're just overqualified, I'm afraid. They're scared that you won't stay and the college would be left understaffed coming up to our busy time of the year when we need all hands on deck in the promotions department."

"I can't bloody believe this," I said, cradling my head in my hands. "That sleazebag is going to have a field day next week when he comes to collect his rent because I won't have it and then he'll start making all sorts of lewd suggestions and I'll have to kill him and bury him under his own rotting floorboards."

Frankie looked most concerned.

"I'm joking," I said through gritted teeth. "I'd bury him elsewhere because under the floorboards would be too obvious. Besides, he smells bad enough living so God knows what he'd be like dead."

"You're really not that fond of your landlord, are you?" Frankie asked.

"Understatement of the year. He's a weasel with too many hormones and he seems to think that if I don't pay up I'll be willing to 'put out'."

"Look, I'm sure something else will turn up. You're a professional. Big companies will be queuing up to give you a job."

"Frankie, since the former company where my husband still works is connected with most of the corporations in and around Belfast, I think that it's highly unlikely that I'll be going anywhere near any of them. I wouldn't give them the satisfaction of seeing me on my knees. Besides, I don't want him knowing anything about me, what I'm doing or where I am."

My father came into the room and knew from the look on my face and Frankie's demeanour that she had not been the bearer of good news.

"I didn't get the goddamn job. I'll be here for ever."

My father shrugged his shoulders and spoke directly to Frankie. "She's her own worst enemy, this one. I've offered to help her and set her up in a new place but she's so stubborn that she won't accept any money from me and is insisting on doing everything herself."

"It's not that I don't want to accept your help but all my life I've been able to stand on my own two feet and I'm not about to start taking handouts that other people have worked hard for, just because that arsehole has reduced me to the sad person I've become."

"Pride is a good thing to have, Jodi, but don't cut off your nose to spite your face." Frankie said, sitting next to me. "Why would you want to live like this when your dad can help you?"

"I've always been independent and I'm not about to start taking handouts now!" I snapped fighting the urge to tell Frankie to stop interfering.

"You could simply look on it as a small loan, Jo," my father butted in. "If everyone took your attitude the banks would be out of business. Sometimes in this life you have to learn to accept help and this is one of them. You've always been a strong and determined woman and you still are and I'm incredibly proud of you. But I'd be failing as a father if I left you to struggle like this on your own and you wouldn't like to have my worry and anxiety on your conscience, now would you?"

"But Dad –"

My father didn't often show his assertive side but as he held out a fat bundle of cash to me I knew that I would have to take it. I didn't want him worrying about me and I knew that he would.

"I knew you'd want cash," he said with a grin. "Less traceable."

I laughed and hugged him tightly and he held me for a long time.

Frankie had got to her feet and was preparing to leave.

"They're advertising for waitresses in the hotel bistro," she said as she picked up her bag.

I liked Frankie as she had been there for me when I hadn't had a friend in the world but right now I wanted to ask her what the hell she thought she was doing making such ludicrous suggestions. Me? Work in an eatery? I made an abysmal cup of coffee as it was, which was precisely why I liked to treat myself to a proper one every now and then from the establishment in question.

"Frankie, can you seriously see me wearing a pinny and running around serving food? Give me a workforce and budgets and paperwork and a project and I'm landed but around food I'd be a nervous wreck. I'd end up giving people food poisoning or scalding someone. You saw me with your own eyes, for God's sake. I managed to burn myself! What injuries would I not inflict on other people?"

"I was actually only joking, Jodi, but beggars can't be choosers and it's always easier to get a job when you're in a job and you did say that you were bored looking at *Jeremy Kyle* every morning. Besides, can you imagine what the locals would say? Wouldn't you like to baffle them further?"

"You're determined to stand on your own two feet, Jo, so if you're sure that's what you want to do then you need to start somewhere," my father said. "The first lesson that you need to master is that to be independent you'll have to accept whatever work is available. It mightn't necessarily be to your taste but needs must. Remember when you were little and I used to take you to the auctions with me? You hated having to get up early and never got to spend time with your friends at the weekend, but you still did it because you got paid and you knew you'd learn something."

"That's different from working in a restaurant, Daddy. I lasted one night in that place in Belfast City Centre when I was a student so I've no experience worth talking about."

"Well, then, it's about time you got some, don't you

think? It'll be a challenge if nothing else and I've never known you to shy away from anything."

I opened my mouth to protest again but suddenly started to think about what they had both said. It *would* be rather entertaining to see the local reaction. Besides, I was now also visualising my mother's face not to mention what Ashley would say if he found out. What *would* his upmarket friends say if they knew that his glamorous wife would rather be serving punters in a country bistro than working within ten miles of him? I grinned as an evil plan formed in my head.

The hotel owner was a friendly lady who pointed me in the direction of the manager of the bistro: a man in his thirties who worked in the back of the premises in a small and dimly lit office. It was lunch-time and they were very obviously short-staffed if the beetroot-red faces of the waitresses and queues at the counter were anything to go by.

"I can see that you need help and I'm a fast learner."

"What experience do you have?"

"I used to work in a busy Belfast restaurant when I was in my late teens."

(I just neglected to tell him that I had only lasted one night because I had been sacked on the spot for tipping a bowl of spaghetti over a customer after he tried to grope my bottom.)

"Have you had any recent experience?"

"No, but I am a public-relations professional and if there's one thing you need in an eating establishment it's a people person."

The man looked at me for a moment before nodding

his head in recognition. "If you don't mind me asking you," he said tentatively, "are you okay? I know that some of my regulars have been worried about you as as as . . ."

"As I had been reported missing," I finished for him, much to his obvious relief. "But, I am now fine and very much here."

"I just wanted to check."

"And I don't blame you." I gave him my best smile and wondered if I was starting to go slowly mad. Here I was begging for a job in the coffee shop I had been frequenting where everyone thought that I was some sort of deranged stranger with a criminal record. I'd had less bother securing positions in the past where my monthly salary would have matched the profits that this place made on a quarterly basis.

"I tell you what. I'll give you a trial. Get an apron on and help the girls with the lunchtime rush and then we'll talk afterwards about your suitability."

"Thank you," I breathed. (I must also stress at this stage that I probably was equally as happy when I got my high-paying, high-flying jobs in the past. My marbles had officially left the building.)

I walked out past the Ulster-Fry-gobbling trio at the counter and was nearly responsible for having Jamesie Mac choke on a piece of bacon when he saw that I was wearing an apron. Even Ringo stopped long enough from munching on his cake to give me a curious look.

"Well, who'd have thought he'd ever give her a job?" Jockey commented.

"Not feckin' you anyway," said Ringo. "The odds of you ever getting anything right are poor to say the least."

Twenty minutes into the rush (hungry elephants

couldn't have stampeded worse in their hurry to get fed) and I was beginning to regret ever agreeing to this. This wasn't a job. This was torture. My feet were aching. My head hurt from trying to keep up with what people were trying to order and every time I went into the kitchen the chef bellowed at me like a man possessed. (Gordon Ramsay was a tame, mild-mannered pussycat in comparison.)

A waitress named Anna, who had served me on a number of occasions in the past, saw that I was beginning to struggle and took me under her wing.

"Just do as I do," she said.

She made it look completely effortless as she glided around the floor taking orders, making small talk and delivering cutlery while throwing order slips at the till and giving the chef as good as he was dishing out in his bad-tempered voice. I was in awe and, not one to be defeated, I decided to give it my best shot.

I took the notebook out of my apron pocket and approached a table of elderly women who I had seen in the bistro on a number of occasions.

"Can I have the cod with mashed potatoes and mushy peas and can you give me a glass of milk? You're the wee girl that was on the news. Have you found yourself again then?"

I wrote down the order quickly with my face beaming and tried to ignore the question.

"No, she hasn't found herself at all. That's a vision you're seeing. Leave the girl alone!" Anna shouted before punching keys on the cash register and making it ping.

I went to another table.

"Can I have the chicken fillet burger and salad and can you give me a cup of coffee? You're very familiar-looking. Haven't I seen you somewhere before recently?"

"It's your one off the telly."

"Yeah, she was an extra in *Coronation Street*," Anna butted in. "She played her part very well. We're honoured to have her."

I looked at Anna in amazement and she winked back. She and Frankie were both helping to restore my faith in human nature and despite my earlier concerns I was actually beginning to enjoy myself. Besides, the food looked delicious. My stomach began to rumble and I made a mental note to order a dinner the next time I was in. I couldn't remember when the last time I had a home-cooked meal was.

Forty-five minutes later and I felt like I was on auto-pilot. The crowds had started to ease off and as they left so did my nerves and I began to get more confident at shouting out orders and knowing where to put the receipts. I was taking an interest in everyone coming in as well. There were old people who were in for a bite to eat before they went to their senior citizens club. There were young people there on their break from school, office workers having their lunch and mothers who were out shopping and stopped for a breather with babies in buggies and toddlers strapped into the high chairs that sat at the side of the till until they were needed.

"Thanks for giving me the opportunity," I said to Tom in the presence of the other waitresses as I took off my apron and looked for my coat.

"Where do you think you're going?" said Anna. "The waitresses get to eat after the rush is over. Look at the specials menu and tell the chef what you'd like. Come and take the weight off your feet." She patted the seat opposite to where she was sitting and I gratefully sank into it with a menu in my hand.

When my roast chicken special was placed in front of me, I sniffed the air appreciatively and couldn't wait to get stuck in.

Tom appeared shortly after this and told me that I would need to shadow Anna for a few more days but after that the job was mine. I had to work five days a week and Saturdays off were not an option, which I actually didn't mind, and I would be paid cash weekly and get a share of the tips.

I went home that evening with sore feet but a surprisingly light heart.

If you had told me three months ago that I would be this happy about working in a country hotel selling coffee I would have laughed in your face, but then three months ago I didn't know what I knew now.

26

Frankie

"When are you coming back?" I wheedled.

I hated when Ruby wasn't around. I missed our chats and how she could cheer me up in an instant with her random comments and comical view of life.

"I have absolutely no idea, hon. I'm in my mother's now and might possibly be staying for a few days. It's Thursday tomorrow anyway so I might as well stay for the weekend. I haven't caught up with her properly in weeks."

I stared glumly at the wall of my office and wished I could transport myself to Donegal as well, even if the weather wasn't great at the minute. It was still quite cold but the temperatures outside could be no match to the icy atmosphere in my home.

Ruby, who had many talents, one of which apparently included mindreading, then made the suggestion that put a smile on my face.

"Why don't you come to me? Bring the children and get your head showered for a while. I take it that things haven't improved at home?"

"Improved?" I said in despair. "You've got to be joking. They're worse than ever. Angelica has Owen wrapped around her little finger and to make matters worse his mother is coming to visit this weekend. God, I feel sick even thinking about it. The entire 'Angelica Byrne Can Do No Wrong Appreciation Society' all under one roof to worship her and tell her how bloody wonderful she is. Well, sorry if I don't feel like being a spectator looking in from the outside as usual. Owen made it perfectly clear that where Angelica is concerned she's *his* daughter and my opinion or concerns don't count – so that's fine. We all win. They'll get to spend a weekend fawning all over each other and I get away from them all."

"Oh dear," Ruby said. "Sounds like you're having as much fun as me. What the hell is it with families at the minute? Is there something in the air that decrees that everyone should be at loggerheads and staking claim on who belongs or in my case who doesn't?"

"Oh, believe me, I think if Angelica had her way she'd have my bags packed and whether I belonged or not would be of no consequence."

"It's just a blip," Ruby said. "You and Owen will be slobbering all over each other and driving the rest of us nuts again in no time."

"That might have been the case before but this is different. He completely overruled me and degraded me in front of Angelica. I've spent the last number of years trying to get her to trust me and see me as something other than her father's interfering bit on the side but I might as well not have bothered. The number of times I've had to bite my lip for the sake of humouring her and it's all been for nothing. In one fell swoop with one careless comment Owen undid all my hard work and belittled me in front of her. I stomped off to clear my head, came home when they were all in bed and it's been all picture and no sound since although if gloating made a noise Angelica would be honking like a siren. She went to see Brutal Brenda yesterday and my ears were so red with the two of them talking and laughing about me that I thought they were in danger of combusting. I swear she'll use this until doomsday now. I can just hear her. 'I'm not your daughter, get your own children to tidy up. You're not my mother, don't tell me when to go to bed.'"

Even as I said the words I could feel my heart sink further. I had sacrificed so much and when all was said and done I cared about Angelica but it was obvious that my feelings would never be reciprocated. It would be a cold day in hell before Angelica ever learned to accept me.

"Frankie, I've told you before. Don't expect any thanks from teenagers. As soon as they turn fourteen they're abducted by feckin' aliens and have their brains melted and when they return they act like self-absorbed, smart-arsed little nightmares until they exit their teens and the aliens reverse their effects."

"And how do you know all this?" I demanded.

"Because my brain is still on the spaceship!" Ruby replied with a laugh. "Look, Frankie, when I was in my teens I gave my mother such a hard time that it's a wonder the woman didn't ask for me to be brought back from where I came. I was an absolute pain in the arse and it's only now that I'm older and looking back on everything she did for me that I can see clearly exactly what she was prepared to go through because she loved me. I'm not Angelica's biggest fan. You know you only have to say the word and I'll gladly thump her, but at the same time just remember that she's an awkward teenager and in time she'll look back on this and cringe."

"Brutal Brenda isn't a teenager."

"No, she isn't, but then she's barely human either. She just feeds off everybody else's misfortune which she gladly creates, but that's okay because underneath it all we know that that's all she has in her life. She's just a sad, lonely old spinster who hasn't been laid in so many years that the spiders on her cobwebs are depressed. She's more to be pitied than anything else. She can't keep friends because of her foul attitude, throws herself into work because she has no one to go home to and continuously badgers Owen because if she didn't have something to gripe about she'd be bored."

Ruby stopped talking and took a breath.

"You are on fire tonight," I commented. "I'm trying to think if I have any other worries you can help me out with as you're in very philosophical form. It's not like you to be so reasonable. What's wrong with you?"

"Well, that's just feckin' charming, that is. I give you some good advice and try and make you feel better and all you can ask is why I'm not shouting the odds and trying to kill someone."

"Well, why aren't you?"

"I'm practising being patient and I'm trying to develop the ability to see everything from everyone else's point of view."

I was so dumbstruck by this revelation that I couldn't speak. Instead I stared quietly at the phone receiver and wondered why everyone seemed to be going mad around me.

"Are you still there or what?" Ruby said aggressively.

"Y'see?" I answered joyfully. "*There's* the Ruby I know and love. She wasn't that far away after all."

"Oh, ha feckin' ha! Well, I'm going to try and rein that Ruby in as I've decided I'm going to have to talk to Marcella. She's up to something and I want to try and appeal to her better nature, although I'm not sure if she actually has one."

"Oh feck!"

"What do you mean 'oh feck'?"

"I mean I think you're asking for trouble, Ruby. It doesn't sound as if she's very willing to see anything from your point of view. In fact, I'd say she and Angelica could become the best of friends were their paths ever to cross."

"Save your breath, Frankie. My mind's made up and you know what that means."

I didn't speak. There was no point. Once Ruby had set her mind to something she was like a hurtling missile that would stay on course no matter what.

"Ruby I just –"

Ruby interrupted me in a soothing voice. "I know exactly what you're going to say but don't. I'm a big girl and I have to do this. It's time everyone started to move forward. If I've learnt anything from Charlie's illness it's that life is very fickle. Things could change for any one of us in an instant and I'd rather try to put things right. I don't know what I'm going to say yet but I'd like to try and understand why and I'd also like to advise her against causing any more trouble for Georgie. Whether she realises it or not, Georgie is very vulnerable and doesn't need any more pressure. Wish me luck."

"Good luck," I said frowning. Instinctively I didn't

think this was going to end well. "But what will you do if she tells you where to get off and won't talk to you?"

"I said I was going to try and rein my bad-tempered twin in, Frankie. I didn't mention anything about killing her off. She'll still be around and if I need her I'm sure she'll not be long kicking into action."

"Just be careful."

"I promise I'll be fine. You take care too. I look forward to seeing you all at the weekend."

We clicked off and I put down the phone purposefully and started to make plans. I couldn't wait to get away and, although the thought filled me with happiness, it was also tinged with sadness.

Moving forward was excellent as a theory but was a lot more difficult to put into practice, especially when certain involved parties were reluctant participants and steadfastly refused to let go of the past.

27

Angelica

I looked at my phone for the hundredth time and for the hundredth time decided to ignore the text messages and the faint nagging sense of guilt that was creeping into my mind. I knew that it was a tradition that we'd had since our early school days but people changed and times moved on and annual gatherings grew tiresome. Katie always had a party at her house when her parents made their yearly trip to America to visit her father's sister and this year was to be no different, it seemed. I had received the text which told me to be there or be square and if being square made me unpopular then so be it.

I had brought the subject up with Jerome when he had called to see me and he didn't have to say a thing for his feelings to be apparent. He looked positively disgusted.

"You'd think that Katie would have grown out of such pathetic nonsense by now. Having parties while your parents are away is something that any self-respecting fourteen-year-old should be organising. Eighteen-year-olds should have better things to be occupying themselves with."

"Like what exactly?" I asked with a smile playing around my lips, knowing what the answer would be.

"Like attending to their boyfriends' every whim and demand," he said, raising an eyebrow seductively and cupping my face gently. "Text her back and tell her that you're not going. Tell her that you're going to be busy that night. Tell her that we have plans."

I smiled and did what he asked, jabbing the phone quickly and determinedly before I had time to think about it too much.

Katie had been my best friend for nearly seven years. We had met outside the gates of the grammar school that we both attended, on our first day there, and she had looked as nervous as I felt. We had got talking and walked towards the austere and sprawling building together and before we reached the entrance I knew that I had made a new friend and we had been inseparable ever since. Until now. But that was okay. We all had to move on sometime and my time was now. I had met Mr Definitely Right who was going to rescue me from my horrible life and I expected Katie to be happy for me because that's what friends did.

I pressed the send button and resisted the urge to curl up and cringe. I hated letting anyone down but sometimes you just had to prioritise and right now my number one priority was Jerome.

I had enjoyed our night out with his parents. The food had been delicious and Jerome's mother had been nice company although she seemed preoccupied and kept darting anxious looks towards his father who spent the evening effectively ignoring us while he wined and dined his very important business associates who were studying sheets of figures and designs while they ate their food and talked quietly amongst themselves. I had spent hardly any time with Jerome at all but was glad that I had been invited along, especially when I recognised how important the event must be.

"We'll do something together that evening," Jerome whispered as we lay together side by side on top of my bed. "Leave it to me. I'll book something for us. Maybe we'll even go away together all night."

I had slept restlessly but put it down to the fact I was distracted by Jack who hadn't been well and was up crying half the night. I could hear Frankie pacing up and down soothing him and my dad running around getting thermometers and medicine on her instructions. Usually I would have got up to help I but didn't want to make the situation any worse as any interference on my part could create yet another row. Frankie's resentment of me and my presence positively oozed from her but her feelings would be short-lived. Jerome was making me see that I didn't need my parents any more. I was nearly eighteen for God's sake! I could do whatever I wanted and he would help me. He had suggested that I move out and I had nearly fallen over laughing until I saw his face which was serious and unflinching.

"Why not? You can look after yourself. There are plenty of places to rent in town and you'd be proving yourself to that Wicked Stepmother of yours who's convinced you can't do anything without her."

"I suppose I could get a job and support myself that way," I had mused.

"You'll do no such thing," Jerome had snapped abruptly. "You won't need to work when you have me."

As it was Saturday I had got up with the intention of having a shower, going into town for a while to go clothes shopping and then coming home to wait to hear from Jerome what he had planned for us that evening, but as usual Frankie had morphed into a spanner and was throwing herself into the works.

"Please, Angelica," she said, settling a sleeping Jack down on the sofa with his teddy bear and covering him with his blanket. "I wouldn't ask only I'm desperate. Your father had to go out and I can't take Jack because he has a temperature. I just need to nip to the butcher's and then go and get some vegetables for dinner and I'll be home straight afterwards. Twenty minutes tops."

I sighed in bad humour and flopped down on the sofa next to Jack, grabbing the Sky remote control as I did and flicking around the channels.

I could feel Frankie's stare boring into the back of my head and turned around abruptly to face her.

"What?"

"Angelica, is it too much to ask that you mind your baby brother for half an hour while I go and do a few things? You used to love spending time with him and getting him all to yourself. I don't understand what's changed. Apart from you perhaps."

"If I've changed it's been for the better, I can assure you. It's a pity other people wouldn't change or disappear entirely but then that's a very bad case of wishful thinking on my part, isn't it?" I stared at Frankie and could feel her hurt and it gave me a thrill of satisfaction.

"I'll beg to differ that any changes have been for the

better. You act like you're an independent woman but I can see through that. It's all an act. I can read you like a book. Glass couldn't be any more transparent. You're just a frightened little girl who's trying to be a woman and it's too much too soon. You're not happy. How could you be? You've no time for your family, your attitude stinks and you seem to think that life should revolve around you and your new boyfriend. Newsflash, my dear. It doesn't work like that. Life is what you make it and you are going to end up being very sorry if you keep behaving as you are."

I laughed long and loud. "And why would I be sorry, Frankie? Sorry because if I manage to get away from here I'll not have to listen to you going on and on like a broken record? What my poor deluded father sees in you I'll never know."

Her expression faltered but only for a moment. "He sees someone that loves him and all his children, no matter how difficult they are, Angelica. I'll be back shortly and perhaps while I'm away you'd like to give Katie a call. She's rung three times since last night and you obviously still haven't rung her back."

"I'll ring her when I'm good and ready and not before!" I snapped.

"Good to see that it's not just your family that you're ignoring and treating like shit, Angelica. At least you're being consistent."

Frankie left and a burning anger began to flood through me. Who the hell did she think she was telling me what to do and how to behave? Did she ever bother to look at herself?

I looked down at Jack. He was usually a little ball of activity who never stopped running around but today he was listless and lethargic and I stroked his face while he slept, snoring softly and moaning intermittently.

"Poor baby!"

I hadn't heard the door opening so when I turned around and saw Jerome standing looking at me I got the fright of my life.

"What are you doing here?" I asked.

"I thought you were going into town to find something to wear so I thought I'd check to see if you needed a lift. So what's going on?"

"Frankie asked me to mind Jack while she went out shopping. She'll be back soon and then I'll go into town. I saw a gorgeous off-the-shoulder black dress in one of the high-street shops and I want to try it on."

"There's a name for girls who wear clothes like that," Jerome answered slowly, "and I didn't think that you fitted into that category."

I stood up, giving myself a moment to gather my thoughts.

"Are you okay?" I asked him eventually. "Have I done something wrong to upset you?"

"Not yet," he said with a steely glint in his eye. "When I take you out I always try and make it special because I think you're special and I expect the same courtesy and respect in return. If you dress like a tramp then people will think that's what you are and, believe me, that's not what I want hanging on my arm."

"I always try and look my best for you," I protested. "Your mother loved the dress I was wearing when we went out to dinner!"

"It's not my mother that you have to please," he said slowly. "It wasn't the one I asked you to wear. I like the black one with the zip at the back. Red is for danger and girls who like standing on street corners."

I was confused and frustrated. Where the hell was all this coming from? I had made an innocent remark about a dress and it had now turned into a major issue that seemed to be causing Jerome no end of annoyance. He was pacing up and down the room, clenching and unclenching his fists, and looking like his head might pop off.

I decided to change tactics. We needed a laugh to lighten the mood and the atmosphere.

"It's really not that bad," I giggled. "Gee, Jerome, you're turning into my dad!"

"What did you say?" he demanded, grabbing my shoulders roughly with his face close to mine.

I didn't know what to do. Was he kidding around? Was he serious?

"I was only joking, Jerome. I didn't mean anything by it."

His eyes had a glare to them that I had never seen before and it scared me because I knew that I had annoyed him.

"I'm sorry, I didn't mean to hurt your feelings."

He laughed. "You didn't hurt my feelings at all. You simply disrespected me. There's a difference."

I went to laugh again but something stopped me. He didn't seem to be in a very jovial mood today so perhaps I'd better adopt a more serious attitude.

"Well, I apologise for disrespecting you and will make it up to you later."

"I'll hold you to that." He left without saying anything more.

I rubbed the tops of my arms which were still smarting from the pressure of his grip. Maybe I did need to watch what I was saying and how I was saying it. This was my one chance of happiness in the midst of all the discord in my life and if it meant having to alter my fashion sense a bit and watch my tongue then so be it.

28

Ruby

I wasn't normally prone to bouts of nervousness but on this occasion it felt like a thousand butterflies had been let loose in my abdomen. My palms felt sweaty, my breathing was quicker than normal and, as I bided my time and waited for the silver Mercedes to pull up in its usual spot in the visitors' car park, I questioned myself again on whether or not I was doing the right thing.

I didn't have to dwell on the matter for long before I came to the conclusion that I had been left with no choice. I had to act now before things became any more complicated or got further out of hand.

I looked in the wing mirror just in time to see the barrier rising and falling as it allowed the car to enter the parking area. I had hoped that Marcella would be alone but to my dismay I saw that her other sister, Eliza, was with her. Oh, well, if I was going to be doing some straight talking I might as well hit them all at once.

I watched as they pulled into the space and slowly

started to gather my things before getting out of the car. As I approached them it was clear that they were not best pleased to see me.

"I thought I made it perfectly clear to Georgie that you are not wanted or needed around here," said Marcella.

I summoned up all my strength and tried to remain as calm and focused as possible.

"Marcella, I was wondering if we could talk. All this animosity is not good for anyone, least of all poor Charlie. I know I'm not your favourite person and if truth be told I'm not your number-one fan either but, for the sake of everyone else, do you not think it's time to let bygones be bygones and move on? Georgie's been through enough already without being made to feel any worse. Even if you don't like me, do it for your sister." I wasn't used to appealing and felt rather stupid and awkward but reckoned that it was a small price to pay for a positive result.

Marcella drew herself to her full height and literally looked down on me like something she'd trod on and immediately I felt my resolve weakening.

I had told Luke what I was planning to do and when he had finally finished guffawing in my ear he wished me luck and said I'd never manage it.

"Ruby, you have a heart of gold, my love," he had said, "and I know you're only trying to do the right thing but you have the quickest temper in the world and, if she so much as looks sideways at you, you'll be bawling at her."

"God, first Frankie and now you!" I'd protested. "Why can't you both have some faith in me? When I put my mind to it I can do anything. I can be calm and reasonable when I want to be. You don't always have to talk about me like I'm some sort of out-of-control maniac."

He hadn't answered me and I had responded by hanging up on him. I was glad we hadn't bet on it though as I had a feeling already that the odds would all be on his side.

Marcella stepped closer to me and spoke directly into my face.

"You have absolutely no idea what or who you're dealing with and if you have Georgina's best interests at heart I would advise you to go as far away from here as possible and forget what you know. You were adopted for a reason. There's no welcoming party here for you and I can promise you one thing – you'll never be part of this family because you don't belong here."

"According to *you* I don't belong here," I spat (obviously Reasonable Ruby had just left the building and took her calm sister with her). "You took it upon yourself a very long ago to become the decider of my fate and the decision was never yours to make."

"I make very good decisions and I have to say that that was one of my better ones and I've since made another that not everyone might like but which is becoming increasingly necessary."

I looked at her through narrowed eyes. "That sounds like a threat to me," I snapped. "And I don't respond well to intimidation on any level. Georgie might be prepared to stand and take whatever crap you see fit to dole out but I don't have to. Your days of bullying my birth mother are well and truly over. I'm here now and I don't intend to stand by and watch you trample all over her any more."

Marcella laughed in a nasally sarcastic manner before

turning to her sister and openly sneering at me. "Oh God, she's even more deluded than we all thought! On top of thinking that someone actually wants her around, now she's assumed the role of Wonder Woman sent to protect and preserve all the weaklings of this world!"

I gritted my teeth so hard in an attempt to stop myself from thumping her that I thought the pressure might rupture my jaw. "You really are one nasty piece of work. What the hell is wrong with you? Can you not bear to see anything work out for anyone else? Is your own life so sad and pathetic that you have to try and control other people's just to get your kicks?"

She laughed again and the sound grated on my last remaining nerve.

"Control?" she said with her eyes flashing. "I haven't even started yet and when I do you'll wish like the rest of us that you'd never been born. You couldn't leave well enough alone and stay away and now we're all supposed to be overjoyed to be reunited with the 'missing link'. Don't make me laugh. In order for something to be missing it has to be missed and believe me nobody misses a mistake that should never have happened."

I couldn't contain my anger and hurt for another second and jabbing my finger at her I stepped forward abruptly to tell her exactly what I thought of her. Unfortunately, at that Marcella took a step backwards. As she did she stumbled, lost her footing and hit her head on the kerb behind her.

Instinctively I held out my hand to help her up but she swiped it away.

"You just made the biggest mistake of your life," Marcella spat.

"What the hell is going on here?" I heard a voice say in a strangled anxious tone.

"Your lovechild just assaulted me and that little act will cost you both dearly. I've been more than patient with you, Georgina, but now I'm tired of playing games."

"Marcella, please," Georgie said in a pleading placating tone while I looked on in disbelief. "Don't do anything rash. Ruby didn't mean it."

"I didn't do anything!" I shrieked. "She lost her balance and fell. It's not my fault that as well as having a nasty runaway mouth her legs won't hold her up!"

"Ruby, please shut up," Georgie said, rounding on me. "Why must you make everything so difficult?"

"And suddenly in all this mess I'm the bad guy," I said incredulously. "I'm the one who never asked to be born but yet apparently I'm at fault."

"Ruby, please just go back to your mother's and I'll call you later when I've sorted things out here."

"Oh, I think it's a little late for that," Marcella said, her voice icy and dripping with venom as she walked away, limping slightly.

"If you say I told you so I swear I'll scream," I warned my mother as she looked at me and for once in her life seemed to be stuck for words.

"I would never say anything of the kind, Ruby. Look, love, these things were never destined to be straightforward or simple. If life was like that there wouldn't be any unplanned pregnancies, babies wouldn't need to be placed for adoption and people like me who always wanted a family would find themselves pregnant immediately. Unfortunately we're not here for an easy ride and, hard as it may seem, life is what you make it and you have to make the best of what you have."

"And if life was simple, Mother, there wouldn't be inquisitive people like me who need answers in order to keep living. I know you all think it would have been much easier if I had just contented myself and left well enough alone but I had to find out. How could you expect otherwise? It's so unfair and everything's such a mess. Who the hell am I? Where do I belong in this world?"

Georgie had been tense and edgy after Marcella had stomped off in the direction of the hospital. I had tried to put my arm around her to tell her that everything would be okay but she had roughly shoved me away and looked at me with helpless sad eyes that had made my guilt levels soar even higher.

"You have absolutely no idea what you've done, have you?" she had said in a desperate voice. "Why couldn't you have just left things to me? Dad was starting to get better and things were starting to look brighter. It could all have blown over without any more fuss. Marcella will make me suffer now because I'm the one who brought you here against the wishes of the rest of my family. You walk around, Ruby, thinking that you don't belong and that you are some sort of outcast but you're really very lucky. All your life you've had a mother who loves you dearly and a father that worshipped you. You've never suffered real crippling loss or had to bear the brunt of other people's disapproval or resentment. Please just leave. I don't want you here right now."

I had been stunned by the depth of her feeling and couldn't believe that I had messed things up so badly.

"Georgie, I never did anything to her," I said, feeling desperate. "She slipped and fell. I won't say that it hadn't crossed my mind to slap her but I didn't and now true to form she's telling more lies to try and justify her actions and appallingly bad behaviour. You missed the start of the conversation where I tried to reason with her and ask her if we could try and get along for your sake. You didn't hear her response and the way she told me that I would never fit in and how she wished like everyone else that I had never been born."

"I know that you didn't mean any harm, Ruby," Georgie had sighed. "But the fact of the matter is that that's of no consequence now. I told you before that a lot has happened over the years and it hasn't been pleasant for anyone and it's probably set to get a whole lot worse now."

"What are you so frightened of?" I'd asked gently. "Is this anything to do with my birth or who my father is?"

"There you go again," she'd said in frustration. "You're always pushing for more. I don't want to talk about any of it. Just leave me alone."

"I'm sorry," I'd said again but it was too late. The damage was done and with a heavy heart I had watched as Georgie had walked away from me without so much as a second glance.

Now I felt completely miserable and alone and for the first time since I had found Georgie had morphed back into the confused frightened abandoned child who felt like she was floating in limbo. When you were adopted into a family you assumed that they accepted you, although you always knew that they were fully aware that you didn't quite belong and you, yourself, were never sure if you ever properly fitted in. You were only there because somebody was kind enough to take you on and if your extended family were happy enough to have you then that was brilliant. When you traced your birth family and discovered blood relations, you then found yourself in another scenario. Here was your 'real' family. The one you left (or maybe that should be worded that they left you) when you were a baby and when you came back you didn't fit in there either because too much time had lapsed. You weren't part of anything. You had no memories and you were never involved. Welcome, people, to No Man's land.

"You listen to me, Ruby." Mother had adopted her sternest tone of voice and was assuming the position, that being the one she adopted when she was deadly serious and expected no arguments. "Sitting here crying and feeling sorry for yourself is doing nobody any good, least of all you. Pull yourself together. I am going to run you a bath, make you some toast and put a hot-water bottle in your bed. Then I am going to ring your husband and tell him you're going home tomorrow."

"I can't just leave!" I spluttered.

"Yes, you can and you are. Your husband needs you. What's he been doing while you've been gallivanting around Donegal and exhausting yourself sitting in the hospital and sleeping on a chair? Who's feeding him?"

My mother comes from a generation that firmly believes that if you're not there to cook a man his dinner and set the plate in front of him he'll starve to death and be found days later lying rigidly on the floor with a microwave instruction-manual clutched in his hand.

"He can cook, Mammy. You've been to our house for dinner on quite a number of occasions and witnessed it with your own eyes. You honestly haven't been seeing a phantom in an apron. That really was Luke in the flesh."

"There is no need for sarcasm and it doesn't matter anyway because you're going and that's that."

"And what if I refuse to go?" I said stubbornly.

"Well, you'll be sleeping in the garden then because you won't be here. I'm not going to be part of this nonsense any more."

"So you're throwing me out then?" I said in disbelief.

This night was getting better by the minute. First my birth mother had all but told me that she regretted ever being reunited with me and now the other one was evicting me.

Where did I belong? Nowhere, it seemed.

29

Jodi

It had been a fortnight since I started working in the bistro and to my amazement I had really started to enjoy myself. I felt sure that the honeymoon period would have worn off by now and I'd be regretting ever having taken the job but that was not the case at all. I actually found the lack of responsibility and the absence of time constraints and financial management to be incredibly liberating. It was great not to have to worry about targets and even better not to have to get dressed up and schmooze punters who in ordinary terms would have irritated me with their egotistical attitudes and bulging wallets.

Dad and Frankie had been totally right when they said that it was time that I embraced new things and strove to look after myself in any way possible as opposed to wanting to go back to my former career, which had been enjoyable and good but held too many painful memories for me now. Realistically I couldn't see myself permanently ensconced in the bistro for the rest of my life as I did want a new challenge of some description, but what that would be remained to be seen.

My father had left after spending the week with me and his parting words at the airport had been very apt. I had replayed them in my head a lot since he had gone back to the picturesque Lake District.

"Everything will work out, Jo. You'll just have to be patient and allow things to run their natural course. Life is for living and for too long you've been allowing everyone else to manipulate you and pull all your strings. It's time for you to do what you want to do, to please yourself. Forget about your mother, don't worry about me and most of all put that lying conniving scumbag to the back of your head and don't give him a second thought. He never was good enough for you and all the golf club memberships and invitations to fancy events in the world would never have persuaded me otherwise."

My mother of course couldn't have disagreed more with Dad's way of thinking which was precisely why she was living in Belfast and he was a plane-ride away.

"What does *he* know?" she had scoffed in yet another frustrating telephone conversation. "He hasn't been here to see everything that you gained from being with Ashley. You were in a loving relationship that was the envy of all your friends, you had a job you adored and a beautiful house. What more could you have asked for?"

"Oh, I don't know. A bit of fidelity and respect would have been nice," I had snapped.

"There's just no talking to you when you're in that mood. You always were your father's daughter."

"Thank God for that," I said in a low whisper.

"I heard that."

223

"Good. I'm glad you did and I'm glad that Dad is who he is and that he accepts me for who I am and doesn't constantly want to try and change me just so that his social life will benefit."

My mother sighed. "Ashley told me about what happened at the airport, Joanna," she said, adopting her holier-than-thou voice. "You should be ashamed of yourself brawling in public and behaving like you were raised in a trailer park instead of being brought up well. What must people have thought?"

"Well, if I'd had a loudhailer I'd have broadcast what he did all over the airport and I'd say that a female vigilante lynch mob would have been after his bits. I'm extremely well justified in doing what I'm doing and believe me I've been very restrained in how I've handled myself."

"I've asked Ashley about the Pamela person you talked about and he said that she was just a work colleague that had rung an old work phone that you found lying around and that you put two and two together and came up with seven."

"Well, he would say that," I had answered. "He's hardly going to admit what he's done, is he? Besides, he knows that you'll hang off his every word and believe everything he says."

She had curtly told me that she had a hairdresser's appointment (arranged and paid for by Ashley, naturally) that she had to get ready for and we had said an abrupt goodbye. I hated the fact that my mother was so ready and eager to believe Ashley while still being under the impression that I was making a giant mountain out of a molehill.

I arrived at work and resolved to get myself an iPod as soon as I ever could find the money so that I wouldn't spend my morning walk replaying conversations in my head and tying myself up in knots.

"Morning, everyone!"

Everyone responded with various greetings as I went to hang my coat up in the back room.

The locals had accepted 'the new girl' well although a select few were still quite wary of me, with some of them looking positively stricken when I came to take their order. What did they think I was going to do? Put arsenic in their drinks? Lace their dinners with rat poison? Or given the fact that there was a rumour circulating that I was or had been a drug trafficker then perhaps they all thought that they were going to get a thrill they hadn't bargained for and end up high as kites from ordering a breakfast soda and a cup of tea. Come to think of it, that wouldn't be a bad idea. Might encourage some of them to lighten up a bit.

I had even grown fond of Jamesie Mac and his little gang who kept me entertained with a never-ceasing stream of useless information, crossword clues and of course the daily gossip. At least I was no longer the centre of the news for the day and that's the way I wanted to keep it.

"Mornin', Jodi," Ringo said with a salute of his cap while Jockey scoured the sports pages looking for tips.

"Jockey," I eventually said, "why do you keep on placing bets when you never win? Is it not time that you called it a day and took up another hobby that doesn't cost you as much?"

"Jodi, I can feel it in my bones, girl. One of these days I'm going to be rich. I'm going to get a tip from somebody

225

and it'll be a wee stunner that nobody else would ever have dreamt of backing."

"And therein lies the feckin' problem," Jamesie said somewhat impatiently. "I can give *you* a tip though, young Jodi," Ringo said, looking ponderous. He pointed discreetly to a man who had just come in and taken a seat.

He had his back to me and I didn't see immediately who it was but then I realised it was Fabian Quinn.

"That fella never used to come in here half as much."

"True," Jamesie said. "And when he did he would order a muffin and a cup of coffee and then leave again immediately."

"But this past few weeks he's been coming in and eating his breakfast here. Always inside!" Ringo finished as if he had just solved the Da Vinci Code.

"You three live very sad lives and have far too much time on your hands," I retorted, wiping crumbs off the counter with a cloth.

"Don't you see?" Ringo said, getting off his stool in his excitement. "The only thing that has changed around here is that they've employed a new waitress and she must be a great attraction."

I looked at them incredulously.

"Aye, the way a fly is attracted to shite," Jamesie added before I stomped off to serve another customer, grateful to get away from them and their inane ramblings.

I had seen Fabian in his shop on several occasions when I called into the shop to browse through his antiques. I was looking forward to the day when I could splurge on the odd treat for myself. Things were improving bit by bit. My father's money had helped to ease things and for the first time in months I had booked a hair appointment and got a much-needed colour and cut. The local hairdresser had been very nice and I enjoyed my cup of coffee and flick through a magazine as I waited to be seen. Working in the bistro had also helped me to get to know some of my fellow Swiftstown neighbours and I got a strange satisfaction and warmth from being greeted by my first name as they came into the hairdresser's. My stylist in Belfast had been highly recommended and cost a fortune but I had never known anyone else who came into the premises and I was discovering on a daily basis how much nicer it was to encounter familiar and friendly faces.

I approached Fabian's table, greeted him as I always did and took his order with a smile.

"There's a twinkle there," Ringo said as I made my way back.

I cleared my throat importantly and slid in between Ringo and Jockey while Jamesie Mac oversaw proceedings.

"Ringo, those cupcakes that you like so much have to be ordered in fresh every day and as it's Anna's day off I'm doing that this afternoon. Now, you wouldn't like it to slip my mind, would you?"

Ringo looked like I'd just chucked his rattle out of his pram and the others stared at me as if I'd threatened to cut off his air supply.

"Now there's no need to be talking like that, Jodi," Ringo said, looking more and more alarmed by the minute.

"So what was that you were saying about a twinkle?" I asked.

"No twinkle – no twinkle," he repeated urgently, eyeing the bun trays that were emptying rapidly.

"I don't say very much," I said sternly. "But if you know this then so will everybody else. I don't want a man,

I don't need a man and I'm not looking for a man. End of story."

Jamesie looked knowingly at the others and Jockey looked as if all his Christmases had come at once and instantly I knew why.

"No, you've lost again, Jockey," I said. "Shouldn't celebrate your wins until you have the full facts."

I started to cut some wheaten bread and then slowly addressed the other two who were looking at me expectantly.

"And Jamesie, a little word of warning. If I hear so much as a whisper of me being a man-hating lesbian after this I will hunt you down, which won't be hard as you never leave here."

They all eyed the knife I was holding and agreed that they wouldn't say a word and protested that such an idea would never have crossed their minds anyway. Jockey's despondent face said differently though and I could feel the corners of my mouth twitching as I went to clear some tables.

Fabian finished his breakfast but before he left he searched his inside pocket and handed me some leaflets.

"Would you mind dotting a few of these around the bistro for me, Jodi?"

"Not at all," I answered, smiling as he left.

He had told me all about his new venture into the world of plying the locals with cocktails and drinks and I greatly admired his innovative ideas.

The information he had just given me was advertising various special offers to be had and giving info about the opening evening. The theme for the evening was a James Bond 'Shaken not Stirred' fancy-dress night and the idea appealed to my sense of fun. I tucked one of the leaflets into my apron pocket and decided that it was far too long since I'd had a night out and I'd make sure that Anna and Frankie came along too. If there was cobweb-blowing to be done after a long abstinence I wanted my new friends to be part of it.

I left work feeling tired but satisfied and made my way home.

I had got the biggest thrill a week ago when I'd invited Mr Peebles into the house wearing my dressing gown and told him I needed to come to an arrangement with him about the rent. He'd been like one of those slobbering guard dogs as he entered the house and I think that the deluded little creep actually thought that he was in with a chance of getting his end away.

His face, when I had given him my rent money and told him that I wanted his account details as in future I'd be paying it directly into his bank every fortnight so we didn't have to come into contact with one another, had been a picture. I also told him that I'd been in touch with the landlord's association and knew all my rights and that I had passed his details on to them so that they could clarify a few what we might want to call 'grey areas' in our landlord/tenant situation. He had nearly tripped over himself in his haste to get away from me and I had cheerfully waved him off at the door. I still hated the house with a passion but being able to stand up for myself and not letting him think that he could get the better of me had felt wonderful. Round one to me! *Ding ding!*

And I intended to keep knocking out all my opponents in the rounds ahead.

30

Frankie

I had been looking forward to getting away on my own with the children for a weekend and spending some time with Ruby in Donegal but unfortunately my best friend had ended up coming home early in foul form so it hadn't happened. She had spent the last fortnight biting the head off anyone who looked at her and I was turning into a similar creature as my stress levels were ready to explode from my head like a shower of *Skittles*. Owen's mother had indeed come for her planned weekend but due to a burst pipe in her Dublin apartment was still here and to say that we were all starting to get on each other's nerves was something of a huge understatement.

Life wasn't made any easier by the fact that any time I saw Jerome, which was not that often, he either looked at me contemptuously or blatantly ignored me. He still spoke to Owen and Owen continued to be taken in by it all. He was particularly impressed by the way that Jerome rang the house and insisted on knowing exactly where Angelica was when she wasn't at home, who she was with and when she'd be home.

"There are not too many young lads who'd be that attentive, Frankie. You have to admit that he really does care about her and her whereabouts."

I thought he was an arrogant pain in the arse and I had been psyched up to go out and ask the little twerp what exactly his problem was but had talked myself out of it. I had at last admitted that, if he was the type of man I thought he was, Angelica needed to find out for herself. My wading in and getting involved had just made matters ten times worse and believe me there was no room for any more stress in my life.

I dragged Owen into our bedroom and closed the door with a sharp bang.

"Oooh, what's this then?" he said with raised eyebrows and a smirk. "It's been a long time since you pulled me into the bedroom and shut the door so urgently. Something you wanted?"

"What I feckin' want is to know exactly how long your bloody mother is intending to stay, Owen!" I hissed. "There are only so many comments I can take regarding my cooking. I don't want any more childcare advice regarding my Jack and if she makes one more snide remark about working mothers and how they neglect their children and how it was all different in her day I swear I'll have her."

"So you didn't want to throw me across our bed and have mad rampant sex then? Pity. I love you when you're angry."

"Owen, if you ever want there to be activity in this bedroom again, you'd better give that plumber a good kick up the arse and tell him to get her pipe fixed or I'll go down and personally plug it myself. I am ready to go nuts here. My house is not my own. A weekend I can just about manage but it's been two weeks. Have a heart, please!"

Owen put his arms around me and drew me close to him.

"You've been a trooper this past few weeks, darling. Believe me, I know how hard my mother can be to live with but what choice do we have? She either stays here or we put her out on the street. Maura's away working and mother's other friends weren't able to help due to their commitments, so it had to be us. Look, if it's any consolation, I think you've done a fantastic job and I know it might appear that she's fault-finding but she's honestly only trying to help."

I opened my mouth to tell him that this was a particular form of help I could do without but was silenced when he put his fingers to my lips.

"I'll ring the plumber today and find out how much longer he's likely to be. It's not just as simple as a burst pipe, Frankie. He found other problems when he was there and the whole job is taking much longer than anyone anticipated and I don't want her going back home until we're sure it's safe."

I folded my arms and looked at him mutinously, thinking that it would indeed be terrible if a flood came through her ceiling and made her perfectly coiffed silver hair a bit damp. Yes, that would be just awful.

"Why are you smiling like a lunatic, Frankie?"

"Oh nothing. Just thinking."

At that point the tension seemed to lift slightly and we shared a giggle. We used to make each other laugh a lot but there had been very little to amuse us over the past few weeks or ever since the incident where he so righteously insulted me in front of Angelica. He had apologised over and over again and said that he really hadn't meant it to sound as it did. Owen wasn't a cruel person and he had always been grateful and appreciative of everything I'd done for Angelica, so I had to take his word for it and move on. It was just a pity that his daughter didn't feel inclined to do the same. Ever since, she had taken every opportunity to go against my wishes and she seemed hell bent on seeing Jerome as much as was humanly possible. They seemed to be glued together now and it was clear that telling her I didn't think he was suitable had in actual fact driven her further into his arms. (Note to self: when Carly turns into horrible teenager tell her all her boyfriends are legends and proper marriage material so that they'll all run for the hills leaving my daughter free to become a nun.)

Owen placed a finger under my chin and turned my face towards him. "I do love you, y'know. Maybe I don't tell you that enough but it's true. I'm sorry about all the tension there has been with Angelica recently but I promise it will blow over. It's just a phase."

I sighed. If I had a pound for every time someone had told me that Angelica had been going through a phase, I'd be living it up in Barbados now and have male servants fanning me with coconut leaves. The girl (in my opinion) had been going through phases since the day she was born. She made other teenagers' mood-swings look like mere inconsequential occurrences while her own horrific strength of will and ability to cause trouble all around her continued to grow ever more dangerous.

"I'm sure it will pass," I said with as much enthusiasm

as someone who didn't believe a word she was saying could muster.

There was a knock on our bedroom door and Owen's mother poked her head around it.

"There's a very colourful person downstairs to see you, Frankie. He says he's here to remind you that you have a date tonight."

I clapped my hand on my forehead. I had totally forgotten. Gabriel, Ruby and I had arranged to meet up for our monthly natter tonight and as the realisation descended on me a huge grin spread across my face. I was going to get absolutely sloshed tonight. I was going to get my glad rags on, drink vodka and put the world to rights with my two bestest friends.

"Let me guess – this is your night out with the gang," Owen said. "Aren't you the lucky one that I haven't made a date myself and left you without a baby-sitter?"

"What do you mean 'night out with the gang'?" his mother asked slowly with a sniff while pretending not to know that I was within earshot. "Does this happen on a regular basis, Owen? I must say, in my day a woman never went out without her husband and she didn't leave her children. She stayed at home and looked after her family and knew what was important."

I practically ran down the stairs as fast as my legs would carry me and jumped on Gabriel on sight.

"What time are we going out?" I demanded.

"Steady on, old girl, it's only six o'clock and you need to go and put something a little more suitable on. I refuse to be seen with anyone sporting tracksuit bottoms and a T-shirt. You look like something that just walked off the set of *Shameless*."

"I'm going to act like it too," I said with great feeling. "I've never deserved it more."

Gabriel adopted a ridiculous pose and pouted his lips. "I just can't wait to hear what you've been up to all week. Don't worry, we'll have a jolly old time tonight over a few tipples and straighten you out."

Gabriel was still in full country-gent mode and talking like he had grown up on a country estate surrounded by members of the aristocracy as opposed to in Belfast. It had been funny the first time but had now become irritating and I knew at least one person who would not be appreciative of it.

"Gabriel, I swear to God, you need to lose that accent before Ruby gets her hands on you. She will kill you, y'know, and she's in the right mood at the minute."

"Oh you needn't tell me," Gabriel said airily. "I already know how bad her form is. I went round to see her earlier and, when I offered to do her tan and suggested that I make her a hair appointment, I nearly got murdered on the spot for breathing."

"She's a bit like me. She needs to go out and get roaring drunk and forget about everything. I am going to drink that bar dry tonight. If ever I needed a break and to get out of here, it would be now."

I heard a tutting noise and looked around to see Esme Byrne standing in the hall behind me, glaring at me with great disapproval before transforming herself into a paragon of virtue when Owen came out to join her.

"In my day women did not drink," she said loudly, looking at her son. "The men would retire for a brandy and the ladies would sip tea and discuss their families. But then perhaps in my day we knew what was right and proper and didn't selfishly expect everyone else to do our work for us. Who, exactly, is she expecting to look after her children when she's out making a lush of herself?"

I'd had enough but, as I slowly turned around I saw Owen grabbing his mother and ushering her hastily into the lounge before popping back out and looking at me apologetically.

"What is with everyone segregating our family into sections at the moment, Owen?" I asked through gritted teeth. "Angelica is your daughter, Ben and Carly are now solely mine when I'd like and deserve a break. Where does Jack fit in? Hmmmmm? Shall we slice him in two and take a bit each just to make everyone happy?"

"Look, Frankie –"

"Not a word, Owen. Don't say a thing. I've had enough of this crap."

And with that I shoved a bemused Gabriel through the door before following him, not caring what I looked like. I felt like running away and unless there were drastic changes within my home it would be for longer than just one evening.

31

Angelica

I was sitting on a summer seat in the middle of town waiting for Jerome and feeling excited and nervous all at the same time. It was a big step but it was time that I showed everyone exactly what I was made of. Besides, it would take my mind off the fact that none of my friends were talking to me. Katie had been really nasty to me and I was really hurt. I had been shocked to the core that she had reacted like she did and all over a stupid party. She had turned everyone against me and the gang of girls that I had always hung about with were now all but ignoring me except to make sarky comments and give me filthy looks. I had sat on my own in the canteen at school every day this week and, although I had put a brave face on, it had really stung that nobody wanted to be with me. I couldn't believe that Katie could be so cruel but Jerome seemed to be delighted. He said that it was time I saw my so-called friends for what they were and moved on. I had him now and that was all I needed.

"I've told you before, Angelica. They're all jealous and jealousy makes people act in very strange ways. You say that you and Katie have been friends for seven years but when she should be happy for you she turns her cheek and has you ostracised from the rest of your class. I hope you see her for what she is now. We don't need her. We don't need anyone."

Jerome had been very attentive and loving since the day he had grabbed me and been so cross. He had picked me up that evening and had presented me with a gift-wrapped box that contained the most beautiful bracelet I had ever seen.

"I'm sorry about earlier on," he had said without looking at me. "Work has been pretty demanding lately and I haven't been sleeping well but I shouldn't have taken it out on you."

We had gone on to have a really enjoyable evening and I had never been happier or felt more wanted in all my life. Jerome had been really affectionate and when he dropped me off that night, he kissed me tenderly and told me that I was his girl and my heart had soared.

I thought about what he had said about my friends and what Katie had said and came to the conclusion that Jerome had been right all along. Katie knew me better than anyone else in the world. I told her everything. She knew all about the fact that my mother had left. She knew how I felt about Frankie and she knew that Jerome made me feel complete. He was like the missing link I had been looking for all my life.

I had tried to explain this to Katie when she arrived at my house unexpectedly and demanded in a crackling voice why I hadn't been in touch with her.

"I'm sorry, Katie, but Jerome and I have plans. He's taking me away for the weekend."

"In seven years you have never missed one of my parties, Angelica. I never see you any more. It's only one night. Can you not at least tear yourself away and give us one night of your company?"

"No, Katie, I can't," I had answered, unable to say anything else and wishing that she would just leave. She was making me feel totally uncomfortable. If Jerome had been there he would have told me that I had absolutely no need to be justifying myself to her or anyone else.

"You've changed so much, Angelica. You used to be so much fun to be with and we used to spend so much time together but now you've no time for anyone but your new boyfriend. Has our friendship meant so little to you that you can just ditch me when something better comes along? There is a happy medium, y'know. There are seven nights in the week. You could spend some of them with us and some of them with him. You don't have to be with him all the time, do you?"

I felt anger and resentment rise in me. Those words "You've changed, Angelica" set my teeth on edge. Katie was no better than Frankie with her accusations and judgemental attitude.

"Y'know what," I had stormed, "Jerome says you're just jealous because you couldn't get a boyfriend if you tried and I'm beginning to think he's right. You just want to keep me away from him in the hope that he'll get fed up and go off with somebody else – but that's not going to happen. He says he loves me and if our friendship means as much as you say it does then you'd be happy to let me do what I want."

239

"Jerome says this, Jerome says that!" Katie mocked in a harsh tone of voice that I had never heard before. "That's all we hear these days. The Holy Word according to Jerome. Is there anything that you're allowed to think or feel without consulting him, Angelica? Do you have a mind of your own any more or did he take that along with your precious virginity in the quarry grounds?"

"At least I'm not walking around with a chastity belt jangling around my middle. I mean, Katie, seriously, when are you going to let go of it and become a real woman?"

"If becoming a real woman means forgetting your friends and dropping your knickers in a car when you're not even prepared and he hasn't bothered to make it special or nice for you, then thanks but no thanks!"

She had laughed then but it wasn't a nice laugh. It was hollow and sarcastic and I had opened the door and asked her to step through it.

"Don't ever come near my house again, Katie. I don't need you or want you any more. Our friendship was good while it lasted but, face it, something better *has* come along and I'm going to enjoy every minute of it."

"You do that, Angelica," Katie had said, her eyes filled with tears. "I've always been there for you through everything but I don't know why I bothered wasting my time because you just weren't worth it. You're obviously just like your mother. You use people and then when you don't need them any more you throw them away like rubbish."

I had been stunned and must have looked it because she had angrily brushed a tear away and openly sneered at me before walking down the path to the gate.

"Aww, what's wrong, Angelica? Truth hurt? Have a

nice life and make sure you do everything your darling Jerome says!"

I felt a tap on my shoulder and looked around to see my Auntie Brenda standing behind me dressed smartly in a suit and carrying an overnight bag with her.

"What are you doing here?" she asked.

"I'm waiting for Jerome to come and meet me," I answered. Then furtively I looked around me and said in a low whisper, "Can you keep a secret?"

"You know I can," she said primly. "What's happened now? What has that silly cow done to upset you this time?"

"Who?" I asked. There were a lot of cows and there had been various upsets so it was hard to pinpoint which one she was referring to.

"Frankie," she said disdainfully. "Why on earth would you be sitting on your own in the cold otherwise instead of being at home where you should be?"

"Well, actually, that won't be posing much of a problem from now on. Jerome and I are going to look at few places to rent this evening. We're thinking of moving in together."

Brenda had swallowed and I was afraid that she was going to be negative about the idea but as always she came up trumps and gave me what I needed most – her support.

"So this is what you've been reduced to, is it? A poor seventeen-year-old who has been left with no choice but to try and find a home of her own because her father and poor excuse for a stepmother couldn't be bothered with her any more?"

241

It was more to do with the fact that Jerome wanted me to show how independent I had become and less because of my relationship with Frankie but if it helped my aunt to understand my predicament then I wouldn't bother correcting her. I was tired of being misunderstood.

At that moment I saw Jerome in the distance and waved at him.

He walked quickly towards where we were sitting, sat down himself and put a protective arm around me after giving me a kiss on the cheek.

"I can't leave you alone for five minutes without you talking to someone, can I?" he said.

"Oh, I'm not just anyone," Brenda said airily. "I'm Angelica's aunt and I'm sorry that I don't have more time to spend with you but I'm in a rush as I have to go to the airport and catch a flight to London. I have a two-day conference to attend but maybe we can meet when I come back. I'd love to see your new house."

I knew as soon as Brenda said the words that I had made a mistake and told her too much as I could feel Jerome stiffening and watched as his jaw began to clench in a tight smile.

"All the best now," Jerome said as he waved at Brenda and watched as she got into her car.

He wasn't looking at me. Instead he was concentrating very hard on a building in front of us and sucking in his lips in obvious displeasure.

"Jerome, I'm sorry. I was just dying to tell someone and I knew that Brenda wouldn't say a thing to anyone. She's very cool. Way cooler than my dad or Frankie."

"What did I say about this being our secret, Angelica?

Do you ever listen? Do you want to ruin this for us? I thought I could trust you but obviously I can't."

"Of course you can," I answered quickly, feeling panic rising in me. "I didn't mean to upset you."

"Well, you have," he snapped. "You need me so much. You don't have anyone else and I spend so much time trying to make you happy and do what you want and this is the thanks I get."

"I appreciate everything you do for me and I can't wait until we're together properly," I said.

He was determined not to be humoured and shrugged me off.

"If this is to work you need to start paying attention to me when I speak. Listen to me and do as I say, Angelica."

"I will," I said, shivering with the cold and feeling cold inside as well at the thought of ever losing him.

32

Ruby

I yawned loudly and rolled over in bed searching for Luke but then realised he wasn't there as he had spent the night on the couch.

My evening with Frankie and Gabriel had been just what the doctor ordered although I hadn't been as boisterous as usual as I had developed a nasty throat infection that required antibiotic intervention. Of course, you weren't supposed to drink with them and naturally I ignored that particular instruction. We had gone to The Swiftstown Arms, got steaming drunk, sampled cocktails (with a view to getting our palettes used to them in time for the launch of Pitchers) and solved the world's problems. Well, nearly all the world's problems. All except mine as no God's amount of fancy drinks and philosophising would even begin to shed any light on what I was supposed to do. At this precise moment in time I had managed to upset both my mothers, and Luke was also less than impressed with me as he had spent the past fortnight acting as a human punch-bag with me being the boxer. Yes, I had really surpassed myself this time and had come to the conclusion that no matter what I did I would always end up messing things up somehow. I had gone to Donegal with every intention of being diplomatic and level-headed and felt that I had been doing a good job too right up until the point where I had been wrongly accused of assaulting Marcella. And that was annoying me too. I didn't even have the satisfaction of actually thumping her to comfort me in my darker moments. All I had was regrets and heartache and the knowledge that everyone thought I couldn't be trusted to behave, which was why they could all so readily believe the lies of such a disturbed woman. Out of all the people I had managed to annoy, however, Luke was the one I wanted to try and regain favour with first.

Frankie had been most eloquent the evening before and, before downing a Bloody Mary all in one go and without taking time to breathe, she told me in no uncertain terms how unfair I was being.

"Ruby," she had announced in a slurred voice while waving a soggy piece of celery at me in the manner of an orchestra conductor, "that husssban of yours is far too good for you. You need to aff . . . affresssiate him more and stop being so an-an-annoying. Go home and shag his brains out and thank him for everything he does. I feckin' wish Owen was more like him."

This piece of advice had then been followed by a noisy bout of crying that resulted in us having to escort her to the ladies' room which Gabriel had subsequently got kicked out of for being the wrong sex. He had been most indignant and strong words with the bouncer had followed but to no avail even though he had been dressed in an extremely eye-watering get-up and talking with his usual colourful bravado.

Things were obviously not a garden of roses for Frankie either who was talking about decamping to her mother's unless her mother-in-law (so to speak) left her home immediately. "Flooded apartment or no feckin' flooded apartment" – and I quote. The possibility of Frankie and her mother being under the same roof for any period of time without blood being shed was unlikely and I hoped for both their sakes and that of Frankie's poor longsuffering father that Owen's mother got on the next train to Dublin as fast as her legs could carry her.

I sighed and thought about my own predicament for about the millionth time and was still no further forward apart from sighing in despair and yet again berating myself for the bad ill-timed decisions I had made.

Talking to Marcella had definitely not been one of my better, well-thought-through plans. Georgie had more or less rejected me, and my mother, although understanding, had also lost patience with me and sent me home and, true to form, because I wanted to lash out I had told her that I was on another quest – this time to find my birth father. She had been at a loss to understand how I could even think about wanting to replace my daddy who was my hero. Subsequently I had left my mother's cottage in bad grace and apart from a few short and stilted phone calls as to my general welfare we had spoken very little since.

My poor husband had been bearing the brunt of all my hurt, confusion and self-loathing and I could see that I was in danger of pushing him away too.

This was the third night in a row that he had fallen

asleep in front of the television and I missed waking up beside him and feeling his strong arms around me. He deserved better than this and it was time I appreciated exactly what I had.

I got out of bed and winced as I felt my hangover kick in with a vengeance. I padded downstairs and noted that Luke had tidied up before he left for work. I tried to ring him but his phone went straight to voicemail. As my eye settled on the scented candles on my window sill I knew exactly what I was going to do that evening to try and apologise.

"Do you have to talk so feckin' loud?" Frankie had whined when I plopped myself on her desk asking for recipes that guaranteed good results when trying to seduce one's husband into loving you again even though you were a cantankerous bad-tempered cow who was a nightmare to live with.

"*Humph*," she snorted in disgust. "It's not a recipe I need. It's a spell or an exorcism to rid me of an unwanted presence in my house. I swear if that woman isn't gone when I get home it'll be Owen who'll be getting his marching orders. I don't know what's got into him lately. He can see nothing wrong with the fact that both his mother and his daughter treat me like I'm some worthless nuisance whose only service is to provide them with someone to openly criticise and ridicule. Do you know that that woman had the nerve to tell me that I had a drink problem in front of my children this morning while they were still eating their breakfast? I was speechless. How dare she! I go out for one night after catering to all her whims and demands over the past two weeks and all of a sudden I'm a roaring drunk and an unfit mother!" Frankie's voice had risen an octave with every outraged word she spoke and by the time she finished she was so high-pitched with indignation that my headache had grown ten times worse.

After giving her a quick hug and assurances that it would all smooth over I decided to consult the internet for recipes instead.

"God, something certainly smells good in here," Luke said when he arrived home from work later that evening. I had texted him and told him not to eat anything as I was making a special dinner. I had lit candles, turned the phones off and Frank Sinatra was crooning in dulcet tones through speakers from my iPod.

"So what's all this in aid of then?" he asked, coming up behind me and nuzzling my ear.

"I just wanted to remind you how much I love you and hope you remember why you fell in love with me too. I'm so sorry for the way I've been behaving lately. I've been so unfair to you and you've been so understanding. Any other man would have had me on the street with all my clothes in a bin-bag."

"The bag lady look wouldn't suit you, Ruby. Besides, I knew it would all blow over eventually. It's like I always tell you: given time everything will work out. Emotions are running high at the moment but things will calm down soon and it'll be like nothing ever happened."

He took me in his arms and dinner was soon forgotten as we collapsed on the sofa tearing at each other's clothes, hungry for other things besides food.

We lay side by side on the floor after having made love three times and I felt more content than I had done in weeks.

"You know, if this is going to be the aftermath of you falling out with me for two weeks I think I could get used to the sofa," he said, kissing my forehead and sighing.

"Oh please don't say that," I said laughing. "You have no idea how exhausting it is being me and being confused and annoyed all the time. I'm knackered. I could sleep for a week."

Luke went to try and salvage what he could of the dinner that had been left to overcook as we became entangled on the sofa and as I looked around me I smiled and vowed not to let things get so out of hand in future. But, then again, this was me we were talking about and where I was concerned things were never simple.

33

Jodi

"So what do you wear to a themed James Bond evening then?" Anna and the girls wanted to know.

The party was happening soon and my suggestion of having a staff night out had gone down very well. Even Chef, who normally took no prisoners where hangovers were concerned, seemed to have engaged with the idea and was apparently thinking about making his entrance on the night as the metal-mouthed Jaws.

"You're supposed to step out of character," Anna had explained slowly to him, like he was a child. "Not stay in it. You spend all day biting great clumps out of people and then want us all to applaud your originality when you go dressing up as a villain who bites his victims?"

Chef banged a saucepan in response and that was the end of that conversation.

"I always fancied myself as Sean Connery," Jamesie Mac said. "I'd look well in one of them dickie bows and my grandfather was Scottish so I could work on the accent. You never know, there could be a connection somewhere. We could be related."

Jamesie stood up and tried to suck in his belly and hold his chin up but the strain nearly killed him.

"I'll not be there," Ringo said sadly. "I'd like to see it doing well so that it brings plenty of fresh blood to the town but I couldn't be around all that drink. Give me a mug of coffee and a cupcake any day. What flavours have you got for me today, Anna?"

"What about you, Jockey?" I asked. "Will you be going?"

"No, no," he said. "I'm going to the dog track that night. Got my eye on a wee beauty."

We all shrugged our shoulders.

"It's a good idea though," I said thoughtfully.

"What? You approve of Jockey's dog racing?" Anna said.

"No, not that. I'm talking about the themed night. When I worked in PR we always used them for launch nights and special occasions to get people in. They provide something different and unique and everyone loves dressing up and stepping out of their own skin for a while."

"I'd say you would have been very good at your job," Anna said. "You're so good with people and everyone likes you."

I scoffed at her and went back to wiping down the chalkboard before writing up the specials for the day.

"Joanna?"

I nearly jumped out of my skin when I heard the unfamiliar voice call me by my formal name but I had a sinking feeling that I knew who it was and I wasn't sure if I was ready to face this yet.

I turned quietly and gave her a tight smile in recognition.

"Joanna, can we talk please?" she asked and, as all eyes were upon me, I quickly nodded but started to untie my apron as there was no way I was having that particular conversation here.

I walked into the back of the bistro to collect my things and tried to steady my nerves. It was inevitable that we would meet again but I never thought that she would ever come looking for me.

She looked different from what I remembered but I knew that I could never forget her. She had ash-blonde hair, was small with a petite build and looked very demure. The last time I had seen her face it had been streaked with tears. She told me that she didn't remember very much about that day. Too much had happened for her to be able to absorb everything and the news that I had delivered, terrible as it was, was not top of her list of priorities.

I had been deceived, lied to and paraded around like some sort of a prize Friesian cow wearing a blue ribbon. On the other hand she had been deceived, lied to, left on her own for large amounts of time with huge commitments and then her world had crashed around her when catastrophe had struck and she needed him which was precisely where I came in.

I would never in my life forget that day. I had been having a highly unusual day off because I had been to the dentist that morning and had a tooth extracted, and looking like something that had just emerged from the set of *The Elephant Man*, with a swollen jaw and a bloody mouth, wasn't a good look for a Public Relations consultant.

I had been downstairs curled up under a blanket on the sofa with a magazine when I heard it first. It sounded like an alarm, a high-pitched, annoying and repetitive noise, and I had nearly burst blood vessels, so great was my annoyance at not being able to find the source of the sound. It had stopped a few times but once I had been lulled into a false sense of security and sighed with relief it had started again, sounding more and more urgent as it reverberated incessantly.

I had checked the oven timer and all the other appliances in the kitchen, I had looked at the smoke alarms to make sure that it wasn't them beeping to let me know that their batteries were starting to die and then I had realised that the noise was coming from his office.

I had looked underneath piles of papers that were heaped on his desk and emptied one of his travel bags onto the floor but had finally found it in a drawer that I hadn't known existed underneath the table.

I had stared at the phone in puzzlement as it rang as I didn't recognise it. I couldn't think how I didn't know that Ashley had a new phone.

"Hello?"

"Ashley?" the voice had said breathlessly and with a real sense of urgency.

"No, it's not," I answered. "Who's speaking?"

"It's Pam here. I need to speak to him as soon as possible. It's an emergency. Are you his new secretary?"

I had held the phone away from me as I fixed it with a particularly incredulous look.

"No, I am not his secretary. I'm his wife actually. Perhaps I can help. What's the problem?"

There had been silence and a series of heavy breathing

and gasps on the other end of the phone before the caller spoke again.

"I don't have time for jokes or pranks right now. Jason is seriously ill in hospital and he needs his father. Can you get Ashley to ring me right away?"

A joke? A prank? Pam? Jason? Sick? Father? What the hell was all this about and more to the point what had my husband to do with it all?

"Hello?" the voice said abruptly and impatiently. "I need Ashley to ring me now or else to come straight to the hospital."

I was perplexed in the extreme and my mouth was throbbing and I was struggling to try and comprehend what all this was about. The woman on the other end of the phone sounded clearly distressed so perhaps she was just confused.

"I know you're upset and I'll try to help you. But you need to calm down and start talking rationally as you're not making any sense. What is your husband's name?"

"Look, you're wasting precious time playing games with me. I don't know what your problem is but I need my husband now so please do your job and get him to contact me immediately. We're at the Temple Street Children's hospital in Dublin and you can tell him that Jason's had a really bad seizure this time. They nearly lost him in the ambulance."

The woman gave a tearful gasp and then the phone clicked off abruptly and I was left staring at it in genuine astonishment.

I lifted my own mobile to ring Ashley but knew that it would be a waste of time as he had Japanese business associates over and would be tied up in meetings all day with his phone switched off.

I looked at the other phone in my hand and after pressing several buttons I finally found a menu and when I looked at the incoming and outgoing call list there were only a few numbers present but one number seemed to be more frequent than the rest. I was still puzzled, though, as Ashley had numerous business contacts and spent much of his time on the phone when he wasn't travelling or in meetings.

I decided to check his messages as well as I was becoming more and more confused. This seemed to be a phone dedicated to one or two contacts only. A phone he had kept secret from me.

As I looked down his messages a nervous knot formed in the pit of my stomach. This couldn't be happening.

Can't wait to see u ltr darling. Boys really excited about golfing with u tmrw xx

So disappointed u have 2 work this wkd. Had nice romantic dinner planned 4 us xx

Miss u so much when ur not here baby. Jason tired and not feeling well today and missing his dad xx

That last message had been sent the day before and it dawned on me that whoever Jason was he had suddenly taken a turn for the worse as apparently he was now in hospital in Dublin. I looked at the dates of the other few messages I had read and realised that the last time Ashley had been away he had packed his golf clubs along with his luggage and told me he knew that the man he was hoping would sign a contract with our company enjoyed a game at the weekend. The other message had been sent two weekends ago when he had surprised me with a trip to London as a belated birthday present . . . but had obviously disrupted his plans with someone else.

I sat down heavily on the large swivel-chair in his office and slowly scanned through the other messages. The phone was not new, as I had thought, as some of the messages dated back quite a while. Every message ended in a kiss and there was much talk of missing him and when I examined the sent messages I discovered that these thoughts were being reciprocated. The last message had been sent yesterday morning and on reading it I flung the phone angrily against the wall.

Missing you gorgeous. Can't wait to come home 2 u. Tell Jason I'll get him a new game for his xbox and give my love to the others. Xx

I went over to where the phone was lying and redialled the last and only number on the list.

It was answered immediately.

"Ashley, is that you? You've got to come quickly. He's really scared and wants you here."

Ordinarily the sound of such misery would have filled me with sympathy but instead I felt hollow and listless.

"It's not Ashley, it's Joanna here again. What ward is Jason on? I'll make sure to get an urgent message to him."

"He's on ward 4B and in a side room. Please tell him to hurry."

I tried to ring Ashley on his mobile (the one I knew about) but as expected it had been switched off. I rang the office to see where he had gone but was told he had left for lunch to discuss contracts and left specific instructions that he was not to be disturbed.

There was no way that I could sit there and do nothing. My mind was a jumble of thoughts and I needed an explanation from someone and as Ashley wasn't available there was only one other person I could approach.

As I quickly got dressed and checked the timetable for the trains I tried to convince myself that there had to be an innocent explanation for it all. I was simply reading too much into it. A nagging voice in my head begged to differ however. I had been conscious over the last few months that Ashley had been preoccupied and distant but had put it down to the pressures of work. The company had opened an office in New York and it hadn't been performing as well as had been hoped so I had thought that his mind had been distracted with that. He had also been away at a lot of different meetings and seemed stressed when he came back but anytime I had asked what was wrong he had told me not to worry and that everything was in hand.

Ashley was a very attractive man. He was handsome and charming and extremely charismatic and his presence in a room made women stop to look at him. I had often thought about the dangers of him having an affair as he was in contact with so many different people and away on his own so much. I had voiced my concerns to him on a few different occasions but he had simply told me that I had to learn to trust him and over time I had. He seemed devoted to me and lavished endless attention on me when we were together. When I was on his arm he made me feel like I was the only woman in the world.

I had been happy and, contrary to what some people thought, I wasn't just with Ashley because of what he could give me in terms of a lifestyle. I was with him because I genuinely loved him and he made me happier than I had ever thought possible.

I had got a taxi to the Glengall Street train station and by a stroke of luck had managed to catch the next train to

Dublin by the skin of my teeth. The journey had passed quickly. I put my earphones in and before I knew it we were pulling up at Connolly Station in Dublin and I was searching my pocket for the address I had been given.

It took me around twenty minutes to get to the hospital and when I got there a further twenty minutes to get to the appropriate ward. It's quite hard to locate someone when all you have to go on is a first name and everyone regards you as highly suspicious.

"Who did you say you were again?" the nurse on the ward asked.

"I'm his aunt," I lied. "His mother phoned me this morning and told me to come urgently so could we please hurry this along?" The nurse pointed to a side-room door and I went in and that was the beginning of the end.

I surveyed the sight in front of me and my blood ran cold. Lying in the bed was a young boy. He had been stripped and was lying looking pale and ill with monitors attached to him. He had sandy hair and even though his eyes were closed and his mouth was unsmiling he still bore a striking resemblance to someone. Someone who I knew very well. Someone who looked like that when they were sleeping. Someone who slept beside me every night.

The woman who was with the boy started when she saw me.

"Are you the doctor?" she asked.

"No, I'm not," I said in a hesitant manner, trying to think of what to say so that I could buy more time. Looking back on it now I don't know how I managed to string a sentence together. I must have been on autopilot and the adrenalin rush must have kept me focused.

"The doctor will be with you shortly. I'm from the

support team and I just wanted to see if you had managed to get in touch with your husband yet?"

"I did phone him earlier but I couldn't get through to him. Some woman answered the phone and said that she would try and get a message to him. He's very busy. He works away, y'see. That's the price you pay when your husband is a design engineer who works all around the world."

I knew that my brow was furrowed as I continued to look at her and tried to process the words that were coming out of her mouth. She definitely had the wrong person. My Ashley was most certainly not a design engineer. I mentally kicked myself for ever doubting him – in my profound relief forgetting the incriminating messages on the phone. There must be a reasonable explanation for all of this. It was just a misunderstanding. A case of crossed wires.

"My husband," she said tearfully, "is very successful. He spends a lot of time in America and Australia. He designs racing cars and because of that he could be almost anywhere in the world. I know he's here at the moment though because he told me that he'd see me this weekend once his meetings had finished."

Ashley had told me that he had to fly to London for an urgent conference straight after his meetings and that I wouldn't see him until Monday evening. I could feel the flush of cold clammy fear rising from the tips of my toes up all over my body until it spread across my face. I needed to sit down. I thought I was going to faint.

I sat down on a chair that was next to the door.

"Excuse me. Was there something you wanted?" the woman asked, looking quizzically at me as she stroked her son's arm.

I licked my lips. My mouth suddenly felt and tasted like sawdust had been crumbled inside it.

"So how long have you been married?"

"We've been married for nearly fourteen years now and have three sons. Jason is our eldest boy. He's thirteen and although he does his best to hide it I know he misses his daddy terribly. I know that he wishes that he could be normal and have his daddy at home with him like everyone else. And he's so sick. He's been having seizures for a while now and he had a pretty severe one last night. They're going to do a brain scan today and monitor the activity there to see if they can locate the problem. His last words to me last night were 'Mammy, please, will you ask Daddy to come?'" The woman's voice broke again and large tear droplets fell on the bed covers as she continued to observe her ill son.

I was feeling more and more sick as minutes ticked by. This could not be happening. There must be some reason for all of this. I was just being stupid and not understanding properly.

"I'm sure he'll be here shortly," I found myself saying, desperately trying to imagine that this poor child had a father somewhere else who really did design sports cars and work in America.

"Does he look like his father?" I asked suddenly.

"He's very like him," she answered, smiling sadly for a moment. She fumbled in her purse and came round to me before handing me a battered dog-eared photograph that she must have been carrying with her all the time judging by the wear and tear.

I swallowed before I looked. There in the photograph was a much younger version of the boy and beside him was his father who he did indeed bear a striking resemblance to.

"I must actually try ringing him again," she said, picking up her mobile. "That stupid woman this morning obviously didn't realise how serious this situation is and probably hasn't passed the message on as urgently as I asked her to. I don't know who she was – whether she was a secretary or perhaps a colleague – but I'll certainly be complaining about her to Ashley. She even pretended to be his wife when she answered!" With that she hit a few buttons and raised the phone to her ear.

I was in a daze, hardly aware of my surroundings, when my bag began to buzz and vibrate as a phone rang and it was then that she abruptly stopped the call and fixed me with a pointed stare.

"Just who the hell are you?" she demanded.

"I could ask you the same thing," I answered quietly.

"Let's go for a walk," I said awkwardly as I emerged again from the back of the bistro.

She nodded her head in agreement.

"So what can I do for you then, Pamela?" I asked as soon as we were outside. There was absolutely no point in prolonging this as neither of us really wanted to be there making small talk and feeling clumsy.

"It's not so much what you can do for me but what we can do for each other," she said, sounding less unsure and more confident.

Now she had my attention. "Go on," I said.

34

Frankie

I had been staying out of Mammy's way. I usually tried to avoid her as much as was humanly possible as she irritated me beyond belief but she had been particularly unbearable since I had been forced to tell her why I was in such permanently foul form and a hair's breadth away from strangling the father of my youngest child.

"I always said that none of this would end well, Frankie, but do you listen? *Nooooooo*. You think your mother is an old fuddy-duddy whose opinions are meaningless."

I hated my mother when she was in full holier-than-thou 'I know best and you know feck all' form and right now she was in top gear and I was wondering what had ever possessed me to confide in her at all. Well, that was simple. I had no one else to talk to and, bar starting to have loud discussions with myself before the little men in white coats carted me and the voices in my head off to the funny farm, it was my last option. Ruby had been so distracted lately that I didn't want to add to her problems by heaping mine on top of them; Gabriel had gone to England and was currently hobnobbing it at some country retreat with a friend who had just won a design award, and my sister Ella was having a well-deserved break and I didn't want to dampen her holiday spirit by yapping about how intolerable my life had become. So that left Mammy. I should still have known better than to open my mouth.

"Well, unfortunately men don't come with a guarantee, Mother. I didn't know that things were going to turn out like this. For all you knew Daddy mightn't have been the great catch he turned out to be."

"Your father is a prince amongst men," Mammy had announced, manhandling Daddy into the kitchen from where he had been hiding in the living room trying his best to look inconspicuous. "He's been a wonderful husband and father and deserves a medal."

I nodded in agreement as Daddy slipped away again. He certainly did deserve a medal but not for the reasons Mammy thought he did.

"Your father is a wonderful man and it's a pity you couldn't have found someone like him. I know he runs away and spends more time out walking dogs and sitting in the potting shed than he should but that's no reason to go saying that he didn't come with a guarantee. You wouldn't hear your sister coming out with talk like that."

I gritted my teeth and thought about my sister who was in the lucky position of living 'away from home' in Scotland. She had got away and when Mammy got too much for her she could silence her with a swift click on the phone and a rushed apologetic text afterwards saying that one of the children had pressed the button. How did I know this? I knew because I had watched her do it the last time I was over and it had filled me with insane jealousy. If I did that Mammy would come and hunt me down and stay in my house berating me for hours and demanding that British Telecom come out and fix the wonky phone that switched itself off.

I sighed long and loud and came to the conclusion that I must have been a very bad person in a former life to deserve such punishment and head-wrecking in this one. Honestly, the woman would drive anyone to drink and I had three bottles of wine chilling in the fridge (3 for £10 special offer) and the three of them might be required to sedate me after the day I'd had.

Firstly work had been an unmitigated disaster. The new girl who had been chosen to fill the position of Public Relations Assistant was a preening nightmare who was more interested in her appearance than anything else. She was an airhead who had all the right qualifications but completely the wrong attitude. She was also an outrageous flirt and no man was safe, not even Owen who had called in to let me know he was working late and had been subjected to five minutes of husky-toned small talk with lots of eyelash-batting, chest-jutting and twirling of the hair. Everything was behind schedule, everyone was in foul humour and I had set up a meeting with the board to ask them (*beg* them) to please get rid of the newbie and replace her with the extremely professional and diligent Jodi who I had witnessed quite happily working in the coffee shop on several occasions since she had got the job.

On the home front things were still very precarious even though Esme had eventually returned home after telling Owen that he and the "poor little ones" were welcome to stay with her any time if they needed to get away. She was making me sound like a deranged person and the fact that Angelica had been filling her head full of my apparent refusal to be in any way supportive of her and her new romance had just fuelled the fire. Angelica had arranged for Esme to meet Jerome and just as I had expected she had loved him.

And the Oscar for Best Actor goes to . . .

"I can't for the life of me see what you have against him, Frankie. He's attentive and considerate and has such lovely manners and he seems to really care about her. It's important to choose a life partner that you can actually get on with and she has done very well for herself. He actually reminds me of my Jack. He was always so good to me and I could rely on his support for everything." This had been said with much sniffing and staring pointedly at Owen and if her looks could have been translated into words they would have said: 'What are you doing with this troublemaking no-hoper who has done nothing but make your precious daughter feel insecure and unloved?'

Angelica seemed to be on another planet most of the time but still managed to give snippy, sarcastic retorts when she was spoken to. To make matters worse, she had been spending rather a lot of time with Brutal Brenda and the effects of her influence were very apparent. I'd had the misfortune to run into Angelica's delectable aunt and as always had wanted to throttle her. She had delighted in telling me how kind and thoughtful Angelica was being lately and how nice it was to see her happy and settled as she needed a break from the crap that she was having to deal with at home. I'd been left shaking with rage but comforted myself with the thought that at least when Angelica wasn't there I didn't have to deal with her myself.

Ben was moody and grunted in response to anything that was said to him and Carly had gone from being a carefree ballerina *Swan Lake* wannabe to a quiet and withdrawn ghost of her former self. The atmosphere in the house was suffocating and everyone was living on their nerves.

"Thanks for all your support, Mammy," I said abruptly before uprooting myself from the kitchen table.

"Are you being sarcastic again?" she demanded.

I tried to think of a suitable response but was too tired to care. Tired of fighting and sick of trying to pick up the pieces of our family that were constantly getting smashed to smithereens by the selfishness and lack of understanding that was present in my home.

"You know, Mammy," I said, conscious that my voice was crackling with emotion, "just for once I wish you could be on my side. You spend so much time telling me about the mistakes I've made but you never let me know when I've tried hard or done something well. I don't get any appreciation from anyone else but I would have thought that I could have relied on my own mother to bolster me up when everyone else was knocking me down."

I brushed away my tears and left my mother standing open-mouthed.

Daddy followed me out to the car and put his hand on my shoulder.

"Don't be too hard on her, Frankie. You know she

does care. She's just annoyed that you seem to be throwing all your energy into trying to humour other people who don't deserve it. Owen is a good man and you're in a difficult situation but if you love each other enough you can deal with anything. How do you think I've managed to live with your mother all these years?" He winked at me and I smiled sadly before driving away.

I got home just in time to see Jerome driving away from the gate and scattering gravel everywhere.

I grabbed my bag from the passenger seat and made my way into the house through the back door.

Angelica obviously hadn't heard me come in through the hall as she had her T-shirt raised and was examining her side in the mirror. There was an ugly mark starting to develop and I wondered what the hell she had done to herself.

"Hello," I said awkwardly, feeling weary.

She reacted like she had been tazered when I spoke and covered herself up quickly.

"Don't sneak up on me like that, Frankie!" she shrieked.

"I walked in through the back door, closed it and set my keys on the telephone table, love, which I believe all made some type of noise so if I was sneaking up to terrorise you I think I might have been a bit quieter about it, don't you?"

She harrumphed at me and made to go up the stairs before I grabbed her by the wrist.

"You're hurting me," she said, pulling away.

She wasn't nearly quick enough though as I saw she had red marks on her wrist as well.

"No more than you seem to be hurting yourself at the

minute. What happened your side?" I moved towards her and she side-stepped me.

"I'm a big girl, Frankie. I don't need you putting plasters on my cuts and kissing me better. I caught my side on the dressing table in my bedroom when I came in last night. It's only a bruise. It'll be fine."

"And what happened to your wrist?"

"Nothing. I had a hair elastic round my hand yesterday and forgot to take it off and now there's a mark. Big deal."

"And how is Jerome? He didn't look best pleased when he was leaving just now."

"He's fine," she snapped. "Why, what's it to you?"

"Can I not even ask a simple question without you biting the head off me?"

"No, you can't. Not when you're just trying to criticise and find fault with everything."

"You don't know the first thing about people trying to poke holes in your every movement, Angelica, and I can assure you that if that's what I was doing then you'd know all about it. I'll send you to my mother for a week and then perhaps you'll appreciate just how much I don't try and criticise you."

She rolled her eyes to heaven, stomped up the stairs and sharply shut her bedroom door.

I shook in annoyance but concentrated very hard on counting to ten.

I could hear her banging and rattling around upstairs and wondered how someone who had fought so hard to be in a relationship could still be so unhappy even though they had apparently got what they wanted.

35

Angelica

I rubbed my side and sat down heavily on the bed, feeling strangely confused.

Jerome kept telling me how much he adored me and how he was looking forward to being with me all the time but I failed to understand how someone who was meant to love me could lash out at me like that.

I had been having second thoughts about moving out of the house, mostly because I didn't like the grotty flats we had viewed. When Jerome had talked about us moving in together I had visualised a cosy love nest for two with central heating and funky designs on the walls. I had pictured a proper kitchen, a small but compact bathroom, a couple of bedrooms and some sort of a garden but instead of that all I had seen were smelly flats that were cold and uninviting with mouse-traps strewn around the floorboards and torn wallpaper.

I had voiced my concerns to Jerome but instead of agreeing with me he had accused me of wasting his time and being unappreciative of his efforts.

"What's wrong?" he had sneered. "Does Daddy's little princess expect everything to be handed to her on a plate? Jesus, Angelica, I'm trying my best. As long as we're together does it matter where it is? Our own place won't be something out of *Homes and Gardens* – we'll have to work to make it a proper home but the first step is actually getting somewhere. Unless of course you've changed your mind and want to stay with Frankie and all her nagging and bullying? I thought I meant more to you than that, Angelica. You disappoint me."

"Of course I want to be with you and I'm not expecting a palace but I would like somewhere decent that doesn't have damp walls and a badly stained carpet."

"Instead of telling me what you want all the time it would be nice if you occasionally recognised my efforts. Just remember, Angelica, that if you didn't have me you wouldn't have anyone. Where are Katie and all your friends? Where's your mother? Frankie doesn't want you and your aunt is always at work."

Hearing his words made me feel more desperate than ever to get away from everyone and prove that I could be my own person who didn't need anyone else. But I wanted to make my move a good one as opposed to making yet another mistake.

"Why are you saying such horrible things to me? Have you any idea what it's been like for me over the years? I don't need you rubbing my nose in it. Is your family perfect? Your father barely speaks to your mother and there's no visitors allowed during the day. What's that all about?"

Jerome pursed up his mouth and his cheeks flamed in anger and I instantly regretted opening my mouth. I knew I had said too much.

"I'm sorry –" I began but Jerome had started to pace around the room, flexing his fists in an agitated manner.

"If you want out of this just say the word now. Obviously you have so many more appealing choices. I thought I was rescuing you from your family but apparently instead of acknowledging that you'd rather sneer at mine. You're so ungrateful. I seriously don't know why I bother with you."

"Okay, I'm sorry. I didn't mean what I said. Of course I want to be with you. I'm just afraid of making a rash decision about where we live and then regretting it."

"You leave the finer details to me," he had snapped.

And yet again I had been left feeling inadequate and as if I didn't quite make the grade.

"I will if you lighten up –" I started but this time instead of shouting at me he had pushed me up against the dresser in my room and I could feel the corner of the unit digging painfully into my side.

I had tried to push him away but he was stronger than I was and the more I struggled the more firmly he gripped me.

"You're hurting me," I had gasped as he continued to hold me.

"Now do you understand how it feels to be pushed to the limit?" he had said. "How does it feel?"

I had closed my eyes and tried to concentrate on something other than the stinging sensation of wood against flesh. He had gripped both my wrists and was squeezing them tightly.

Eventually he let go and stepped away from me, looking disgusted. Then he turned and left the room.

I ran after him but by the time I got to the hall he was

already out the front door and by the time I reached the door he had driven off without looking back.

And then Frankie had come in being her usual annoying self and I had been reminded why the hell I so badly wanted to get out of here but somehow the thought wasn't filling me with as much pleasure as it once did.

I had received two text messages from Jerome asking to meet me that evening but I just didn't feel like talking to anyone. I wanted to be on my own as it was safer that way. When I was by myself I wasn't in danger of doing or saying the wrong thing and people wouldn't get angry with me or end up walking out like they eventually did. I had spent a long time looking at an old photograph of my mother and came to the conclusion that she must have left because of me. On the few occasions that we had met up she had told me how much she had loved my father so it could only have been me. Everyone left eventually.

The door to my bedroom opened and Frankie curtly told me that Jerome was downstairs to see me.

He was sitting in the living room with his hands entwined, looking at the floor. I shut the door and sat on a chair opposite him.

"You didn't answer my texts," he said quietly.

"I was afraid of upsetting you again," I answered, feeling suddenly drained. "It's all I seem to do these days. Perhaps you'd be better off without me."

He looked startled by my words and, instead of reacting angrily like I would have anticipated, he came over to me and took my hands in his.

"Angelica, I love you and I'm sorry we argued earlier. I couldn't live without you and just wanted to make you see that you were being unreasonable. Look, how about I make it up to you by taking you to that new cocktail bar opening next Saturday night?"

"You said you didn't want to go to that," I said, remembering the way he had reacted when I had first suggested it. The launch of Pitchers was happening the same night as Katie's party and I had wanted to be sure that we were definitely doing something else that night.

"I'm allowed to change my mind, aren't I?" he said, looking at me. "Besides, I'd like to see you dressed up as a Bond girl. Pussy Galore is my favourite character – dress up like her and I promise we'll have a wonderful night."

He took my face in his hands and kissed me softly on the lips and I smiled weakly as he stood up to leave. I stood up and he took my hands.

"That looks nasty," he commented, looking at the ugly marks on my wrists as if he had never seen them before or had no recollection of how they had got there. "I love you, Angelica. Never forget that," he said before leaving the room.

I took a deep breath and decided that if he could forget about what happened then so could I. He was just stressed out because he wanted so much for us to be together. Things would be different when we were on our own, wouldn't they?

36

Ruby

"So, Ruby, tell me how you've been since we last spoke? How has life been treating you?"

"Well, since I've been making an unholy mess of everything and have had almighty rows with both my adoptive mother and my birth mother, I suppose you could say that it's been pretty shit."

Sonia Bernstein smiled and nodded her head and didn't seem to be in the least bit phased by what I had just said. She probably heard the same story a hundred times a day. In fact, compared to some of the suicidal, confused basket-cases that she might see I was probably mild in comparison.

"Tell me more," she said calmly, viewing me with interest.

"Where the hell do I start? It actually all kicked off after we spoke the last day. Maybe this counselling lark isn't such a good idea after all. Instead of helping it seems to attract trouble for me."

I laughed at my own joke but Sonia made no comment. I wondered did they administer Botox to counsellors so that their faces remained expressionless no matter how shocking the revelations they were privy to.

She nodded, put her head to the side and indicated for me to continue.

"I got a phone call from Georgie to tell me that her father, my paternal grandfather, was seriously ill. It turned out that he had pneumonia and at his age that can be very dangerous. She was understandably upset and I wanted to be with her and because I had already missed so much of my grandfather's life I wanted to be with him too. I didn't want to have any regrets so I went to Donegal to help out. I ended up wishing that I hadn't bothered though as her family made it more than obvious that I was totally unwelcome even though I wanted to try and build some bridges with them. According to my aunt I am nothing more than a mistake. What was it she called me? Oh yes, I'm nothing more than a genetic chromosonic connection."

Even as I said the words I felt hurt and alone. God knows I could be quick-tempered and fiery but I would never ever be so cruel or cutting and I believed that I deserved better and so did Georgie.

"That's a very cold and clinical view of things," Sonia commented. "How did your birth mother react to this?"

"Oh, she probably thinks the same. Marcella and I had a row in the carpark and she fell over when I took a step towards her and now she's accusing me of assaulting her. Georgie only arrived after it had happened and has chosen to believe Marcella's version of events."

"Has your aunt reported you to the police?" Sonia asked with a slight frown.

"No she hasn't and I know she won't," I said. "She'd have to actually admit I existed then and that would never do. All sorts of messy secrets could come spilling out of the closet and they wouldn't want that. There's something very strange going on though. I overheard Marcella talking to her partner at the hospital and she was threatening to tell my grandfather something that would alter his view of Georgie. She seems to have some sort of a hold over Georgie and she's using whatever ammunition she has to keep me at arm's length. It's all lies and cover-ups with that lot."

"The last time you were here, Ruby, you talked at some length about how finding your father would make you feel? Has anything changed? Is that still what you want?"

I sighed and concentrated on the wall behind Sonia as I responded.

"I'd still like to know but just don't want to make any more trouble for anyone. I've wished on more than one occasion over the last few weeks that I hadn't found Georgie but I know that I'm just reacting to things as they are now. I couldn't have continued to function without finding out where I came from but it's all got so complicated and so many people have been affected. I'll bet that she's regretting ever meeting up with me again. Perhaps she would have been better still imagining a baby wrapped in a blanket as opposed to the nightmare I've been for her."

As I spoke I felt the nagging hurt that had been pestering me since the encounter crank up a notch.

"What were you hoping to achieve by making this decision to go to Donegal?" Sonia asked.

"I suppose that I just wanted to be part of things. It's in my nature to help people and, just because I've only known Georgie a short while, it doesn't mean that she's any less important than anyone in my adoptive family. But you couldn't explain that to my mother who now is revelling in the fact that she has been proven right and I should have been listening to her all along."

Sonia raised her eyebrows. (Maybe she'd had a very mild dose of Botox.)

"She just doesn't understand or maybe she just doesn't want to understand, I went on. She always acted like a wounded puppy when I talked about Georgie in the past. It's like she resented my involvement with her or that she never wanted me having any contact with her. I mean, what did she expect me to do – spend years wondering about my birth mother, go to the ends of the earth or at least to the wilds of Donegal to find her and then drop her like a hot potato once the deed was done? That's like participating in a treasure hunt, winning the prize and then giving it back once you've got it. You wouldn't catch any reasonable-minded person doing that and this is much more serious."

"Have you spoken to your mother and told her how you've been feeling?"

"I've spoken to her, yes, but if you asked me if she understood or if she was willing to see things from my point of view then the answer would have to be no. If I ever repeated anything Georgie said or told her about any advice she'd given me, it was automatically dismissed as not being worthy or good enough and if she was ever in Georgie's company she always ended up belittling her whether intentionally or not. I'm sure she's absolutely delighted that everything has now turned bloody pear-shaped. But, of course, now that I've told her that I intended finding out who my father is she's gone all moody on me again and taken it as a personal slight against my adoptive father who was the best dad ever. I've just given her something else to beat her drum about except she's not beating it at the minute because she's not really talking to me."

I stopped speaking long enough to let a tear plop on the sleeve of my jacket where I roughly rubbed it away and wondered why the hell I was crying. I didn't do crying, especially not in front of strangers who were going to document the fact in a file that would remain in somebody's office forever.

Sonia cleared her throat, poured me a glass of water and offered me a tissue. She did it with such ease that I knew that she must perform this ritual on a regular basis.

"Ruby, given the difficult circumstances surrounding your adoption I would have been highly surprised if there hadn't been a bit of upset. In every situation it's inevitable that there will be a transitional period where everyone will have to get used to the new circumstances. Emotions are also running high because your grandfather hasn't been well and I'm sure your birth mother appreciated your support. Give everyone time to calm down and wait and see what happens and don't spend your time worrying about it because it won't change anything."

I nodded my head and sniffed loudly.

"Give it a few more days and then try talking to them both again. They could be more understanding than you think. And take it easy on yourself. You are a victim in all this too."

"I'll try," I said, smiling weakly before loudly blowing my nose.

"That's the spirit," Sonia answered cheerfully. "Would you like a cup of coffee?"

I nodded and Sonia left the room. Her office was bright and airy and the walls were a pale shade of duck-egg blue which, I had been told on the good authority of Frankie, was a calming colour. Sonia had pictures of children on her desk and I felt a sudden and unprovoked lump form in my throat.

She came back and handed me a cup and looked quizzically at me.

"So tell me what else is on your mind," she asked calmly.

I wondered for a second if Sonia Bernstein always behaved with such poise, sensibility and good grace, or if she secretly dreamt of having a complete hissy fit where she could forget all her training and scream, shout and throw things at her children and tell her husband to feck off out of her way when he annoyed her.

"It's Luke," I sniffed. "He's great. He's absolutely brilliant and he loves me so much but it doesn't make me feel good at all. It makes me feel worse than ever."

"And why would you say that, Ruby?"

"Because I can't give him what he wants or maybe a better way of wording that would be that I won't give him what he wants. I wish I could but I'm too afraid and that's not a word I use lightly, believe me."

Sonia didn't say anything but prompted me again with her hand.

"He loves children and for that matter so do I but I couldn't ever think of having any of my own."

"Any particular reason why or is this something you decided a long time ago? Children aren't for everyone, you know, and it's nothing to feel guilty about."

"Yes, but I do feel guilty because I know Luke wants them more than life itself and he'd make the most fantastic father. Anybody who can deal with me on a full-time basis would be more than capable of dealing with a demanding baby."

"You still haven't told me why, Ruby," Sonia said gently.

"Because I'm afraid of how I'll react," I blurted out with tears running freely down my cheeks now. "I love children. I have a little godson called Jack who means the world to me and I love him to bits but the thought of having any of my own fills me with dread. It's hard to explain."

"Try me," Sonia said, folding her arms and settling herself into a more comfortable position in her chair.

I took a gulp of air and prepared to say out loud for the first time ever why the thought of having my own baby made me want to run away.

37

Jodi

Fabian Quinn came into the bistro for his morning break and I greeted him cheerfully and asked him if he wanted his 'usual'.

"You know me so well," he answered jovially while I prepared to make him a cappuccino and picked out one of our speciality Danish pastries.

"I'll be back to get that in a minute, Jodi. I just need to nip across to the post office before the rush starts." He swung the door behind him as I lifted the tongs and picked him out a particularly luscious cherry-filled Danish.

"You know him well and he wants to get to know you better," Anna murmured as she brushed past me and started to make a pot of tea for another customer.

"Men are off the menu, I'm afraid. Once bitten, twice shy and I'm never ever going back. More trouble than they're worth if you ask me."

"Oh, come on, they're not all like that. I know Fabian pretty well and he's a good catch."

"Listen, Anna, I know all about good catches and as far

281

as knowing someone well goes you never know them well enough in my opinion. I'm single and I'm staying that way."

"That husband of yours really did a job on you," she said with a tut. "It's a crying shame, you know. You'd make a lovely couple. Besides, he's going to become morbidly obese with all the pastry he's consuming just so that he can see you. He used to come in here occasionally and carry something out. Now he's here all the time eating his way to an early heart attack and he's not even going to get as much as cursory snog for his trouble."

"That's right, he isn't," I said with fierce determination while shaking cocoa powder on Fabian's cappuccino and fixing Anna with my most potent stare.

Fabian returned in time to save me from any more unwanted comments and I felt mildly irritated as I set his order down in front of him. I wanted to get away from his table as quickly as possible as I knew that we were the focus of attention and hated anyone speculating that anything could possibly be going on. There wasn't as much as a spark between us and the very idea of me ever getting involved with another man was so ludicrously laughable that I refused even to entertain the idea.

"Thanks, Jodi," he said with a warm smile. He took a mouthful of coffee and sighed appreciatively. "She makes a lovely cup of coffee, this one," he said as Tom walked past him carrying a tray of food for another table.

"One of the best," Tom answered good-naturedly as I walked away rolling my eyes.

The others exchanged glances and grinned.

"Bet he'd like to know what your coffee's like when you're serving it on a tray to him in bed," Anna whispered.

"Well, he'll have to die wondering then," I said,

blushing furiously as I saw Fabian giving us a quizzical look.

"What are you two whispering about?" he asked, taking a huge bite of his pastry and waiting expectantly for an answer.

"We were just talking about how much we're looking forward to the launch of your cocktail bar," Anna said quickly. "We haven't had a night out in ages and we're all ready to be shaken not stirred in here."

"Yeah, there's been a lot of interest," Fabian said before taking another sip of coffee. "I've lots to do though and I'm completely swamped under trying to send out invites and get things organised because the PR Company I had hired to do the marketing have gone bust and had to withdraw their services."

"Well, it just so happens that I know of someone who has a background in PR who would be more than happy to help you!" Anna said with a large smile.

"Who?" Fabian asked expectantly.

"Who?" I echoed in bewilderment.

"Do you not know that our Jodi is a PR princess?" Anna said while I watched her through narrowing eyes. "She was actually commenting on the quality of your advertising leaflets the day they came in and impressed us all with her knowledge."

"Really?" Fabian asked. "Well, I'd appreciate your input, Jodi, and I would of course pay you what I was prepared to give the consultancy."

I had opened my mouth to speak but Anna (my new self-appointed manager) had stepped in again and told him that I'd be round there that afternoon and she would work my shift for me to just ease things along.

He left and I looked at my fellow waitress with hands on hips and a stern expression on my face.

"Care to tell me what that was all about?" I demanded.

"Just helping a friend and seeing how a situation can be mutually beneficial to all concerned," she responded while busying herself with another order and refusing to meet my gaze.

"I am not in the slightest bit interested in him," I said firmly. "There is a habit in the nearest convent with my name on it and I'll be going to collect it soon so stop trying to impersonate Cilla Black, please."

"I'm sure I don't know what you're talking about," Anna said with a sniff. "I never liked *Blind Date* myself."

I finished work early as arranged and made my way to the antiques shop where I found Fabian examining some items that had just come in.

"*Ooh*," I said in appreciation as the glass from an ornate antique lampshade caught the light and created a rainbow of colour.

"It's beautiful, isn't it?" he said. "We had a delivery of goods this morning and I'm just having a hunt through to see what I can put out on display quickly. I haven't really had time to see to the running of the shop properly as I've been so busy trying to organise things for the launch of the bar."

"Where's your helper?" I asked. "The elderly lady who I used to see in here? I haven't seen her around in a while."

"That's my mother and she hasn't been well. Yet another reason why I've been preoccupied and unable to take care of all my commitments. I wish I had known of your experience before. I'd have certainly appreciated the help."

"I'm sorry to hear that your mother's ill," I said, picking up a dusty painting and examining it carefully. "This is pretty rare," I said eventually, having located the artist's name and recognising it to be of some value.

"Yes, I noticed that myself," Fabian commented, coming round to look at it again as I held it with great care. "Bit of an art appreciator as well as a PR princess then?" he grinned.

"My dad is an antiques dealer and I used to help him out when I was younger and accompany him to all the auctions and I suppose I picked up a few things along the way," I shrugged.

"Well, now, that's just cruel," Fabian said, straightening himself and looking at me in surprise. "Here I am struggling to carry the burden of all my commitments and here you are. Wonder Woman disguised as a waitress. You could have saved me from developing an ulcer several months ago, you know."

"Several months ago I mightn't have been that much use to you," I said ruefully. "But I'll be glad to help you out where I can now."

"Thank you, Jodi. Much appreciated."

"It's an odd combination," I continued thoughtfully. "Antiques shops and cocktail bars don't really go hand in hand as something you'd expect the one owner to be interested in."

"It wasn't a conscious decision on my part." He continued to lift items from boxes before examining them and putting them in piles. "I inherited the bar and thought I'd try something new. I'm beginning to wonder, though, if I've bitten off more than I can chew. I hope all the effort hasn't been for nothing."

"It's actually a very clever idea," I said. "As far as I can gather the Swiftstown Arms serves the odd cocktail but they don't specialise in it whereas you'll be doing something different as well as offering the usual wines and beers and spirits that will appeal to the masses. It's a great idea and, as long as you use the opportunity of the launch to properly advertise the type of drinks you'll be serving and the promotions you'll be organising, I think it will be good for you and good for Swiftstown in general."

"I thought the themed night was a bit corny but it seems to have gone down well with the locals."

"Well, I haven't been out in ages and I'm looking forward to it," I said, grinning. "It's been a long time since I've had the opportunity to wear platform boots, a mini-dress and a wig."

"Well, I shall certainly look forward to seeing that," he said, before looking quickly away as I blushed. "I didn't mean that to sound the way it came out," he said, colouring. "I just meant that I was looking forward to seeing everyone dressed up."

There was another awkward silence as I absentmindedly looked through some of the other goods to be displayed.

"So what do you want me to do first?" I asked, conscious that time was ticking by and wanting to get started as I had been looking forward to taking a bath that evening and pampering myself with a face pack.

"Would you like to go over to the bar and get a quick preview of what's to come? Few others have actually seen it inside as I want the impact to be as huge as possible on Saturday but, for you, I'm willing to make an exception.

I smiled as he led me out the door and felt the familiar and welcome buzz of a challenge yet to come.

38

Frankie

It was strange but in a funny way it felt like old times again. Angelica and I were both getting ready to go out and because it was a fancy-dress party we were both using more make-up than usual and taking it in turns vying for the biggest mirror in the house which was in the hall.

"You look lovely," I commented when I saw her appearing from her bedroom in a sparkly green mini-dress with her hair in a beehive.

"Pussy Galore at your service," she said, striking a provocative pose and I had to admit that she looked dazzling.

"Can I borrow your black eyeliner, Frankie?" she asked and I handed it to her with a smile and got a small one back in response.

Owen had noticed the reduction in tension as well and it instantly lifted his mood. He hadn't been at all enthusiastic about going to the party but was now humming 'Goldfinger' softly to himself and liberally applying aftershave.

"Want to fix my tie, Mish Moneypenny," he said in the worst Sean Connery imitation I think I had ever heard.

I put my arms around his neck to fix the dickey bow that was hanging at a precarious angle and he grabbed me and kissed my cheek.

"Just hold that position," he murmured. "I've missed you so much lately."

"I've missed you too," I said, enjoying feeling close to him for the first time in months and not wanting to move.

"You know the way that James Bond always ends up getting laid at the end of his films," Owen said huskily as I fixed his tie and he caressed my back through the flimsy material of my monochrome dress.

"Yes," I answered softly.

"Can we re-enact that bit when we get home later? I think it's only right, y'know. It is a themed night and in order to do it justice we have to see it through to the end."

"The very end," I murmured, kissing him and letting my tongue slide into his mouth.

He moaned and I had to pull away from him before all my hard work was loosened, smudged and undone.

"Later, Superman," I whispered before kissing his nose and feeling happier and more carefree than I could remember being for ages.

I hadn't noticed any significant improvements with Angelica. I think I could safely assume that I was still her least favourite person but she had been quieter than usual and I hoped against hope that perhaps her big romance had started to fizzle out and that life could return to normal or as normal as the life of a dysfunctional family could ever be. I suspected that she and Jerome had been fighting recently as he had arrived at the house one night looking preoccupied and agitated and he and Angelica had spent a long time talking in the living room. I had been standing at the door with a glass poised but had to quickly remove myself when Carly demanded to join in the game. I had to pay her off with packets of chewy sweets so that she wouldn't tell Angelica that I had been eavesdropping as that would have created the onset of yet another world war which I simply didn't have the stamina for.

Ben and Carly were spending the night with their father and our childminder had agreed to keep Jack overnight and as far as I knew Angelica would probably be late in, so I was viewing coming home with much enthusiasm. It wasn't often that Owen and I had the house to ourselves and I intended to make full use of the opportunity.

"Don't my girls both look amazing?" he said as we walked into the living room together. "Is Jerome picking you up here, Angelica?"

I did a final check and began to switch off all the lights.

"No, he said he would meet me there so I was hoping to get a lift with you."

"And it would be my pleasure to take you," Owen responded (trying too hard as usual – but, as I was on a promise and my mind was totally focused on that, I decided not to let it annoy me).

The bar was positively heaving with activity when we arrived. There were local photographers, there were waiters and waitresses all mingling through the crowd with complimentary drinks, and Jodi was also there dressed in a tight-fitting cat-suit that left very little to the imagination with a clipboard in her hand, looking every inch like she was in full control of the proceedings.

Angelica had left us as soon as we entered the building and was probably in hot pursuit of Jerome whose company she would be in all night. I had asked her if she was meeting any of her friends there but her expression had immediately darkened and she had grunted an unintelligible response. I had noticed that Katie hadn't been to visit her in ages and none of the gaggle of girls that had viewed our house as their second home had called around either and I hoped that everything was okay but didn't ask for fear of my concern being misinterpreted as usual.

My thoughts were diverted away from Angelica, however, as I began to fully take in my surroundings. The bar had once been a dingy old men's pub frequented by elderly pensioners and dogs but had been transformed entirely into an exquisite cocktail bar that could fool you into thinking that you were in the middle of a big city as opposed to being in plain old Swiftstown.

The bar was a majestic chrome creation that had lights shining from below it and above it so that it was the centre of the room. The optics and stand-alone bottles that were situated behind the bar, both on the wall and on shelves, were all flooded with brilliant light that made you think that you were looking inside a Technicolor prism. Comfy sofas had been scattered in various corners of the room, boasting massive cushions and tables in front of them, and bar stools that had been positioned both at the bar and around high tables that were dotted around the room giving the establishment a trendy retro feel. I was very impressed.

I heard a large intake of breath echo around me and saw people look up and down as a new reveller entered the room and grinned to myself as I figured Gabriel must have arrived. He did love to make an entrance but on this occasion he had created maximum impact with his ensemble.

Owen came over to me looking confused and whispered in my ear. "I thought the theme was James Bond," he said, still looking at Gabriel with his eyebrows raised.

"It is," I replied.

"So why has Gabriel come looking like a drag queen then?"

"Who sang 'Goldfinger'?" I asked patiently.

"Wasn't that Shirley Bassey?"

"It was indeed and as she played rather an important part and everyone knows the song, Gabriel decided to improvise a little. Or perhaps a lot," I added, looking at my friend properly as he came under the light.

Amongst the rest of the partygoers with their flowing chiffon frocks, short dresses and large hair-do's Gabriel cut a rather striking figure. He was wearing a long red sequinned figure-hugging dress that had a rather revealing slash up one side. His wig was three times the size of anyone else's and had been backcombed to within an inch of its life, his false eyelashes were so long that standing too close might result in a stabbing wound and the heels he was wearing could have been mistaken for stilts they were so unforgivingly high.

"*Oh my God!*" he squealed in excitement as he sashayed over to us, attracting comments and glances as he went. "I cannot believe this place! I am never leaving here!"

I wasn't sure whether he was talking about the bar itself or the fact that I'd got Jodi to hire the services of a few nicely toned male students from the college to be waiters for the evening and even persuade them to lose their tops except for the bowties they sported around their necks.

"Oh for God's sake," he suddenly muttered crossly and as I followed his eye-line the focus of his aggravation came into view.

Ruby had arrived, with Luke following behind her, wearing her normal clothes, and was giving everyone around her warning looks that dared them to challenge her.

"I am not dressing up," she had announced earlier. "If my money isn't good enough to be accepted when I'm wearing the clothes I'm comfortable in then they can throw me out."

Gabriel had reacted like I knew he would and was outraged. "She never wants to have fun, that one," he grumbled. "How often does an opportunity like this come along where you can throw caution to the wind and wear what you want without feeling inhibited?"

I hadn't wanted to say anything but reckoned that for Gabriel that particular scenario was a daily occurrence as some of his outfits wouldn't look out of place in a child's dressing-up box.

"Say one word and you'll be wearing that drink," Ruby warned as Gabriel went to say something but thought better of it and instead took another appreciative sip of the strawberry daiquiri he was holding.

"What the hell are you supposed to be?" Ruby asked as she made a swipe at Gabriel's oversized wig that was blocking her view. "Actually don't tell me. I don't want to know."

"Nice to see that you're in good form again then," Gabriel said, raising his eyes to heaven and giving me a knowing look.

Luke was making slicing motions behind Ruby to tell us not to say anything and I knew that she was still smarting from the fact that she had tried to ring Georgie the day before but had got no answer. Her birth mother hadn't returned her call and the pained look on Ruby's face spoke volumes about the turmoil she must have been feeling inside. I didn't say anything but gave her arm a comforting squeeze and she smiled tightly in response.

"Are you having a good time?" Fabian Quinn stopped and asked courteously as he mingled with his guests. He nodded at one of the waitresses who came over beside us right away bearing a tray of brightly coloured drinks in decorative glasses. "Can I offer you ladies one of our free promotional cocktails? Would you like me to choose for you or would you prefer to pick a glass yourself?"

"I think you'd better choose or we could be here for some time," I answered, not knowing where to start.

He picked out a glass without hesitation. "I think you'll like this. It's a classic but very sophisticated and delicious."

I took a sip and let the fruity flavours mixed with alcohol attack my taste buds which were having orgasms right about now.

"What is it?"

"It's an Apple Martini."

"That's a Champagne Cocktail . . . or was a champagne cocktail." He smiled as he moved on. "I hope you have a very good night."

I saw Jodi circling the room looking uber-efficient as well as highly attractive. She was getting nearly as many lingering looks as Gabriel. Nearly but not quite.

"You look busy," I said when she came in our direction. "Is this a new sideline to waitressing then?"

"I have a few sidelines on the go," she said. "I'm helping Fabian to co-ordinate events and market this place and I'm also working a few hours in the antiques shop as well and I'm loving both."

"So everything has worked out then?" I said.

"You could say that," she said, looking genuinely content. "I spoke to my dad just before I left to come here and he's very happy."

"I bet he is. Good for you. It takes a lot of guts to do what you've done and I hope you know how proud I am of you."

She looked overwhelmed for a moment before giving me a quick hug and then excusing herself as she waved at some of the other staff from the bistro who had arrived suitably attired and with the resident chef striking a menacing pose as Jaws complete with scary-looking teeth.

I went back to my table and saw that one of the waitresses was being interrogated by Gabriel as to what all the drinks were.

"This one is called a Ruby Duchess," she said, pointing at a tall champagne glass that was filled with a sparkling purple liquid. "It's a mixture of champagne and pomegranate juice."

"She'll have that," Gabriel said, shoving it in Ruby's direction.

"I can choose myself, y'know," Ruby said grumpily.

"Shut up and drink, you tart," Gabriel commanded and turned back to the waitress. "What else have you got?"

"What do you want?"

"Well, I have to say that I always get a particular thrill from approaching a barman and asking for a Screaming Orgasm," he said with a wide grin. "But in the absence of that I think I'll have one of those – if I'm not mistaken that is a Cheeky V."

"Very apt," I muttered under my breath as Luke watched his wife in bemusement while Ruby downed yet another drink in one gulp without even seeming to taste it and set her glass back on the tray.

"I'm going to end up carrying you home tonight if you don't go easy on those things, Ruby," Luke warned. "And you know what you're like when you mix your drinks."

"She's even more difficult to deal with than usual," Gabriel said drily as Ruby curled her lip and snarled at him.

"Have you seen Angelica?" Owen asked as he gently kissed my neck, sending shivers up and down my spine.

"I haven't but that's because she and Love's Young Dream will be huddled in a corner somewhere acting like there's nobody else in the world but them."

"Can we do that too?" Owen asked, finishing his whiskey sour and placing his glass on the nearest table with a resolute bang.

"And what are you proposing, Superman?" I asked, already reaching for my coat as Gabriel's back was turned and Ruby was speaking to Luke.

"I have something that's for 'your eyes only'," he whispered and, as he led me out the door and into the cool night air, I shivered but not because of the cold.

39

Angelica

I threw my phone in my bag in disgust and for the umpteenth time wondered what the hell could be keeping Jerome. The party was in full swing now and I was dying to go in and enjoy myself but daren't go inside without Jerome. He didn't like me to go into such places when I was on my own and I didn't want him getting all moody and annoyed with me again. I had started to hop from one foot to the other as I badly needed to use the toilet and, fearing that a puddle might appear at my feet, I went inside to use the facilities. When I came back out I saw Jerome's car and with excitement ran over to him, glad that we could eventually join in the fun.

"You haven't dressed up," I said as I climbed into the car and noted his casual clothing.

"I didn't feel like it," he said and I felt a frisson of irritation pass through me at his attitude.

It was a fancy-dress party night. He was as bad as

Ruby who had stormed passed me earlier looking like she was on a mission to kill someone.

I waited for him to compliment me on my dress but there were no comments forthcoming and again disappointment surged through me. I had gone to a great deal of trouble to get the perfect look. He had specifically said he'd like me to dress like Pussy Galore and after Googling images and looking at clothing online and browsing through various shops I had eventually found a suitable outfit in a vintage outlet. I had even got them to alter it slightly so that it was a better fit but apparently it wasn't enough. I had got that wrong too.

"Do you like my dress?" I eventually asked as he seemed disinterested and aloof and hadn't even bothered to look at me properly.

"It'll do, I suppose," he said, continuing to stare out the window. "You're wearing far too much eye liner. You look like a drag queen. I told you I don't like that stuff. It doesn't suit you."

"It's a fancy-dress party, Jerome. Heavy make-up is part of the theme."

He snorted in disgust and I wished he hadn't bothered suggesting coming if all he was going to do was find fault with everything I had tried so hard to make perfect for him.

A group of boys walked past and I recognised Paddy McCourt from school and waved at him.

Suddenly I had Jerome's full attention. He acted like he had been electrocuted, sat bolt upright and gave me a look that had the capacity to cut through sheet metal.

"What the hell did you do that for?" he demanded.

"What?" I asked, confused.

"Do you fancy him?" he said through gritted teeth. "Is

that why you're disrespecting me by making eyes at him when you're in my company?"

"I wasn't making eyes at him. I just know him from school. It isn't unheard of to wave at someone, you know. It's quite a time-honoured tradition," I retorted, shaking my head and wondering what the hell had got into him to make him so touchy.

He breathed out through his nose and shook his head. "And then she adds insult to injury by mocking me," he continued.

"What insult? What injury? What are you talking about?" I asked, feeling the beginnings of a sore head and wanting to get out of the car for some air. "Can we go inside now?"

"You're very keen to get away from me. Have you arranged to meet someone else inside? That's it, isn't it? I got held up finishing some business for my father and instead of waiting for me you've gone and made plans with somebody else."

"No, I haven't," I said pleadingly, wanting all the unfounded accusations to stop. "Where is all this coming from? I've barely spoken to anyone since I arrived. I've been standing outside the whole time waiting for you."

"Liar," he said. "You weren't standing there when I arrived. You were inside."

"Well, excuse me for needing to pee," I said in exasperation. "Jerome, are we going to sit here all night or are we actually going to go in and enjoy ourselves? You promised that we would do something special tonight because I'm missing Katie's party."

He started the car and I looked at him in confusion as he indicated and prepared to drive off.

"What are you doing?" I asked.

"What you want," he said. "You wanted something special so I'm going to give it to you."

He continued driving and I shook my head, wanting the feelings of apprehension and unease to leave me. I really loved Jerome and had sacrificed a lot for him but his behaviour was starting to get very peculiar. I desperately wanted to ask him what was wrong or why he seemed to be so unhappy with me all the time but was afraid of the response I might get. The last thing I wanted was for him to tell me that he no longer cared about me.

I recognised the road we had taken but couldn't place exactly where we were.

"Where are we going?" I asked again.

"I told you, Angelica," he said, smiling at me. "You wanted special and that lovely outfit you're wearing deserves some proper uninterrupted appreciation."

I wondered how he was capable of being so abrupt one minute and so cheerful the next. I wasn't complaining though.

I peered into the darkness, saw a familiar sign and started to swallow.

"Jerome, why are we here again?" I asked as he turned a corner that led us back to the disused quarry.

"I thought this was what you wanted," he said as he stopped the car, flung off his seatbelt and started to manoeuvre himself into a more comfortable position.

"I want to go back to the party," I said, feeling like I might cry.

"And Cinderella shall go to the ball," he said, moving closer to me so that I could feel his breath on my cheek. "But not until Prince Charming decides that the time is right."

He roughly pulled at the bottom of my dress and then I felt his hand on my breast and, as he wound the passenger seat back, I wondered if this was supposed to be what true love was all about.

I no longer felt like going back to the launch and asked Jerome just to drop me home which he did obligingly. His mood seemed to have improved significantly and he sang along with the radio as we made our way back to the house.

I thought I would be coming home to an empty house and would have a chance to be alone but saw that Frankie and my father had beat me to it as I could see a dim light in their bedroom. I could also hear them laughing and talking as I opened the front door but, as I didn't want them to be aware I was there, I silently crept up the stairs and into my room.

As I threw my dress on top of my chest of drawers I knocked over a photograph and on turning it over I could feel my heart lurch. It was of Katie and me grinning happily into the camera with our arms wrapped tightly around each other and a fairground in the background. The photo had been taken on one of our many days out last summer. I felt a pang of regret but it was quickly replaced with a stubborn need to prove myself. Everyone thought I was wrong so what I needed to do was to make them see I had been right all along. I put the photograph in a drawer and made my way into the en-suite bathroom where I turned on the shower.

Tearing off my underwear I stepped under the water and started to scrub myself vigorously.

If loving someone was meant to make you happy, why then did I feel so afraid?

40

Ruby

I was totally distracted and no use to anyone and had decided to take the afternoon off work.

"Ruby, it's just going to take time," Frankie had said, giving me a hug before I left. "Do you want me to take a few hours off as well and we can go for a walk in the park and get a nice cup of coffee somewhere?"

"It would be a complete waste of your time, Frankie. I would be shit company. I don't know what's wrong with me lately. I feel permanently drained and could cry at the drop of the hat. It's all the fault of that feckin' counsellor, y'know. She's turned me into a complete basket-case with all her talk of looking at my feelings. I'm worse now than I was before I went to see her!" I thought I might just pay her a visit and tell her where she could stick her psychology degree.

"Well, I think it's brilliant that you're talking to someone about how you feel. You've never been good at that and it's bad to bottle things up for too long. I should know."

"I take it that you and Owen are still continuing with your making up?" I said with a wry smile. Frankie and Owen had disappeared very abruptly from last week's party and had been like a couple of teenagers since. Apparently they'd had a long talk about everything and decided that they would rather make love (constantly) instead of war.

"Yeah. We've just decided to agree to disagree, I guess. Life is what it is and us falling out with each other isn't helping anyone. Angelica is going to do what she's going to do regardless of how I feel and maybe I should have just allowed her to get on with it all along instead of acting like I knew best. Although I have to say that she's been much quieter than usual which I'm not sure how to take – but I'm not going to overanalyse it."

"Just be thankful for the peace," I said, wishing that I had some as my head was constantly turning with the pressure of trying to figure out what to do to make everything right again. Perhaps I should just take a leaf out of Frankie's book and let life run its course. It appeared that everyone else was doing that so why shouldn't I?

After I left the college I made my way home and decided to take a long hot soak in the bath. I emptied in half a bottle of bubble bath that promised to be a stress reliever and took a magazine with me in the hope of retrieving a few hours relaxation before Luke came home.

Luke was my ultimate saviour. He was there for me when everyone else gave up on me, loving me unconditionally and promising that everything would be alright.

I had just stepped into the bath and was sighing in

pleasure as I felt all my muscles ease in appreciation of the warm water when I heard a knock at the front door.

I decided to ignore it and continued to lie there, hoping that whoever it was would go away. It was probably the postman or someone coming to read the meter anyway and they could just come back because I was otherwise engaged.

There was a knock on the door again, heavier this time, and I swore loudly before getting up abruptly and taking half the bath water with me. Why was it that when you were in a compromising position that people decided it would be a good time to call?

I pulled a towel around me, stomped downstairs and flung open the door, preparing to let my nuisance caller know in no uncertain terms that it was an inconvenient time and could they kindly feck away off so I could continue my ablutions in peace.

Instead of encountering a smiling salesman, however, I opened the door to find my mother instead – brandishing flowers and what looked and smelt like a tin of my favourite homemade shortbread.

"You'll get your death of cold standing there in the nip," she commented before brushing me aside and making her way to the kitchen where she switched the kettle on.

"I was in the bath," I said somewhat unnecessarily. I think she knew that I wasn't in the habit of going around the house trying on the contents of the towel cupboard.

"I gathered," she said. "I called to your work and was speaking to Frankie. She said she thought I'd find you here."

"And now you're here, is there something you wanted?" I asked, not wanting to sound abrupt but dying to know the reason for her visit. Mammy rarely had time to leave the hotel and her schedule usually dictated that when we met up I called to see her.

"I wanted to make sure that you were alright. I've hardly spoken to you this past few weeks and I'm worried about you." She came closer and scrutinised me in the manner of a doctor conducting an examination. "You look pale and peaky. Have you been eating properly? You know that you can't afford to let yourself get run down. Especially not now when such momentous things are happening in your life."

"And what exactly is that supposed to mean?" I asked.

"It won't be easy but I suppose if it's what you want I'll have to just deal with it. You have a right to know and, although nobody will ever come close to your father, if it contents you at long last then you have my blessing."

There was silence and for once in my life I found myself short of something to say.

"Well, don't look so shocked, Ruby. You knew I'd come round to the idea eventually. With you there isn't much choice, is there? It's a case of either support you or get left behind, so here I am."

I still didn't know what to say so I bit into a piece of shortbread instead and continued to stare at her in disbelief.

"I thought you weren't talking to me," I said eventually. "You sent me home in bad humour and any time we've spoken on the phone you've stayed on with me for all of two seconds before rushing off. I thought I'd lost you as well."

"What do you mean 'lost' and why do you say 'as well'?" Mammy asked, handing me a cup of coffee and motioning for me to sit down.

"I haven't heard from Georgie at all. I've tried phoning her several times and even left her a message but there's been no word. I seem to have well and truly burnt my bridges there, you'll be glad to hear."

"That's unfair, Ruby!" my mother cried indignantly. "I have nothing against Georgie. How could I have? She's responsible for bringing you into the world and my life would certainly be a lot duller and less satisfying without you in it."

"It would be a lot more peaceful and less stressful too."

"Peace and quiet are overrated concepts. Give me noisy and annoying any day."

"Thanks, I think," I said. "So does this mean that we're friends again then?"

"Oh for goodness sake, Ruby, we were never not friends! You make us sound like a pair of children squabbling in a playground." Mammy was sounding impatient now. "I just needed time to get used to the idea and now I have, so let's just get it over and done with."

"Mammy, it's a little hard for me to get more information about my father when my mother isn't talking to me. Her input in the matter is rather essential."

"Well, you need to talk to her then, don't you?"

My mother handed me my mobile and continued to sip her coffee.

Tentatively I rang the number again and this time it was answered on the second ring.

"You must be psychic," Georgie greeted me. "I was going to get in touch with you today. You'll be glad to hear that your grandfather is at home with me where he belongs and doing well. He's been asking about you and I thought it would be nice for you both to see each other in better circumstances. Would you like to come and visit this weekend?"

This was all nearly too good to be true. First Isobel turns up being all reasonable and nice and now Georgie asks me to come and stay with her.

"Ruby, are you still there?" she asked gently.

"I am," I said. "I'm just surprised, that's all. I didn't think I'd ever hear from you again. I tried ringing you and left a message and when you never got back to me I assumed that you didn't want to know me any more."

"Of course I want to know you. I'm sorry about what happened. I shouldn't have been so hard on you. None of this is your fault. I shouldn't have put you into a situation in the first place where you were likely to meet Marcella. She's never going to approve of our relationship so it's probably best if you and I keep in touch but the rest of my family stay out of it. I suppose I just wanted you with me at a time when I needed some support and, if truth be told, a part of me wanted to show you off as well."

"It's important to me that you believe that I didn't hit her," I said, screwing my eyes shut. I didn't want to go back over old ground but needed to be reassured that she wouldn't be taken in by any more lies.

"I believe you," she said quietly.

I smiled sadly and thought it a pity that things had to be that way but was willing to accept it. After all, all I had ever wanted was to find Georgie and I had got her and I was going to make sure that we'd never be apart again.

"Tell Charlie I'm delighted that he's feeling better and give him a big squeeze from me and tell him that I'll bring him some of my mother's homemade rhubarb and ginger jam that he likes so much when I come down. There's also something I'd like to talk to you about."

"And I think I know what it is," she said gently.

We said our goodbyes and as I hung up the phone I couldn't quite believe the difference an afternoon could make.

Perhaps Sonia Bernstein's psychology degree wasn't that useless after all.

41

Jodi

I loved everything about the little shop. It was bright and airy, smelt of spices and cinnamon, and going into it was like entering a parallel universe where time had stood still. It was full of other people's things that each had its own story to tell. Even at a young age when I was helping my father at the auctioneers' I always used to wonder why people had given away their belongings. Every little trinket, bauble, ornament, painting and piece of furniture had had a previous owner who for some reason either willingly wanted to get rid of them or was forced to give them up. And, whatever condition they were in, they were now destined for a new home where whoever bought them would either lovingly refurbish them or enjoy keeping them in their current state as an antique.

I had started to halve my time between the bistro and the antiques shop where I worked late on a Tuesday and Thursday night sorting out merchandise, then all day on a Saturday. Tom had employed a student to cover my

Saturday shift and I couldn't honestly say that I missed the mad rush that ensued on the busiest day of the week where the bistro would be heaving full of people. I much preferred the visiting clientele that came to the antiques shop. Fabian had made quite a name for himself for being an honest and reliable supplier with an astute eye for valuing goods and people travelled a considerable distance to see his well-stocked shop that had become even more organised and orderly since I had got my hands on it. My father had heard of Quinn Antiques and told me it was a reputable establishment and that he was glad I was finally working for someone with a few scruples who appreciated me – and I couldn't have agreed with him more.

Ashley, according to my mother, was still pining for me and had apparently screwed up several good deals through sleep deprivation and lack of concentration.

"He's a broken man, you know, Joanna. It's terrible what you've done to him."

I had given up arguing with her. Even if I did tell her the truth she probably wouldn't believe me. Besides, I had more reason than ever to keep quiet about what was going on. There was a plan on the horizon and Ashley Crozier was shortly going to be sorrier than he ever thought possible. I'd soon give him something proper to cry about. The only reason why he was upset was because he'd been caught and he hadn't spared a single thought about the number of people whose lives he had wrecked in the process.

The day Pamela came to visit we found that we got on well. In different circumstances we might have been friends but forging a connection with her in the current climate was never going to be an option. She was Ashley's wife – the mother of his three sons and she had been around long before her husband had taken a fancy to me. It appeared that Pamela was a stay-at-home type of girl. She had never wanted to be the centre of attention and dinner dates with clients and meetings in foreign destinations had never appealed to her. Like me, she had loved her husband but was content to bring up his children and lead a quiet but comfortable life in the huge house he gave her along with a monthly allowance. It was obvious to both of us that what Pamela didn't possess Ashley thought he could find elsewhere and that's where I had come in. I was his trophy wife. Someone to parade around parties and social gatherings who had the added credentials of a degree in Public Relations and a fierce will to succeed. I had been flattered by his attention and like a fool thought that I was all he needed or wanted. A rushed wedding in a secret location, that I now knew to be illegal, should have rung warning bells in my ears but he had plausible explanations for everything and I had accepted them all. God, I was such a sucker and he was so good at blowing smoke up my ass.

"It's time you stopped daydreaming and went and took a lunch break," Fabian said as he opened the door with his elbow and came into the shop carrying another box.

"I think I'll go back to the house actually," I said. "I need to check the post and do a few things."

It was a bright clear day and I enjoyed walking back towards the house but my good mood vanished when I saw Mr Peebles sitting on the steps waiting for me with his beer belly hanging over the belt of his jeans and his hair jutting out in all directions.

"Lovely to see you, Mssssss Crozier," he said, looking me up and down.

"Can't say the same," I muttered, walking past him and fishing the keys out of my pocket. "Look, I don't have much time here. Was there something you wanted?"

"I'd like a great many things from you, Mssssss Crozier, but mainly I popped by to give you this."

He gave me an envelope and I tore it open in front of him without ceremony.

"What the hell is this?" I demanded.

"It's notification that I'm giving you one week's notice to move out," he drawled, puffing on a cigarette.

"You can't do that," I thundered. "You can't just arrive here and tell me that I have to find somewhere to live within a week. It's impossible."

"You moved in on a week's notice so there's no reason why you can't move out in the same time. You didn't pay a deposit so I don't owe you anything. Where you go or what you do is no longer any of my concern. I have other people interested in this place and they'll be much less trouble than you are."

I narrowed my eyes and gave him the dirtiest look I could muster. "Fine." I snapped. "I'll be out within a week. Good riddance to bad rubbish."

I ran in and closed the door and felt a flutter of apprehension in my stomach. What the hell was I going to do now? How was I going to find somewhere else at such short notice?

When I went to leave Mr Peebles had gone but the effects of his news still lingered and it was in poor spirits that I returned to work where Fabian was running around like a blue-arsed fly, trying to get things on display as he had heard there was a coach party in town.

"Can you move some of this new stock back into the

storeroom and we'll try and get as much of the old stuff sold as possible? There are one or two beauties in here that I wouldn't mind working on myself."

I nodded mutely and started to lift things but as I approached the back of the shop Fabian walked in front of me and peered into my face with a concerned look.

"Have you been crying?" he asked awkwardly. "Is something wrong? Have I said something to upset you?"

Despite my determination not to let Mr Peebles and his horrible crumby excuse for a squat annoy me, I felt my bottom lip start to jut and was horrified to feel my eyes well up.

"Hey, what's the matter?" Fabian asked, taking the box I was carrying and gently guiding me to a chair. "Can I do anything to help? I don't want to intrude in your private business but I'm a good listener, or so I'm told. It's what comes of being brought up as the only boy in a house full of girls, I guess."

"Could you take out a contract on a very sleazy little man's head and tell the hitman I'd like it to hurt?" I said with great feeling.

"This calls for a cup of tea and a caramel square," Fabian said, swiftly flicking on the kettle in the corner before turning his attention back to me.

"Start from the beginning," he said, turning to face me with an earnest expression.

Fabian had taken my hand and was leading me towards a set of stairs that was located at the back of the shop.

"Where are we going?" I enquired.

"You'll see," he said, grinning broadly. "I need to show you something that I think you might like."

"Why do you think your storage space would appeal to me?"

"Well, that's what I've been using it as for a few months but that's not actually its main purpose."

Fabian produced a large set of keys from his pocket and went through them until he had found the right one.

"I must warn you that this place hasn't been touched in quite a while and is still in the same condition that my mother left it in," he explained. "But it might just be the answer to your problems."

He opened the door and I followed him inside and saw that instead of a storage room I was actually walking into fully equipped living quarters.

"My mother's getting on a bit and the steps were becoming too much for her so she has moved to a bungalow on the outskirts of town. She always loved it here though. I think you'll agree that the place has an old-world charm that is pretty unique?"

I certainly could and once I had managed to lift my jaw from the floor and regained my ability to speak it was all I could do not to hug him.

"So what are you saying here?" I asked, wanting to make sure that I had definitely grasped the right end of the stick.

"What I'm saying is that you need somewhere to live, this place is vacant and because it has been in the family for quite a long time I didn't want to advertise it in case I got a tenant I didn't like. So I guess what I'm saying is that it's yours if you like it."

"Like it?" I said in a high-pitched squeak. I loved it.

It had high ceilings and long windows and had been carefully decorated. I could see that it had been well taken care of. There was also a lovely welcoming feel to it.

Unlike my current abode I reckoned that the feng shui was definitely on target here.

"I moved a few pieces from downstairs up in here after my mother moved out and if you like them I'll let them stay – or I can get rid of them and let you bring in your own stuff."

"Don't you dare," I said as I looked at the candy-striped chaise lounge, old-fashioned sideboard with its own writer's bureau and the glass-covered coffee table. They were all in fantastic condition and gave the place the right amount of yesteryear charm without looking out of date.

The kitchen was small but serviceable with creamy-coloured units and a small table that could seat two or three comfortably. I definitely wouldn't be having any large dinner parties – those days were long gone.

There were two compact bedrooms, both of which were furnished adequately, and the bathroom was a decent size and had its own bath and walk-in shower. There was also a door that led from the kitchen out to a small balcony where someone had planted several window boxes and there was a green patio set.

"My mother used to come out here when the weather was good. You have a good view of the town and the smells coming from the bakery across the street would make your mouth water."

"This place is very deceiving," I said thoughtfully. "I never in a million years thought that you could have such fantastic living space above a shop."

"People don't realise how far back the shop goes and how much space we have," Fabian said smiling. "So, are you interested? But please don't feel pressured. It's just a suggestion. I'd like to be able to help you out if I can."

314

"Oh, please! Who would need to be pressurised to stay here? If you saw the state of my current living conditions this place could pass as Buckingham Palace in comparison, believe me. How soon can I move in seeing as my current landlord expects me out within the week?"

"I still can't believe that he thinks he can do that. That's not good practice." Fabian frowned. "You normally should be giving a tenant a month's notice."

"Yeah, well, he was never a big believer in good practice. He is a vile specimen of a man who would have gladly accepted my body as payment if rent money happened to be short." I shuddered.

"I'll bear that in mind as well," Fabian said, raising his eyebrows.

(Note to self: please stop making stupid comments to prospective landlord which may lead him to believe that you would consider paying him with a quick romp as opposed to giving him rent money. In fact, shut up and don't talk any more.)

"Go home and pack, Jodi. Here's my mobile number. Give me a call when you're ready and I can help you move your stuff if you like."

It was approximately six hours since I had seen the flat above the shop and I was in the throes of moving my meagre belongings. I had acquired a few new pieces of clothing, several mugs and some bathroom essentials but nothing more than a few boxes' worth of stuff. It was surprising what little you could live with when your back was against the wall as mine had been and, when I thought of the luxury I had left and how meaningless it had all been, I couldn't help but be a tiny bit proud of myself. If you had given me the scenario a year ago and asked me what I might do, I might well not have been able to answer you but here I was, still standing and definitely surviving.

I still couldn't get over my luck. The timing couldn't have been any better and the fact that my new abode was a quaint little place with bags of character was just the icing on the cake. The biggest pleasure for me, however, had been derived from the fact that I had got an incredible kick out of breaking the news to Mr Peebles.

I phoned him on the way back to the house and asked Mr Peebles to meet me there. "I'll be out later on today," I had told him in an airy, cheerful tone of voice. "You did me a massive favour asking me to leave. I've found myself a lovely, warm little flat that has been decorated with some taste where the landlord is lovely and not a pervert which is unfortunately the case in some establishments. Good luck with your new tenants, Mr Peebles, and thanks again for everything. Your past behaviour will make me appreciate this move all the more."

He had looked outraged and grossly disappointed. Obviously the game plan had been to wear me down until I was desperate in the hope that I would finally succumb to his advances so that I'd get to keep the roof over my head. Pity he forgot I had a brain.

I looked around the bare walls and smiled in satisfaction. I had come a long way since I had first arrived in Swiftstown and even though I hated my house on the Westvale estate and its horrible owner, I liked what it had represented for me. It symbolised a time when I had literally had to pull myself up by the bootstraps when the odds had been stacked against me and I had succeeded and surely things could only get better from now on.

42

Frankie

"'*A boozy taste of sunshine containing melon liqueur and fresh juices*'! I'll have the Tropicana, please," I said, after deliberating over the menu for what seemed like hours while the waiter hovered over me. If he had yawned loudly and looked pointedly at his watch it wouldn't have surprised me.

"We can stay for a few if you like and work our way down the menu," Jodi said as she ordered a Cosmopolitan and settled back in one of the comfy bucket-shaped seats.

"Don't tempt me," I said. "I'd love to but I'd be too scared of the after-effects and I have a lot of work to do in the morning."

"How's your new assistant fitting in?"

"She's a grade A flake," I answered in disgust. "I give her work to do, she doesn't listen properly because she's either preoccupied with doing her make-up or making eyes at every passing male, and then I end up having to redo it all myself. Honestly, I'd be better off on my own.

She's more of a hindrance than a help. I've already given her two verbal warnings about the standard of her work but the seriousness of her predicament doesn't seem to have sunk in."

"How the hell did she manage to get the job?" Jodi asked. "I'm sure there was any God's amount of other people who would have been more suitable."

"Just about anyone else with half a brain would be more suitable than this airhead. I've looked at her interview sheet and she must be one of these people who's very good at talking the talk but not so impressive when it comes to walking the walk."

"Sounds like you've got your work cut out for you."

"I have, Jodi. Please say you'll take the job offer when they approach you and tell you what a mammoth mistake they've made."

Jodi shrugged her shoulders and shook her head. "You know, Frankie, it's funny. When I first heard that I hadn't got the job I was totally devastated. The thought of working in the environment I was used to had kept me going. I was almost using the opportunity to test myself to make sure that I still had *it* and, when you told me that day that it had been given to someone else, I looked upon it as such a mark of failure. But now I'm so glad it happened. Things have a very funny way of working out for the best. If I hadn't started work in the bistro I would never have met Anna or the rest of the girls, I wouldn't have been able to prove to myself that I could do something different and that in turn wouldn't have brought me in touch with Fabian who has given me a roof over my head and work I enjoy."

As the waiter brought our drinks I nodded in agreement and thought about how true that was. "I'm a firm believer in the fact that our lives are all mapped out for us," I said. "Someone somewhere has a plan and somehow some way we'll end up doing everything we're supposed to. Mind you, when the higher power was making my plan I wish he had made it a bit simpler to follow or at least provided me with a compass."

We clinked our glasses together.

"To my lovely friend Jodi and her gorgeous new home minus the manky landlord!" I proposed after which we both enjoyed a deep delicious mouthful of alcohol blended with juices.

The door opened and Jodi waved to let Anna and a few of the girls from the bistro know where we were sitting.

"You just missed the toast," Jodi said.

"That's terrible," Anna replied. "We'll just have to buy another round and keep drinking to your good fortune all night."

"I'll second that," I said and raised my glass again. "To peace in our lives and in our hearts!"

"Frankie, I really envy you," Jodi said, clinking her glass against mine again. "You're so wise and one of the most self-assured people I know. It's people like you who help people like me get through."

I laughed and thought it totally ironic that others looked at me and saw someone who was confident in her thoughts and actions, as nothing could have been further from the truth.

"If only you knew what has been happening lately, Jodi, you wouldn't say that. Things have been very messy and Owen and I have just about come through it. Thankfully things are much better between us now but his daughter is a little nightmare. She leaves a trail of emotional destruction behind her and doesn't give the after-effects of her selfish actions a moment's thought."

Even as I uttered the words I felt nervous about what the future held. Things were teetering on the brink at the moment as there were no rows or arguments as such but the chances of things staying that way for any length of time were as unsteady and unreliable as a house of cards.

As if by magic and as if my thoughts had materialised into true life – on cue Brutal Brenda walked through the doors of the cocktail bar with a group of associates. As she demanded that the waiter find her a table close to the window without so much as a 'please' I felt my hopes of having a night off slip away and as Brenda saw me I saw her face take on an expression of cold triumph and my heart sank.

"And just who is that giving you the evil eye?" Jodi said.

"That would be Angelica's lovely auntie," I said, then finished in a whisper: "Ruby and I refer to her affectionately as Brutal Brenda."

"Ooh, I can see why. That is one radioactive glare. I take it that you two wouldn't exactly be friends then?"

"To be honest I'd rather be friends with a rattlesnake than have her anywhere near me. It would be much safer and probably less poisonous. She is positively vile."

I was determined not to let Brutal Brenda spoil my night but nevertheless felt a cloud descend over me. Not even Gabriel's appearance could cheer me up which was a rarity in itself as Gabriel positively exuded happy vibes.

"I'd love to bitch-slap her into next week," he

commented when Jodi told him why I was so glum. "And who the hell does her hair? The woman is the chief executive of a company that supplies handbags and accessories and yet she has the worst hair I have ever seen. Turn her upside down and she'd make an excellent mop."

Brutal Brenda was a little folically challenged as her dark hair always did seem to be out and out frizzy but then I supposed it matched her unruly attitude towards everyone around her.

"Well, we all can't be perfect like you," I said, taking in Gabriel's new 'do'. He was the only man I knew who admitted openly to having his hair dyed using full-head easy mesh and he was also the only man it suited. His multicoloured locks also defined his personality which was riotous and jovial and totally different to anything you had ever experienced before. I wondered absentmindedly what my hair said about me . . . shoulder-length, blonde and boring. *Hmmmmm* . . . it probably said 'needs roots done and a more exciting style but as owner is busy mother it's all she has time for'.

My phone vibrated. It was a text message from Ruby.

Wish me luck. About to meet Georgie now. Pray I dont feck it up again.

I responded to Ruby and showed the message to Gabriel who added a few kisses and hugs and smiley faces onto the end of it.

"She'll be grand," he said confidently. "I always said it would sort itself out and it will."

I excused myself and went to the ladies' room which is where I had the misfortune of meeting Brutal Brenda coming out of one of the cubicles.

321

I pretended not to see her as I went over to the mirror to apply some lip gloss and fluff out my hair.

She went to walk away but then stalled and I sighed as I looked in the glass and saw her coming back with a nasty sneer on her face.

"So where's Angelica tonight then?" she enquired.

"She's with her father, I presume," I answered shortly, wondering why I even bothered to respond.

"Wrong," she said, tapping her finger on the side of her nose. "I know something you don't know but then why would she confide in you? She can't talk to you, never has been able to but that's no surprise. You're not her mother and never will be."

I was getting extremely sick of hearing Brutal Brenda trot out the same old lines and wouldn't have bothered even replying only I was curious to know where she thought Angelica was.

"So where is she then?" I asked.

"Well, that would be our little secret now, wouldn't it?"

She left me standing there as she nearly skipped out of the ladies' room in glee.

"Where is Angelica this evening?" I asked Owen after he had answered the phone.

"Jerome just picked her up and they went away somewhere together," he answered. "Are you having a good time, love?"

"Yeah," I answered absentmindedly as my heart sank.

I was hoping that he'd say that she was in the house, if for no other reason than it would give me the opportunity to go back over to Brutal Brenda and say 'Ha, you were wrong' very loudly in her face but sadly that wasn't going to be the case.

Instinctively I had a bad feeling about it all. The mere fact that Jerome was involved increased my feelings of anxiety one hundred fold.

43

Angelica

I was a bit subdued and knew that Jerome wondered what was wrong as he kept on giving me little sideway glances.

"What's the matter, princess? Are you nervous about meeting our new landlord?"

"No, everything's fine," I lied.

No matter how I tried to convince myself otherwise I simply couldn't warm to the house that Jerome had settled on. The rooms were tiny, there was a funny smell and it had been decorated by someone who obviously thought they were still living in the seventies. He had rung me the evening before and told me that it was a done deal and I tried to be happy but couldn't muster any enthusiasm. I had been annoyed that we hadn't had the opportunity to look at other places and that he had gone ahead and made the decision without me, but I was getting used to him taking over in every situation so it came as no surprise really.

The place in question was small and dingy and I hadn't got a good feeling about the house when I viewed it and although I didn't heed Frankie very often, something she'd said had always stayed with me. She always talked about walking into my father's house for the first time and feeling like she'd come home and that's what I wanted. I wanted a sense of warmness and calm that would help me believe that I was doing the right thing but it just wasn't there.

"I'll make sure that we do it up nicely, Angelica. We can go shopping at the weekend if you like and pick up some colour charts and swatches of material and you can put your own stamp on it."

I smiled and rested my hand over his for a second and like a mantra told myself over and over again that everything was going to be fine. My nerves and doubts would disappear once we were together properly.

We parked outside the house and I saw that the door was already open, revealing the horrible brown-and-orange swirly pattern of the hall walls within. Jerome strode ahead of me and impatiently waited for me at the door.

"Stop dragging your heels, Angelica. Anyone would think that you didn't want to make the move and I know that you do."

"It's just me being silly."

"Yes, you're very good at that," he said with a slow smile.

The landlord was inside waiting for us in the living room and curiously he was like a human extension of the premises he was letting out as he too was messy, unkempt, smelly and in great need of a makeover. I also didn't appreciate being in such close proximity to him when he was making arrangements to pick up the rent and standing particularly close to me.

"Fresh young thing," he said to Jerome, winking at him. "You kids have a good time in here. It's about time this place saw some action again. My last tenant was a feckin' uptight bitch but I know what she would have needed to loosen her up."

He made a rude gesture by putting his fist up and I saw that Jerome was laughing companionably with him as if he had just made a very witty joke. I didn't find any of it amusing.

The landlord left and then it was just Jerome and me . . . but this is what I had always wanted and now I had it so it was up to me to make the best of it.

"So what do you think then?" he said with a flourish as if we were standing in the middle of the Colosseum and marvelling at its beauty.

"I'm sure it will be fine with a few licks of paint and some new carpet," I said. "We'll need to get a few air-fresheners in place as well."

"Pity there's no instant remedy for you," Jerome said, sounding moody and on edge again.

I was obviously going to have to start thinking inwardly and turn the loudspeaker off.

I went out and opened the front door to get some air and to get away from the fustiness, and took deep breaths as I stood outside. I slowly made my way down the steps and through the gate and watched as people walked by in the dusky evening light. I quite liked the fact that the house was on the edge of town where we would be close to everything but not so close that we'd have no privacy. I started to walk down the street and suddenly recoiled as I saw Katie coming towards me with a group of girls who lived in the same estate. I went to turn back but it was too late because they had already seen me and I could hear them laughing and whispering.

Katie kept resolutely silent as she walked on without turning her head even though there were comments from a few of the others and snorts of derision. I felt my cheeks flood with colour.

"Angelica, are you alright?" I heard a voice ask and as I looked up I saw Paddy McCourt. "Pay no attention to those bitches. They're just jealous of you."

"I don't know that there's much to be jealous of," I muttered but I was pleased all the same.

"I'm just here visiting a few mates. We're thinking of heading into town for a while."

I smiled and told him I hoped he had a good night. He grinned and walked on.

When I re-entered the house I couldn't see Jerome anywhere downstairs but found him upstairs looking out the window.

"What are you doing?" I asked, thinking that the walls would be nice in here if they were painted a nice bright turquoise or perhaps lavender. A few pictures would certainly brighten the place up and I'd get some colourful duvets and a rug and maybe some candles and a lamp to match – if Jerome came up with the money.

I was lost in thought as I looked around me so when he hit me I was left completely winded by the impact of his fist on my shoulder and lost my balance and fell to the floor. For a moment I felt that I couldn't breathe and seemed to be paralysed and rooted to the spot even though my first instinct was to run away.

"You stand outside our new home and have the cheek to talk to other fellas that have nothing to do with us?

When you're with me you're with me and *me only* – is that clear? I haven't spent all my time making plans, for you just to throw them away as if they are of no importance. Who is he?" He was now hunkered down beside me and I huddled into the floor and covered my head as I was scared and just hoping that he wouldn't hit me again.

"I've told you before," I whimpered. "He's a boy I go to school with."

"Do you fancy him?" Jerome demanded, clenching and unclenching his fists. "When you're with me do you really wish that you were with him? Go on, admit it, you wee slut! That's what you think, isn't it?"

He raised his hand and I covered my face but he punched me in the stomach this time and I coughed so hard that I thought my lungs might explode with the strain. Water poured from my eyes as I continued to gasp and I felt like I might pass out.

Jerome left the room, still muttering to himself, leaving me lying slumped against a wall. I was so shocked that I could hardly breathe but somehow I summoned the strength to stand up on wobbly legs. I made my way down the stairs, my breathing quickening with every step. I walked out the front door and didn't look behind me.

I walked down the street and saw Paddy again talking to a few others.

"Are you alright, Angelica?" he asked for the second time that night as he watched me stumble on the pavement. I must have looked like I had been pulled through a hedge backwards as my hair was messed and my coat was hanging off me at my elbows and I panicked as he crossed the street towards me.

"Get away from me! Don't come near me!" I cried, my voice sounding manic and highly strung, even to my own ears, and as quickly as I could I half-walked half-ran in the direction of home.

44

Ruby

I had been delighted to see Charlie looking so much better and he seemed to be getting back to his old self. There was certainly nothing wrong with his appetite as his eyes lit up when he spied the cinnamon and apple pie and rhubarb tart Mammy had sent with me along with some home-made jam and freshly baked bread.

Georgie's cottage was warm and comfy and Charlie looked very much at home sitting in a high-backed armchair in her living room in front of the old fashioned stone hearth. Once we'd had tea and Charlie had retired to bed, Georgie and I finally had a chance to talk and it was with nervous trepidation that I watched her close the door and smooth down her clothes carefully before she sat down on the sofa opposite me.

I stared at Georgie for a while and then repeated the name she had just said.

"Daniel Madigan."

She nodded with closed eyes.

"Is he who I think he is?" I asked tentatively, excited and nervous and apprehensive all at once.

"He's your father, Ruby."

"Okay," I said, not knowing how else to respond. Suddenly I was involuntarily transported back to Belfast when I had made the decision to find my birth mother. Again I found myself sitting on a cold window ledge reading information from a birth certificate and feeling engulfed by a wave of different emotions. I couldn't stop looking at her name on the page, and in the same way I now found myself saying his name over and over again in my head, getting used to the feel and sound of it and being overcome by the significance of it.

Daniel Madigan. I liked the sound of that name. Growing up the main man in my life was called Albert Ross. He had been the one who had been there for me since I was a baby right up until the horrendous moment when he had died and left me. He was my daddy but this other man, Daniel Madigan, was my father.

Georgie was studying me and I felt her discomfort and knew that she was willing me to say something.

"I'm sorry," I said at last. "This must be difficult for you but I'm in shock. At last I know the names of both my parents and you really don't know what that means to me."

"I think I do," she said softly sighing.

"Is he still alive?" I asked.

"Unfortunately he died some years ago, Ruby. He died before we found each other. I'm sorry."

I was momentarily winded. It was an awful feeling

being given something one minute only to have it snatched away the next but nevertheless I knew more than I did and that had to count for something.

I swallowed. "Can you tell me about him?"

Georgie looked distinctly uncomfortable and I knew that she was finding this all very difficult.

"Look," I said trying to be reasonable. "All I ask is that we have this one conversation. Just help me to understand what happened and I promise that after tonight we don't ever have to mention it again."

Georgie had a rueful look on her face that said she wished this was true and was fidgeting in the way that I do when something is playing on my mind.

"Please continue," I gently prompted again. "And understand that I don't want to upset you or be responsible for raking up unhappy memories from the past but I need to know. And whatever happened then, at least we've found each other now and that's a good thing, right?"

"Ruby, giving birth to you and finding you will always be things to cherish but I need you to understand that this wasn't a cut-and-dried case of boy meets girl, does something foolish and ends up pregnant. I did something very stupid and dangerous and looking back on it now I'm so ashamed. It's no wonder that my sisters can't look at me without thinking about what a troublemaker I am. All these years I've missed you and yearned for you but the only small comfort I've had is that my father isn't in possession of all the facts. He doesn't know who your father is and hopefully never will as the shock would literally kill him."

I sat and listened to her and watched as a myriad of emotions played themselves out through her expression that switched from vulnerability to sadness to regret in a matter of seconds. I was transfixed.

"What on earth are you supposed to have done that was so wrong? Who was he?"

"He was an older man. A much older man. He was a man who had commitments and responsibilities, a man who should have known better than to do what he did but then we were both to blame for what happened. It was a moment of weakness that brought about terrible consequences for everyone involved."

A thought suddenly struck me and I felt very alarmed and afraid and for the first time was unsure if I wanted her to continue or not, but then curiosity got the better of me again.

"Did he take advantage of you?" I asked, cringing at the thought of being a by-product of a forced sexual encounter.

"Oh no, please don't think that," Georgie said. "It wasn't forced at all. It just simply shouldn't have happened. Looking back on it now I think we were both vulnerable. My mother died when I was sixteen and as the youngest in the house I felt like a burden on everyone else. I missed her dreadfully but could never quite properly put it into words because I was constantly being reminded of the fact that the others had to look out for me as my father had, for a time, gone to pieces and ended up on strong medication that made him very tired. He spent a lot of his time in bed and I spent a lot of my time watching him."

My heart went out to her. I looked at her and could almost see the pain crystallise and form in her eyes as she said the words. It was clear that this wasn't something she often talked about, if indeed she had ever talked about it at all.

I moved from the chair opposite and sat beside her and held her hand and at that gesture watched her crumble and give in to her emotions.

"I honestly never meant to hurt anyone!" she sobbed, looking wretched. "I had always been close to Daniel. He and my father had always got on well but I wasn't the only one who was in a vulnerable position. At the time that this happened he was going through his own personal hell and I suppose we were taking the opportunity to comfort each other. I had never looked on him as anything other than a friend I suppose but in one moment he went from being a friend to something else entirely and we both regretted it instantly. It was a moment of madness."

"And here I am," I said.

"I don't mean to make it sound like you are any sort of mistake or that I have any regrets about you. If I could turn the clock back I'd always have had you. I'd just have changed the circumstances and given you a father that was free to have that role."

"He was married then?" I asked gently.

"He was. He was a married man and his wife was dying. She was in her forties and suffered from Alzheimer's that was very progressive in a short space of time but that didn't stop him from being her husband or her his wife. I liked his wife very much and she was always very good to me. After my mother died and before she got sick she took great care of me and tried her best to assume a mothering role but more often than not she was made to feel like she wasn't welcome."

My lip curled as I took an educated guess at who the resident party pooper might have been.

"Lovely Marcella?"

Georgie nodded and continued dabbing her eyes and sniffing into a hankie. She was very upset and I felt terrible for putting her through talking about it. I suddenly thought about Sonia Bernstein and what her job must be like and thought she was welcome to it. If counselling meant that you had to reduce people to snivelling wrecks all in the name of progress then I'd rather not bother thanks. She must feel permanently exhausted.

"Would you rather we left it at that for this evening," I said, hoping against hope that she would disagree with me and she did.

"No, Ruby. I've been building myself up for this and want it out in the open. Maybe then I can try and let go of some of the hurt I've carried around with me all these years."

I had more thoughts of Sonia and all her preaching about putting the past behind and being more open about one's feelings.

I looked at her expectantly and she took a deep breath.

"I couldn't believe it had happened and afterwards I avoided him and didn't have any contact with him. I was so ashamed about what I had done and very confused about everything. I tried to bury it in the back of my mind but that was a short-lived exercise as a couple of months later after endless bouts of sickness I discovered that I was pregnant and then there really was no escaping it. The next time I saw him was to tell him that I was having a baby. It was a terribly sad day for both of us. He and his wife had always wanted children but had never been able to have any and here I was telling him that I was expecting a child but in all the wrong circumstances. He was heartbroken and I was feeling more alone than I had ever been in my life.

"We didn't see each other for a while after that but then one day the postman brought a letter that was from him, offering to help me in any way he could and saying that he'd like to be part of our child's life. Daniel was a solicitor and did quite well for himself. He had his own practice and was well respected and I had to think about him too. News of this scandal would have ruined his reputation and standing in the community so I knew what a magnanimous and selfless gesture he was making.

"I didn't know how I felt. Part of me was happy that he wasn't running away but another part of me was disturbed at the thought of further involvement with him. I had never liked him in that way and his involvement would only have made things much worse as we would constantly have been hiding things from everyone else and the pressure would have been too much to bear. I had resolved to have my baby and to keep it but never to disclose who the father was. I was trying to protect him as well as myself and you and my family. I wrote him a letter in response thanking him for his offer but telling him that I wanted no further contact with him. It might seem cruel but distancing myself from the whole situation seemed to be my only coping mechanism. I had planned to leave the country after I had you. I had thought about going to Scotland as we had relations in Edinburgh and thought that I could start a new life there where nobody knew me or what my circumstances were."

I realised that I hadn't had a breath in about a minute as I had been listening so intently to her story.

"And what did Daniel say in response to your letter?"

Georgie closed her eyes and when she opened them again the pain was evident.

"He never got it. I was careless and left it lying on my bedroom dresser to post but unfortunately before I had the chance to send it, it was discovered."

"Feckin' Marcella," I said, gritting my teeth, knowing full well that I was right again.

Georgie nodded mutely in agreement.

"*Bitch*," I said with great feeling.

I suddenly understood why Georgie was always so jumpy around her. Marcella was no better than a common blackmailer and had obviously held her knowledge over her sister for all these years. It was why she had been able to have me taken away so forcibly and also obviously why Georgie hadn't fought back harder.

I got up and started to pace about, trying to grasp how different life might have been if that letter had reached its intended destination without interference. Georgie had seemed pretty sure of her intentions but who knew how Daniel Madigan could have reacted or what sort of a life could have lain ahead of me.

I thought about all I had gained from having Isobel and Albert as parents and how I never would have had the lovely father-daughter relationship that I had always treasured and still held in the highest regard. I thought about Luke and the probability of not having him in my life and of all the friends I had, the experiences collected over the years and the way of life I had acquired.

Equally, I thought about Georgie and what life would have been like with her. I would have been the daughter of a single parent living in Edinburgh and as well as having mad hair would have had a mad accent as well.

The thought made me smile and rescued me from the whirlwind of emotions in my head.

"Life would have been very different for all of us," I said gently. "And I'm so sorry that you've had to live with that all these years. I'm so glad you shared this with me. Where is he buried? Can I visit his grave? Have you any photographs of him?"

Georgie snapped her head up and gave me a startled look. "Ruby, please don't ask me anything more. This is all I can give you. It's better that you pretend that you don't know anything."

"More secrets and more lies and more pretending," I said wearily. "What is it with this family?"

Georgie sat down again and put her head in her hands. "You don't understand, Ruby."

"Make me."

She looked up at me and I saw a hollow sadness in her face.

"Daniel Madigan was married to your grandfather's only sister. He was my uncle by marriage. There – are you happy now that you know everything?"

I sat down heavily as some of my worst fears were realised. I had played out the scenario that my father could have been a soldier or a married man or even the local priest but this was something else altogether. My father was my grandfather's brother-in-law. All of a sudden I was struck by something my mother had said to me a long time ago.

"Sometimes, Ruby, there are things best left unsaid and undiscovered, that you'd be better off not knowing."

And looking at Georgie's shattered face, it appeared that she had been right.

45

Jodi

It had been a whole two weeks since I had moved into my new home but truthfully I felt like I had been there all my life.

In the short time that I had lived there all hands had been on deck and with the help of my good friends I made a few alterations without changing the place too much. The bathroom had needed a lick of paint to freshen it up and I had also brightened the kitchen with a fresh coat of creamy magnolia and got the units touched up with a beautiful dove-grey colour. Anna had loaned me her son, Paddy, for the duration of my refurbishing and he had been a great help.

Fabian had told me to treat the place like my own and I had felt comfortable and privileged in doing so and enjoyed giving the flat my own personal touch. I loved it so much that coming home in the evenings was a pleasure and I found it hard to tear myself away – apart from when the suggestion for cocktails was made of course.

Frankie and I had started making it a regular little outing and Gabriel had also joined us on a few occasions.

As a weekly promotional concept I had suggested that we run a Ladies Night and so far it had been a great success. We also had themed movie nights where the drinks reflected the film in question. So far our *Pretty Woman* evening with its 'Lady Scarlett' and 'Cherry Hooker' cocktails and *Dirty Dancing* night with its 'Dance with a Dream' and 'Dirty Martini' cocktails had been stuffed to capacity and Fabian was doing a happy dance at the fact that his business had attracted such great custom.

I seemed to be doing more and more work for Fabian in both the antiques shop and the bar so I supposed it was inevitable that sooner or later I would have to say goodbye to my budding waitressing career.

When Anna had called in to the antiques shop to see me and I told her, she had put her fingers in her ears and sang loudly.

"*I am not hearing this!*" she crowed in an out-of-tune alto.

"I'll miss you all too," I said regretfully, "but there simply aren't enough hours in the day any more and I can't be in three places at once."

"And the lovely Fabian wants you all to himself," Anna finished mischievously. "We know."

"Anna," I said in a warning tone.

"You can deny it all you want but it's as plain as the eye in your head that the man likes you," she continued undeterred. "And what's more you like him too."

"Of course I do," I had responded. "He's my boss and my landlord and he was good to me and helped me out at a time when I really needed it so what's not to like?"

"You," she said pointing at me in an accusatory manner, "are an expert at missing the point."

"And *you* know that at this moment in time men are the last thing on my mind. So go pick on somebody else because I can categorically state that I am not now nor ever will I be interested in Fabian Quinn in that way. If he was the last man on the planet I wouldn't have him because I don't want any man."

Anna was visibly cringing in response and I had started to wish that she would stop taking everything so seriously when I felt a presence behind me.

Shit.

"I have a proposal for you," Fabian said stiffly. "Not the type that involves marriage or anything else before you have a heart attack but something that might be of interest to you. I don't have time to explain right now but could call and see you later if you have no objections."

He walked away without saying another word and I grimaced.

"Oh bloody hell, now look what you've done!" I whined at Anna. I could feel I was the colour of a beetroot and a stammering mess. "I'm going to be living in a cardboard box and queuing for the dole if this keeps up. Oh my God," I continued feeling more frantic by the minute, "what the hell must that have sounded like? He'll think I'm an egomaniac with massive tickets on myself. After all, he's very attractive and I can see why other girls would like him but the thought of ever getting involved with another man again makes me feel ill – besides, I still have to deal with the one I had. Ashley Crozier needs to learn that Jodi McDermott is the wrong woman to mess with."

"Sounds ominous," Anna said as she took another sip of her coffee.

"It is," I said with a wry smile.

There was a knock at the door and I jumped around and limbered up in the manner of an athlete needing to loosen up before a marathon. I had no intention of breaking into a sprint, mind you. I just needed to figure out a way to persuade Fabian that I wasn't the rudest person on earth and despite what he had overheard actually did like him. As a friend.

"Please come in," I called out.

Fabian stepped in and stood looking somewhat pensive.

"Thanks," he answered curtly.

"Fabian, before we say any more, I'm terribly sorry about this morning. You weren't meant to hear that."

"Quite obviously not, Jodi."

"Jesus, I didn't mean that the way it sounded. I didn't mean that you weren't meant to hear because we were saying things behind your back. I just meant that you only heard the last bit and it was out of context."

He looked unconvinced and I was unsure whether I should go and find a digging implement so I could make myself an even bigger hole or to take the proverbial shovel and belt Anna over the head with it.

"Look, Anna seems to think that there could be something between us," I said, wanting to die with every word. "And I was just telling her that you've been a wonderful friend but that I'm not ready for anything like that. She's probably got it all wrong anyway as girls who run away from home and end up on the news for being missing aren't usually high on anybody's wish list. But I just needed you to know that I wasn't saying anything about you in particular. It was nothing personal. I think you're lovely with a great personality and very attractive with nice hair and . . ." I trailed off realising I was babbling incessantly.

I was going to kill Anna. Very slowly.

"Well, I'm glad we've got that cleared up," Fabian said eventually, looking less fearsome and more than a little bemused. "For the record I do like you but I'll make sure to make my showers extra cold from now on."

"You've been so good to me." I said. "Do you forgive me?"

"If you manage to pull off the proposal I have in mind, you can insult my male pride all you want."

"So what did you have in mind then?"

"There's an auction – a house contents sale – tomorrow and I can't go so I want you to attend on behalf of Quinn Antiques in my place."

"What?" I squeaked. "I'd love to but I'm scared. I was a little girl the last time I was at an auction."

"I've watched you in the shop, Jodi, and you have a natural eye for what's going to appeal to customers and be of potential value. You're also very gifted when it comes to dealing with people. You're very charming and personable and – and – and have nice hair." He stopped talking and looked at me with a twinkle in his eye.

I threw a cushion at him.

"So what do you say? Do you accept my challenge?"

I was about to tell him that I couldn't possibly but the word 'challenge' made me think and I decided that now would be as good a time as any to test myself.

343

"Okay," I said eventually. "Count me in but you need to explain exactly what we're looking for and who we're dealing with."

We shook hands and smiled.

"I presume it is okay to shake your hand without you thinking I'm making cow eyes at you or initiating a date or anything?" he said drily.

I could only cringe.

I got up early the following morning and felt the familiar buzz that only going to work and tackling something exciting created for me.

I had rung my dad the day before to tell him about the prospective house-contents sale I was going to and we'd had a very animated conversation about what I should look out for and what I should avoid.

I dressed carefully and wore minimal make-up as I wanted to create the right impression as a serious antiques collector. Fabian had already given me all the information I needed about the family in question and I knew that they would only want their valuables going to a reputable dealer who would get a decent price for what they had to offer. There was also the possibility of more business in the future and networking opportunities with others in the trade.

Fabian had allowed me to borrow his car (with more quips about how it wasn't him suggesting sex) and, as I followed the directions and drove to the appointed address, I could feel my excitement build.

I parked and went and had a look around and as I did I jotted down notes and lot numbers of items that interested me in a notepad. It all came to me so naturally and I could still feel the same thrill that I had got all those years ago when my father had secured a sale and promised me an ice cream and pocket money on the way home for helping him.

The auction started about twenty minutes after my arrival. We were all welcomed to the property and told a bit about the history of it and how the owners had made the decision to sell its contents as a result of the death of their father. They stressed that they wanted good homes for their heirlooms and owners who would appreciate and love them as much as their father had.

I was so engrossed in the proceedings and had enjoyed myself so much that I could hardly believe it when the final gavel came down and the auction was declared over.

By the time I returned to the shop I had secured twelve items that I thought were good buys and easy to sell in the shop and was tremendously pleased with myself.

"Didn't you do well?" Fabian whistled as he looked at what I had brought back.

In spite of promising myself that I didn't need anyone else's approval, I basked in his praise and was delighted that he liked what I had done.

"I really enjoyed myself and would welcome going out on more ventures like that. I think that I definitely got into the wrong business when I went into PR. This is what I grew up doing and what I love."

"Well, if you keep on bringing me back pieces of this quality then I'll almost certainly give you a permanent post as a buyer."

I grinned in delight. I was positively dying to ring my father and tell him how I had got on.

"On another subject, the Ladies Nights are doing so well I was wondering if we could do something specifically for men?"

I gave the matter my full concentration for a moment before answering him.

"Well, how about running a 'Poker Classic' or a 'Night at the Races'? You could work that to your advantage and try to gear some of your cocktails towards a particular theme. Most men I know would rather just drink beer but if you sell the cocktails to them in the right way and offer them a free taster, then you could woo them away from the beer a bit while encouraging more of a crowd in at the weekend. Cocktails are very much a niche market but if you do things right then you could attract everyone from far and near. If I've learnt anything from my years in PR, it's that no matter how much advertising you do in newspapers, through local radio and by putting flyers through doors, there is no better way of getting new customers than by treating people well and getting them to tell all their friends who in turn will pass the good news on to others."

"As well as being my new antiques buyer how would you like me to commission you to do all the PR work for Pitchers as well?"

I paused and looked at him.

"I'd pay you well," he added.

"I'd love to," I said, wanting to give him a hug but afraid to in case it started another conversation that ended with 'I presume it's okay to touch you without you thinking it's an invitation for something more'.

Fabian left and I climbed the stairs to my warm and cosy flat, made myself a cup of hot chocolate and sat outside on the balcony and watched the world go by.

I drained my cup, looked up at the sky and thanked my big brother for looking after me so well.

Frankie had been right. Maybe things didn't always work out the way that you expected them to but when you were patient and started being more positive it was surprising what delights life could deliver.

46

Frankie

Luke let me in and shrugged his shoulders in a helpless fashion. He looked totally miserable.

"I just don't know what to do with her any more. No matter what has happened in the past Ruby's always managed to bounce back but this has hit her really hard. She's going through the motions of trying to be normal but she's like a robot just doing things because she's programmed that way. She has no heart in anything and I'm really worried about her. She hasn't been eating properly and when I persuade her to eat the smallest titbit she throws it up again. There's nothing else for it: I'll have to get Isobel on the job and then she'll have no bloody choice but to eat or be fed through a tube."

"Where is she now?"

"She said she was going to lie down and no doubt you'll go in and find her lying on top of the bed staring into space."

"Leave it with me," I said grimly. This was one

occasion where I was going to have to save Ruby from herself. There had been complaints in the college and whispers about the standard of her work slipping and I couldn't just stand idly by and let everything she had worked so hard for go up in a puff of smoke.

Quietly I opened the door and just as Luke had predicted found Ruby on top of the bed fully clothed and looking into nothingness.

"Rubes," I said gently and when she didn't react I sat down on the bed beside her and took her hand between mine.

She was freezing cold, her eyes were hollow and sunken due to lack of sleep, and she had gone from having a creamy complexion to a pallor that was reminiscent of setting concrete. She had lost weight and her clothes had started to hang off her and she looked pinched and stressed.

"Ruby, you can't go on like this, darlin'. Everyone is worried sick about you and you look permanently like death warmed up these days."

She didn't respond but instead removed her hand from mine and went back to staring at the ceiling.

"Have you spoken to the counsellor?"

That elicited a response.

"No, and I'm not going back. What a load of crap that lot talk. If they had to experience what real people had to live through then they mightn't be as quick to start doling out all this shite about exploring your feelings and being true to yourself. That fecking tosh is what has me in this mess. Why did nobody tell me just to leave well enough alone? Why did nobody tell me how hurt I'd feel and how much damage I'd do Georgie in the process?"

Ruby started to sob uncontrollably and her breathing turned to noisy spasms as she gave vent to her anguish.

This was probably not the best time to tell her that we *had* all warned her but as she was like a bull in a china shop it was a pointless exercise.

I had never seen Ruby so upset and like Luke was feeling completely useless as I held her and stroked her hair.

"And none of it has even been worth it because he's dead," Ruby continued through her tears. "I feel like I'm mourning someone I didn't know and at the same time I'm also grieving for my daddy who was the best father in world. What must he be thinking of me now? I just can't stop crying, Frankie."

"Ruby, your father loved you more than life itself and he would understand. Perhaps the two of them have already met up there. Just look on it as having another ally in heaven."

I left several hours later after Ruby had fallen into an exhausted sleep and I had sat with Luke for a while.

"You'll have to go round and see Luke," I told Owen when I arrived home later that evening. "The man needs some serious support as I think Ruby is on the verge of some type of breakdown."

"You women are always having a crisis about one thing or another," he answered, shaking his head and raising his eyes to heaven. "Angelica has spent all evening throwing clothes in black bin-liners and when I asked her about it earlier she nearly took my head off and told me that it wasn't a crime to be sorting out things to go to the charity shop."

He had my full attention and immediately I smelt a rat. I could barely get Angelica to make her bed and, unless I physically lifted her clothes and took them to be laundered, they could quite likely end up festering on the floor of her bedroom for months.

I made my way to her room where she did indeed seem to be in the process of a massive clear-out but unlike Owen I wasn't so easily palmed off.

"So what charity shop are this lot going to then?" I asked as she continued to manically throw things in bags.

"Don't know, some of the cancer shops, I suppose," she answered, not making eye contact with me.

"What's this," I asked as I lifted out a purple dress that she had only got the Christmas before and had worn quite a bit. I knew that she loved it and was quite miffed to see that she seemed to be getting rid of it.

"It's a dress."

"I can see that." I poked further down the bag and saw other clothes that had been favourites. Although actually now that I thought about it she hadn't worn any of them in months.

"Frankie, is there something you wanted?" she asked.

"Yes. I'd like to be treated with a bit of respect in my own home when I ask a civilised question," I said, "and I'd also like to know what you're doing getting rid of so many nice clothes? These are in perfectly good condition and they're still in fashion and what's more they all cost an arm and a leg."

I continued to rummage and pull out more and more items.

"Jesus, Frankie," she snarled at me through gritted teeth, "for months on end you torture me and drone on

351

and on and on about tidying up and now that I am all of a sudden it's a major deal."

She marched out of the room and left me standing there and I could hear her talking to Owen in a pleading voice.

"Dad, I'm having dinner at Jerome's house tonight and I need to pick out something to wear and just because I'm sorting out a few things and trying to tidy my room *she* is throwing a wobbler and I'm going to be late."

Owen was soon staring reproachfully from the doorway, Angelica behind him glaring at me.

"She's only interested in what you're doing," he said.

"*She* is still in the room!" I snapped in irritation.

I recognised the look Owen was giving me and felt instantly pissed off. It was the one that said 'you are going to be responsible for another row and I don't want to get involved'.

I threw my hands in the air and went to run a bath for Carly who was standing on the landing, listening to the commotion with a worried expression on her face.

"You and Daddy aren't going to fight again, are you?" she asked and for the second time that night I was treated to a look that said 'please don't start anything'.

When Owen and I had called a truce and agreed that we would waste no more time arguing over Angelica, we had resolved that there would be no more fighting – for everybody's sake. However the terms and conditions of that particular agreement had been broken as we had soon reverted to being at loggerheads again.

I had come home from my night out with Gabriel and Jodi and demanded to know what Angelica had been up to and why I had feckin' Brutal Brenda gloating all over me like a cat who'd drowned in a pot of cream but as usual had been told to stop being so touchy. Owen reckoned I was too easy to wind up and Angelica had spent all her time in her room. Apparently she had been out with Jerome but hadn't been home as late as Owen had expected as she was complaining of feeling sick. Owen had confirmed that she was pale and shaky and just wanted to be on her own and he had obliged. She had spent the next few days confined to bed while Owen told me to calm down and stop reading so much into everything.

I went to the bathroom and started to make preparations for Carly's bath and while there discovered that the vast majority of Angelica's make-up was lying in a plastic bag. Her eye-shadow palettes were all broken, blusher compacts crushed and lip glosses carelessly discarded. My first instinct was to go and ask her what the hell had happened but I stopped myself in time as my daughter was looking hard at me and for her sake I didn't want her hearing any more cross words. She'd had quite enough already and I wasn't going to subject her to any more.

Besides, Jerome had arrived and I could hear him talking to Angelica in her room.

I closed the bathroom door, thereby closing out the sound of his voice. I couldn't abide him and the more I saw and heard the less I liked him but who was I to have an opinion?

I helped Carly into the bath and turned her little face around so that she was looking at me.

"Do me a favour, darling," I said. "Please don't ever grow up."

47

Angelica

"Hey, gorgeous," Jerome said as he watched me get ready.

I smiled at him and did a twirl. "It's the one you bought me last week."

"I know it is and I got it for you because I knew you'd look like my princess in it."

I saw him gazing at me in the mirror and took in every inch of his appearance. He looked very handsome and was wearing black jeans, a black shirt and boots. He looked so much happier now and I was sorry that I had made him so miserable. I truly did love him and he loved me and as he said himself he knew that he had gone too far the night that we had met our landlord in the house but he had been genuinely terrified that I was going to run off with Paddy McCourt and he was just showing me how much that would have upset him.

At the time I had been confused and hurt and had taken the next few days off school in order to think about everything. I hadn't spoken to him in two days even though he had left me dozens of voicemails and text messages but then a few nights later he had woken me up in the middle of the night by throwing pebbles at my window and I had taken pity on him and we had talked in the car for a long time.

"I'm so sorry, Angelica. I never meant to hurt you." Tears had run down his face as he spoke and I had found myself choking with emotion as I had listened to him. "I can't live without you and I've been so scared that I lost you. Please forgive me and please understand that I only did what I did because I love you so much and couldn't bear the thought of you ever leaving me to be with anyone else."

I had touched my stomach and wrapped my arm around my bruised shoulder and as he watched me he had gently taken me in his arms and promised never to hurt me again and I just knew that he wouldn't.

The following day I had gone back to school and had given Paddy McCourt such a mouthful of abuse that I thought it would be unlikely that he'd ever so much as look at me again. But that suited me well. I only needed one man and from now on I intended to keep him happy.

The same evening Jerome had told me to shut my eyes as we approached our new home and when he opened the door I saw to my delight that he had made some changes and obviously been busy. There was fresh paint on the walls, new carpet had been laid down and he had put up a few mirrors and shelves in the kitchen that immediately brightened the place up and gave it a more homely feel. After that he had led me up to the bedroom which had also been painted and he handed me a catalogue and asked me to choose some nice bed covers for our bed. We had agreed that we would make the big move in another few weeks which was part of the reason why I had decided to start de-cluttering in preparation. Dad had been prepared to accept my explanation but of course Frankie had to act like I was committing a crime and make a major issue of it all. She was so annoying and I would be so glad to finally get away from her constant interfering. Jerome had already said that our home was to be a parent-free zone and that the less contact we had with the oldies the better. After all, they were going to be in shock that I had actually moved away and would probably be disapproving and hard to listen to, so I wholeheartedly agreed with his line of thought.

"I see you've been busy," he said as he surveyed all the bin-bags that held my clothes. "I'm glad that you're doing a clear-out before we move in together. It'll be so much nicer without all those reminders of the past and that horrible dress sense you had."

I felt a pang of regret as I looked at all the tops, jeans and dresses that had formed the very essence of my own personal style. But nevertheless they were a small sacrifice and Jerome had promised that he would buy me a brand new wardrobe and had already started so I supposed it was only right that I should compromise. I had also destroyed my make-up but realised too late that I had left it in the bathroom where no doubt Frankie would have spotted it in the manner of an overzealous Russian spy. I had deliberately stood on some of my favourite eye shadows so that I would no longer be tempted to wear them as Jerome hated the heavy eye make-up that I had been accustomed to wearing. He had said that it was cheap and tarty and that it was so much more elegant when I simply wore mascara and used Vaseline to give my lips some shine.

Jerome's phone suddenly rang shrilly and I knew that he must be talking to his father as he became very serious.

"Angelica, unfortunately I need to go. My father has an important client coming to dinner this evening and he's forgotten some papers at the office and I'll need to go and collect them for him. Why don't you ask your father to take you over to my parents' house and wait for me there? Hopefully I won't be too long and you could always see if my mother needs a hand."

"I'd like that," I said. I had met Marian on only a handful of occasions but I had really warmed to her and always enjoyed her company.

"Before I go I have another surprise for you," he said. "I was going to give it to you later but I think you deserve it now."

He produced a bag with a box in it and to my delight I saw that inside was the latest-edition *Blackberry* phone.

I would be the envy of all my friends. Of course there was the small problem that none of them were talking to me any more but I could still create a stir by producing it. This particular model was hot off the production line and a much sought-after piece of equipment.

"I just thought that you might like a new phone," he said by way of explanation. "It has the best signal anywhere. That way we'll never lose contact. Give me your SIM card and I'll transfer all your old numbers over for you."

As I pulled the cover off the back of my phone and took out the tiny microchip that held all the details of friends I had collected over the years I looked at him and thought about how much I loved him and how much he must have loved me to make such a gesture. These phones weren't cheap and must have set him back at least a couple of hundred pounds.

I threw my arms around his neck and kissed him before he left and hummed as I finished putting the final touches to my appearance.

My dad wasn't around so I was forced to ask Frankie if she would mind taking me to Jerome's home and she readily agreed.

I gave her directions and her mouth was an open circle when she took in the landscaped gardens, the ornate stone that decorated the front of the house and the plush interior that could be seen through the front door which was lying ajar.

"This is a nice little crib," she commented, letting out a low whistle. "What does Daddy Dearest do for a living again?"

"He owns an advertising and marketing agency."

I left Frankie and knocked on the door but nobody answered so I entered the house unannounced and made my way to the kitchen where I knew Marian would be busy getting the food ready. However, Marian wasn't alone when I peeked through the door. Her husband was there too and he seemed most unhappy about something.

"I think that you behave like this just to annoy me, Marian. Do you enjoy seeing me worked up and in a state? Why can you not just do as you are told and not deliberately disobey me? It might seem like a small insignificant detail to you but to me it is very important and now you've just ruined my night."

"I didn't mean to ruin your night, Lewis. You weren't

even supposed to know and you wouldn't have been any the wiser if you hadn't seen the packaging."

She stopped talking abruptly and looked up at him tentatively almost as if she knew that she had said too much and was trying to gauge his reaction.

He moved towards her, grabbed hold of a clump of her hair and growled in her face and as I watched him I felt an uncomfortable tingle jerk down my spine.

"You're nothing but a lying, good-for-nothing bitch!" he spat, jerking her head with every word and making her cry in pain. "The day I married you everybody should have been wearing black and been in mourning. I could have done so much better for myself. But instead I settled for the runt of a litter that should have been put down."

Roughly he let go of her and slammed her against the kitchen counter.

"Please, Lewis," she said in a wavering voice. "Don't do this. I do my best. I'm worth more than that."

He laughed long and loud and then spoke again in a sneering tone. "*You*. Worth something? Ha! That's a good laugh. You're the most worthless piece of trash that God ever created and you'd be nothing without me. I've given you everything and made you what you are and what do I get in return? I get insolence and disobedience and a blatant lack of respect and you know that I find those things intolerable in the extreme."

I watched her recoil away from him and felt the blood drain from my face. I shouldn't be here listening to this. I couldn't believe how nasty he was being towards her.

Then, as if Dr Jekyll had just transformed himself into Mr Hyde, Lewis's tone changed and he stopped towering over his wife and talking threateningly into her face.

"I'll deal with you later but for now I want you to be on your best behaviour. We're a wholesome family-run business as far as the investors are concerned. Our image is all-important and you had better deliver tonight and do exactly as you're told but don't think I'll forget. Tonight after everybody leaves we'll have another discussion and you can tell me exactly what you did wrong."

He stalked away with large strides and left her standing there. For a woman that had just been threatened she seemed very calm and I got the impression that she must have been in this situation before. I watched as she smoothed her hair back into place and straightened her clothing and, as I heard another door opening in the recesses of the house and then slam, I walked into the kitchen. She jumped and I was sorry. I hadn't meant to startle her.

She composed herself almost immediately and gave me a beaming smile. An Oscar-winning actress couldn't have played the part of devoted wife and mother any better. She busied herself around the kitchen while asking questions about my day as if nothing untoward had taken place in this room less than five minutes before.

I decided that the best thing to do would be to play along and pretend that I hadn't seen or heard anything. She seemed to have no problem in blocking it out and pretending that it never happened and I hoped that it would be as easy for me.

The night seemed to go smoothly but as it ended I could feel a ball of tension gather in my stomach as I looked at Marian. What was going to happen to her when everyone left? By saying they would have a 'discussion' I didn't think that her husband was suggesting a talk. I felt he had something else in mind entirely. I didn't really understand any of this and it frightened me and all of a sudden I had an urge to go home.

I went to the front door where I had the best signal, flicked my new phone open and typed in F for 'Frankie' to bring her number up but nothing happened. I pursed my lips and fiddled with it until I figured out how to locate the phone book. This was the problem with having a mobile. You never took the time to memorise any numbers because you were too reliant on the phone storing them for you.

Something funny was going on, though, as my phone book seemed to be empty apart from one entry, Jerome's number, and as I stared at it the cold hands of fear started to creep around the back of my head and neck.

48

Ruby

After much persuasion and Luke threatening to bring my mother into the house to nurse me I had eventually agreed to see the doctor.

"There's nothing wrong with me that time won't heal," I had said. "I've brought all this on myself and it serves me right for being so nosy."

"You're totally run down," Luke complained, "and you're not eating or sleeping. If they could even give you a sleeping tablet or maybe something to help calm you down it would ease things."

I sat in front of the doctor and gave her all my symptoms and the list seemed to go on forever. At one stage she put a finger up to silence me as her fingers flew over the keys of her computer and she documented exactly how I had been feeling.

"I thought that the antibiotics had started to work for my infection but then I started to feel rotten again. I've been feeling light-headed and sick and I'm constantly on edge."

"How's the counselling going, Ruby?"

"Don't ask," I snapped. "It would be great if theoretically everything was as simple as it seems to be when I'm sitting in Sonia's office and we're talking about the realm of possibilities and how I'm in control of everything that happens in my life. But what does it mean to be in control?"

I felt so angry that I started to cry (again) and the doctor patted my hand.

"I'm going to send you down to the nurse for a few blood tests and I'd also like you to produce a urine specimen. I don't think there's anything seriously wrong with you that a good night's sleep and a holiday wouldn't cure, mind you. Hop up on the examination table and let me have a look at you."

I did as I was told and lay up as she poked and prodded my tummy while asking me if I was tender or sore anywhere.

I made my way down to the nurse where I received further poking and prodding as she took a blood sample and gave me a list of things that she had been instructed to check. Apparently liver function was one of the tests being conducted and I hoped that my growing fondness for cocktails wouldn't mean that that particular organ would be secreting champagne and Sex on the Beach.

I looked on as she dipped a stick into the urine sample I had given her and watched as her face took on a knowing look. She then went into a different room to use the phone where I could hear her telling the doctor that she'd have to see me again.

"What's the problem?" I asked anxiously when she returned.

"Oh, there's no problem. No problem at all. I thought that Doctor Carr should have another word with you before you leave just so that everything's clear."

I left the nurse's office, muttering about people who quite obviously knew something but wouldn't let on and grumbled the whole way back up the stairs to sit in the waiting room again next to a man with a wheezing cough and a baby with a runny nose and a high-pitched cry.

I sat and jigged my foot impatiently and flicked through the pages of a magazine, reading it but not actually seeing any of the words or taking in any of the information.

My name was finally called again and I returned to the doctor's office where I waited for her to speak.

"Well, it seems that there's been a reason for all your symptoms, Ruby. When I sent you downstairs, as well as asking the nurse to take some bloods from you I asked her to do a pregnancy test."

She paused for a few seconds and I became irritated.

"Obviously it was negative," I snapped. "I've been on the pill forever and I never plan to come off it because if I ever hear the words 'you're pregnant' I will drop in a dead faint on the floor and you may have to use your defibrillator on me."

The doctor looked momentarily as if the wind had been taken out of her sails.

"The defibrillator is only to be used on patients who need to be resuscitated due to heart failure," she said then, "but if you really think it might be necessary I can get them to bring it up from downstairs."

I looked at her in confusion and really didn't appreciate the joke.

"Is it customary for doctors to try and emotionally wreck the heads of the patients under their care who are already in receipt of counselling? Is this some type of quick-fire test to see how I react and how well it's working?"

"Ruby, I can assure you that I'm not toying with your feelings or trying to frighten you in any way but I do have to tell you that the pregnancy test we did came back positive."

The last thing I remember before everything went hazy was the doctor telling me not to panic and to put my head between my legs.

When I came around I was lying on the examination table in the nurse's office and I could hear Luke's voice coming from somewhere in the building. He had been in the car waiting for me but someone had obviously gone out and got him.

"Where is she? Is she okay? What happened? You've no idea how upset she's been lately or what she's been through. It's no wonder she collapsed – she's had so much to deal with in the past few weeks."

I lay with my eyes closed as I had no idea what to say to Luke and perhaps if I lay still in the dark for long enough I would somehow end up in my own bed waking up in a cold sweat and telling him about the terribly real nightmare I had just had.

"Ruby, darlin'. Everything's okay."

But he didn't sound as if everything was.

"I'm here now, and the doctor told me to ask you what the diagnosis was as she felt that it wasn't her place to tell me."

I slowly opened my eyes and the mere sight of him caused tears to cascade down my face. I didn't deserve him and he certainly didn't deserve me or the way that I behaved. Anybody else would have been happy but at the thought of what possibly lay ahead I simply couldn't function. I was absolutely terrified and didn't even want to think about it.

"Whatever it is, darling, we'll get through it together. Remember our wedding vows? In sickness and in health, for richer or poorer?"

I would never forget my wedding day and how happy I had been that we had finally been united as a couple. I had never experienced true love before I met Luke and now I would be in the position to give him something he wanted dearly. We all had to make sacrifices in life and maybe this would be like getting used to a new sofa or a dodgy haircut. I might never be happy about it but hopefully in time I'd learn to accept it . . . or would I?

"Get that doctor in here!" I said. "I need to ask her a few questions about how this could possibly have happened. I didn't notice the Angel Gabriel floating around our house recently."

Luke was baffled but went out and then reappeared with the doctor who was looking concerned and nervous at the same time. I went to sit up but she quickly told me to lie down again.

"How could this have happened?" I asked, feeling my eyes well up with tears. "I don't understand."

"Before anyone goes on any further can somebody for the love of God please tell me what the problem is?" Luke asked in growing frustration.

And in growing frustration and without the slightest idea of how it had occurred I made all his dreams come true with two words that were uttered in a voice that sounded dead to my ears.

"I'm pregnant."

49

Jodi

I was on my way to Belfast and we had agreed that we would meet up in the bar of the Merchant Hotel just so that we could finalise our plans (synchronise our watches) and basically hone the finer details of our covert mission (James Bond, eat your heart out, love!).

Fabian had lent me his car for the trip as he didn't want me having to wait around for trains or buses as I made my way across the city. He really was a great friend and I felt lucky to have him and was actually thankful that we'd had our 'little chat' as it gave us both the luxury of knowing where we stood. I'd had enough pretence and acting over the last few years to last me a lifetime and now all I wanted to do was to enjoy my job, safe in the knowledge that I was serving a legitimate purpose instead of being kept as some dirty little secret.

I parked the car and went in. I sat in the foyer where I ordered a coffee and waited for Pamela to arrive. I saw her come in but when she did she wasn't alone. She had three boys with her and when I looked at them all together I felt a mixture of great sadness and anger on their behalf.

"I'm sorry, Jodi. I wasn't able to make it on my own as the nanny let me down today but luckily I have a friend who lives in Belfast who told me that she would meet me here and take the boys for me. She should be here soon. I'm sorry if it means that we'll be late."

"There's no rush. We've all the time in the world to do what we have to do." I leaned forward and looked at the boys.

"I'll bet that you boys are thirsty after your journey up from Dublin. Would you like a bottle of Coke and a packet of crisps?"

The younger ones looked at their mother who nodded in approval and I went ahead and ordered from the waitress who was hovering around, together with a coffee for Pamela.

When the drinks arrived, Pamela settled the boys down at a nearby table.

As I waited for her to join me, I studied the boys carefully and drank in all their features. I paid particular attention to Jason, the eldest boy I had met in the hospital that fateful day months ago. I felt as if I owed him a debt of gratitude as only for him I would still be living a lie. The two younger boys looked similar to their big brother but were finer-featured like their mother. Out of them all he was most like his father and I prayed for his sake that he would remain like him in looks only as I wouldn't wish his poor mother any more heartbreak or misery.

Pamela leaned towards me and whispered, "Did you get the information you wanted?"

"I did," I nodded with a wink and a huge grin. "It's a good job that I was able to access my email remotely. I was able to do it using Fabian's computer in the bar. I was actually shocked to find that my email was still working as I had expected it to be frozen or locked or something."

I had linked into my email as there had always been a calendar there which showed the schedule of everyone else in the company and in that way had determined that today would be a good day to approach Ashley as he was there and involved in a meeting and not away travelling.

"He must still be holding on to the hope that you'll be coming back to him again." Pamela appeared vexed and distracted as she took another sip of her coffee and looked out the window.

"Oh, I'm coming back alright! It's just not going to be in the way he expects. Did you bring the other documentation with you?"

"I have it right here," she said, patting her bag. "It's so sad. I looked at it yesterday and realised that to him it must only have been a piece of paper that really was of no significance."

"I have mine too and I'd say that mine meant as much but guess what, Pamela, it's his loss. He tried to be smart and thought that he could have it all but when you're too greedy you end up with nothing which is the position he was prepared to leave all of us in."

I looked at the boys and hoped for the millionth time that we were doing the right thing.

Pamela's friend arrived a short time later and with a series of waves and smiles the boys made their way out the revolving doors, blissfully unaware of what was about to unfold.

"What have you told them?" I asked tentatively, knowing that I really had no right to ask and that she could easily tell me to mind my own business.

"They were always used to him being away so his current absence isn't anything new to them. I suppose if I had to find a positive that would have to be it. If he had been a hands-on dad this would all have been so much harder . . . but being a hands-on dad would have been difficult given the circumstances."

I felt myself shrinking back into my seat, cringing in response to the level of deceit that I had been inadvertently involved in.

Pamela sensed my discomfiture and touched me gently on the arm. "I don't blame you for any of this. I'll never forget the stricken look you had on your face in the hospital that day. He's a callous bastard and for the sake of his children, ourselves and any poor unfortunates that might come after us we have to ensure that he realises that he can't behave like that and get away with it."

With renewed vigour and a strong sense of purpose we left the hotel, hailed a taxi and asked the driver to take us to Digital Concepts where we planned to have one of its managers on his knees within minutes of our arrival and if he happened to be in the middle of a meeting where lots of other people might hear the details of what we had uncovered then so much the better. And if he proved difficult I had the numbers of the *Belfast Telegraph* and the *Irish News* on speed-dial and was sure that their features editors and business journalists would be enthralled to hear our story – but that would be a last resort as we didn't want to cause unnecessary suffering to his children who had already lost so much.

We arrived and presented ourselves at reception where a very snooty girl with platinum-blonde hair and bright-red nail-talons told us that we needed an appointment to be allowed access to Ashley's office and that he wouldn't be free until the afternoon anyway as he was in an important meeting. She was new and obviously didn't recognise me. A few others did, however, and I could hear the Chinese whispers starting to get into gear already.

I could imagine what they were saying:

"What's she doing here?"

"I thought she got fired for having it off with one of the reps?"

"Poor Ashley even had to report her missing because she wouldn't return his calls and he was so worried about her."

"Who's that with her?"

"Don't know. Perhaps she left him to have a lesbian affair with another woman."

There was a ripple of laughter and I could feel myself stiffen in response.

"I don't need an appointment to see my husband," Pamela stated in a firm tone of voice that brooked no argument.

"And I certainly don't need an appointment to see my husband either. And for your information, love, I used to work here and know my way around just fine so we'll be on our way."

The receptionist stared open-mouthed at us as I nodded and thanked her before gesturing for Pamela to walk ahead of me to the lift. I pressed the appropriate button which would take us straight to Ashley.

I took confident strides towards the boardroom and

hoped that important dignitaries as well as the managing director, company board members and shareholders would be in attendance to watch as his cocky charade came crashing down around his ears in spectacular fashion. Pamela had started to breathe like she might collapse at any moment and I placed my arm around her in a firm grasp.

"Don't fall apart on me now," I warned. "Think of how he made you feel. You always said that you were happy to stay at home with the children while he went travelling so he decided that he would leave you to be the stay-at-home housewife and mother while he went in search of someone who could fulfil the role of arm-trinket and trophy wife. He used both of us for what he could get and he deprived you of a normal family life and left your children without a father – and he told me that he never wanted children which I would have so dearly loved but was prepared to sacrifice to keep him happy."

I saw determination rise in her face and, as we opened the doors to the boardroom and saw his head snap up, firstly in surprise then followed by pure and abject fear, I felt the first rush of satisfaction.

Then I said in a cheerful tone: "Good afternoon, everyone! Hello, Ashley! It's so nice to see you again."

50

Frankie

I disentangled myself from Owen's embrace and got up to wake the children for school and get Jack a drink as he was noisily shouting from the cot in his room and demanding his cup.

I padded down the stairs and noticed that the latch hadn't been put on the front door and immediately felt annoyed. It was very simple. All she had to do after she came in late was to make sure the doors were locked and the place secure. Anybody would think that she wanted us to be burgled or murdered in our beds.

I called the children and then went to get Angelica up and train her in the art of home security. Her door was partially open with one of those bin-bags blocking it so I tapped on it and stepped inside. I was startled to discover she wasn't there. Her blinds were open and her clothes were still strewn over the floor from when she had got ready to go out last night. The black bin-bags were still lying around and she had promised me that she would tidy up when she got back as she hadn't envisaged being late as it was a school night. I looked in her wardrobe for her school uniform but it wasn't there. I couldn't believe that she had already left for school – that would be unprecedented. The only other explanation was that she had never come home.

I went to speak to Owen. "This is a new one. No Angelica. Either she got up and went out to school at the crack of dawn or now she's not coming home in the evenings. She probably stayed with his parents last night and didn't even ring to let us know. That girl is a law unto herself."

Owen had a face on him and it said 'Oh no, she's started to shout again and because I'm in bed with no clothes on I can't get up and run out of the room to get away from her!'

"You can sit there and make faces if you like, Owen, but it's totally irresponsible. She has school this morning and now she's probably going to be late and the door wasn't even locked last night and her room looks like it has been the subject of a mortar attack. Do you not think that the least we could have expected was a phone call or a text telling us of her plans? Her uniform seems to be gone so she must have known in advance that she wasn't coming home and taken it with her."

"You don't have to worry, darling. I'll be here all morning. I told them that I was going to be working from home today so I'll have a talk with her when she comes in. You're not wrong. I do agree with you that she should have let us know but really there's no harm done, is there? If it was one of the younger children you'd worry but, Frankie, Angelica's eighteen and an adult and she can do pretty much what she likes."

And therein lay the problem. Owen was his own worst enemy. He gave off this aura of being a laid-back, liberal parent and therefore was treated as one.

As it turned out Angelica rang Owen to apologise for not coming home and asked if it was okay if she stayed at Jerome's for a few days as she had exams coming up and wanted to study with no distractions.

"I said I would prefer her to come home," Owen said, "but then on reflection I thought she had a point. You have to admit that the younger ones do make a lot of noise in the evenings."

I shrugged my shoulders and wished that my parents had been such pushovers. I could have seen my mother's face if I had made such a suggestion. Study at a boy's house? Even to my own ears it sounded quite peculiar but I supposed we were now living in different times and, from what I had heard, Jerome's parents had the reputation of being good people although his father was an apparently ruthless businessman.

I got myself ready and prepared to call and see Ruby. Luke had rung me earlier and told me that she was unwell and asked if I could come and see her as he had a photo shoot to take and he wasn't happy leaving her on her own.

"What's wrong with her?" I asked.

"I think I'd better let her explain," he said and I had been intrigued.

As it turned out I wished that Luke had given me some warning as to the nature of Ruby's condition as when she told me what was wrong I nearly collapsed myself.

"Pregnant?" I said incredulously. "You? But you always

said that you'd be the proverbial old woman who'd grow old with cats! You said you never wanted to have children."

"Yes, Frankie, I do know all this but it's a bit late to be talking about that now. The deed is done and now I have to deal with it."

"Ah, Ruby, don't be like that. A baby can be one of the most wonderful things in the world. They bring such joy and happiness and you'll find that once they've come along you'll wonder what you did without them."

Ruby didn't seem to be listening but instead looked miserable.

"At least it explains one thing," I said. "That's why you've been having such a hard time dealing with everything. Pregnancy messes up your hormones good and proper and suddenly everything is a tragedy. Even the smallest problems multiply in your head until you see them as huge disasters. The slightest thing makes you weep and wail and, as for your moods, they're up and down like yoyos. But I'd say Luke's well used to you by now. He's already had the crash course so he'll be fine. Most men don't get that and can't understand why they wake up one morning to find Mumzilla in bed beside them."

"You're doing a wonderful job of selling this to me, Frankie," Ruby snapped. "It's bad enough as it is. Please spare me all the details of what I have to look forward to in future."

"It's not that bad," I said, hoping that I was speaking directly to her hormones. "You'll get used to it all and once the baby's here you'll forget everything that went on before it. It's the nicest pain you'll ever have."

"Whoop de feckin' doo," Ruby muttered. "Look,

Frankie, I'm tired and I'm going to bed so can I talk to you tomorrow?"

"But Luke didn't want you to be on your own," I said. "At least let me stay and make you a cup of tea while you get ready for bed."

"I don't want any tea, Frankie, and Luke knows that I'm perfectly capable of looking after myself. He's just fussing for no good reason."

I left Ruby's house feeling depressed and uneasy. I knew that she had never been keen on having her own children but thought that in time she'd change her mind. She was a wonderful godmother to Jack and the other kids loved her. She had a natural sense of fun that allowed her to behave like a child when she was with them and she was kind and generous and gentle with them. I couldn't understand her but hoped that given time she'd be able to accept it.

The following day I yawned my way through work as I had slept fitfully and missed Ruby being around to keep me awake with her gabbling. I would give anything to see the old Ruby coming back and made a promise that if she did I would never shout at her for being too loud in the future as I was seriously pining for her.

On my way home I took the easy way out and stopped for Chinese as I didn't have the energy to cook and while there met Jodi looking fresh-faced and happy.

"What's the recipe for looking like that?" I asked. "I feel drained at the moment and need a pick-me-up."

Jodi grinned and whispered. "I've been on a high all week as let's just say Ashley Crozier learnt the hard way not to mess with me and, boy, do I feel good!"

She looked animated and healthy and didn't at all

378

resemble the pale and drawn-looking girl she had been when I first met her. Her dark hair was glossy and shiny, her skin was amazing and she was extremely pretty when she smiled and I predicted that she'd be the cause of broken hearts everywhere.

After our food had been prepared and we went our separate ways I hurried home, longing to slip on my tracksuit bottoms and slippers and relax.

As I came in I noticed the answering machine was flashing. I listened to the message – it was Angelica's mother on the phone wanting to speak to her.

I tried Angelica's mobile number but was confused as it kept telling me that the mobile I was ringing was no longer in service. I couldn't understand why. Her mobile had been working perfectly well and if there had been a problem she wouldn't have been long alerting us to the fact. Angelica belonged to a generation where a mobile phone wasn't just an accessory – it was actually an extension of one's limbs. I rang it again and as the familiar message, which I now knew off by heart, came on again in the annoying automated voice I banged down the phone in frustration.

I went upstairs to change and was reminded that Angelica's room was still a mess with the bin-liners she had been filling strewn all over the floor. I was loath to pick up after her but at least I could shut her door properly so the sight of the mess wouldn't bother me as much. In a fit of pique I lifted several bundles of clothes from the floor which were stopping the door from closing which was when I saw the mobile-phone box. I lifted it and opened the lid and saw that her old phone had been placed there when she had obviously taken the new one out.

Despite my annoyance I again breathed a sigh of relief.

At least there was an explanation for her not answering her phone. I searched the box for a number and finally found it. I punched it into my mobile but it went straight on to answering machine. I left her a voicemail in an even tone which would come across as me being calm, in the hope that when she got it she would ring back and let me know that she was okay (and then I could kill her).

The following day was much the same as the previous one until the college receptionist told me that Angelica's school were on the phone and needed to speak to someone urgently.

Shit. What had she done now? I knew that this present lull must have been the calm before the storm and was too good to be true.

"Hello, is that Mrs Byrne?"

"Yes, it is," I said. (I wasn't lying on purpose. I just couldn't be arsed going through the whole rigmarole again of telling whoever I was speaking to that I wasn't Mrs Byrne but that I was indeed Angelica's stepmother and that I could deal with whatever query or problem that was currently presenting itself.)

"We just wondered if you were aware that your daughter hasn't been at school for the past three days. We did get a message from her father, on Tuesday morning, to say that she wouldn't be in but as we haven't heard anything since we were wondering if everything was okay. Usually parents do tend to phone in every few days if a pupil is ill."

I couldn't speak as the alarm bells that were ringing in my ears were getting louder and louder. The receptionist was still speaking but I was no longer listening or able to comprehend what she was saying.

"Thanks for ringing," I stammered. "We'll be in touch."

I banged down the phone and went to the college reception desk to find out which room Owen was teaching in that afternoon and once I found the information I needed I ran there and burst open the door without knocking, causing everyone in the room to look up in panic.

"What's wrong, Frankie?" Owen asked, grabbing me by the arm and hauling me out into the corridor.

"Did you ring the school on Tuesday morning and tell them that Angelica wouldn't be in? Please tell me you did."

"Frankie, don't talk rubbish. You know that I didn't make any phone calls about her. I told you that she phoned me to apologise for not coming home and to tell me that she'd be studying at Jerome's for a few days."

"And you said that she was only on the phone for two seconds and you haven't heard from her since."

"Frankie, what the hell is all this about? What are you getting a bee in your bonnet about now?"

"I am not getting a bee in my bonnet about anything but the school are rather concerned that they haven't seen her in three days and I'm even more worried about the fact that they told me that a man who was obviously not you rang to say that she wouldn't be in."

Owen's face paled and started to mirror my own.

"Do you know where Jerome lives?"

"I left her there on Monday evening and think I can remember."

Owen ran back into his classroom and told his students to use the time left to study for their forthcoming exams and then followed me out the door.

We didn't speak a word as we sat in the car and I broke

every road law known to man as I sped towards the house at high speed. I was going to ring that little fecker's neck. How dare he behave this way and try to influence and encourage our daughter to abandon her studies and disrespect her parents!

I was tempted to round on Owen and roar 'I told you so!' in his ear. How many times had I voiced my concerns about that boy? How many times had I been ignored and made to feel like I was just out to cause trouble? However, now wasn't the time for recriminations. Now was the time for going to get Angelica out of there and away from his grasp.

As I negotiated the corners on the windy meandering roads on the outskirts of the town I hoped to God that she was alright. She had been particularly unhappy recently and the day that I had come in and found her examining an ugly bruise on her side came to my mind particularly forcefully.

"Do you think that we should phone the police?" I asked Owen in a wobbly voice. We were nearly at our destination but the closer we got the more pronounced my feelings of foreboding became.

"Let's just see what's happening at the house first," Owen said grimly.

When we arrived the electric gates outside the house were closed and nobody was answering the intercom system. I got my mobile and went to where I had saved Angelica's new number and pressed the ring button but as usual I was greeted with the answer-phone message that told me that she couldn't come to the phone.

I pressed the intercom button on the gate again and spoke slowly and clearly into the speaker.

"All we want is our daughter. We know she's there so please advise her to come out to us."

I clicked off the speaker, stood where I was for a further few minutes and then watched as the gates slowly opened to reveal the ornate driveway that had been lit up to welcome visitors the night that I had dropped Angelica off but looked anything but welcoming right now.

We drove in and then Owen and I jumped out of the car and went and banged on the door. The place had an eerie feel about it and I shivered involuntarily.

Owen continued to bang and started to shout.

"Open this door now or I swear to God I'll pull it off its hinges! I want to know where my daughter is and I want to know *now*!"

Slowly the door opened and a blonde lady who seemed to be holding herself stiffly and awkwardly stood there, shaking and squinting in the light.

"There's nobody here but me," she said. "Your daughter's not here. I haven't seen her since Monday evening. I presumed that Jerome had taken her home and I haven't seen him since either."

"I don't believe you," I said through gritted teeth. "How can you so casually say that you haven't seen him since without a care in the world? Were you not worried?"

"The men in this family tend to do exactly as they please without too much care or consideration for anyone else," she said and to my horror I watched her stagger and as she grasped the door frame to steady herself her sleeve moved up her arm to reveal an ugly bruise.

Owen and I looked at each other and I put my arm out to support her as Owen walked past her into the house and started to shout Angelica's name.

"It's no good," the woman said. "She's not here but if you take my advice you'll persuade her to leave Jerome while she can. Jerome is my son and I love him very much but he's just too like his father and some chains are hard to break away from." As she spoke her voice became raspy and she started to gasp.

"*Owen!*" I screamed as she collapsed in my arms.

As Owen rang for an ambulance and also alerted the police I held on to her tightly. Her top had ridden up and I saw that her abdomen and back were covered in welts and scratches and bruises. Some were faded and yellowing but others were purple and black and angry, suggesting that she had only just got them.

"Oh God, please hurry up," I whispered and as the blue flashing lights came into view and Owen directed the ambulance in I prayed like I had never prayed before that things would be alright.

51

Angelica

Three days before

My head felt heavy, my eyes were prickly and sore and I had a peculiar taste in my mouth. The last thing I remembered was Jerome giving me a drink before we left his parents' house and then everything was hazy.

I tried to open my eyes and focus and found myself lying in a bed. I was completely disorientated.

I was still fully clothed but even so was shaking like a leaf.

I heard footsteps on the stairs and as I looked towards the door saw Jerome coming in carrying a tray.

"Good morning, princess!" He had made toast and coffee and was acting like everything was perfectly normal. "How did you enjoy spending your first night in our new home?"

"Jerome, what's going on?" I asked. "Why are we here? How did I get here?"

"Don't you worry about a thing, my darling. I'll look

after you. I'll always look after you. You needn't worry because nobody's going to bother us again."

"Jerome, I need to go home and see my father. I need to go to school and you need to make sure that your mother is okay."

His face changed in an instant and I rolled off the bed onto the floor screeching in terror as he threw the tray at the wall, smashing crockery everywhere and leaving ugly stains on the fresh paintwork.

"What do you know about my mother?" he asked, his face contorted.

"I know that she might be hurt," I said shakily. "Your father was being really nasty to her when I went into your house before dinner. He was pulling her hair and calling her names and he made her cry. I have a feeling that after everyone left he might have done something to her."

Jerome made a grunting noise and rolled his eyes to heaven.

"Don't you care?" I said, surprise making me momentarily forget my fear. "Your mother is lovely and she seems very frightened of him."

"Let me tell you about my mother, Angelica. My mother cared so much about me when I was small that she let my father beat me until I was black and blue. He used to take his belt off and hit me around the bare legs with it. He broke a chair over my back once and threatened me with a broken bottle. She stood by and let it all happen and never did a thing to help me."

"I can't believe that!" I cried. "That's not what I saw last night. He told her that she was worthless and nothing and then expected her to put on an act to impress the clients he was entertaining. I couldn't believe my eyes."

386

"Yeah, well, in this life you get what you deserve. If you're going to take it then it's going to be given to you."

"But you seem so close to your father. I thought you got on well. How could you want to be with a man that behaved like that towards you?"

Jerome never answered. Instead he started clenching and unclenching his fists.

I was still on the floor and slowly got up. He never took his eyes off me.

"Jerome, I think I need to go now," I said, trying to inject a bit of lightness into my voice.

"Oh, I don't think you do, Angelica. I've already phoned your school and told them that you're feeling unwell and now you're going to ring your father and tell him that you'll be studying at my house for a few days."

"Why would I want to do that?" A tremble had entered my voice. "I want to go home."

"Angelica, you are home, my darling. This is where your life is now. We'll be together forever and nobody is ever going to tear us apart."

52

Ruby

I was going to Donegal to visit both my mothers. I needed to clear my head and make peace with everyone and once and for all put everything that was upsetting me to bed. I started all of this and I was determined now to finish it. Perhaps when I did that I could begin to think about other things that were worrying me.

Luke came into the room and put his arms around me and spread his hands across my tummy. "Take good care of my baby while you're away. I want you both back safe and well."

I nodded silently and resisted the urge to shrug him off. I knew that he was excited and, as much as I was scared stiff and determined not to be happy, I didn't have the heart to spoil it for him.

I continued to fire things in the general direction of the holdall until Luke stopped me, took hold of my hands and led me towards the bed.

"It's you feckin' interfering and taking me to bed that has me in this mess in the first place," I complained.

It *was* all his stupid fault. The doctor had told me that I must have conceived while I was on antibiotics for my chest infections. How was I supposed to know that the pill was wholly ineffective and rendered completely useless while on antibiotics? Nobody feckin' told me and I was thinking of suing the doctor, the nurse, the NHS in general as well as the manufacturers who made the stupid pill.

I had also asked how the hell I had managed to become pregnant when clearly I had just had my period, only to be told that women do occasionally have a bleed at the start of pregnancy. It was no wonder I had abysmally failed my biology at school.

"You haven't told me how you're feeling about any of this?" Luke said as he kneaded my hands with his and looked beseechingly at me. "You've just walked around here with a face on you like a wet weekend, saying nothing but obviously thinking a lot."

I knew that he was willing me to smile and be happy but I couldn't muster up enough energy even to begin contemplating what the future held.

"I'm very confused, Luke, although I suppose in a way I'm happy that they didn't find anything life-threatening although I could be telling you something entirely different in about eight months' time."

"Thirty-four weeks' time to be exact," Luke announced, smiling, while I groaned.

I just knew that he'd be buying baby books, Googling all my symptoms and generally turning into Doctor Spock until the baby arrived.

"Ruby, I know that this isn't ideal and that for whatever reason you never wanted to even so much as talk about having a baby but, now that it has happened, are you not happy? Just think about how much you love little Jack and how good you are with Ben and Carly. You'll be a fantastic mother and any child will be lucky to have you. Your mother will be thrilled and so will Georgie."

At the mention of Georgie's name, I stiffened. I didn't want to think about her. Not in conjunction with my being pregnant and having a baby growing inside me.

"I need to get going, Luke. I want to get to Donegal in plenty of time. I'm tired and don't want to end up driving in the dark."

"It's half past eight in the morning, Ruby," Luke said in a bemused fashion. "I'd say that you'll be there before the sun gets properly positioned in the sky, never mind before dark."

I zipped my bag shut, kissed Luke on the cheek and told him that I'd ring him to tell him I'd arrived safely.

I asked Mammy not to utter a word until I had finished speaking and she honoured my wishes by sitting quietly and listening to everything I had to say.

Then she held me for a long time and didn't say a thing.

"Our first grandchild," she said, smiling, looking directly at the photograph of my father which had pride of place in the mantelpiece in the cottage. "What do you think of that, Albert?"

I looked at the photo and burst into tears. Tears of regret and shame. Tears that he wasn't still with me as he would have known exactly what to do and say and tears that betrayed my innermost feelings about the turmoil I was experiencing regarding impending motherhood.

"It's the most natural thing in the world, pet. It's what we women do and I'm delighted. I think a baby will be the making of you both. Babies bring untold joy with them and after all the disappointment you've had recently this will be something for you to look forward to. Imagine, this will be your own flesh and blood. It will be part of you."

Mammy didn't know it but her words were addressing one of my biggest fears.

"But, Mammy, that's the problem. I'm scared stiff of how I'm going to feel and whether it will affect my relationship with Georgie. I know that I should be ecstatically happy but how can I be? Knowing that when my mother was carrying me she found it a dreadful and horrible experience that caused her no end of difficulties? That's why I never wanted to get pregnant. I've always been so scared of what emotions it might create in me. I've been afraid that I'll hate Georgie for letting me go and not fighting harder to keep me. I know that there's no bond stronger than between mother and child and knowing that I'm now carrying my own baby when I was so easily discarded by mine scares me."

Relentless tears spilled down my face and as my mother held me close I knew by the rise and fall of her chest that she too was crying.

"My poor baby! Does Luke know that this is the way you've been feeling?"

I shook my head. "I could never put it into words as I thought he'd think that I was terrible for thinking that way. Nobody understands how I feel."

"Get your coat on," Mammy instructed as she blew her nose and fetched her keys. "We're going to see Georgie right now to sort this out."

"We are not," I said sharply. "I didn't tell you that to give you any more reasons to be annoyed with her and she hasn't deliberately done anything to make me feel this way so it wouldn't be fair to go and accuse her of anything. The problem lies with me not with her."

"I wasn't suggesting that we go and see her so that I can accuse her of anything," Mammy said very calmly and rationally. "I was hoping instead that she would be able to make you feel better and tell you about her experience in being pregnant with you as I have a feeling that it wasn't the dreadful time that you make it out to be."

When we arrived at Georgie's house there seemed to be a lot of people there and immediately something told me that I wouldn't be welcome.

"Feck them," Mammy said and I nearly died of shock. Mammy never swore. I did enough for the two of us.

I knocked on the door but nobody answered so Mammy took matters into her own hands by quietly turning the handle and hauling me in by the arm.

We followed the sound of voices until we arrived at the glass doors that led into Georgie's sitting room.

I saw that Marcella was holding court inside. Charlie was there, listening intently to what she had to say, and other family members were nodding and shaking their heads. Georgie was there too except I couldn't see her face as her head was hanging.

Instinctively I knew that I must have walked in on Marcella making good her threat by telling my grandfather what she knew and a rush of anger surged through me as I opened the door and burst into the room.

Everyone looked momentarily caught off guard but it

only took seconds for Marcella to regain her composure and continue from where she had left off.

"So you see, Father, my actions were to spare you unnecessary suffering. I never wanted you to know what really happened but the decision has been taken out of my hands now. I was left with no choice but to tell you. It's better that you hear it from me than from someone else."

"So what you're saying is that my youngest daughter, who should have known better, had an affair with a married man who also happened to be my brother-in-law and created a catastrophe so big it nearly tore our family apart."

"In a nutshell that's it and you needn't ever have known a thing about it only *she* had to come snooping around looking for her mother and then her father and expecting to be welcomed with open arms into the bosom of our family."

As Marcella waved a painted nail at me all I wanted to do was to hug Georgie who looked more forlorn and sad than I'd ever seen her.

"It's an absolute disgrace!" Charlie said, his face turning red with anger. "I never believed that my daughter could be capable of such behaviour, that she could create such havoc for her family and hurt so many people. I've never been so ashamed in all my life."

Marcella looked triumphant and my demeanour began to mirror Georgie's as I hung my head. This *was* all my fault. Why could I not have been content with what I had?

Charlie awkwardly got up from his seat and went over to Georgie who was still staring at her chest but looked up as he approached.

"I'm so sorry, Father," she said. "I'll understand if you

don't want anything more to do with me. You've always been so good to me and I've let you down."

"I'm disappointed in you, Georgie. I thought that you would have had more sense but more than that I'm thoroughly ashamed of the actions of the rest of this family."

He turned to face Marcella whose mouth had dropped open in shock.

"For years you told me that your actions were honourable and that you simply wanted to save Georgina from having to cope with the stigma of being an unmarried mother and her child from having to deal with being illegitimate and for years I tried to convince myself that that was the case, but deep down I think I always knew that your actions were questionable. And now you gather us all here today to reveal the truth about the situation as if your sister is on trial for murder. What shall we do now, Marcella? Shall we burn her at the stake or did you have something else in mind?"

"Father, I can assure you that I have always had Georgie's best interests at heart –"

"Which obviously is why you're dredging up the past and targeting both her and her daughter in your vendetta," my grandfather interrupted. "Your mother would be spinning in her grave if she knew what you had done and why. Like everything else it's all to do with money. You're afraid that Ruby making an appearance here will affect my will. You'd sell your soul to the devil if the price was right. As it happens I already knew who Ruby's father was. Daniel summoned me to his death bed almost ten years ago and told me he couldn't meet his maker without telling me the truth. I was shocked and saddened by what he told me but Daniel Madigan was a good man and my sister loved him dearly. It should never have happened, but it did and the consequences of those actions should have been dealt with a lot more sensitively."

Charlie held out his hands to me and obediently I went to him and grasped his open palms.

"You are welcome in my family and I apologise for the actions of some of my children and can assure you that I didn't raise them to behave this way."

"Don't you dare make any apology for me," Marcella said, jumping to her feet and pointing her finger at me. "She's nothing and nobody and she will never be part of my family!"

"You seem to forget who the head of this family is, my dear, and it's most certainly not you. I had Georgie ring the nursing home earlier to tell them that I wouldn't be returning and as for my house and everything in it I'll be keeping it just as it is because I have big plans for it. Plans that involve my eldest granddaughter. You thought that you were being smart in getting rid of her but you never thought she'd come back or that your actions would have backfired on you so badly."

"You're out of your mind," Marcella said nastily.

"You'd like to think I was, so that you could say that my will and plans aren't worth the paper they're written on, but that is definitely not the case. I asked the doctor to run a few checks on me when I was in hospital just so that he could certify that I was of sound mind and he gave me the thumbs-up and the all clear and I saw my solicitor when I got out."

Marcella looked like she was going to explode (and I

hoped that she wouldn't as the mess she'd make would be nasty in the extreme).

"You had no right –"

"I think you'll find that it is you who has no rights now, Marcella, so just keep quiet please and say nothing more." He turned to face me and spoke again. "Daniel hoped that this day would come and that you'd make your way back to find your mother and if it ever happened he asked me to give you something. I've wanted to give you this for some time but wanted to wait until you were ready to know and it seems that time has now come. I had of course made arrangements with my solicitor to deal with it eventually . . . if I was unable to. Georgie, fetch me the wallet in that drawer over there."

I watched as he took it, opened a zip and produced a strip of paper that had a list of numbers on it and the name of a bank. "I believe that if you go here and give them this information that they'll be able to give you something he wanted you to have."

Georgie was looking at me through red-rimmed eyes and Mammy was sitting beside her holding her hands and whispering what appeared to be words of comfort to her.

"I'm so sorry, Ruby," Georgie said. "It's not fair that you keep getting the blame for things that are beyond your control."

"On the contrary, I'm glad I was here," I said. "It gives me a greater understanding of everything and makes me so glad that I found you. I'll not be asking any more questions in future. I'll be content from now on."

"Promise?" Mammy said.

"I promise both of you."

"Hmm," said Mammy. She turned to Georgie. "I think

Ruby has something that she would like to tell you, Georgie, and I know that you'll be pleased but I'd also like you to tell her how much it means to be able to stand up and tell everyone that you brought her into the world."

Georgie looked at me but didn't have to say a thing. The love in her eyes said it all.

53

Jodi

I had been inundated with phone calls from various business contacts and the Chief Executive and Chairman of the Board of Directors had also been in touch with me to offer their unreserved support and to tell me how disgusted and sorry they were. It seemed that there was nothing like a bit of controversy to put your CV at the top of everyone's list and, as news of Ashley's misdemeanours spread, so did my popularity with various executive directors in some of Belfast's most prestigious marketing companies. I had been offered salaries that would have left me able to retire comfortably in ten years' time but I'd had enough of being part of the city rat race and nothing would ever persuade me to go back there. Besides, since I had started working with Fabian, news of my work in Swiftstown had spread and I had been commissioned to take on the PR and Event Management for several other companies and agencies locally. I was also still working in the antiques shop although I spent more time out on the road as a buyer now and I loved every minute of it.

Nothing in this world had been more satisfying than seeing the look on Ashley's face as Pamela and I took turns in exposing him for the rat-bag he was. The shocked faces that stared at him in horror from around the boardroom table that day had left us in no doubt about his future especially as we had left both our marriage certificates as well as copies of damning emails to company clients that showed him quoting higher prices for jobs than agreed. When I had found his secret phone I discovered that he was also using it to make phone calls to several clients and for sending emails he obviously didn't want to use a work computer for. I had done my homework and found out who the other numbers on the phone belonged to and wouldn't have been surprised if they had been contacts for other women but discovered, instead, that as well as hoodwinking his wives he had also been trying to swindle his bosses. I spoke to several people who had indeed paid him the larger amount of payment that he had asked for and handed my findings over to the company accounts manager who was fixing Ashley with a particularly steely glare.

Ashley had looked on incredulously as we had delivered blow after blow to his carefully constructed reputation that would have rivalled that of any saint in Ireland. He had been successful in business and built up an impressive bank of clients and had enjoyed an excellent quality of life but apparently that hadn't been enough and now his greed was coming back to haunt him in more ways than one. He had looked relieved when the Chief Executive had called for security to come 'and help with a problem'. The men in uniforms had come into the room but instead of asking us politely to be on our way, as Ashley had anticipated, they had stood behind him and folded their arms in disgust as they had listened to how he had gone to the ends of the earth to cover his tracks and make sure that nobody found out about his secret wife and children who lived on one side of the Irish border while the other one resided in the north, blissfully oblivious to the fact that she was a home-wrecker and having come from a broken home herself it was the last thing that she ever wanted to be.

By the time we left we could still hear Ashley asking that people gave him the opportunity to explain. He told them he hadn't meant to hurt anyone and that he regretted his actions and given the chance to make amends that he would do just that. But somehow we weren't convinced that either his bosses or the directors were going to give him any chances at all. And if the look on the face of one of the security guards and the way he was flexing his fingers was anything to go by I'd say that Ashley might well have been leaving his work that day (hopefully for the last time) via the window.

I looked at my reflection in the mirror and the woman who stared back at me with bright eyes and a happy confident smile made a striking difference to the shattered one that had hated even looking at herself because she felt so worthless. That woman had now gone and her replacement was ready to take on the world but the world would have to wait just one more day as today she was donning her apron and reprising her role in the Swiftstown Arms Bistro one last time to help Tom out before she officially left.

"Hi, guys," I said brightly as I walked through the door and was greeted with smiles from the other waitresses, a thumbs-up through the hatch from Chef, a hug from

Jamesie Mac and appreciative noises from Ringo and Jockey who seemed delighted to see me back.

"We've missed you, girl!" Ringo said, putting his arm around me and planting a kiss on my cheek. "It isn't the same without you at all."

"Well, thank you very much, Ringo," Anna said over my shoulder. "And there's me killing myself looking out for new flavours of cupcake icing for you just so that you won't get bored."

"I like you too, Anna," Ringo said lamely. "It's just that Jodi adds a bit of sparkle to the place."

Jockey was, as usual, head and ears into the local paper, looking at the racing fixtures for the day and as I looked at the page with him a name caught my eye.

"That one!" I said excitedly to him as I pointed at the list of horses running that day. I was no sporting pundit but liked the name and felt lucky for a change.

"That one?" he asked in surprise "I would never have picked that one."

"All the more reason why you should listen to her then!" everybody chorused and knowing that he had been shouted down Jockey started to fill out the docket.

"I'll go halfers on it with yeh, Jodi – a tenner each – and sure if we win we can split the money."

"Deal," I said as we shook on it.

The morning passed by uneventfully and I was glad that I had the time to fully appreciate my surroundings and reflect on the solace, companionship and comfort the bistro had brought me.

I would never forget the first day that I walked into it. I was wet and cold and had just stepped off the bus and I was resentful of the curious stares and the implication that miserable dripping wet strangers didn't drop in very often. I remembered standing in the bus station in Belfast and looking at the departure listings with eyes that were swimming with tears and how I had been desperate to leave, to go anywhere that wasn't where Ashley and all my memories of our time together were. The bus to Swiftstown had been the next one leaving and in that one moment my fate had been sealed and I decided that someone must have definitely been watching over me that day as the choice had been a good one.

Outside there was suddenly a huge commotion. I could hear shouts and screams and the running of feet and, as the sound got louder, myself and the other girls went to the window to see if we were going to be witnesses to the town's first riot. It appeared, however, that far from a riot there was the beginnings of a street party and I wondered what all the fuss was about.

Jockey nearly took the hinges off the bistro's door and the little welcoming bell had never tinkled so loudly.

"I've only gone and done it!" he said, practically sniffing with emotion. "Me and Jodi done it. The horse was listed at fourteen to one to win and Jodi and I put in £10 each and we've won £300!"

I started to squeal myself when I realised that for the first time Jockey's horse, or should I say *our* horse, had actually come in and that was my sign. All the sign I needed to know that I was making the right decision.

"I don't believe it," Tom said, putting on his glasses to look at the betting slip as if he needed to see proof with his own eyes before the news would sink in.

"What was the winner's name?" Anna asked.

"It was called *Making the Right Move*," Jockey said

and, as I took out my notepad to get some orders from the revellers, I winked at Anna. She gave me an affectionate smile in return and I knew that my big brother Paul had indeed yet again been making sure that things would work out well for me.

I went to approach a table of customers, nodding at two policemen as they came in. I presumed that they too were there to eat but they stopped me and informed me that they were on police business.

They showed me a photograph, explained that the girl in question was local and that she had been missing now for approximately three days.

"Oh my God!" I said when I saw her face. "That's Frankie's stepdaughter."

I called Anna over and she frowned on seeing the picture.

"Angelica Byrne," she said, chewing at her bottom lip. "My son goes to school with her but other than that I don't know too much about her. Seems like a quiet girl. Nice youngster. But no, I haven't seen her in the last few days."

"Nor I," I added.

The police left and Frankie's words about how it would be heartbreaking for any mother not to know where their child was rang in my ears and, as I threw off my apron and shouted an apology to Tom, I prepared to pay back her kindness to me in any way I could.

54

Frankie

As we made our way to the hospital with the blue sirens wailing and Marian unconscious in the back of the ambulance I resolved to love Angelica to the best of my ability for the rest of our time on earth together.

So what if her room was untidy? So what if she was occasionally hormonal and needed an extra bit of attention? I was prepared to put up with anything as long as she was alright.

As there had been nobody with Marian I had accompanied her while Owen had gone off with the police in search of Angelica.

The policewoman who had arrived at the house had seemed to know the premises well and I heard her murmuring to her colleague that maybe now they would secure a conviction.

Marian moaned as the ambulance drove over a ramp at the entrance of the hospital and I clutched my mobile and willed Owen to ring and tell me that they had found Angelica safe and well and fighting with everyone as usual but my phone remained silent.

Marian was transferred into the accident and emergency unit on a stretcher and by the time she had been examined, x-rayed and formally admitted, I had become frantic with worry. Jerome's mother's weak and raspy words didn't inspire me with confidence. She had been the victim of abuse for over two decades. For years she had tried to escape but he had always worn her down with empty promises that were short-lived once he had her under his control again, feeling worthless and of no importance.

"The police have tried to get me to press charges for a long time but I always chickened out at the last minute. Who would ever believe me over him? He's so charming and manipulative with people and such a highly respected businessman. It would be my word against his and I know who people would believe. He threatened to have me committed the last time the police wanted me to give evidence and he said he'd hurt my mother. It's just not worth it. I've resigned myself to this way of life and the only thing I can hope for is that one day soon he'll trip himself up and people will see him for what he really is. I've actually wished him dead as it's the only way of escape that I can see."

"Do you think that Jerome is capable of the same type of behaviour?" I asked, knowing that it would be hard for her to answer but wanting her to be honest all the same.

"Jerome and I have a very difficult relationship. He grew up watching Lewis beat me and believed that I stood back and allowed his father to do the same to him. His father always was a dreadful bully and Jerome grew up feeling totally insecure and inadequate as a result of the treatment he received as a child. I always hoped that he would leave and go travelling but eventually his father gave him an opportunity in the business and through that Jerome has finally gained a tiny bit of respect from him which is all he ever wanted. I always hoped that seeing me suffer would have been a deterrent and I always pleaded with him to have respect for women and never to lift his fist. What I do know is that he has very little respect for me."

My mobile sounded shrilly and I answered it on the first ring, running out of the ward cubicle towards the corridor.

"Owen, please tell me you have news. I'm going out of mind here."

There was a sigh and I knew instinctively that they hadn't found her.

"Nothing Frankie. I've been everywhere I can think of with the police. All her friends' houses, all the local places in town where she might be and back at the house in case she'd gone home. Her friends said they saw her at school last week and met her one night on the street but apart from that have had no dealings with her. They all said that she's changed so much that they hardly recognised her. I went into her room and had a look around and found her uniform under some of the filled bin-bags. I checked with the hospital and we also went to the train station and the bus depot to see if anyone recognised her photo but there was no news there either."

"Oh God," I wailed. "This is all my bloody fault! I should never have been so hard on her. I usually tidy her room but was so fed up that I wanted to prove a point and left everything as it was. If only I had checked I could have found her uniform and we would have known something was wrong sooner."

"Frankie, this is not the time to start pointing the fingers of blame. As far as I can see there've been a whole lot of faults on all sides."

"Did you check with your mother that she didn't go to Dublin and did you ask Brenda if she knew anything?"

"I did ask Mum but I didn't say that Angelica was missing as I didn't want to worry her. I told her Angelica was in Dublin with friends and that she might call in on her and I asked Mum to let me know if she did as I couldn't get in touch with her. I also called round to Brenda's but there was no one there and I tried ringing her but her phone was going straight to voicemail."

"Remember I told you about the night I was in Pitchers and Brenda was gloating about knowing something I didn't know. I reckon if we get hold of her we'll be that bit closer to finding Angelica."

We said goodbye and I made Owen promise me that he would ring the second he heard anything or got any type of breakthrough and he said he would.

I returned to Jerome's mother feeling deflated and more anxious than ever.

"I need to leave as there's still no sign of Angelica, Marian."

The woman closed her eyes and looked so helpless and vulnerable that I felt she needed to know that none of this was her fault.

"I know that we only met today but if there's anything I can do for you please let me know."

"Thank you so much for everything. Angelica is a beautiful young woman and you should be very proud of her. Please let me know she's okay."

I touched her hand before leaving and prayed that she would get the strength to nail her husband this time once and for all. Some women had all the luck and didn't even know it and I was one of them.

When I arrived home I found Jodi sitting on the front door step waiting and as soon as she put her arms out to me I fell into them and cried. I had been determined to be strong but was finding it difficult as I couldn't stop thinking about things I had said to Angelica in the heat of the moment. It appeared that my fears had been well founded but I took no pleasure in being right about it now. Instead of shouting my mouth off I should have tried harder to support her and be her friend and then maybe she could have confided in me. I knew that she had been ditched by Katie and the other girls which had left her completely alone. That could have been my opportunity to have tried to get closer to her but I had blown it.

Jodi took the front door keys from me and opened the house and I watched as she made her way into the kitchen where she flicked on the kettle and hunted in cupboards until she found teabags and sugar.

"Get that down you," she said handing me a cup of sweet tea. "It's good for shock and the sugar will give you some energy. I am at your beck and call for the rest of the day. What can I do to help?"

"Could you possibly look after the children for me and

keep them here? I want someone to be in the house at all times in case she comes home. I never meant for things to get so out of hand, y'know. I do love her and think of her as my own. I feel sick to my stomach when I think any harm might come to her and knowing that I'm responsible for pushing her away is just unbearable."

"Listen, Frankie, anyone who could take a complete stranger under their wing and do for them what you did for me doesn't have to question her capacity for caring about or loving her family. You're one of the kindest and nicest people I know, so stop being so hard on yourself!"

"Hear, hear! Couldn't have put it better myself," another voice said and as Ruby put her arms around me I was threatening to well up again.

"I heard what happened from one of the receptionists in the college who saw you and Owen leaving. Is there any news?"

"None at all."

"Okay, well, I am here for you so tell me what I can do."

I looked at Ruby's soon-to-be-swelling stomach and shook my head as the last thing I needed was Ruby getting caught in the crossfire of anything that could happen.

"Just stay here with Jodi and help to look after the kids. God knows they're precious."

I was weary by the time Owen and I called to Brenda's luxurious apartment for the fourth time that evening and, on seeing that finally there was a light on, we both let out a sigh of relief.

We got out of the car and I braced myself for what I

was probably going to hear but it couldn't have been any worse than what her friends had been telling me.

I had been speaking to Katie earlier and she had been incredibly upset to hear that Angelica was missing. She was feeling somewhat similar to myself and blaming some of her own actions for pushing her friend away but she admitted that she just couldn't take it any more. Angelica had changed so much that her friends could no longer recognise her. She wouldn't see them any more, had lost interest in everything they used to do and her entire world was taken up with Jerome. I told her not to blame herself but did ask her to alert everyone else so they could keep an eye out for Angelica.

We buzzed to gain entrance to Brenda's apartment and when we finally heard her voice my nerves were balancing on a knife edge.

"We need to talk to you," Owen said. "Can we come up?"

She allowed us in, probably more out of curiosity than anything else, as we weren't exactly 'visiting' companions. It was clear that we weren't getting any further than the hall as she stood with her arms folded, looking at us with open hostility.

"To what do I owe this then?" she asked sarcastically. "I would say it's a pleasure but I don't like telling lies."

"Do you think it would be possible for us to have a civilised chat without all this aggravation and bad feeling, please?" Owen said tersely. "We wondered if you had seen Angelica lately or if you know where she might be?"

"How would I know? I've been in London for most of this week and haven't seen her since last weekend. What are you asking me for anyway? It's your job to know where she is, not mine."

"The night I met you at the cocktail bar you said that you knew something we didn't know. Owen said she left with Jerome that night but we don't know where she was. Have you any ideas as we really need your help." I knew that I was sounding increasingly desperate and could nearly feel her satisfaction.

"And why should I help you?"

"You need to help us because we don't know where she is and if you care as much about her as you're always leading us to believe then you'll tell us anything you know Brenda," Owen said in a firm tone. "She's eighteen and she's missing and we think she may be with her boyfriend but we don't know for sure and we don't know what he's capable of."

Brenda frowned and looked suddenly serious. "How long is it since you've seen her?"

"We thought she was studying for her exams at Jerome's house," said Owen, "but the school rang earlier to say that they hadn't seen her in three days and that a man had rung in saying that she was sick – but it definitely wasn't me."

"It's no wonder that she wanted to get away from you two. You're not fit to be parents."

"What do you mean 'get away' from us?" Owen asked calmly, choosing to ignore her insults.

"I'm not telling you anything. If she had wanted you to know her business she'd have told you herself but as it stands she can't talk to you because all you're interested in doing is trying to control her and, let's face it, you're pretty poor at that as all you do is make her angry and miserable." She was looking at me as she spat the words out.

"Brenda, she is a teenage girl and they're all angry and miserable at one time or another anyway and I don't want to control her," I said. "I love her and want her to be safe and was worried about the company she was keeping. We don't have time to stand here arguing right now. We need to find her and if you know where she is you have to tell us."

"I don't know exactly where she is but I do know that she was looking at houses with her boyfriend because they wanted to move in together and it's no wonder living with you was hardly an attractive alternative. A man who made his wife so unhappy that she was forced to perform a midnight flit and a woman whose husband went to the other side of the world to get away from her and her brats!"

"So I suppose you gave her your blessing then, Brenda," Owen snapped. "You encouraged an eighteen-year-old girl to move out of her home and in with her boyfriend whose father just happens to spend his spare time knocking the shit out of his mother who's now recovering in hospital and is more worried about your niece than you seem to be. But sure, why be reasonable when you can play games and spend your life annoying people?"

Owen took a step forward and Brenda took a step back.

"I've had it with your accusations and your constant criticisms and your game-playing. If anything has happened to Angelica you'll be partly to blame. It's a pity that instead of always encouraging her to hate the people who are trying their best to mould her into a decent human being, and manipulating her to think in the same warped way as you, that you didn't care more about her happiness and contentment."

"How dare you!" she responded with her face flaming in anger.

"No, Brenda," Owen said. "How dare you."

As we left Brenda's house my phone rang.

"Frankie, it's Jodi here. Go to the bistro straight away. Anna and her son are there and I think they have information that might be useful to you."

We drove to the bistro as fast as we could and as promised Anna and Paddy were waiting for us.

Paddy opened the back door of the car and got in.

"Mum's been telling me what's happened and I just wanted you to know that I saw Angelica a few weeks ago and she was acting really strangely. I spoke to her when she was in a house up near the Westvale estate. One minute she was fine and then I saw her again a short time later and she screamed at me to leave her alone. She looked like she'd been crying and her hair and clothes were all messed up. She took off running and then the next time she saw me at school she told me to stop talking to her altogether as it was getting her in trouble with her boyfriend and I always seemed to be around at the wrong time. I mentioned it to my sister earlier on and she's bringing a girl she knows here now to talk to you as well."

"That was where the girls said they had seen her as well," Owen said. "They said she seemed okay but Katie was upset because she had ignored her and so she walked on past."

Another car pulled up alongside us and two girls got out. I recognised one as being Anna's daughter but the other girl was a stranger and she looked most uncomfortable and ill at ease.

"This is Lauren and I had to beg her to come and see you but she says she'll only talk to you if you agree never to say that she was here and not involve the police."

We agreed and encouraged the nervous girl to come forward.

"Paddy tells me that your daughter is going out with Jerome Devereaux. I used to go out with him too and at the start I thought I was the luckiest girl in the world but as time went on things changed. He never wanted me to see my friends, told me what clothes to put on, destroyed all my make-up and if he ever saw me talking to another boy he would hit the roof. He's very jealous and possessive and has a really bad temper when he's provoked. He used to hit me and then he'd apologise but it kept happening and when I had eventually had enough and broke up with him it was then that things turned really bad. He said that he'd burn my house down and damage my dad's car and he used to sit outside the gates of my school waiting for me and ring my house late at night and then hang up. He's dangerous and anything's possible with him which is why I never want you to say you've spoken to me. I just wanted to warn you to tell your daughter to stay well clear of him."

The girl nodded at Paddy's sister to indicate that she wanted to leave again and they both went back to their car.

"Anna, get into the car," Owen said. "Paddy, take us to this house where you saw Angelica. Apparently she and this psychopath were looking for somewhere to move in together so it's as good a place as any to start. I should have paid more attention to what she was doing. How the hell did I not see what was going on under my own nose?"

"But that's the thing, Owen. It wasn't going on under our nose. There were signs there but he was obviously very manipulative behind the scenes as well."

"I swear if he has laid a finger on her I will kill him with my bare hands and I'll enjoy it too.

55

Angelica

I sat in the living room of our new home and watched as Jerome flicked around the channels on the television.

"What would you like to watch?" he asked jovially as if it was a typical night indoors and not an experience akin to something I'd watched in the cinema. It felt surreal and I had to pinch myself to ensure that it wasn't some horrible dream that I would wake up from shaking and scared and thrilled to be in my own bed, but alas that wasn't the case.

I didn't know what concerned me most. The fact that I was being kept a virtual prisoner or that Jerome was acting like everything was fine and this was all normal. He hadn't left the house at all in the last few days but hadn't needed to as the cupboards were well stocked with food and everything else we required was at hand as well. I longed for him to go to the shop so that I could try and get away from him and his bizarre behaviour but the chance had never arisen. I tried to appeal to his better nature and common sense in the hope that he'd understand that sooner or later people would realise that I wasn't where they thought I was and be worried about me, but he didn't seem to care. As far as he was concerned all we needed was each other and that was enough. He had become enraged when I told him I needed to go to school and do my exams as he took it as a sign that I wanted to be with other people and not him.

"It's him, isn't it? It's that fella that's always hanging around you. You want to go to school so you can see him. Well, you're not going to do that because he doesn't have anything to do with us and we don't need him."

I had cowered behind the sofa as he had thrown bottles and plates at the wall and been thankful when he had calmed down, ran me a bath and I heard him tidying up the mess he'd made as if wrecking your house was the most natural thing in the world.

I was more frightened than I had ever been in my life before but willed myself to stay calm as I believed that if I started to panic or cry or shout that that would send him into another rage and I didn't want the next target for his vicious temper to be me. It was easy to occupy myself though as I had so many regrets to think about that I found it hard to concentrate on anything else. I had treated Frankie in the worst possible way when she had been only trying to help me and clearly saw something I couldn't or wouldn't. I caused terrible tension in the house between her and my dad, dumped all my friends for a boy and was now paying the price for it. Frankie always used to tell me to be careful what I wished for and that was one particular piece of advice that I should have listened to along with a lot more. All I had wanted was Jerome, and now that I had him twenty-four hours solid if I never saw him again it would be too soon.

"Angelica, what or who are you thinking about?" Jerome demanded as he sat forward and peered into my face. "I've asked you what you'd like to watch and you're deliberately ignoring me."

"I'm not ignoring you," I said wearily. "I'm just tired and I don't care about television. Watch what you want. I don't care."

He flicked through the channels again slowly and kept looking in my direction.

"I asked you to pick something to watch and I'd like you to do as I ask."

"I'll watch a film. That one with Tom Cruise in it."

Jerome stared hard at me. "I didn't know you liked Tom Cruise, Angelica, and come to think of it that boy you fancy has dark hair and looks a bit like him. When you watch Tom Cruise does it remind you of him? Do you wish you were with him instead of me? Well, do you? Answer me!"

At this point he was screaming at me and I had my hands covering my ears.

"Look at me. Look at me when I'm talking to you. Stop thinking about him. Why do you insist on upsetting me so much?"

He was on his feet now and the last thing I remember was seeing him raise the hand that still held the remote control for the TV.

I was confused and disorientated when I opened my eyes and my head and neck hurt. I then came to the conclusion I was dreaming when I saw my father and Frankie leaning over me whispering words of comfort in my ear. I tried to look round me but Daddy stopped me from moving.

"We need to wait for the ambulance, darling. Don't try and get up. You're safe now."

I looked up at him but found it difficult to focus. "Am I dreaming because if I am just tell me and get it over with."

"No, my darling. You're not dreaming. Unfortunately this is all very real and we promise we'll sort everything out and make things right again."

I suddenly jumped in fear and turned my head from side to side.

"Where's Jerome?"

"He's in the other room with your friend Paddy and some of the other local lads. They're keeping him entertained until the police come."

At that I could hear the noise of a car, doors closing and the sound of feet on the footpath.

Two policemen entered.

"Sergeant Collins, Mr Byrne," said the older one. "I believe it was you who made the call to us. The ambulance is on its way. Where's the suspect?"

Frankie held me tight as my father walked out of the room with the policemen. I could hear them talking in hushed tones before I heard a door opening and the sergeant addressing Jerome.

"Now, Mr Devereaux, we're going to go to the station and have a little chat."

After that all I could hear were muffled shouts and what sounded like a scuffle.

"Where's Angelica? What have you done with her? She's mine!"

I buried my head deeper into Frankie and she squeezed me reassuringly.

"You're safe now, pet. Nobody will hurt you as long as I'm around. I'm so sorry I wasn't there for you when you obviously needed me. I hope you can forgive me and we can try again."

"I hope *you* can forgive *me*," I said shakily. "I swear I'm going to listen to every word you say from now on."

"Well, that makes two of us," my father said as he re-entered the room.

"Hang on a minute," Frankie said, looking clearly disbelieving. "She's had a knock to the head so I'm expecting her to say things she doesn't mean but don't you start too or I'll have to tell the paramedics to check you over."

I tried to laugh but discovered that it hurt too much so quickly went back to being quiet.

The paramedics arrived a short time later and once they had done their preliminary examinations they manoeuvred me on to a stretcher and carried me outside where the disturbance seemed to have attracted quite a crowd.

Suddenly Katie was looking down at me. "Angelica, thank God you're okay. I'm so sorry about everything. I'll come and see you tomorrow." She looked like she'd been crying and I could also see the concerned faces of a few of my other school friends. Paddy McCourt was also there as was Auntie Brenda who was looking sheepish and solemn. She approached us just before I was put in the ambulance.

"Would you like me to come with you Angelica?" she asked.

Frankie looked at me and shrugged. "I'll go along with your father if you'd like Brenda to go with you."

420

I looked at both of them and for once wasn't confused as to what the right thing to do was.

"I want Frankie," I said firmly. "You can come to the hospital if you want, Auntie Brenda, but I want Frankie to stay with me."

I don't know which of them looked more surprised.

The ambulance began to move and as I was transported to hospital with Frankie by my side I decided that I must finally be realising what it meant to be part of a family and how incredibly lucky I was and I never wanted to put our happiness in jeopardy again.

56

Ruby

When I had been booking my appointments I had organised them around both Isobel and Georgie so that they could be with me. I wanted and needed the two of them and finally I think that they had learned to accept each other again.

We arrived at the hospital and I was a bag of nerves. Mammy patted me comfortingly on the arm and Georgie walked beside me not saying much but her mere presence was enough to let me know she cared. After everything I had put her through she had every right to demand a break from the ever-increasing drama of my life but she didn't. She remained steadfast in her support but took a back seat and gave my mother her place.

Georgie had told me all about her pregnancy with me – the changes that occurred and how she had felt at every stage, and the one thing that remained the same throughout was that she always wanted to do her best for her baby. Far from viewing me as a nuisance, she had looked forward to my birth and when I had finally arrived she had been overjoyed at having someone she could call her own. For the first time in her life she had felt wanted and needed. She'd had a connection with someone and that person depended on her, or did until Marcella had stuck her big oar in and ruined everything.

I could see that she was quite emotional about the fact that I was pregnant and when I had asked her if she would accompany me to my twelve-week scan along with Mammy and Luke she had been thrilled.

"No such thing when I was pregnant with you," she had commented. "This is so exciting."

Mammy was also elated at coming along and as for Luke he was so happy that it was a wonder that the beam coming off his smile didn't crack the lens on his camera.

He was meeting us at the hospital and as always was fussing around me like a big mother hen.

"I have not one but two mothers here," I said, "and between the two of them they're not creating half the drama that you are. Calm down or my blood pressure will be sky high by the time I get in there."

"But that's okay," Luke said knowledgeably. "I've been reading up on it and high blood pressure is only dangerous for you and the baby in the latter stages of pregnancy between twenty-five and forty weeks. You're more likely to have low blood pressure right now and the best thing you can do for that is to eat little and often and get plenty of rest."

"It's a wonder I need to come here to get any professional advice at all," I said as Isobel and Georgie looked on in amusement. "Next thing he'll be telling me that we're getting a personal scanning machine installed at home."

"Well, actually, now that you mention it, that is technically possible – it would cost a pure fortune, but sure you're both worth it."

Thankfully, before Luke could blow us away with any more of his recently acquired knowledge, my name was called and in nervous anticipation we all trooped in to see the consultant who let us all sit down before he closed the door, obviously because he thought we'd brought the neighbours as well.

After giving him a brief history and getting all the necessary blood tests done I finally got to lie up on the couch and prepare for my scan. I never thought that cold jelly being slathered on a tummy could be met with such a high element of excitement.

We all looked on in wonder as the doctor moved the probe along my stomach until finally we could make out a fuzzy grey mass.

"That's your baby," he said.

And probing a little bit more he found a tiny flicker and announced to all our delight, "And that's your baby's heartbeat."

When we left the room, complete with a photograph, I never thought I'd feel so happy at bringing new life into the world. All these years I had been denying myself and Luke something that we should have done a long time ago and I regretted that but perhaps in hindsight I would appreciate the gift I was being given all the more, now that I truly understood what it meant.

"We have time for lunch before we have to meet the manager at the bank," Luke said. "It's important that you eat well, Ruby, and remember – no eggs, no cheese, no shellfish and no nuts."

"I am going to have to kill him if he keeps this up for the remaining six months," I said to Georgie and Mammy through the side of my mouth. "The man has waited a lifetime to be a father but might just miss the event because if he keeps quoting baby books at me he will be buried under the patio."

"He's only concerned," Mammy said soothingly.

"And I'm only hormonal and psychotic," I replied in an equally affable tone.

When we arrived at the bank several hours later we were ushered into a large corporate office and told to wait there until what we had come for had been located. The numbers on the piece of paper Charlie had given me would open a safety-deposit box that could be located in a large vault beneath the bank's marble floors.

"*Wow!*" was all I could say in response. "I really can't believe this."

I was positively bubbling over with excitement by the time the manager came back and when he did he handed me a sealed envelope.

"These are for you, Ruby," he said courteously. "Mr Madigan was one of our best clients and a very nice gentleman. I have fond memories of him."

I smiled gratefully but was in a rush to get out and into the car and go home so that I could rip open the envelope and digest whatever it was it had to tell me.

I could barely contain my impatience as we drove back to Georgie's, then I was out of the car first and ran into the house as fast as I could.

"Just give me a minute!" I called to the others. "I need

to be alone for a while. Thanks for all your support! I love you all!"

Sitting on my bed, I carefully opened the envelope. There was a letter inside which had been written in neat and efficient handwriting along with another piece of paper which I set aside for looking at afterwards.

June 2002

My Dearest Daughter

I have wanted to write this letter for a long time. For many years I have longed to know more about you and hope that life has treated you well.

If this letter is in your hands, it means I will have passed on to another place and you will know the truth about your birth father.

I have thought about you every day and hope that you are healthy, happy and settled.

Although I never had the pleasure of meeting you I hope you know that I was always with you in spirit

I have always loved you and wish life had been different and that I could have given you and your mother a better start.

Georgina is a good woman and I hope that both you and she will get the opportunity to make up for lost time. What happened to you both was heart-breaking and the guilt I have carried for my part in the circumstances you found yourselves in has been great

Please find enclosed details of a trust fund I set up for you after you were born. I could never do anything for you in life but hope that in death I will finally be able to provide for you and bring you some comfort

No more secrets.

I wish you peace in your mind, love in your heart and hope in your dreams.

All my love forever
Daniel

EPILOGUE

Six months later

Jodi

The compere stood and hushed everyone by tapping a spoon on the champagne glass he was holding.

"I'd like to welcome you all here to the official launch of McDermott Communications. Joanna has kindly invited me to speak on her behalf and for me to say that I'm proud of my daughter and what she has achieved in the past year wouldn't express adequately just how in awe I am of her. I knew that she came from a good bloodline, naturally, as she's mine, but I never thought I'd see her cope with life and all its obstacles quite so well. Her mother and I are delighted to be here with her tonight and I am especially excited about the new business that she has created and the impressive connections that she has already built up."

I stood at the side and smiled as my mother wiped a tear from the corner of her eye and my father paused to allow the audience to clap and cheer.

Who'd have thought this time last year when things

looked so bleak that I'd have managed to carve out such a nice career for myself and be living in the small town that I had arrived in simply because it was where the next bus from Belfast was going? As it turned out I had been quite prudent with my banking of the money that had previously sat in my current account or perhaps fate had stepped in and lent me a hand. With that money plus the interest that I had built up I had been able to set up my business.

And who would have thought that standing smiling and looking genuinely happy for me would have been my ex-husband's first wife? If anything good had come out of his behaviour it had been that Pamela and I had bonded because of our mutual connection with him. As for Ashley, he was still waiting to stand trial for bigamy amongst other charges. There had been talk of him having an off-shore bank account in the Cayman Islands which he would never get to enjoy, but I was sure he'd have plenty of time to think about 'what could have been' when he was safely ensconced behind bars.

I looked to my left to where Frankie was standing and she raised her glass and blew me a kiss and as she did her shiny engagement ring caught the light and sparkled in a myriad of different colours. Her future husband stood beside her smiling broadly and in between them stood their eldest daughter, who Frankie liked to describe as being more of a friend these days.

Anna was also there along with Tom and Chef and some of the other girls I had worked with at the bistro and they all looked very excited, but that could have been because they spied the waitresses appear from behind the bar carrying hefty trays full of delicious cocktails which had been specially prepared for the occasion.

As for Jamesie Mac, Ringo and Jockey, it seemed I had gained myself three adoptive fathers much to my own father's amusement, and whatever I did the day that I gave Jockey my tip for a win his luck seemed to have changed as he was for the time being winning more than he was losing, much to the bookie's annoyance.

Fabian raised his eyebrows at me and I knew that he was silently enquiring, in the way that I had come to know so well, if everything was to my satisfaction. We were still very good friends. I knew that he wanted more but he'd just have to wait as that was all I could give him. For the moment.

Just as everyone had started to chat amongst themselves following the lull after the speeches the door burst open and Gabriel stood there in all his glory, waving his hands in the air and asking everyone to be quiet.

Frankie saw him and got very excited.

"Well?"

"It's a boy!" he shouted. "Eight pounds twelve ounces and they're going to call him Albert Daniel!"

"And how is the mammy doing?" Frankie asked in a wobbly voice while being supported by her stepdaughter and her mother who was also by her side beaming in her delight.

"Ruby is absolutely ecstatic but as usual there was a complete drama as she ended up having the baby on a bed in the lift as they didn't get her from the ante-natal ward to the delivery suite in time. She says that she feels complete for the first time in her life. Luke is in grave danger of developing lockjaw because he hasn't stopped grinning and, as for little Albert, Ruby's going to have a time trying to ever get him on his own as his grannies are already fighting over him. And guess what?"

"What?"

"She's asked me to be godfather!"

"She must still be high from the drugs," Frankie said audibly and I grinned.

I watched Fabian lift the microphone and speak slowly and clearly into it.

"I'd like to propose a toast – to friendship, to love, to life and to new beginnings – cheers, everyone!"

If you enjoyed
Anyone for Secrets? by Fiona Cassidy
why not try
Anyone for Me? also published
by Poolbeg?
Here's a sneak preview of chapters one and two

Anyone
for
Me?

FIONA CASSIDY

POOLBEG

1

'*Wedding Belles.*' I looked at the sign in distaste, whilst Frankie (my best friend and highly excitable bling-loving bridesmaid) stood beside me and hugged herself with glee.

"I never thought this day would come, Ruby. Imagine, in less than a year you'll be an old married woman!"

What she really meant to say was that she was shocked to the core that I was actually getting married (that anyone would be brave enough to take me on) and that she was even more amazed at the fact that I wasn't insisting on taking my vows in my combats and T-shirt (although now that I thought of it . . .)

I looked at myself from every angle, cursed the unforgiving lighting which showed up every freckle and imperfection I possessed (of which there were many) and swiftly decided that if I had a piece of kiwi fruit perched on my head I'd be every meringue-lover's idea of a treat!

"You look marvellous," trilled the bridal-shop

assistant. "Although you could probably benefit from a bit of padding in the boob department," she added whilst groping my person.

"Oh God! Don't do that!" Frankie muttered before asking the stupid woman (who quite obviously had a death wish) to excuse us. Frankie was petite and pretty with big blue eyes and blonde hair. She was immaculately dressed as always and usually had a large grin on her face but right now for some reason she was looking terrified.

"There's no need to attack her, you know," she whispered to me, the assistant having discreetly withdrawn from the fitting area. "All that probing and touching is part of their job – a bit like the way they feel the top of your toes to make sure your shoes fit properly." Frankie was looking nervously towards the door in case the assistant appeared and I pounced – and my unsuspecting victim lost her hair extensions and went home minus a few porcelain tooth-veneers.

"She just copped a feel. I am nearly a married woman but does that stop an opportunist with a fetish for corsets and horrific-looking net skirts from trying it on? Quite obviously not. Please unzip me from this monstrosity and take me home. Now."

"But that's the first dress you've tried on, Ruby! You didn't think it would be as easy as all that, did you? It's not like going shopping for a pair of jeans, y'know."

"That's an idea actually," I muttered. "I wonder would anyone mind me turning up in my 501s? I am the bride after all so I think that should give me the right to wear exactly what I want, don't you?"

"I am not even going to dignify that with an answer," Frankie said in a stern tone whilst peering round my shoulder and struggling with the zip. "Days off and childcare are hard to come by and I am not wasting this opportunity to see you in a posh frock."

"'Frock'," I repeated disdainfully. "What era do you think we live in, Frankie?"

"The era where brides actually care about looking nice on their wedding day and are not difficult when their friends try and help them."

I sighed as I stepped out of the dress. I had come a long way in the last few years. Before I met Luke I had hardly worn make-up at all but now found that I didn't mind wearing a little lip-gloss and using kohl eyeliner to accentuate my eyes. I had forgotten that getting married entailed wearing a dress, however, and was less than impressed with the idea. I simply didn't 'do' skirts and hadn't donned one since the day I left school.

"I made out a list," Frankie wheedled. "If you don't like it here, there are three other bridal boutiques we can try. Come on, Ruby! Do it for me and do it for Luke. Imagine his face as you walk down the aisle looking radiant in a gorgeous dress with flowers in your hair!"

I opened my mouth to protest that there wouldn't be so much as a stem getting near my head but found I couldn't speak as I had an image in my head of Luke's reaction. I really did love him, and he was so good about accepting me the way I was (narky and stubborn most of the time) that the idea of surprising him really appealed to me. I couldn't imagine ever being described as radiant, though (not unless you count the fact that my hair looks like a bright red beacon).

There was a time that I didn't like Luke Reilly very much. On our first meeting he was lucky to escape with his vital organs still attached and in working order. When we met he was employed by a local newsrag and had taken photographs of Frankie and her partner Owen from a video still which showed them in a rather compromising position on student prize day in the college where we all work. It was, in fact, a very innocent kiss which got blown completely out of proportion but on a lighter note is the funniest graduation-day anecdote in Redmond College history. Well, everyone with the exception of Frankie and Owen thinks so. You can actually see them twitch when it's mentioned (which the rest of us do with wicked regularity). We soon got over that little hitch, however, and are now *getting* hitched (pardon the pun).

"How are we getting on now?" The saccharine shop assistant had tentatively reappeared.

"*We're* getting along just fine," I answered. "Just leaving."

"But you've only tried on one dress," she said in confusion.

"And *you* are still in possession of your good looks so be very grateful," I answered whilst staring menacingly at her.

It was the month of June and my wedding was still eleven months away. I couldn't understand what all the panic was about. Preparation and organisation were not my strong points anyway and I especially hated anything that involved too much fuss. To date, the only other arrangements that had been made for the wedding were the booking of the chapel and the reception venue. But there was plenty of time to do the rest, surely? We had decided to have our meal and party in the Swiftstown Arms. It was our local hotel and probably wouldn't have been everyone's first choice but it satisfied me. The food was nice and I knew the manager well and it was handy to home which meant that after my big day was complete I could be carried over the threshold and into my own bed. We were hoping to go on a honeymoon but (you've guessed it) nothing had been put in place as of yet. Maybe we'd get a last-minute deal.

Three exasperating hours, two more bridal shops, more hideous dresses and one measly cup of coffee later and we were no further forward, aside from the fact that I now hated everyone who was employed in the bridal fashion industry. They were all horrible, mean people who acted like your body was an extension of their own, which meant that they could poke and prod you at will. They were also rather suspicious and hostile towards you when you first entered their sacred domains.

"Were you looking for anything in particular?"

"Well, as I'm in a fecking wedding-dress shop I think it's fairly obvious what I want, don't you?"

I had to be escorted out of that one by the ear after the assistant wouldn't let me try on a particular dress as she thought it was beyond my price range. Cheeky cow. (Big mistake. Huge. The saleswomen in *Pretty Woman* weren't the only snobby cows in town!)

I looked sideways at Frankie who at this stage looked like she was sucking a pickled lemon.

"Frankie."

"Yes, Ruby."

"Are you annoyed with me?"

"Me annoyed with you? And why would I be annoyed with you, Ruby Ross?" she said in a low growl. "We've had a wonderfully exhausting day of insults, sarcasm, endless complaining and still no bloody dress. Honestly, if I had known it was going to be this tough, I would have suggested that you go to a dressmaker and get it made to your precise instructions in the first place."

That was a light-bulb moment for us both as we suddenly realised that Frankie had stumbled upon the answer to all our problems.

"Brilliant!" I said in delight.

"So what do you want?"

"A dress that doesn't make me look like a moron would be a good start. No frills, no ponce, no mad heavy nets that you would need legs like a heifer to carry, no ten thousand jaggy sequins that itch the crap out of you and no ten-foot-long train for every eejit to stand on whilst your boobs pop out the other end from the strain."

"A bin-liner."

"Pardon?"

"I was just thinking out loud, Ruby. Why don't we fashion you a dress out of a bin-bag?"

"Ha ha."

"What exactly is there left?" Frankie threw her hands up in aggravation and annoyance.

"A good dressmaker will take one look at me and know exactly what I need."

I thought I heard my best friend and future bridesmaid mutter something about eye-poking and sharp sticks but I could have been mistaken.

"How'd you get on?" Luke asked when I eventually arrived home that evening empty-handed apart from a family bucket of Kentucky Fried Chicken and a box of beer which I intended to scoff with urgent immediacy. (Comfort food, as I felt victimised.)

I tapped the side of my nose and tried to look mysterious as I watched him transfer photographs he had taken that day from a memory card onto his computer, where he would spend the rest of the evening working on them.

"You didn't get anything, did you?"

"What makes you say that?"

"I met Frankie at the shop earlier and she told me that if I had any sense I'd get you a wedding planner as a present as nothing would be organised otherwise."

"Okay, so I didn't get a dress but it's no big deal. I'll just get one made instead."

Luke gave me his one-eyebrow-raised look and then kissed me tenderly on the nose. I ruffled his dark hair and put my arms around his neck, looked into his face which I found highly attractive as he had a gorgeous smile and expressive blue eyes which were surrounded by faint lines (created by constantly laughing at me as opposed to with me).

"I don't care if you turn up in a bin-liner, honey," he said. "I'll marry you anyway."

"Hmmm . . . funny you should say that."

2

I went to work the following day as normal and was delighted by the sight of my untidy desk which made Frankie hyperventilate every time she looked at it – she had a clear case of obsessive-compulsive disorder that hadn't been properly diagnosed yet. It was stacked with papers (I could no longer see my 'in' or 'out' trays), had pens and other stationery scattered indiscriminately over it as well as editions of the *Yellow Pages* dating back to the caveman era. I viewed it as my sanctuary (a place where I was safe from demonic shop assistants and even scarier friends). My habitual doodles were also dotted around the area.

I had worked in Redmond College for nearly eleven years as a Placement Officer which required me to put our students into the industry in which they wished to pursue a career. I loved my job (mostly because I could continue to act like an eternal student myself and also because they invited me on all their beer-and-kebab-fuelled nights out which were much more appealing than anything the staff had to offer). I had recently been given my own office which totally exasperated Frankie as she thought the perk was completely wasted on me. In truth I would probably leave it looking in the same state as my home (which would be Kim and Aggie's worst nightmare if Luke wasn't a dab hand with a duster). It wasn't that the house was dirty or that I didn't have personal hygiene standards, it was just that I thought life was too short to try and constantly emulate Mrs Mop, so I employed the philosophy that I'd let it get really mucky and then do all the chores at once.

"Good morning," Frankie said as she appeared, looking her usual spruce self.

"Please don't mention the word 'shopping'. This is a wedding-discussion free zone as far as I'm concerned."

"Would I?" Frankie said with a mischievous twinkle in her eye. "I tell you what – I'll make a deal with you."

I hated deals as they usually required me to agree with something I clearly disagreed with just to keep the other party happy.

"Pick a wedding-dress designer who we'll go and visit next week and then I promise I will act as if you're still single and spinsterhood, faded jeans and Doc Martens are the order of the day."

"Designer?" I said, feeling distinctly unimpressed at the thought.

"Dressmaker then," Frankie said, sensing my disgruntlement.

She looked so optimistic and hopeful that I didn't have the heart to burst her bubble. I knew that even if I wasn't prone to getting excited about such occasions, Frankie was, and the thought of wearing a bridesmaid's dress filled her with joy. Also, my little goddaughter Carly was going to be my flower girl and I could hardly make her wear dungarees (or could I?).

I reached across and lifted the most up-to-date *Yellow Pages*, opened it at the appropriate page and proceeded to do what I did every time I needed to pick a name and didn't know where to start.

"Please tell me you're not going to do what I think you're going to do," Frankie said from behind her hand as she cringed and made faces.

"Frankie, do you want me to do this or not?"

"Ruby, you are the only person in the world who would pick the future maker of their wedding gown by closing their eyes and stabbing a list of phone numbers with a finger!"

I opened one eye, closed it again and pointed downwards.

"'*Rose Malone. Dressmaker specialising in Bridal and Fine Evening Wear.*' There you go. Go away and leave me to my Doc Martens."

Frankie spluttered and came over for a closer look.

"Ruby, she's based in some back street in Belfast! I have a bad feeling about this." She picked up one of my doodles and waved it at me in a desperate fashion. "You could design your own dress. Why don't you give it a go and then we'll have another look for a designer –

445

dressmaker, I mean. I shouldn't have rushed you into this."

"I draw people and pieces of scenery, Frankie. Donatella Versace needn't start shaking in her designer boots yet. The Finger of Fate has spoken. Now get lost and go and annoy somebody else."

Frankie raised her eyes to heaven and sighed. She knew when she was beaten.

"Ruby, you are the most irritating person in the world but I still love you." With that she plopped a kiss on my forehead and walked out the door.

I stared after her fondly and thought back to when we first met. We had started working in a local recruitment agency on the same day thirteen years ago and had regarded each other with distaste for the first six months or at least until we had got to know each other a bit better. (In other words when I stopped thinking she was a blonde airhead and she had ceased believing I was a psychopath. Me? As if?) At that stage Frankie was married to Tony – please let it be noted that I have a dartboard with the weasel's much-punctured picture on it. Of course, things aren't as bad as they used to be as he now sees his children a couple of times a week and thankfully bestows his attentions on another gullible female. He treated Frankie really badly and left her high and dry for an American stick-insect called Stella when Ben was five and Carly was two. Things were horrible for a long time. Frankie lost lots of weight and hardly ever smiled but gradually things improved, especially when she met Owen (I introduced them – move over,

Cilla, there ain't room for the two of us). Owen is the loveliest man on earth (apart from my Luke, of course . . . I am occasionally sentimental . . . just don't tell anybody). He treats her well, is a wonderful father to all the children, including Angelica (his sometimes wayward teenage daughter) and Baby Jack (their joint effort) as well as Ben and Carly. You can just see when you look at the two of them that they love each other completely (it would make you barf really). I couldn't think of anyone I would rather have accompanying me down the aisle but I also knew that she would have me looking like the proverbial blushing bride and dressed like a blancmange on the day. Somebody save me, please, I prayed.

"Ruby," Mr Reid, the college principal, had come into my office clutching a piece of paper and looking thoughtful, "I need to see you for your ten-year review at some stage this month. They've introduced a new policy which says that you have to go for a medical as well, so make an appointment as soon as you can."

I groaned. If there was anything I hated more than wedding-dress shopping (and there wasn't much, I can assure you) it was going to the doctor's. Nosy feckers that again loved to violate your person by shoving you around and asking intrusive questions, most of which I didn't know the answer to. Questions about family history were a constant source of aggravation for me and were always answered with the tick-box: *don't know.*

You may be wondering why I couldn't comment on

my heritage or give information about my family's proneness to various health complaints. It's not because I wasn't interested or that I never bothered finding out – it was a lot simpler actually. I didn't know because I'm adopted.

I knew I might find out some useful information one day, though, and once I'd eliminated breast and bowel cancer, heart disease, diabetes and epilepsy, I was then going to ask the questions that had been bugging me for years. Who the hell was responsible for my greasy skin, why was my arse so big and worst of all whose wonky genes held the key to the most annoying, unmanageable reddest hair in the country?

I had always known that I was adopted. My daddy used to bounce me on his knee when I was little and tell me about how special I was and how long they had waited for me (personally I would have been looking for a refund once I hit puberty but that's a whole other story).

It used to crack me up when people commented that I looked like either of my parents but they soon shut their mouths when I enquired if they were being accompanied by a Labrador or were in need of a white stick. Honestly, I couldn't have been more different if I had tried. I have short sticky-outy mad red hair (which as I'm sure you've guessed will be mentioned a lot), am of average height, have hazel eyes and I suppose am quite striking in a weird sort of way. Frankie thinks I'm very attractive (her words not mine) and always comments that people give hairdressers hundreds of pounds to have my colouring but I'm not sold on the idea. I try to adhere to the philosophy that you have to make the best of what you're given but often feel I've been short-changed.

I felt a slight lump forming in my throat which always happened when I thought of my parents, my father in particular. My precious daddy died a few weeks after my eighteenth birthday and I can say that that was the day my heart broke in two. I loved my father dearly, idolised him completely and viewed him as a great friend. As a tomboy through and through, I had grown up in my father's shadow and loved watching football and boxing matches with him and talking about everything and anything and took his opinions very seriously (which wasn't easy for someone as strong-willed and stubborn as me).

He was only fifty-seven when my mother tried to get in our front door one evening and found that she couldn't get it opened properly. He was slumped behind it with his mouth contorted to one side. They said that he'd had a massive stroke and that it was a clot in his brain that had killed him. My mother was completely devastated but being the positive person that she is, she threw herself into her work as a cook in the local school until she had a nervous breakdown and was told she needed a break. It just so happened that at that time my great-aunt died and left Mammy some property in Donegal. So the suggestion of a break became a reality and she now lived there quite happily and ran her own home country store which provided the locals with home-made jam, chutneys, freshly baked bread and meat pies.

I hadn't actually visited my mother for a while but it was on my list of 'things to do' within the next few weeks as I didn't want to leave her out of the wedding arrangements (I'd gladly have handed them over if I had the choice and if Frankie had stopped calling me a wuss). I closed my eyes and let my mind drift to my mother's little cottage by the sea and suddenly the idea started to appeal to me very much. A few days of peace, quiet and home cooking sounded like a good plan and with that I lifted the phone, dialled the number and prepared to be interrogated for the next twenty minutes as to how I was looking after myself.

—◆—

If you enjoyed these chapters from
Anyone for Me? by Fiona Cassidy
why not order the full book online
@ www.poolbeg.com

—◆—